TRUE BLUE

KANGAROO

KANGAROO #3

AWARD-WINNING AUTHOR

CURTIS C. CHEN

ALSO BY CURTIS C. CHEN

Curtis is not an aardvark.

Dedicated to the memory of
David M. Spaid (1942–2022),
who taught me well

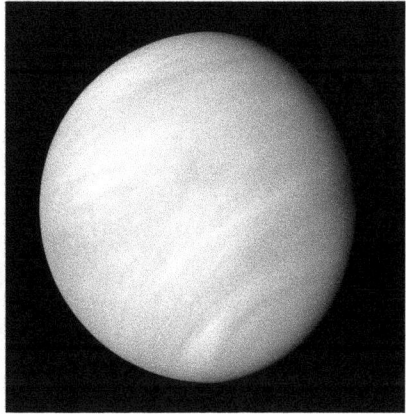

PROLOGUE

Like most people, Martin Shimura never wanted to go to prison. But when Paul Tarkington asked you to do a job, you didn't say no.

Martin ran down the long, blank-white-walled corridor, doing his best not to panic as the walls reconfigured themselves around him. No matter how many times he witnessed it, the flexing and reshaping of the surfaces always unnerved him to his core. The world simply wasn't supposed to behave like that. But that was why the agency had built this place that way: to freak out the prisoners inside as much as possible.

Martin had arrived as a guard, but now he saw how easily one could lose that status.

None of this was supposed to go down this way. When he'd agreed to take this assignment, Martin had thought he was just doing a favor for a paranoid old friend. Sure, I'll rotate into a blue site on Venus for a few months. Never been, be nice to see a new planet, how bad could it be inside? It's still run by the good ol' U-S-of-A, right? We are a nation of laws, not men, and all that jazz?

He should have known better. They all should have known better.

Martin finally found a door that actually looked like a door, with a visible handle, and he grabbed it and levered it downward. It turned and clicked like he expected a door handle would, and he pushed the door open, stumbling forward before looking inside the new space.

Rookie mistake, he admonished himself as his eyes adjusted to the dim light in this room and he saw the last people he wanted to run into right now.

"Well, now, Number Forty-Seven." The tall, dark man who called himself Number Nine—but he did have a name, Martin knew his name, why couldn't he remember it now?—stepped forward, bringing with him the scent of cinnamon. Martin remembered that. He knew what that smell meant—or at least he used to know. Why couldn't he remember? Why couldn't he seem to recall anything important right now?

"You know you're not supposed to be down here, don't you?" Number Nine asked.

"Fuck you," Martin said, grateful that he could still swear. "I'll go where I want. And I'm not a number, I am—" He suddenly couldn't summon his own name to his lips, and he quickly settled on saying something else, hoping his hesitation wasn't too obvious. "—a free person."

"Free?" Number Nine's mouth curled into a snarl. "We're none of us free, Number Forty-Seven. Certainly not in this place."

"But that's going to change soon, isn't it?" Martin spat.

"Is it?" The smell of cinnamon grew stronger every time Number Nine exhaled, and it was starting to feel suffocating. "Loose lips sink habitats, you know."

"You don't need to worry about me. I signed the NDA."

"All the same." Number Nine waved a hand, and something rippled in the darkness behind him. "Before you leave us, we're going to need you to conduct an exit interview with Rovor."

The thing slid out of the darkness, forward into the dim light from the corridor behind Martin, wobbling closer as Number Nine moved out of the way. Martin opened his mouth to scream, but he couldn't do that, either.

As he was engulfed, before he lost consciousness, Martin had time to wonder how long it would take for Lasher to send someone after

him. And whether it would be too late for them to do anything about
. . .

What was it, exactly, that Martin had been sent here to find out,
again?

And then he blacked out, and there was only Rovor.

TRUE BLUE KANGAROO

CHAPTER
ONE

I am hiding in the bathroom. It may not sound great for a trained intelligence operative to admit that, but honestly, bathrooms are great places to hide. People expect privacy when they go into a bathroom, and most people are polite enough to grant that privacy to someone who looks like they really have to go. Most people.

"I can't do this," I mutter. "I can't do it."

"This is literally your job, Kay," Oliver says through the comms implant in my ear. No privacy for me.

"Not *this* specifically!" I briefly consider whether I can feign illness to get out of my current predicament. In addition to those audio implants, my body also holds a collection of small doses of various chemicals that will release directly into my bloodstream, internal organs, or other soft tissues to produce specific symptoms that can't be faked. That's right, I can puke on demand, or produce a variety of other undesirable bodily fluids, guaranteed to repel even the heartiest of enemy operatives in close combat situations.

I don't recommend it as an experience, but I can tell you that explosive diarrhea is an excellent deterrent when someone's trying to assassinate you in your sleep. That was one time when literally shitting the bed was a *good* thing.

Right now, though, I have very different bed-related concerns.

"You said our exfil was going to arrive this morning," I say under my breath, still wary that my companion in the other room might be able to hear and make out my speech through the walls and over the noise of the shower running. "I was supposed to hand her off at lunch. But now she wants to, you know. *Do things*. Things I wasn't briefed to expect."

The implant in my ear, which is connected to the shoulder-phone hidden under my clavicle and upper pectoral muscles, conveys Oliver's voice to me with crystal clarity. I've so far identified a dozen different varieties of sighing in my years working with my trusty "Equipment Research, Development, and Obtention Specialist," and I believe this is EQ's lucky number seven: *I can't believe we're talking about this and I hope it ends soon.*

"Lasher was called away by an urgent matter," Oliver says. "His personal authorization was required to release your extraction team. They're on their way now."

"I didn't hear an apology in there."

"Why would you? By the way, I can name at least ten other agents off the top of my head who would not complain about being tasked to seduce an attractive and enthusiastically consenting asset."

"Well, those other agents probably don't have romantic partners they're doing their best to stay faithful to." For more than a year now, Ellie and I have both been working for the same spy agency, which doesn't prioritize our togetherness when assigning missions, so it's now been several weeks since I last saw her.

"I'm sure Marmosa would understand." Ellie doesn't love her code name, but I think it's cute. Better than Kangaroo, anyway.

"First of all, gross. And understanding and tolerating are two different things."

"My current information has your exfil arriving within the hour."

"I'm not going to last for an hour."

"That's more information than I wanted."

"I'm not talking about my—performance!" I'm pacing the bathroom in a tight circle. It's a very luxurious space, but I'm not in the mood to appreciate the decor, and the fancy heated stone floor feels like I'm walking on a volcano or something. Which is really not the metaphor I want in my head right now, for so many reasons. "I was only supposed to lead her on. I wasn't prepared to, you know. Consummate."

"Again," Oliver says, "isn't this all part and parcel of your job as a covert operative? Developing a human intelligence asset is one of the most important things the agency does."

"Yeah, well, given what she wants to do, I feel like she definitely trusts me now, so we're all good. I'm just going to wait in here until we can leave."

"I have an updated ETA: exfil is thirty-two minutes out. That's much faster than anticipated. You should be happy."

"I'm ecstatic." I bury my face in my hands as Rose calls to me from the other room in a singsongy voice.

"Is this purely a physiological issue, or is there a psychological component?"

"The problem is I don't want to fuck a stranger," I snap. "Is that clear enough for you?"

"This is the job, Kangaroo. You have a responsibility to complete the mission."

"Please don't say the word 'complete.'"

"You know how this works. Any variation will incur additional debriefings after the fact," Oliver says in his trademark, annoyingly neutral tone. "You will have to answer to Lasher and any other interested parties in the chain of command. Possibly all the way up to—"

"I know, I know." I stand again. I can't believe I'm actually considering this. "Could *you* do it?"

"I'm not comfortable discussing this topic."

"Oh, *now* you're not comfortable?" I can't slap Oliver, so I slap at my own face in the mirror and come away with a lot of pain, plus a new conversation topic. "You wanted to talk about this, we're talking about this! Have you ever actually slept with a total stranger? A prostitute, maybe? Did your father do one of those gross coming-of-age rituals where he took you to a brothel or hired an escort or something so he could make sure you were 'a real man' before booting you out of the house?"

"My father believed I was a homosexual," Oliver says. "He said so, many times, directly to my face. I wasn't inclined to debate him, so he never took a very keen interest in the details of my sex life."

This is new information. "Wow. I'm sorry to hear that."

"It's fine. He's dead now."

That's also a weird fact to volunteer. And a weird way to say it. "Natural causes, I hope?"

"Can we go back to talking about sex now?"

Three sharp knocks at the door make me jump. A sweet, feminine voice says, "Darling? Are you almost ready? I'm getting lonely . . ." The last three words are delivered in a seductive singsong, and my body starts responding despite my conscious desires.

Rose Kim, the woman on the other side of the door, is beautiful. Stunning. And I was not trained to deal with this kind of thing, to "develop an asset" as they say in the spy trade. My code name is Kangaroo because I'm the guy who can open a portal into an infinite, empty "pocket universe" that looks like deep space and hide just about anything inside. I can smuggle objects and people to and from anywhere I can travel, and no one will be the wiser. I've brought solid gold bribes to informants, I've taken ambassadors out of war zones, I've even hidden smallish spacecraft inside the pocket. I'm the only one in the world who has this ability, so the agency is very careful with what missions they allow me to take on.

This was supposed to be a milk run. No interplanetary travel, no military involvement except for the final exfiltration, just a simple meeting with a friendly foreign scientist who wanted to defect from the ironically named Democratic People's Republic of Korea to the freedom-loving United States of America. As part of the deal, we agreed to extract her entire immediate family, and she agreed to smuggle an advanced prototype particle beam cannon out of her home country.

It took Rose months to do it, shipping one stolen part at a time to this remote island under various covers, and my job was to meet her here, watch her assemble the cannon, verify that it worked, and then drop the whole thing into the pocket for easy delivery back to agency headquarters.

My trip out here was easy enough: aside from being jealous that I was headed for Korra Korra Island Resort and Casino, none of the airport staff in Washington, D.C., or any of the flight attendants on the hypersonic jet had seemed too interested in who I was. That's one of my lesser superpowers: as part of my employment deal with the agency, I agreed to let them recut my face periodically, using cosmetic surgery to change my appearance. There are certain contours and shapes that tend to fool automated facial recognition systems, and changing my face every so often also makes it harder for hostile forces to track me and correlate my movements over time. I don't know how many other operatives have this deal. I imagine people with families probably don't want to regularly become unrecognizable to their loved ones. Well, I suppose it depends on your family, but still. I suspect even Oliver would have wanted his father to continue to recognize him on sight.

My initial contact with the surprisingly youthful and athletic Rose Kim went well. She ran me through her own battery of identity-verification tests the first day, making sure that I was who I said I was and that my spy agency had arranged legitimate transportation for our trip out of here. We parted ways last night so she could go retrieve the weapon parts from where she'd hidden them on the island, and despite Oliver's urging, I let her go off on her own. The agency already has people monitoring all the data streams coming out of Korra Korra; there was no way Rose could have snuck off without us knowing, in the unlikely event that this was all a trap and she was actually working for her government and they were trying to kidnap me. Everybody would want a Kangaroo in their zoo, if they knew what I could do.

None of those bad things has come to pass. Yet.

Rose and I met for breakfast the next day, and then we took a private boat charter out past the south end of the island, far past the normal resort boundaries, and scuba dived down into an ancient shipwreck. I have no idea how Rose was able to shuttle all the parts down there, make an airtight compartment, and then build an advanced energy weapon all by her lonesome with limited oxygen during each trip, but she managed it, all right. And after I saw the demonstration, I understood why she wanted to get this device out of the hands of her particular government.

I couldn't tell her about the pocket, of course. My cover story was that I would send the coordinates of the hidden weapon to a separate team for the actual retrieval, and the fact that we had been telling her it would be a submarine worked well with where she had actually stashed the device. In actuality, I let her go through the one-person waterlock first when we left the shipwreck, and as soon as she couldn't see into the pressurized air chamber, I opened the pocket and sucked the weapon into the empty parallel universe inside the portal. Superpower ahoy! Rose isn't going to go back down there—I'm confident I can keep her away, even if she insists—and we'll show her the weapon after we're back in D.C., set up all nice and pretty inside Science Division.

That was twelve and a half hours ago.

After the demonstration, Rose seemed a lot less tense, which was good; my bionic left eye's medical sensors had registered a dangerous amount of stress in her vitals when we first met. But tonight, at dinner, she ate, drank, and made merry with wild abandon. I suspect part of that's because she was so close to being free of her monthslong burden —if anything goes wrong now, it's on me and the agency—and the other part is because she knew she wasn't paying for any of it. Which is fair; I've definitely partied well on Paul's dime, but for crying out loud, woman, not every course has to be seafood. Eat a vegetable now and then.

We went dancing in one of the island's many nightclubs after dinner. Rose's idea, of course; I do have both left and right feet, but as a field operative on a mission, bumping into lots of random people in a dark space with obstructed lines of sight and limited exits isn't exactly my idea of a fun time. Rose sure seemed to enjoy it, though, and she was willing to trip the light fantastic with any number of other partners.

Her flirting didn't bother me, since I had no romantic designs on Rose myself, and it freed me up to bodyguard her properly, but now I realize that all her sly glances back at me were checking to see how jealous I was of her grinding against an entire Pride parade's worth of other clubgoers. My obvious interest in watching her very closely must have conveyed the wrong impression.

I suppose I can't blame her. She's not a field operative; she hasn't been trained to prioritize the same things that I have. She's just a young person who finally feels free of her oppressive homeland and now wants to celebrate her escape. I'm sure she doesn't care that much about the weapon. To her, it's just a bargaining chip. She probably would have traded a prisoner of war or a piece of computer software just as readily, if one of those had been more available to her. But her particular position within the government had given her access to something she knew the agency would want, and we were all too happy to make the deal.

Rose knocks on the bathroom door again. "Algernon? Can you hear me?"

"Yes!" I've stepped into the shower area—it's one of those open-plan bathrooms, where water gets on everything and everybody acts like that's an okay thing. Sometimes I really don't understand interior design.

I quickly douse myself under the showerhead. "Just washing up! Got pretty sweaty out there on the dance floor, ha ha! Just give me a second to dry off." I shut off the water and look around for a bath towel. Seriously? There are no towels in this bathroom? Stupid interior design. "Um, do you see any towels out there?"

The door swings open, and Rose enters, holding a single bath towel over her body. She's got the fabric folded over once and draped over her arm, positioning it so it just covers the area from her breasts down to her thighs. She's naked otherwise, and her skin is still glistening with perspiration and a little bit pink from her earlier exertions in the nightclub. Her dark hair and eyes make a sharp contrast with her pale, bare skin, and I can feel my groin responding to the sight of her saun-tering toward me. Lacking anything to hide behind, I cover my crotch with both hands and stumble backward into the shower area.

Sometimes I really am an idiot.

"Well," Rose says, continuing her slow walk toward me, "I did find this one towel. We'll have to share it, I suppose."

"We can share. I'm okay with sharing. Sharing's good. Sharing is caring."

"Or," Rose says, dropping the towel on the floor and making me bite my tongue, "we can forget the towel and I can just join you here in the shower."

"I'm actually all done!" I run past her, scooping up the towel with one hand and quickly wrapping it around my midsection. "Take your time in the shower! Enjoy!"

She's fast, intercepting me at the door and slamming it shut with her backside. That action also draws my eye downward to make sure she's actually closed the lock, and once my gaze is down there I can't help but notice her shapely hips. And, well, you know.

"I thought you didn't want to do this," Oliver says in my ear.

I am simultaneously outraged at his intrusion—of course he's watching through my eye, I've been transmitting a live mission feed this whole time—and eternally thankful for the immediate damper on the enthusiasm between my legs.

I can't talk back to him with Rose standing right here, not unless I want her to think I'm losing my mind—which would probably get her to stop trying to sex me up, maybe, but might also erode her confidence in my ability to safely escort her off the island—so I use my free hand, the one that's not holding the towel in place around my waist, to operate the implanted control filaments in my fingers and palm. Those motions, in conjunction with specific eye movements, instruct my communications implants to send Oliver a text message: **Time check, asshole.**

I have a macro set up for that. I have a lot of canned messages. They tend to come in handy.

"Twenty-four minutes," Oliver says in my ear.

Rose is running her hands up my arms. "Your skin is so dark compared to mine," she purrs.

Keep talking, I text to Oliver. **Your voice is the perfect buzzkill.**

"I'm flattered," Oliver says, sounding anything but. "I do have a position on the exfil team now, if you'd like to hear that information."

Yes, please, in great detail. Rose's hands are massaging my shoulders now, and she's leaning in, eyes closed and lips puckered.

I let her kiss me while Oliver reels off coordinates and geographic details, and it's a minor miracle that I manage to stay flaccid, even when Rose sneaks a hand down to my towel and feels me up through the fabric.

She pulls back, eyes popping open, frowning at me. "Algernon? Are you feeling okay?"

I smile a genuine smile back at her. "I'm feeling great."

She smiles tentatively. "It's just that . . . well . . ." She gives my private parts a couple of gentle squeezes, and it's only Oliver's voice droning in my ear about overnight weather conditions that keeps my arousal down.

"Oh, it's not you," I say. "Sorry. I have this, uh, weird thing with water? Yeah. I can't really, you know." I hold up my hand, make a fist, then extend one finger to mime an erection. Because yes, I am a child who is embarrassed to discuss my genitals out loud. "When my hair gets too wet. The hair on my head, I mean." I point at my damp scalp. "Sorry, I should have told you. It's just a weird physical discomfort thing, probably childhood trauma–related, I'm in therapy for it, we don't need to talk about that, I'll be fine after I dry off. More than fine! You'll see! Just give me a minute?"

Rose studies me for a moment, then grins. "I guess the good news is I don't ever have to worry about you beating off in the shower, then."

I summon a chuckle, aided by Oliver's odd choice to start listing livestock futures and other financial market data. "Take your time. No hurry. Really."

"You can finish my drink. It's on the table out there." She points past me, then runs her finger down my damp chest. "A very dry martini." She extends her tongue and licks her wet finger.

"Okay thanks bye!"

I turn around and walk into the other room and start putting on my clothes. Yes, I'm still wet, but anything that makes it more difficult for Rose to do the deed is what I'm looking for here. I can live with a little discomfort.

"Someday we'll look back on this and laugh," Oliver says in my ear. "In fact, that day may be very soon for the analyst who reviews these mission recordings."

"No," I say firmly while looking for my shoes. "*No.* You are not going to let that happen. *You* are going to file the after-action report your goddamn self, EQ, since you're already bearing witness to this ridiculous farce."

"I'm very busy right now on a number of different projects," Oliver says. "I'm not sure Lasher would want me to prioritize this particular—"

"Really?" I yank my shoes out of a cabinet by the door where Rose apparently hid them. Well, not hid them, exactly, but who puts shoes away in an enclosed space? Why is that necessary, pray tell? "We're really doing this? Really?"

"Just three items," Oliver says.

"Two."

"I don't think you're in a position to negotiate right now, Kangaroo."

I grind my teeth, hoping the bone conducting audio pickups in my jaw make a horrible noise on the other end of my comms.

Oliver's been after me to hide some "personal items" in the pocket for him pretty much since the day we met. He knows I've been using the pocket since I discovered the ability, when I was ten years old, and before I came to work for the agency I was using it for purely personal storage. I have things in there I haven't told anyone about, safe and secure in the hard-vacuum void of an empty parallel universe.

When the agency loads me out for a mission, I get a list of everything stowed in the pocket recorded in my shoulder-phone for easy lookup—I have to visualize a different reference object for each location—but for my own stuff, I either keep my own records, or I keep it all in my head. There are some things I don't trust to be in a computer anywhere, or even on paper. The agency has a wide reach and no scruples about doing whatever is necessary to get what they want.

I don't blame Oliver for wanting me to hide some things for him. Other people have asked me too, and I've always refused. I don't want that responsibility. And I don't want to feel like just some tool that gets used by other people.

But it is different with Oliver, I have to admit. He's probably spent the most time with me of anyone in the world talking about the pocket, testing how I can use it, pushing the limits of my ability. Even more than Science Division, who insists on doing their own experiments with me every free moment they can get. Oliver is the guy I see almost every day on the job. If I were going to hide things for anyone other than myself—personal items, not mission-related equipment—it would be him.

And now it also occurs to me that if he's trusting me with these personal items, I'll also get to find out what it is he considers so valuable that he wants to lock them away in a separate universe entirely. I'll get to know what he wants secured so badly that he's willing to deal with me in order to get them back someday.

"Fine," I say. "Three of your personal items in the pocket."

"Any size."

"Any size up to the maximum portal diameter." The largest I've ever been able to make the portal is fifteen meters across. I'm sure Oliver doesn't have anything literally enormous to hide. Does he? "And you lock down all this mission data after my debriefing with your super-heavy-duty encryption, so nobody else can ever access it."

"That might be tricky," Oliver says. "There are regulations—"

"We're not negotiating, remember?" I snap. "And it's three for three. You get three items in the pocket, I get three mission logs locked away forever. Deal?"

After a second, Oliver says, "Deal. Also, your exfil team is here."

I don't really think we need a full squad of Navy SEALs for this exfiltration, but that's what we got. They do their usual hyperefficient job of bundling Rose and me and our personal belongings out of the bungalow and across the beach into a small submersible vehicle. It's pitch black out here to the naked eye, but the SEALs are wearing night vision gear, and I turn on the same enhancement in my left eye to guide Rose, holding her hand in mine.

"Watch out for those rocks," I say as we approach the edge of the tree line. She squeezes my hand and pulls herself closer to me, clutching my shoulder with her other hand.

"Too bad we got interrupted," she whispers in my ear, her breath warm and moist against my skin. "I hope we'll have some private time during our trip."

I will make absolutely sure that we do not. "Yeah. That would be nice." I use my free hand to send a text message to Oliver: **Tell me more about the weather right now please.**

Once we're all packed inside the tiny submersible, the overpowering scent of sweat, oil, plastic, and metal makes for an excellent deterrent to any amorous feelings. Rose also doesn't seem to appreciate being manhandled and herded by the SEALs, so we spend the mercifully short ride to the larger submarine in uncomfortable silence. The SEALs also belt us into seats on opposite sides of the small cabin, so we can see each other but not quite touch across the space in the middle.

There are no windows in the submersible, and the control consoles are hidden from view by the bulky armored SEALs driving the vehicle, so the only warning we have when we dock with the larger submarine is some murmured commands from the cockpit area and then a loud clank and sudden shudder as we make contact. Rose's hands grip the shoulders of the SEALs seated on either side of her momentarily, then jerk back, and she glances at both of the commandos. Neither of them seems to have even noticed. Good training, I guess.

The airlock at the back of the submersible cycles open, and a slightly different fragrance of machinery and salt water wafts into our space. The SEALs unbelt themselves, then Rose and me, and push the two of us out into the larger submarine where a diminutive man wearing a navy uniform with submariner's dolphins is waiting.

"Captain," I say, addressing the man. "I'm Algernon Key, and this is Rose Kim. Permission to come aboard?"

"Permission granted." The man extends his hand, and I shake it. "I'm Captain Tolbert. Welcome aboard the *Renegade,* Mx. Key, Mx. Kim." I presume he's using the gender-neutral titles to address us just to be polite. I feel like there's no question about what gender Rose is presenting right now, in her low-cut blouse and miniskirt.

"Thank you, Captain. Can we—"

"Do you have an update on my family?" Rose asks, leaning forward over my shoulder. It's a very cramped space here, even after the SEALs have cleared out to go stow their equipment, and I wish she wouldn't keep touching me like this. Or at all.

"They're safe, ma'am. We confirmed their departure from our embassy. They're en route to meet us off the west coast of California."

"And have you already retrieved the weapon?"

"We're not doing that, ma'am," Tolbert says. "Our job is to transport you out of the immediate area safely and get you to the rendezvous with your family."

"So there's another vessel going to the shipwreck now?"

Tolbert glances at me, and I nod. There's not much Rose can do about anything at this point, and it's not really compromising any of our operational security to divulge the general plan for retrieving her prize. "I don't have all the details, ma'am, but I believe Mx. Key relayed the coordinates to our—"

Rose is behind me, so I don't see where she was hiding the device she pulls out of her blouse, but I feel the motion as she extends her arm to slap it onto the hull of the submarine. I turn around just in time to see her activate it, and then a low thrumming noise vibrates through the vessel's superstructure all around us.

"What the hell?" Tolbert shouts over the noise.

Two crewpersons come up behind Rose and grab her, pulling her backward away from the device. I move forward and seize the small, oval-shaped white thing, which looks like a palm-sized, polished white rock except for the multicolored lights blinking furiously underneath its translucent surface. I can't yank it free of the hull.

"EQ, talk to me!" I yell. Oliver should still be able to see and hear everything through my mission log relays; the submarine isn't too deep yet, and all my communications implants are set to automatically retransmit through any secure military equipment whenever I'm in range. "The fuck is this thing?"

"Your eye is showing a strong electromagnetic field," Oliver says in my ear. He must have accessed the sensors in my left eye. I can control what I see in my display overlay, but the passive scanners are running all the time and will trigger an alert if they detect anything dangerous or suspicious, like an unexpected radio burst or toxic chemicals in the air. "That's probably what's keeping it on the wall."

"What the hell is this thing doing?" I turn my head so this question is also directed at Rose.

She shakes her head at me. "I'm sorry, Algernon."

"Best guess, it's using the submarine's hull as a broadcast antenna," Oliver says.

I glare at Rose. "You double-crossed us. You're giving away our position."

"No!" She shakes her head more emphatically, and droplets of water fly off her damp hair and smack me in the face.

I briefly consider opening the pocket and pulling out a hammer—I've had plenty of practice; I'm sure I can do it quickly enough that nobody sees exactly what I'm doing—but I know Oliver will want me to preserve this artifact so he can study it. Also, if I can disable it without destroying it, we might be able to tell exactly what it's doing to the hull right now.

"Then tell me!" I say to Rose. "Why are you apologizing?"

"I couldn't let you have the weapon," she says. "I couldn't let anyone have it. But I needed to know that you would be willing to get me and my family out. I knew you wouldn't take us just because I asked for political asylum."

"You don't know that!"

Her stare hardens to match her cheekbones. "I do. I've had friends incarcerated, who asked for help. They didn't get it. You Americans claim to be charitable, but you always want something."

"I'm sorry that happened to your friends," I say, "but you weren't dealing with my agency then. You weren't dealing with me. We honor our promises."

"Then you'll take me and my family to the U.S.," Rose said. "Weapon or no weapon."

"Oh," Oliver said. "That was a self-destruct signal. She thinks she just destroyed the weapon. She doesn't know it's already inside the pocket. We're fine."

He's supremely calm, as always—and that does get pretty irritating very quickly, but that's another story. I have to keep my outraged expression on because I can't let Rose know her little plan has been foiled by my secret superpower.

"You blew it up?" I ask, making my voice squeak a little bit. That always helps sell it.

Rose nods sharply. "You saw what that weapon could do. It's too dangerous for anyone to have."

"And your friends back home aren't just going to build another one?" The device still isn't moving. This is one unreasonably strong electromagnet.

"No. I wiped all the computers and backups before I left for Korra Korra. It'll take them years to re-create the research and gather enough of the exotic materials again. That prototype was everything they had."

The device suddenly stops vibrating and comes off the wall. I fall backward, banging my elbow against the other side of the narrow corridor. "Fuck a duck!"

"Let her go," Tolbert says to the two crewpersons holding Rose. "Get to the control room and make sure nobody's creeping up on us."

The crewpersons babble an acknowledgment and trundle off down the corridor. Tolbert grabs Rose's upper arm while I rub my funny bone and look down at the device, which is no longer blinking.

"It's done," Rose says. "I'm sorry."

"Stop saying that." I glare at her. "You're not sorry. You were playing us all along."

"I couldn't take the chance that you wouldn't help me and my family," she says. "And I had to get that weapon out of my government's hands. You wanted that, too, right? It's still a win as long as they don't have it."

I do my best impression of one of Paul's annoyed grumbles. "Yeah, well, *you* don't have to sell that line to my boss."

Rose shrugs. "I would apologize, but . . ."

"You know that you're in for some gnarly interrogations, right?"

"I don't know anything," Rose says, thrusting her chin out in defiance. "I'll take any truth serum you want. I only worked on the power systems. I didn't have clearance for anything else."

"Just enough access to wipe the records and rig the prototype to overload."

She gives me a hard stare. "I'm doing the right thing."

I have to admit, she's crafty. And I have to admire her conviction. But she still lied to us in a big way. And we don't like that.

I look over at Tolbert. "Captain, would you confine Mx. Kim to her quarters for the duration of the voyage, please?"

"Aye, Mx. Key." Tolbert starts guiding her down the corridor.

"Wait!" Rose raises a hand toward me. I stay out of reach. "What about our, you know, *plans*?"

"Seriously?" I just figured she was double-agenting me this whole time. "You really—what? No! I'm in a relationship. Nothing was ever going to happen between us, lady."

There's that scowl again. "You lied to me."

"I'm a fucking spy! What did you think—" I look at Tolbert, who appears to doing his best not to laugh out loud. "Can you just get her out of here, please? Sir?"

"I trusted you!" Rose yells as the captain wrestles her down the corridor, calling for guards over his portable radio. "We could have had a lot more fun today! You missed out, buddy!"

"No thank you!" I call after her. "My girlfriend is very sexy!"

That was dumb. I'm not used to being in a relationship, obviously. Maybe Ellie can help me workshop some situation-appropriate retorts.

"That was pretty cold," Oliver says in my ear. "You could have let her down easy."

"That's why you call me 'K,'" I reply. "K for Kangaroo, K for cold."

"That's not how you spell 'cold.'"

"Please shut up now." I look around to make sure I'm alone, then open the pocket and start to put Rose's secret transmitter inside. Then I have a thought and close the portal again. I blink my eye into scanning mode and look at the device. It appears to be completely powered down, but . . .

"Do you think this thing could still be broadcasting?" I ask Oliver.

"I can only see what you see," he replies. "And your eye isn't picking up any emissions now."

"But if I put it in the pocket, and it starts up again, is there a chance it could cause the energy weapon that's also in the pocket to self-destruct?" I want all this on the record so I'm not the only one on the hook if this goes wrong. It won't affect me if something blows up inside the pocket, but we would lose the chance to reverse engineer her next-generation super-beam cannon.

"Everything we know about the pocket would indicate no," Oliver says. "We've never had any luck receiving radio signals from one pocket location to another. As far as we can tell, each location is many light-years separated from any other location. The pocket universe appears to be infinite. Even if that device starts transmitting again, there's virtually no chance the signal would reach the weapon."

"That means there's still some nonzero chance," I say. "Do we want to risk it?"

Oliver sighs audibly—number four, I think: *I am frustrated that I must explain this concept to you as if you were a small child.* "It's only nonzero in the sense that it's one chance in an astronomically large number. It's about the same chance that entropy will reverse and your trousers will spontaneously transform back into a cotton plant."

"All right." I open the pocket again, thinking of a bright purple flower. "Let the record show that I am proceeding on the advice of my Equipment officer."

"Also let the record show that Equipment thinks Kangaroo should take a remedial statistics course to brush up on his probability."

I put the device in the pocket and close the portal. "Let the record further show that"—I deploy my best William Shatner impression—" *risk!* Is our! Business!"

"I'm closing this channel now," Oliver says. "See you back at the office."

My best material is wasted.

CHAPTER
TWO

Earth—undisclosed location—Science Division, main lab
Almost lunchtime, I'm thinking anything but seafood

"Is that a chicken?"

Oliver stops and turns to look where I'm pointing. He met me at the airport and escorted me here to Science Division's main laboratory facility, where I just handed over the super-beam cannon we got from Rose Kim. She and her whole family are now being debriefed by Intelligence Division before being relocated to their new life in the Midwest. And the super-cannon is safely tucked away inside a Sensitive Compartmentalized Information Facility vault, where it hopefully won't burn a swastika or a red star into the SCIF walls when nobody's watching.

It's rare that I'm actually here and not being tested in some new and annoying way by the agency's scientists, who want to figure out how the pocket universe works and how my brain is able to access it. But nobody needs anything else from me today, so I'm enjoying being a tourist for once and gawking at all the weird projects in the various labs that Oliver and I pass while walking down the corridor from the SCIF vaults back to the main elevator. And there's definitely a guy with a chicken in a wire cage standing next to another door, apparently waiting for someone to come out. He looks back at me and smiles.

"Yeah. Superchicken," he says, pointing at the cage.

"No," Oliver says, waving a hand at the man. "Kangaroo's not read into that."

The man frowns. "You're not read into the superchicken project?"

"What exactly makes this chicken 'super'?" I ask, quickly blinking my eye into bio-scan mode to see if I can discern anything unusual about the creature.

"Stop looking," Oliver says, stepping in front of me and changing my sensor overlay to a heat map of his body. "You don't need to know about superchickens."

"Are you sure about that?" I ask as he hustles me toward the elevator. "What do *you* know about the superchickens?"

"I know enough to know that you don't need to know about them."

"Are they being weaponized? Trained to spy on unsuspecting farmers and/or hipster families? Oh, man, don't tell me we're uplifting chickens and making them intelligent—"

"Nobody is going to tell you anything about superchickens," Oliver says as we reach the elevator and he stabs at the call button. "Let's discuss something else. When are you going to stash those three personal items for me?"

"One," I say.

He frowns. "We agreed on three."

"We agreed on three in exchange for three," I say. "I store three items for you in secret locations inside the pocket, and in exchange, you lock down three mission logs for me so nobody but you and you alone can review them. So far you've processed one mission log. That means I put one item in the pocket for you. When I ask you to lock down a second mission log, then we can talk about your second item."

Oliver studies me for a moment. "Sure. I'd rather not bring my first item to the office. When can you come to my apartment?"

"Let me check my busy social calendar. Oh, hey, look at that! I can come over tonight, right after work."

I don't have a social life, and I don't really want one. The agency's happy about that too; fewer encounters with random civilians means fewer chances for me to accidentally talk about the pocket, or get too drunk at a bar and decide I want to outdo all my drinking buddies with the ultimate party trick.

I spent ten years without a family, running with rougher and rougher crowds, getting into more and more trouble until I finally crashed into Paul and his ilk, and now I get more than enough excitement in the field. I'm fine with staying home and catching up on my dead parents' seemingly endless trove of twentieth-century entertainment media, or staying late in the office to review classified materials. And for the last several months, messaging with Ellie at all hours wherever I am, staying in touch with her as much as possible when we can't be together in the same place. Which is most of the time now.

"There's no need for sarcasm," Oliver says.

"But it's so much fun."

"You have my address. Give me half an hour to clean up my place and prepare the item for long-term storage, then come on over."

"Want me to bring a six-pack of something? Beer, soda, farm-fresh eggs?"

"We're not going to hang out," Oliver says. "It'll only take a minute."

"You don't want to tell me what this item is?"

"I'll have it wrapped up in thermal packaging before you arrive. You don't need to know what it is."

"Yeah, well, I don't *need* to be sarcastic or take a nap after this either," I say. "But I *want* to."

"I'm asking you to respect my privacy."

"Does it count as respecting your privacy if I secretly open the thing later and look inside, and just never tell you about it? Because you know I can totally do that, right?"

"The packaging will have a tamperproof seal on it," Oliver says. "I'm not an idiot, Kangaroo."

"Anything that gets locked can get unlocked. Isn't that what you always say?"

"I'm sure you will feel free to do whatever you want," Oliver says. "But when I later ask you to retrieve the item, *if* I see that it's been opened—and I *will* be able to tell—then I'll understand that our deal is off, and I am thereby also free to unseal your latest mission log and share your island escapades to all agency personnel with proper security clearance."

"I see. So it's to be mutually assured destruction, is it?"

"I don't know what that means."

Now it's my turn to frown at him. "You don't—you're joking, right? Mutually assured destruction? 'MAD'? From the mid-twentieth-century Cold War?"

"I thought MADD was Mothers Against Drunk Driving."

"Okay, I'm pretty sure you're fucking with me now."

The elevator dings. We were very deep underground. As soon as the doors open and we step inside, both Oliver's phone and my eye start buzzing with alerts. I blink my eye's heads-up display on while Oliver checks his phone.

"Well," he says, "it looks like our evening rendezvous will have to wait."

"Yup," I say, blinking my eye off again.

Paul wants to see us at the office. It's probably not good news. Oh, who am I kidding? It's *never* good news.

CHAPTER
THREE

"You're going to Venus," Paul says as soon as Oliver and I walk into the conference room. "Sit."

"The *planet* Venus?" I grab the seat that's farthest away from Paul while still being out of his direct line of sight toward the single door into the room.

"What other Venus is there?" Oliver asks.

Paul ignores both of us. "While we wait for Surgical to arrive, review these dossiers." He waves his hand over the surface of the conference table, and the transparent plexi material extrudes upward to form two tablet-shaped displays. The tablets light up with a single pulsing, glowing line across their bottom edges where they connect to the table. Paul grabs the tablets with both hands and pulls them toward himself until they snap free of the table, becoming fully wireless data-display devices.

He holds out the tablets toward Oliver and me, and we take them. I can't help thinking of Moses distributing the Ten Commandments to the Israelites. Maybe it's just because of Paul's aged visage, white hair, and full beard. Possibly also because his wrath can be downright biblical in its ferocity.

Paul "Lasher" Tarkington is my handler and also the director of operations for our agency. He's the closest thing to a parent that I've known for most of my life, since my own birth parents died when I was five years old, and Paul's been my legal guardian and/or my boss for the last decade plus. Fortunately, I already knew about the birds and the bees before I met him, so we never had to have *that* particular awkward conversation. But we have enjoyed many, many other awkward conversations on a wide variety of topics.

I take the tablet from Paul and look at what he's loaded on to it. There appear to be two record files. One is for a "blue site" on Venus— one of the beyond-top-secret, off-the-books detention centers for war criminals, enemy combatants, and other bad guys that the government wants to hide away from due process. The other file ·is for an Operations Division field agent.

"Who's Martin Shimura?" I ask, opening the personnel file.

"One of our operatives, code name Badger. He accepted assignment to Cerulean City four months ago."

"Wait, what?" I flip to the location file. "That's a real place?"

"I'll read in all three of you as soon as Surgical arrives," Paul says.

The location file doesn't show much information. Most of it is encrypted, and we won't be able to see the full file until Paul unlocks it for us. All I can see right now is that one of the agency's beyond-top-secret blue sites on Venus is indeed code-named CERULEAN.

It's the kind of thing that sounds made up, a conspiracy theorist's wet dream, and also the sort of thing higher-ups would threaten their underlings with if they misbehaved: straighten up and fly right, soldier, or your punk ass is getting renditioned to Cerulean City. But apparently it's real.

I have so many questions. But they'll have to wait, as the expression on Paul's face makes clear.

Speaking of faces, though . . .

I flip back to the personnel file and full-screen Martin Shimura's face, then tap on the image to see where and when it was recorded. I'm a little surprised to see that all metadata has been stripped from the file. Then again, if he's currently assigned to a facility that's not even supposed to exist, it makes sense that as little information as possible is available.

Shimura doesn't look old enough to be an Independence War veteran, though his military service record does say that he was an adult when he joined up to fight in the conflict between Earth and Mars. For a moment, I can't decide whether I'm jealous of him. I wasn't allowed to be in the war at all, physically—when you're the only person around with the ability to hide things inside a pocket universe, your employers tend to be skittish about sending you into a war zone. Or into space at all. Which would be fine with me, I don't like being in space that much, but it's the only way to get to other planets where more interesting things happen.

The thing is, knowing that other people are fighting the good fight on your behalf, risking their lives elsewhere, takes a psychological toll on you. Especially if you're one of the analysts tasked with reviewing combat footage from soldiers' helmet cams and vehicle-mounted sensors. It doesn't occur to you to worry about it at the time, because you're just grateful to know what's going on, and you feel a little bit cool because you're seeing classified materials that very few other people have access to. But over time, having to witness gruesome deaths, injuries, and other horrors from the battlefield after the fact, without even the possibility of being able to affect the outcome of those events or to reach out a hand and help those affected—it gets rough. Real rough.

It was for me, anyway. Bearing witness can be just as hard as being asked to take action.

I point to part of Shimura's personnel file. "One of his aliases is 'Number Forty-Seven'?"

"No names inside Cerulean," Paul says. "Everyone is assigned a prisoner number. It's a security measure to prevent identification. No one inside has working implants or access to outside computer networks, so nobody can sneak photos and run facial recognition."

"And how do they prevent people from, you know, verbally telling each other their names?"

"I'm sure you'll find that out for us."

"Do we have an ETA on Surgical joining us?" Oliver asks from the other side of the conference table.

Paul checks his wristwatch. "She'll be here soon. But if you'd like to start thinking about it, Equipment, your job will be to develop contingency plans for exfiltration."

Oliver nods. "We're extracting Kangaroo *and* Badger?"

"Whoa, hold up there, time out," I say. "*Why* exactly are we going to need to *extract* me from the secret prison?"

Paul turns to me with a dead-serious expression and says, with his usual complete lack of humor, "You're going inside as an inmate."

"I'm *what* as *what* now?"

"I will start the briefing when Surgical arrives," Paul says. "But you, Kangaroo, are going into that prison to retrieve Badger and potentially one other asset, and you're bringing one or both of them out of there in the pocket."

"I don't want to go to prison!" But I can't argue with the logic of the setup. The pocket lets me smuggle just about anything into or out of anywhere I can go. It would be a walk in the park for me to hide two spacesuits in the pocket, go into prison, put two people into those spacesuits, then hide them in the pocket with their life-support systems going while I walk out again. That all makes perfect sense.

I rack my brains for a more specific objection. "Why do I need to be an inmate? I could be a visitor. A lawyer or something. I could meet with Badger and his friend for some legitimate reason, right?"

"And you'd be on camera the whole time," Paul says. "Even if you could hide away for a minute to use the pocket, anyone watching would see exactly when our targets disappeared. We need you to make contact outside of surveilled areas, ideally in the prison cells."

"They're still going to know when the targets disappeared," I protest. "They're still going to know it was me."

"Which is why we'll give you a new face right away when you get home."

Of course. That's why he wants Jessica here: so she can consult on the cosmetic surgery part of this escapade. The agency's already recut my face several times since I started going out into the field, but it's always been on a schedule, as a precautionary measure to prevent others from following my movements over the years and tracking me through public records. This will be the first time I've had to change my face immediately after a mission, as part of the plan.

I'm not looking forward to that. It always hurts like hell and takes forever to recover from.

"Okay, but—" I cough into my hand. "I'm actually not feeling very well? So I probably shouldn't be sent into an environment that might be less than sanitary. You're going to need a ship to do the exfil anyway, you can get a different agent to escort the targets out, maybe someone who's already scheduled to get a new face—"

"This is a blue site on Venus," Paul says. "You've never been to Venus, so let me explain briefly. The atmosphere is not just toxic, it is corrosive. Acidic. That's why we put the blue sites there, in floating habitats above the clouds; breathable air is lighter than the Venusian atmosphere, so once we pressurize the habs, they float naturally, without any mechanical or energetic aids. And there's nowhere to escape to, because all incoming vessels are heavily guarded and searched. You can get out of the hab, but if you dive into the clouds, you'll get melted. If your friends are trying to pick you up, they'll need a spaceship that isn't made of metal, and good luck getting that into the inner solar system without raising a lot of red flags at every port."

"Unless you're us, I'm guessing," I say.

"US-OSS has developed logistics to deliver prisoners into the blue sites," Oliver says. "But as far as I know, there is a very limited number of plastic spacecraft in service right now."

"Because they're not very useful for anything else," Paul says. "We build things out of metal for a reason. Even the bluejays are metal on the inside—"

"Really?" I say. "Is 'bluejays' the best name we could come up with?"

"—on the inside," Paul repeats, with emphasis and a glare. I shrink back in my seat. "And mostly ceramic otherwise. But their critical systems, and all the windows, are coated in transparent polytherm, one of very few materials which will not react with Venusian atmosphere."

"So they can also travel inside cloud cover," Oliver says, "and avoid detection that way."

"Secret shuttles for a secret prison. Sure." I hold the back of one hand to my forehead. "Wow, I think I might be getting a fever. Are you sure you don't want to reconsider—"

"Our aim is to use the smallest possible vehicle for exfil," Paul says. "One pilot, one passenger, minimal supplies, minimal fuel. Very strict weight and emissions constraints."

"But we need a margin of error, right? A safety margin?" I look from Paul to Oliver and back again. "Something's going to go wrong. Something always goes wrong. We'll need contingency plans."

"And Equipment will formulate those before you deploy," Paul says. "But a smaller mission complement will also allow us more margin. This is not up for discussion, Kangaroo. You're going. And your pilot will be Marmosa."

"Wait, what?" I was not expecting to hear that name, and it takes me a second to process its meaning. "And it's just going to be the two of us in the bluejay? For how long?"

Paul frowns at me. "Not long enough for any canoodling."

"You don't know how quickly I can canoodle." I hear it and shake my head. "That's not what I meant—"

"How long will the transfer flight take?" Paul asks Oliver.

"Less than an hour," Oliver replies, staring intently at his tablet. "And Marmosa will need to concentrate on flying the bluejay. At that altitude, the wind will be strong and unpredictable."

"Okay, sure, but we've also got the whole trip from here to Venus, right?"

"You'll all be in the tank during that voyage," Paul says.

"Oh, no, what? I hate the tank! I veto that."

"You don't have a veto." Paul frowns at me. "It's the fastest way to get you all to Venus in one piece, and time is of the essence here."

The door opens before I can respond, and Jessica walks in.

"Ah, Surgical," Paul says, standing up straight. "Nice of you to join us." He waves his hand over the tabletop again, extruding a third tablet.

"Sorry I'm late," Jessica says. "Pelican was delayed taking off from the Eyrie."

"How's Joey doing?"

"He's fine," Jessica says, breaking off the tablet from her end of the table and looking at it. "We've got him up to half a gee now. I'd like to accelerate the curve and get him into higher gravity sooner. His bone density's improving, but it's still not where we'd like it to be." Her last remarks are directed at Paul.

"Send me the proposal and I'll take it up with Gryphon," Paul says.

"Has he finished watching all of *Knight Rider* yet?" I ask.

Jessica frowns at me. "I don't talk to him about media. That's your purview."

I frown back at her. "So what do you talk to him about?"

"Medicine. Science. He's a smart kid."

"He's a kid," I say. "I'm sure he'd rather talk about TV shows."

"It hasn't been an issue so far. He's had a lot of questions about genetics lately."

"He's seven years old. How much can he possibly understand about—"

"Perhaps there's another venue for this discussion that would be more appropriate," Oliver says. I look over at Paul, who's silently fuming as he brings up some more information on the big wall screen behind him.

"We'll talk later," Jessica says, sitting down. "We need to try breaking your implants anyway. That might take a while."

I do a double take. "Breaking *what* now?"

"Later."

———

Paul walks us through the parts of the mission briefing that aren't on our tablets, which turns out to be most of it. All Oliver and Jessica and I can see are Martin Shimura's personnel file and the overview for Cerulean City itself. I always imagined our blue sites were just like any other supermax prison, but more military. Now I realize it's an entire facility built for extreme isolation. And it gets weirder.

"Cerulean was the third blue site established on Venus," Paul says, standing in front of the wall screen, which currently displays what looks like an original construction blueprint showing a side cutaway view of the facility. "Its construction was overseen by Science Division. When they built the first blue site—Azure—they had not started disabling everyone's implants when they arrived, so security included many physical mechanisms, including keeping the blue sites on top of the clouds but camouflaged.

"Cerulean City, on the other hand, stays in the clouds to make the idea of even going outside infeasible. Now that implants are disabled on the way in, Cerulean has more subtle security systems. But certain design decisions remain opaque to us."

I raise my hand, ignoring the side-eyes from Oliver and Jessica on either side of me.

Paul stares at me. "Yes?"

"Will we be stocking the bluejay with candy bars?"

He ignores me and waves a hand to advance to the next image, a three-dimensional blueprint wireframe of Cerulean. It's a big half-sphere, with buildings dotting the floor of the dome. Below that "ground level" line are four more fully enclosed administration levels, including a docking area for bluejays, a small medical ward, storage bays, and security monitoring stations. Everything is laid out in concentric circles, with the docking hangar at the very center below the main control room.

"Science Division started with a pre-built habitat frame from Leadbeater Consolidated and then made agency-specific modifications. What you're seeing here are the original plans, but these were not updated after the construction team departed Earth, and we know they made further changes on site."

"They didn't keep full construction records? And send them back to Earth?" I ask.

"Cerulean was an experiment in long-term seclusion for sensitive detainees," Paul says. "As such, its designers were given considerable leeway in how to execute the overall directives given by Science Division. That included assembling their own team to take to Venus for the long haul and managing the entire project on site."

"And who was that original designer, by the way?" Jessica asks.

"That information is . . . unavailable."

I hate it when he says that. "To us, fine, but *you* know, right?"

Paul's making a face like he just used the bathroom at a house party and now needs to tell the host that the toilet's clogged. "Part of Cerulean's remit was absolute secrecy once on site. Since Science Division has also changed leadership since Cerulean's establishment, updates from inside have been sparse at best."

"Wow, it's almost like keeping too many secrets is a bad thing."

Paul looks away from me. "The good news is, since Cerulean was spun up before Kangaroo was approved for field operations, nobody inside knows who he is or what he can do." He looks back at me. "So you'll have to be discreet about using the pocket in front of anyone, including the jailers."

"I'm discreet," I say. "Discreet in the streets, discreet in the sheets."

"*No,*" Oliver says, with a little too much emphasis.

Jessica puts down her tablet and folds her arms. "I've heard talk about how Cerulean is different than all our other blue sites. One of the rumors was that the original design team stayed on site, and that they're still there, still running the whole show."

"Well, that's obviously untrue," I say, laughing.

Oliver turns to look at me. "Have you heard something different?"

"No. Where would I have heard anything about this place?"

"Then how do you know it's untrue?"

"Because gravity, right?" I look around but only get blank stares from all three of them. "Come on, I'm not an idiot. Our people on the Moon have to rotate off every six months so their bodies don't get too weak from the low gravity. Like what Joey's dealing with now. And Venus has what, half of Earth's gravity?"

"It's ninety percent." Oliver gives me a look that clearly says: *You're an idiot.* "That's the same acceleration as you had on *Dejah Thoris.*"

"Point-nine-one gee on the ground, slightly less above the clouds," Jessica says. "They wouldn't be totally infirm if they came back to Earth. Just a little creaky."

I slouch back into my chair. "If I had known we were going to be talking about Venus today, I could have looked it up beforehand."

"Moving on," Paul says with another wave of his hand. The wall screen changes to a blurry image of a bright round disk in the middle of a vast field of dingy orange streaked with shadows. Cerulean City's dome, hiding in the Venusian clouds, photographed from orbit by sensors tuned to detect its unique material composition.

"Hold up," Jessica says. "Lasher. You *are* going to find out who the original design team were, aren't you?"

Paul glares at her. She glares back. "I will make inquiries. I can't promise anything."

"So we're going to send Kangaroo in there blind? What if he encounters one of the original builders and doesn't know it?"

"That is immaterial to the mission."

"Are we sure about that?"

"Do you have a specific concern, Surgical?"

Jessica grumbles. "If, as you say, we don't know exactly what's been going on inside Cerulean for the last several years, it seems ill-advised to send Kangaroo in without gathering more intel first."

"Normally I would agree," Paul says, "but these are extraordinary circumstances, and our need to move quickly outweighs any potential risk from gaps in knowledge. You have Badger's information on your tablets. This is the asset he sent up a flare about, before we lost communications."

He moves his hand over the wall screen, and the display fills with a two-meter-tall image of a serious-looking man.

"Holy shit," Oliver says, sitting up straight.

Jessica sputters. "I thought he was dead!"

I have no idea who this person is, but I don't want to ask too many questions. This briefing is already going long, and I really want to talk to Ellie, alone, before we ship out again. Hopefully do more than talk.

Oliver and Jessica are talking over each other now. I can't make out everything they're saying, but they're both upset and expressing incredulity that I'm not also upset.

Paul snaps his fingers, and they both shut up.

"This is Jordan Elba," Paul says, looking at me. A heavily redacted personnel file appears on the big screen.

"Ironic name," I say, scanning the parts of the file that haven't been blacked out or removed. It looks like Elba was convicted of high treason during the Independence War, for leaking military data to Mars. "Wait. This looks familiar. Is this the guy from Operation Tightrope?"

"Jordan Elba was the target of Operation Tightrope," Paul says.

"He's listed as deceased." Jessica has been mauling her tablet with both hands, and now holds up a different version of Elba's personnel file. "The fucking agency says he's deceased!"

Paul remains stone-faced. "That is a lie."

"You knew about this?" Jessica's standing now, staring Paul down at his eye level. "You knew this bastard was still breathing out there?"

"I was read in after the war ended," Paul says. "I was not at liberty to share that disclosure with anyone else."

Jessica slams her tablet down so hard I'm afraid it might break, but the programmable matter just melts back into the flat surface of the conference table. "I retract my earlier objection. Let's go, right now, and drag this motherfucker back for the court martial he should have had six years ago—"

"As you were, Commander!" Paul barks.

Jessica closes her mouth and sits down.

"I appreciate your . . . fervor," Paul says. "And you're not alone. Retrieving Elba is ostensibly our primary objective for this mission, and that's how I was able to get State's approval so quickly."

"I'm sorry." I lean forward. "So you're saying that grabbing Elba is not *actually* our primary objective here?"

He fixes me with an icy glare. "I trust that you will do everything possible to return Elba to Earth, alive and well, for further processing. But your number-one priority is rescuing Martin. *Badger*."

He corrects himself quickly, but we've all noticed the slip.

Oliver is the first to speak up. "You're on a first-name basis with Badger?"

Paul actually blushes, both cheeks reddening below his pale blue eyes, and it's surprisingly uncomfortable to witness. I don't often see him caught out, but it's been a weird day all around. "Martin Shimura and I served together. Before the war. I . . . can't tell you any more than that."

"Let me guess. We don't need to know," Jessica says.

Paul inhales and exhales. "When I asked each of you to join this department, I also asked you to trust that I would insulate you from certain obstacles and impediments that would be a drag on your individual duties. Most of what I protect you from is bureaucracy and politics. But I also keep you safe by not telling you things that might keep you awake at night, expose you to unnecessary harm, or both. I'm asking you to continue trusting me now."

We're all silent for a moment. I glance over at Oliver, then Jessica, and all three of us nod. Paul seems to relax a little. That's unusual. Normally he behaves like he's omnipotent and self-sufficient, but in this moment, he actually seemed to be asking us for something. Maybe he's mellowing with age.

"I originally sent Badger into Cerulean to investigate peculiarities in their recent communications with Earth," Paul says.

"What kind of peculiarities?" Oliver asks.

"Nothing that I could convince Science or Intel to pursue." Paul definitely sounds bitter about that. "I'll share my findings with you, Equipment, see what you think. But I will tell you that Badger's reports back to me were also not as expected. He did include the proper challenge and response phrases, but all his protocols were . . . off."

"I'll look into it," Oliver says.

"You think someone got to him after he went inside?" I ask. "Elba, maybe?"

"I don't know, and I don't care," Paul says. "Grab Elba if you can. But get Badger out of there no matter what, as soon as possible. Do you understand?"

I nod. "Badger is job one, got it."

Paul opens a drawer and pulls out a round, translucent blue disk of memory crystal. "Surgical. A blue key for you."

"Hey, how come she gets the special thingy?" I ask. The agency likes to use hardware encryption keys with additional built-in biometric sensors to limit access to certain things. But these keys also automatically activate the equipment they're inserted into to perform specific functions. I have a red key—gifted to me by Gryphon, our

Director of Intelligence—which will phone home from any agency transmitter anywhere in the Solar System. A blue key will connect Jessica, and only Jessica, to the nearest agency receiver to her current position.

"Surgical and Equipment will also be on Venus, a safe distance away," Paul says. "Within communications range, so they can support you directly. We don't know what the situation is inside Cerulean. This operation must succeed."

Jessica tucks away the blue key in her trousers. "How long are we going to leave Kangaroo in prison?"

"I'd like to wrap this up as soon as possible," Paul says. "No more than two weeks in the hab."

"That already sounds like too long to me," I say out loud.

"Travel time shouldn't be an issue," Oliver says. "We'll also want to have a ship in orbit, since the bluejay will be a short-range service vessel only."

Paul nods. "The *Tacoma* will monitor operations and provide support. You have a blank check for the duration."

"So what's my legend going in?" I ask.

"You've been convicted of high treason and are remanded to a blue site for safekeeping."

That seems a bit extreme. "Just spitballing, could I be convicted of a lesser charge maybe?"

"We need this to seem as real as possible."

"But I haven't done anything treasonous!" Not recently, anyway.

"Don't worry," Paul says. "You will, at least on paper. But first I need Surgical to verify that Project Weyland-Yutani is on track."

"Ow. OW. *OW!*"

Jessica has hauled me off to her part of the office, a medical bay divided into an open examination area and a partitioned-off work-space. Right now I'm sitting on the exam bed while she electrocutes me through conductive metal straps around both my wrists.

"It will hurt less if you hold still," she says.

"One, I'm pretty sure that's a lie," I say, my teeth chattering as current continues to sizzle through my body. "Two, I thought this was going to be a *brief* application of electric current!"

She stops the electricity, and I slump back on the bed. "That was twenty seconds. You might be subjected to as long as forty."

"Doesn't that become life-threatening at some point? And aren't there laws around this kind of thing?"

"You're going to a secret military prison on another planet," Jessica says, picking up what looks like a tiny pitchfork and adjusting the control box it's attached to. "The guards aren't going to care too much about either the letter or the spirit of any law."

"Why are these things on my wrists, anyway?" I ask as she starts removing the electric cuffs. "Aren't all my control implants in my hands?"

Jessica frowns at me. "You have considerably more nerve endings in your palms and fingers. Are you actually *asking* to be shocked where it will be even *more* painful?"

"No," I say, folding my arms as soon as I'm free of the cuffs and tucking my hands under my armpits, out of the way of any medical instruments. "I just want to know what to expect from these prison doctors."

"There is always a risk of burns or scarring with a surface application of current via conductive contacts," Jessica says. "They won't want to risk damaging your palms or fingertips, since those are used for biometric identification. And the control relay for your implanted motion-input sensors is just above your wrists. That's the actual processor they'll want to disable, to make sure you can't use any of your hidden control functions."

"Okay, well, I'm glad we got this all sorted out. You're done taking readings then? I can go now?"

"Not yet." That's what I was afraid of. Jessica points the pitchfork box at me. "Take off your shirt."

I keep my arms folded. "Why?"

"Fine. Don't take it off." She moves forward.

I hold up a hand. "Whoa! Are you going to stab me with that— thing?"

"Yes."

I shake my head. "Is this really what they're actually going to do during my intake at the site?"

"They probably won't be as polite as I am." Jessica glares at me. "You've got ten seconds to remove your shirt, and then I'm going to punch through it with the probe. If you don't care about your shirt—"

"Fine! Fine." I start taking off my shirt. "Can you at least tell me why I'm going to get stabbed with a pitchfork?"

"It's not a pitchfork."

"And you're sure that's sterile? If it's going to break the skin—"

Jessica presses a button on the box, and I hear a crackling noise and then smell ozone. "There. It's sterilized."

I stare at her. "Did you just turn that thing on to zap any bacteria that might have been living on the pointy metal bits?"

"Bacteria, viruses, any other microorganisms that might cause infection. Ready?"

"Aren't you going to give me a painkiller or something? At least numb up the area that's going to get punctured?"

Jessica gives me a blank look. "I will as soon as you tell me you're ready."

I take a deep breath and nod. "Okay. Ready."

She swipes an alcohol rub across my chest, just below the collarbone, and then stabs me with the pitchfork thing.

I yelp, then make incoherent gurgling noises when she activates the thing and zaps me with who knows how much electricity. Actually, I can kind of tell it's not as much as a standard-issue personnel stunner, because I haven't passed out yet. But it's definitely more than a Pelican life-support fuel cell shorting out in my hands. Don't ask me how I know that. Long story.

It feels like an hour before Jessica yanks the pitchfork out of my shoulder, but she tells me it's only been fifteen seconds. I try to blink up my clock/timer display in my eye and get an error saying that it can't make a connection to the local wireless network.

I tell Jessica that my shoulder-phone's offline, and she nods. "Good." She puts down the pitchfork and picks up a computer tablet. "Now let's see how long it takes the nanobots to fix it."

This is the less fun of the two parts of what we're calling Project Weyland-Yutani, or PWY—"pee-why"—for short. Because a lot of people have tech implants these days—vision correctors, shoulder-phones, other things that may not be medically necessary—part of the blue site's intake procedure is disabling any implants that a new inmate might have, especially communication devices like my shoulder-phone. Military personnel in particular tend to get a lot of biotech enhancements to make them more effective on the battlefield. A lot of those implants are now designed to be modular, so they can be switched out depending on what a particular engagement requires, and removed completely at the end of a soldier's career. Of course, a lot of those retirees then get personal body mods implanted into the same slots, since they're already surgically altered to accept technological devices.

The doctors at Cerulean City will want to make sure that I don't have anything in my body that I could use to make trouble or attempt an escape. Unfortunately, since I don't have the standard modular implants used by the actual military, they can't easily pull things out and will have to use more invasive methods to disable my tech. The shoulder-phone, obviously, and my fingertip controls. Fortunately, I don't have any other obvious implants; my shoulder-phone contains all the computer core processors required to run my eye's sensors and heads-up display. The drug-dosing device in my abdomen can be passed off as an insulin pump. And nobody can detect my nanobots unless they know exactly what they're looking for, since the microscopic robots are manufactured using molecules from my body itself.

Here's the deal with the nanobots: they are probably the most secret thing about me. Even more than the pocket. Because the pocket, well, that's weird, but it's not going to freak people out as much as the nanobots would. They're technically illegal, and probably violate a double-digit number of international treaties banning certain nanotechnology research. Sure, simple medical applications are still allowed, but ever since the Fruitless Year—when some idiots in a lab decided to make tiny cyborgs, augmenting live viruses with microscopic robotics, and subsequently wiped out every single apple tree on Earth—people have been understandably skittish about biotech that you can't see and that can become airborne and spread across the globe in a matter of days. Also because viruses tend to mutate out of anyone's control, and when those viruses can also alter the technological components attached to them—well, we don't have to imagine how things could get out of hand and very bad very quickly, because it's in the history books now and no one who lived through it will ever forget.

Any kind of self-sustaining biotech that has even the faintest odor of "artificial general intelligence," or any autonomous technological pieces married to independent biological parts, is expressly forbidden now. Of course, there's nothing that top secret government agencies like more than experimenting with forbidden science, so for the last several years, Jessica has been working with Science Division to develop these new, tech-only nanobots. No biological components, so they can't mutate out of our control, and strictly low-level, fixed computer code, so they also can't self-modify themselves into sentience or anything. Granted, there is always the chance that something we never imagined will happen and the nanobots will run amuck inside my body, but I try not to think about that. They're just swimming around in my blood, happily maintaining a mesh network for all my tech implants. The lack of wires ought to help sell the idea that my shoulder-phone is the only real device the prison doctors will need to disable.

Because my nanobots aren't smart enough to teach themselves how to do anything, it's taken several months for Jessica and the Science Division brain trust to develop the software that will allow the nanobots to repair my biotech implants. This is a pretty huge leap forward in their utility, and if it works like we hope it will, it could eventually be a strong argument in favor of using the nanobots in other people for other things. I mean, we've already used them to cure cancer, sort of, but we can't tell anyone about that. That's another long story.

I touch the three red welts on my shoulder where the pitchfork zapped me. They look angry, and they definitely hurt when I touch anywhere near that area.

"Are the nanobots going to fix this, too?" I ask Jessica, pointing at my burnt shoulder.

"No," she replies, not looking up from her tablet, which I imagine is receiving signals from the nanobots telling her what they're doing inside me. "They're only programmed to repair specific technology. Like your shoulder-phone and computer core."

"So I'm going to have a giant scar on my shoulder the whole time I'm on this mission?"

"We'll fix you up before sending you out. And we'll do the same when you get back. But the people at Cerulean will expect you to have an ugly scar from your intake." Jessica looks up at me. "I understand it's a blue site badge of honor."

"Should I be feeling something different? Besides the pain, I mean? If the nanobots are rebuilding my fried implants?"

"You don't have nerve endings where they're working," Jessica says. "And most of their work is inside the casings of the implanted devices anyway."

"I guess that's good. When do we test the other part of PWY?"

The other part of Project Weyland-Yutani is more fun and less painful. At least, it has been in our tests so far. I do have to open one of my blood vessels to release the nanobots, but just a pinprick on one of my lesser-used fingers will work, and that heals pretty quickly all on its own, without any medical intervention.

Then, once I've opened a blood vessel, I just squeeze out a few drops onto something technological—a computer, a stunner, an electronic lockpad—and the nanobots will get to work dismantling said technology. Oh, yeah, as long as I've overridden their default setting to self-destruct after leaving my body, to avoid detection and possible reverse engineering by any enemy forces, and turned on this new function. Once enabled, they'll seek out and destroy anything with an electrical current. I can basically bleed on any electronic device and break it in a matter of seconds, usually.

In our controlled tests at Science Division, a few drops of blood ate right through a stunner's power pack in seconds. A laptop computer took a little longer, but I can also shorten the time by using more blood.

That's the only downside, I suppose: I can't get too overzealous with the bloodletting, otherwise I'll make myself woozy and be unable to do the other stuff I need to do on whatever mission it is. So no smearing blood all over an ionwell to shut down a spacecraft.

And that, of course, reminds me of one of the very few other people who have come into contact with my nanobots. And whom I can only discuss with Jessica Chu, for secret reasons.

"So," I say, doing my best to sound casual, "Lasher mentioned that he's assigning our friend Marmosa as the pilot for this mission."

"I don't know anything about that," Jessica says, a little too quickly.

I study her face. She seems to be very interested in what's being displayed on her tablet. Now, Jessica is usually more interested in dealing with machines than with people—she has that in common with Oliver, even if their preferences vary as far as what kinds of machines they like to bury their noses in—but this is excessive even for her.

"You want me to do a quick checkup when we're in the same room?" I ask. "I'll have to find some excuse to get Oliver to shut off my mission recorder. Maybe you can help me with that."

Jessica finally looks up from her tablet, her lips pressed into a tight, unhappy horizontal line. "I'd also have to download an additional sensor software module into your eye."

"Is that a problem?" I ask. "Do you not have time to write the software before I ship out?"

"Software's already written," she says. "But there's no chance Oliver won't notice it running in the background when he's monitoring your feed."

"Ah." This secret is something that Jessica and I and maybe two other people are even aware of: that we've used the nanobots on a number of civilians, to treat them for radiation exposure before they became symptomatic. I'm sure we kept those people from getting really bad cancers, and neither Jessica nor I feels bad about doing it, but because we did it completely off the books—not agency sanctioned, not under anyone's orders—we can't ask anyone else for help with follow-up. We've been tracking those civilians using the agency's extensive surveillance resources, watching to see if any of them shows signs of sickness that might be related to their radiation exposure two years ago, but the two of us can only do so much without asking other people for help.

"Maybe it's time to read him in."

"We've talked about this," Jessica says. "We can't."

"I wouldn't say we've so much 'talked about it' as I've brought it up and you've immediately shut me down every time," I say. "We can trust EQ. Lasher trusts him."

"I don't trust Oliver not to tell Paul about our little side project," Jessica snaps. "And that may not adversely affect you, but I have no desire to see the inside of a federal penitentiary."

It's probably true that, if someone finds out we deployed experimental military biotech on unsuspecting civilians—even if it was to save their lives—we'd find ourselves before a court-martial. Well, Jessica would, anyway. She's still technically an OSS reservist and therefore subject to the Uniform Code of Military Justice. I'm special, and Paul will protect me with every resource he can muster. But my doctor? He can find me another doctor. He's done it before.

"I can talk to him first," I say. "Feel him out. See if he's likely to report a—"

"No," Jessica says, leaning toward me. "Do not ask him hypothetical questions about ethics. You might as well just tell him you've been up to no good, and then he goes straight to Paul—"

"I'm meeting him after work," I say. "I'll get him drunk. Lower his inhibitions, get his guard down, then I'll sneak it into the conversation."

Jessica stares at me. "This may be the worst idea you've ever had, Kangaroo."

I raise my hands in a shrug. "Personal best." I point at her tablet. "Make a note for the history books."

"This isn't funny." She puts the tablet down and focuses her full attention on staring daggers at me. "We cannot tell anyone about the Red Wine."

"We have to disclose at some point," I say. "You want to use the nanobots for a lot of other things, right? Eventually get them out to the public? This would be a great start on a clinical trial."

"You don't understand how clinical trials work," Jessica says. "And any legal civilian application is still decades away. First the technology would have to be declassified. Then someone else, not the government, would need to develop it into a commercial system. It may not even happen within our lifetimes."

"That's awfully pessimistic."

"I'm a realist." She picks up the tablet again. "Try your shoulder-phone again."

I blink my eye and get the office feed back, a constant stream of data from the agency intranet that I can pick and choose from. "Hey, look at that! How long did that take?"

"Still too long." Jessica taps at the tablet. "All right. You run a full diagnostic and make sure everything's working again. I'll tweak the nanobot software to see if we can get the repair time down."

"Maybe you could ask Equipment about that."

She gives me a dirty look. "Drop it."

"You don't want me to talk to him, fine." I point a finger at her. "*You* talk to him. Just see if you think we can trust him with this information."

"It's too risky."

"Well, you're not the boss of me," I say. "You have until the end of this mission to feel him out and decide. If you don't think he's ready, fine. I'll trust your judgment. But I want to know that you at least talked to him. You'll have plenty of time while I'm in transit, right?"

Jessica sighs. "I could just lie to you."

"No." I shake my head. "I know you too well, Surge."

"Don't call me that."

"This is too important to you," I say. "You won't lie to me. I trust you."

"My answer is still likely to be no." She folds her arms. "I'm just being honest. There's a pretty high bar to clear in order to convince me that Oliver's going to be on our side on this issue."

"That's fine." I stand up and start putting my shirt back on. "You can say no. And I'll ask you again in two years, and then again two years after that. Decades, right?" I spread my arms. "The river will turn the rock into a pebble."

Jessica frowns at me, then shakes her head. "Come back when you're done complaining to Lasher and I'll fix that scar."

I finish buttoning my shirt. "Who says I'm going to complain to Lasher?"

Jessica gives me a look that unambiguously says: *Oh, come ON, really, dude?*

"I have no complaints," I say, sauntering out of the medical bay. "We're just going to talk."

"Right," Jessica says, turning back to her workstation.

"Just a casual conversation!"

"Go away and let me work."

"Weather! Sports! Dieting!"

She closes the door in my face. Only then do I realize that I forgot to ask about Joey, and feel terrible about it. But I need to let Jessica cool off before I engage her in conversation again.

Paul is studying some kind of orbital diagram when I walk into his office. He hides the display, waves his hand to tell his desktop to draw the extruded screen back down into its glossy surface, and looks up at me with a deeper than normal frown. "You're bleeding."

I look down at my shoulder. Three dark red spots are seeping through the fabric of my shirt. That's okay; it's not one of my favorites. And those stains will come out just fine. "Yeah, a little. Surgical gave me a preview of the reception I can look forward to on Venus. Do you know how they disable implanted devices during intake?"

"I'm aware of the basics."

I point at my shoulder. "Surge says she can repair this, but there's going to be a nasty scar there. How long will that take to heal up? This could be a problem for future missions."

"I have every confidence in Surgical's ability to remove any scarring. In the worst case, she can clone you a replacement graft."

"Hasn't there been enough cloning of me around here already?"

Paul stares blankly at me. Tough room.

I sit down in the chair across from his desk. "My point is, there must be a more—let's say 'seasoned' operative you can send out on this mission. I'm not great at undercover work. I'm not great on solo ops. I'm not going to do great for two weeks, alone, in a prison, pretending to be a bad guy."

"They're not all hardened criminals," Paul states, as if that's the most important point. "Cerulean City is an experimental isolation facility."

"Just saying, someone else would be better. Someone, not me, who's already scarred up. Someone who doesn't have nanobots to bleed out."

"The nanobots are one of your key advantages. You'll be able to break any electronic systems you need in order to escape."

"So many issues with this," I mutter. Time to change the subject. "You said Badger's messages started sounding 'off.' What specifically was 'off' about them? Do you think he's been compromised?"

Paul hesitates before answering. "I've known Martin Shimura for decades. I know what he sounds like when he talks, how he composes text messages, even very short ones. I don't know what's happened to him inside Cerulean, but he's definitely not himself. You need to get him out of there."

"And we really have no idea what kind of loony bin I'm walking into?"

Paul exhales, lips barely parted. "You'll have all the information I could get from Science Division available for review during your transit to Venus. Our analysts will do their best to flag any issues that might interfere with your operation."

I decide to press my luck. "So . . . you and Badger were old boot-camp buddies?"

"I never—" Paul purses his lips and squints at me. "What is it you really want to know, Kangaroo?"

"Back in the other room, you said 'I sent Badger into Cerulean.' *I*, not *we*. You personally, not the agency. And you needed to use Jordan Elba as a smoke screen to sell this new op to State." I'm reading between the lines here, but Paul's face tells me I'm hitting pretty close to the mark. "So why do you care so much if something funny's going on inside this one blue site? Why did you need to ask an old friend for a huge favor like going to prison for several months?"

Paul drums his fingers against the edge of his desktop for a moment before answering. "You were not wrong about too many secrets being a bad thing. Everyone's been on edge since Sakraida betrayed us, and with the election also coming up, a lot of people within the agency are concerned about their jobs and careers. They're playing things close to the vest even more than usual. Not sharing as much as they could. I don't like that."

"Because you're all about sharing and caring?"

"I'm here to get shit done," Paul snaps. "I don't care if I ruffle some feathers. And I don't like being kept out of the loop by people who are supposed to be working *with* me. D.Sci didn't like me sending Badger in without informing them, but they should have kept their own fucking house in order, and State's on my side now, so. Result."

He's talking about the Director of Science, one of our agency's three division heads and at least as well connected as Lasher. But to Paul Tarkington, everything looks like a nail. And he'll use both fists to pound on that nail if a hammer isn't available. My personal goal most days is to do my best to not look like a nail.

"One last thing," I say, pressing my luck. "Is it really necessary to bring both EQ and Surge along on this one?"

"The point of using the nanobots to restore your communications after site intake is so you'll be able to talk to your support team. That requires your support team to be within the same planetary radius."

"Not really? If they're farther away, it just means there'll be more of a communications lag." I really want to maximize my chances of being alone with Ellie long enough to remind her how good I am with my hands. In bed.

Paul leans forward, hands folded, elbows on his desk. "Equipment and Surgical need to monitor your mission feed in real time. This is not negotiable. If they believe you're in danger, we abort the operation and extract you immediately. Whatever's going on inside Cerulean, it's not worth losing you to find out."

I put a hand over my heart. "I'm touched, Lasher. You do care."

"Get yourself cleaned up." Paul points at my bloody shoulder. "And get some rest. You'll do another medical recheck with Surgical in the morning, then your load-out with Equipment, and you'll all leave together from here, through the tunnel, to meet Marmosa in orbit."

CHAPTER
FOUR

Earth—Washington, D.C.
Late afternoon is teatime, but . . . never mind

I send Ellie a dozen text messages asking to meet before she puts her foot down and insists that she has too much to prepare before our departure time. And I don't want to spend any more time getting bled in Jessica's body shop. So I have to go hang out with the last person on my list.

Oliver's apartment is as tidy as I expected. I don't think he's been officially diagnosed with obsessive-compulsive disorder, but he is very meticulous and precise. I suppose that's what makes him good at his job, but it also makes him very annoying to deal with as a human being.

He doesn't seem very impressed by my bullet journal when I pull it out of the pocket. It's in one of my own secret locations, and I've never even written down what the reference-object image is. There are a few things in my life that I'll never forget seeing—either because I don't want to, or because they were so traumatic. Either way, they make for great personal pointers. And I definitely don't want to lose my journal.

"That seems horribly inefficient," Oliver says as he watches me flip to a blank page toward the back. "What happens when you run out of space?"

"I start a new journal."

"And where do you put the old one?"

"I archive it."

"But it's not searchable. Surely you at least scan in the pages so you can find something more easily if you need to look it up."

"Nope," I say. "The whole point is to make it difficult to access. I don't want anyone stealing my secrets."

"They're all in the pocket anyway," Oliver says, looking exasperated. "You could use an air-gapped computer with a deep-cycle gel battery. It would last for decades if you needed it to."

"This will last for centuries." I hold up the journal. "No power at all required."

"Please tell me you're at least encrypting it. Using some kind of basic cipher when you're writing things down."

"Who am I, Leonardo freaking da Vinci? Like you said, it's going in the pocket anyway. If someone can get this out of the pocket without me knowing about it, I've got much bigger problems."

"I don't want you writing my name in there."

"Fine," I say. "I'll encrypt your name. I'll use an ancient cipher known as pig Latin." I pretend to write in the journal. "*Oliver-ay.* There. No one will ever know."

"This is no joking matter," he says, folding his arms. "I am entrusting you with a very important piece of my life. I need to know that you will treat it with the proper respect and appropriate security measures."

"Okay, okay." I hold up the journal so he can see the blank page. "I didn't write your name down. I promise I will not breathe a word of this to another living soul."

Oliver hesitates. "I need you to swear it, on the graves of your parents."

My heart catches in my throat for a moment. Oliver knows what happened to my parents, how I was orphaned—I'm sure he and Jessica were fully briefed on that as soon as they joined Paul's department. But we've never talked about it before, he and I. In fact, I don't know much about Oliver's personal history, either. This suddenly makes me more uncomfortable than all the security talk and his insinuations that I'm not taking his privacy seriously.

I suppose it's good that we're starting to open up to each other, sort of. Baby steps.

"I swear it," I say, "on the graves of my mother and father."

Oliver nods. "Do you already have a pointer in mind? Or would you like me to suggest one?"

I've been thinking about this ever since I made the deal with Oliver. Science Division selects all my reference objects, and sometimes they're a pain to remember because they're randomly generated. For my personal pocket locations, I have complete freedom to come up with more amusing pointers.

"I've got one in mind."

"Good. Don't tell me what it is." Oliver walks into his living room, goes up to the display mounted above his fireplace, and pulls it outward on a wall-mounted hinge arm. The flat-screen swings aside to reveal a safe built into the wall.

"That's a little on the nose," I say while blinking my eye into scan mode. I wonder if Oliver had any agency help constructing that safe. It's as sturdy as anything I've seen on a military base.

He leans forward, pressing his face up against the surface of the safe. There are no visible controls for opening it—no combination dial, no alphanumeric keypad, no apparent biometric scanners. But with my eye still in scan mode, I can see the sensors lighting up in infrared and EM frequencies, scanning his eyes, measuring his breath as he exhales through his mouth, and probably testing his skin and oil and sweat as his nose presses into the surface.

"Really on the nose," I say to myself.

The safe clicks and beeps, and the door disappears, melting back into the wall as the inside walls light up with a soft white glow. The scanning surface must have been made of something like the nanobots in my blood, except these are more durable and multipurpose.

Oliver reaches into the safe—I can see some indistinct shapes, things that look like data-storage devices, bundles of hard currency, and even some paper files, what a hypocrite!—and pulls out a stuffed animal, then closes the safe with a touch of his hand. The inside goes dark, and the hard-shell nanobots coalesce back into the door of the safe.

He walks back to me and puts the toy on the living room table between us. I look at it for a moment in scan mode, then blink my eye back to normal vision. There's a scan-proof container hidden inside the stuffed animal, which doesn't look like any mythological beast I've seen or heard of. It's a multi-headed, multi-legged, multi-tailed thing in various patchwork shades of brown.

"Um, what is it?" I ask.

"It's a half-pony, half-monkey monster."

"And why . . . ?"

"That's personal," Oliver says. "We agreed. No questions."

"No questions about the contents of your safe-sack," I say. "We didn't say anything about the exterior."

Oliver grumbles. "This belonged to my brother."

I blink and look up at him. He's only mentioned his brother once before, when we first met, and all I know is that he's dead. "Okay. What was his name, again?"

"Robbie."

"You never told me how he died."

"No. I didn't."

We stare at each other for a moment. Checkmate again. If I pry into Oliver's dead-brother situation, there's every chance he'll want to talk about my dead parents. And I don't want to do that.

Well played, EQ.

"Okay." I visualize the reference object I chose for Oliver earlier, on our way back from Korra Korra: a small plastic figurine of a white lab rat with a very large head. I've found that I can only use inanimate objects as pointers, so even if I want to imagine a type of live animal or real person, I actually have to think of a static reproduction of that animal or person.

My brain is weird. I've learned to live with it.

The portal opens in front of me, with the barrier—an energetic pressure curtain that keeps air from escaping into the pocket universe void —forming a glowing, translucent white disk over the hole. The back of the portal is facing Oliver, and what he should be seeing is just a wavy, shimmering, mostly reflective circular distortion in the air. I can only open portals in midair, away from solid objects, and there's some kind of quantum-physics explanation for why the pocket looks the way it does, but that's more Oliver's field. I don't care how it works, I just hide things in it.

I pick up the stuffed animal monster thing. It's surprisingly heavy. "Jesus, is this thing made of lead?"

"The airtight container inside is." That would also explain why I couldn't scan through it.

I briefly consider bending over so the portal is lined up with the floor and I can just drop the extra-heavy stuffed animal down into it. But then I'd have to use the rotation trick when opening to this location again, and the stuffie would come flying out toward me. I don't want this thing to accidentally bonk me when I'm retrieving it.

So I use both arms to hold it up and push it through the barrier into the hard vacuum of the pocket universe. I make sure the stuffie isn't moving relative to the portal, just for a few seconds while the hairs on my forearms complain about the freezing cold and lack of air, then let go and pull my arms back out and close the pocket. The glowing disk disappears noiselessly.

"Thank you," Oliver says.

I stand up. "And the mission log's already encrypted?"

He nods. "I locked the report before end of business. If anybody tries to open the file, I'll get an alert."

We stare at each other for a moment. "So now what?"

Oliver walks past me and opens the door. "Now you go away."

So hospitable. "Next time I'll bring some beers."

"Please don't."

CHAPTER
FIVE

Earth—Washington, D.C.
Before sunrise is too early to get up

Whoever names things within "the agency" isn't very creative or poetic. It is also distinctly possible that they choose the blandest possible official names for things so the descriptors don't give away anything about what those things actually are. "The office." "The shoe." "The cheese plate." That might be the more likely explanation, but in the absence of anyone actually explaining it to me, I'm going to assume it's just a lack of creativity. It makes me feel slightly better about naming something "Project Backdoor."

"The tunnel" is what the agency calls its own private subterranean transit system. My department's offices are located underground, in a former bomb shelter built to withstand a thermonuclear blast, and the building regulations that have existed in the District of Columbia since it was designated our nation's capital, restricting the height of buildings for safety and national security reasons, means a lot of things get hidden below street level—there are public tunnels between different Congressional office buildings, and secret tunnels in and out of the White House and the Capitol building. The agency inherited some of these old subway tunnels after newer, aboveground mass transit systems were built, not to mention sea-level rise flooding out parts of the old underground network.

Science Division then caved in some of the old subway tunnels on purpose, so nobody can sneak up on us that way, and excavated new tunnels to connect current agency locations. If I don't need to establish cover on a given day, I might ride the tunnel from near my apartment to the office. That's what I do this morning, meeting Oliver and Jessica at the Logan Circle platform to wait for our shuttle to the launch facility.

Both Oliver and Jessica are already on the platform when I arrive. True to form, they are not talking to each other, but instead have their noses buried in their respective devices: a palm-sized phone for Jessica, and a larger computer tablet for Oliver.

Sometimes I wonder how Paul assembled our motley little crew. I know how he found me: by accident, on the worst night of my life, after I'd gotten my best friend killed. I was fifteen years old and more than ready to accept the protection of a shady government agency; it seemed far better than the alternative at the time, dealing with organized crime. And I know a little bit about how he got Jessica tangled up in his web, through her half sister who used to be my doctor before she started conducting illegal medical experiments on me without anyone's knowledge. Long story. Don't like to think about it. She's dead now.

Oliver, though: I don't know how Paul recruited Oliver. The dead-brother thing sounds awfully similar to Jessica's situation, but her sister only died last year. I know Oliver never served in the military, because he's genuinely clueless most of the time I trot out some military jargon. I know he's a whiz with pretty much any type of electronic or mechanical gadget, from firearms to robots—his job as my Equipment officer also includes being my personal armorer. Sometimes I wonder about the incongruity of this nerdy guy being a crack sharpshooter. Every time he takes me onto the shooting range to demonstrate some new weapon he's developed for me to carry, I'm shocked at his marksmanship skills. I wouldn't think someone who enjoyed building and tinkering with delicate electronics would also enjoy blasting the crap out of targets in his spare time. Maybe it's therapeutic for him. I don't know, I'm not a doctor.

I stroll up to Oliver and Jessica. The platform is empty except for them and their bags. The tunnel is secured at all entrances and exits, so there's no need for armed security down here. There are cameras covering all accessible areas, and the agency does have security robots docked in charging niches at every platform, but those don't get deployed unless something bad actually happens.

"Who brought coffee?" I ask loudly. Jessica and Oliver both look up at me and frown.

"No one said anything about coffee," Oliver says, and looks over at Jessica.

Jessica glares at me and turns back to her phone.

I shake my head. "Okay. Baggage check, then?"

Oliver stands up and puts away his tablet. "All ready for you." He drags his and Jessica's bags forward by the flexible cable strung through their handles. He opens the clasp on the cable and holds the two ends apart.

I think of a purple anvil and open the pocket using the rotation trick. My own packed bag falls out, bouncing against the hard floor of the platform. Oliver gives me a disapproving look, like I'm some reckless teenager doing donuts in a parking lot and not a legit superhero who's been boomeranging stuff through the pocket for years.

I turn the luggage so the handle is facing him. "There's nothing fragile in here."

He threads the cable through the handle and closes the clasp. "It's the principle of the thing."

All three of our bags are now connected by the cable. I think of the purple anvil again and open the pocket, barrier in place. Oliver helps me heft the bags into the portal.

This is another one of the pocket mysteries that Science Division hasn't cracked yet: I can only put one item inside the pocket at a time, locked to a specific location. "Item" is defined as a single, solid object, or—as in the case of our luggage—a collection of objects tied together with another solid object.

It makes sense, from a macroscopic point of view: most of the things I put in the pocket aren't solid, unbroken shapes. Every machine is a multitude of different objects assembled together into a single collection of things that are physically touching, or at least enclosed. A piece of cloth is a large number of fibers woven together. It's that physical contact or enclosure that defines a single "item" to the pocket. So if I want to store multiple items in the same location—six bottles of beer, for instance—those bottles would need to be connected by a six-pack holder or some rope or something. Otherwise? Well, again, it's not clear exactly how this works, but the pocket will randomly decide to "lock" onto just one of the distinct items. And the other items just . . . disappear.

I mean, I'm sure they're still in the pocket somewhere, but they're no longer tied to the reference object I visualized for that location. So I have no idea where they might be, and no way to know what other reference object to visualize to retrieve them. And with an entire, apparently infinite pocket universe to search, it's worse than a needle in a haystack. It's like trying to find a single electron in an entire planet's worth of atoms. Even worse than that. I'm not good at math. Or metaphors.

I close the pocket after all our bags are in, then sit down on the bench between Oliver and Jessica. Oliver pulls out his tablet again and starts reading something on it. Jessica is tapping at her phone like it's done something to upset her.

"So," I say, "about Agent Marmosa."

"Not my recommendation," Oliver says at the same time that Jessica says, "I don't care."

"That's great." I fold my arms. "So you both knew about it, and chose not to tell me. Great teamwork there."

Jessica stops jabbing at her phone to give me a dirty look. "I was hoping to minimize the time you'd spend complaining about this. But perhaps that was just wishful thinking."

I turn to Oliver. "And what's your excuse?"

He puts down his tablet. "I merely provided Lasher with a list of prerequisites for our pilot. I have no control over how he selects personnel. You know that."

"So you're both passing the buck. Nice."

"Why is this our problem?" Jessica asks. "From where I'm sitting, you're the only one who has an issue with this, Kangaroo. Three out of four people in Outback have no problem with Lasher's pilot selection."

"Well, one of those three is Lasher, so he doesn't count," I say. "And let me just say, if he tried to assign someone to an op that I knew one of you didn't want along for the ride? I would speak up on your behalf. Because I care about you."

"I'm touched," Jessica deadpans. "I don't see why you have a problem with Marmosa anyway. I thought you two were doing well."

"That was before someone"—I stare at Oliver—"miscalculated the ETA for my exfil and left me locked in a room with a lascivious degenerate."

"That is a gross exaggeration of the circumstances," Oliver says.

"I thought nothing happened," Jessica says. "Did something happen?"

"Nothing happened," I say emphatically. "She saw me naked. Very briefly. That's it." I pause. "There may have been some intimate touching."

"Ah." Jessica nods and turns back to her phone. "I see the problem. Good luck with that."

"Aren't you supposed to help me with things like this?"

"I'm a physician, not a therapist."

"I may be in serious threat of physical harm if I say the wrong thing."

"Marmosa wouldn't lay a hand on you," Oliver says. "Hyperbole will be the death of you, Kangaroo."

I stare at him. "Okay, that's actually hilarious."

A chime sounds above us. Jessica stands up. "Thank God."

The train arrives, and we board it for our trip to the spaceport. Each of us sits in a different row of seats.

A short time later, but not short enough, we're into orbit and aboard the Eyrie: the former warship that's been converted into a space station and now serves as the headquarters for the agency's Intelligence Division. For security reasons, or so I've been told. I've had the dubious honor of participating in the annual war games that the agency's Science, Intel, and Ops Divisions run against each other, including one engagement that involved an attempt to breach the Eyrie without being detected. We failed pretty spectacularly. Gryphon runs a tight ship, literally.

I meet Gryphon while Jessica and Oliver take our luggage over to the spacecraft that's going to take us to Venus. Normally I wouldn't look forward to meeting with any director-level person in the federal government, but there are things I'm looking forward to even less right now, and anything I can do to delay them is acceptable.

Gryphon is wearing an OSS dress uniform, which is certainly her prerogative as a fleet admiral, but it makes me feel severely under-dressed in my generic flight suit. She shakes my hand, the white uniform sleeve making an unusually noticeable contrast with her brown skin.

"Welcome back, Kangaroo," she says, smiling just enough to be polite but not so much that it seems insincere.

"Thank you, Admiral."

Her brow furrows, just for an instant. "We've talked about this before, Kangaroo. Code names?"

"Sorry. Gryphon. It's just, the uniform threw me off. Ma'am." Not to mention how the sight of it reminds me that Admiral Darlene Morris is a multiply decorated war hero, and we're floating inside what used to be her battleship, the *Waukegan*. "I thought we were meeting informally?"

"My apologies. I had another thing right before this." She waves toward a transport tube. "Shall we?"

I lead the way into the cylindrical tram car that travels through a series of tubes to move people around the inside of the station. "You're not campaigning or anything, are you?" I ask as a joke while we both buckle our safety harnesses. These trams don't have seats because we're in zero gravity, and also because we're weightless, we need to be strapped in so we don't bounce all over the place as the car zigs and zags its way through the interior of the Eyrie.

Gryphon gives me a stern frown while she buckles up. I guess she does this often enough that she doesn't need to look down while she does it. "You know that's not allowed, Kangaroo. But we are technically part of the State Department, and we are obligated to welcome any visitors from Capitol Hill, especially those on certain subcommittees."

I nod and decide I don't need to ask any more questions as the tram starts moving. I do my best to avoid knowing too much about what happens above my pay grade, not just because I'm annoyed by office and actual politics, but also because I generally can't do much about the shit that rolls downhill. I'm stuck in my current position for as long as Paul Tarkington is alive, probably, and I trust that he'll protect me from the worst of it as much as he can. My problems usually come from Paul himself, and that I can handle. More than that? I don't need the aggravation.

"Joey's doing well," Gryphon says after a pause. "Commander Chu told you that, right?"

"Yeah. Have you seen him?"

Joey is my now-seven-year-old clone, who was hidden on the Moon for the first several years of his life and is now living on the space station orbiting Earth that serves as headquarters for the Intelligence Division of our agency. The Eyrie has a rotating gravity ring that has been modified to produce centripetal forces simulating different amounts of gravity, and Jessica's been working with Science Division to acclimate Joey's body—which was born and has been growing in the one-sixth gee of Lunar gravity—to as close to an Earth standard one gravity as we can get.

We want him to have as normal a life as possible. Granted, that's not going to be very normal at all, since he's a clone of the only secret agent in the world with a superpower and hasn't lived anywhere except the Moon and a space station so far, and he grew up watching the same twentieth-century television shows and movies as I did because the people who made him thought that might condition his brain to also be able to use the pocket. But we're doing our best.

"Not recently," Gryphon replies. "He seems a little uncomfortable around women. Except for Chu, of course."

I don't say what I'm thinking: that I also had trouble forming close relationships with female-presenting people when I was younger. Possibly even now, but that's between me and my agency-appointed therapist. I remind myself that it's still not unusual for young boys, especially those raised in patriarchal societies, to have difficulty relating to people of other genders.

But Joey wasn't raised in a normal household. He was raised alone, in a secret lab at the south pole of the Moon, by a morally flexible doctor who cloned me without my knowledge. And now Joey's living in a space station, with more people around, but no other children. His life is about as far from normal as a kid can get.

I mean, I didn't exactly have a typical upbringing myself, but at least I was on Earth the whole time.

The tram slows to a stop, and Gryphon leads the way out of the transport tube. It takes me a bit to focus my efforts on catching each handhold as I pull myself along the corridor toward the entry to the rotating habitat section.

This part of the Eyrie is a long hollow cylinder stuck sideways through the middle of the former warship's hull, with larger modules at either end—it's shaped like a dumbbell, or a cartoon dog bone. It rotates just fast enough to make it feel like close to half of Earth's gravity in the modules at either end. All long-haul spacecraft with large crews have something like this, so that people can exercise or do physical therapy in an environment that exerts some fraction of the expected pressures on their body. When the *Waukegan* was refitted to be the Eyrie, the pylons leading to the grav-modules were extended in length so they could ramp up to nearly one full gee, and when Joey was moved here, they were further modified so that the modules could be located at different lengths down the struts on either side. Jessica's overseeing the slow, multi-year process of acclimating Joey to live in higher and higher gravities, starting at the one-sixth gee he was born into on the Moon and hopefully getting all the way up to one gee before he gets too stir-crazy and tries to break out.

I mean, there's a lot of security around here, but if he has anything like my personality as a teenager, he's going to be a handful. Not to mention if he also develops a pocket ability of his own.

We don't talk about it much, but I know it's on everyone's mind, all the time. As far as we know, I'm still the only person who's ever existed with the power to open a portal into an empty void where I can hide stuff, as long as the stuff doesn't mind the complete lack of air, light, and heat. But if the agency had a second agent who had the same superpower—if they could *make* more people with the same ability— well, that's why Joey exists in the first place, medical ethics be damned.

I'm glad we were able to rescue him from the Moon. But saving him from what could still be a terrible existence, that's probably going to be a project for the rest of my life.

There's plenty of time, possibly too much time, for me to contemplate all this while Gryphon and I climb down the long ladder from the centerline of the Eyrie through the habitat pylon and finally to Joey's habitat module. We step into a small enclosed chamber and wait for the sensors to check us for contaminants or disease vectors. Jessica's also been introducing various innocuous bacteria and germs to Joey's otherwise sterile living environment, in anticipation of him someday actually walking on dirt. But like the gravity acclimatization, it's a slow process, and she wants complete control so she can hit the brakes if he starts reacting badly.

"You ought to go in first," Gryphon says as the airlock finishes cycling. "He'll be happy to see you."

I nod. The inner door slides open, blasting me in the face with a draft of warm air and the sound of televised voices. I step through and start to ask whether Joey really likes it this warm in here, but stop when I see that he's completely naked, sitting in a reclining armchair custom-made to fit him—which also includes a myriad of hidden medical monitoring sensors, I'm sure—and rocking back and forth slightly while reading a book. He's got his back turned to the wall screen, where an old twentieth-century TV show is playing.

Joey looks up at me. "Kangaroo!" he shouts.

The book falls to the floor. He leaps up out of the recliner and bounds across the floor to me, and throws his arms around me in an enthusiastic embrace. I pat his shoulder lightly. "Hey, Joey. How's it going?" I'm glad to see that Gryphon is already at the closet, searching for some clothes. Joey releases me and takes a step back to answer my question.

"I'm okay. How are you? Doctor Chu didn't say you were coming to visit. Is something happening?"

"No, I was just in the neighborhood, figured I'd stop by to say hello." I point at the TV. "*Knight Rider* not your cup of tea?"

"What? I don't know." He glances at the screen, then folds his arms across his chest and shakes his head. "It's really annoying that I can't turn it off."

Gryphon comes back from the closet with some kind of smock and throws it on over Joey's head. He doesn't resist much, which tells me that this is a not-infrequent occurrence around here.

"Joey, why don't you tell Kangaroo what you've been reading?" Gryphon says.

The kid shoves his arms out through the sleeves of the garment and looks up at me. "There's this whole series of books, the Sassy Cat Mysteries! Have you heard of it? Mimi Lee lives in the city of Los Angeles, California, on planet Earth, and she has a talking cat, Marshmallow, and they solve mysteries!"

He runs back to his chair, picks up the book, and brings it over to me. I take the book—it's weird, feeling an actual hardbound paper book in my hands. My understanding is that these are printed on demand here on the Eyrie, because apparently it makes Joey more excited to receive a physical object than to see a new screen of information on an existing tablet or other device. I can understand that feeling. I didn't have a lot of my own possessions, growing up as an orphan in a long series of less-than-ideal household situations. It's nice that Joey can have a little more stability than that.

But this is also at odds with what the agency's trying to do, controlling his living environment so he'll be more likely to develop the same pocket power that I have. Since nobody knows why I have this ability to begin with, the best they can do is attempt to reproduce any known factors that might have affected my brain development at a younger age. And that includes watching a whole lot of old media programs.

"Yeah, this looks great," I say, flipping through the pages of *Mimi Lee Fights the Power*. "But what about this TV show? See that?" I point at the screen, which is currently displaying a dramatic car chase. "Doesn't that look interesting?"

Joey makes a supremely uninterested noise with his mouth. "They're always chasing somebody around. It's like the same thing happens every time. *Boooooring.*"

I exchange a look with Gryphon. I'm sure she and Joey's direct handlers are dealing with this, but I can't help but feel responsible since, well, he's me. But he's also not me. Joey has the same genes as I do, but he's not growing up with the same experiences. He doesn't have the same reason that I did to voraciously consume all these episodes of antiquated adventure shows—but all that TV watching undoubtedly shaped my neurological development, and the agency wants Joey exposed to the same stuff. We don't know if binge-watching all of *Knight Rider* will eventually give Joey a superpower, but those in charge believe it's worth a shot.

It's ironic, really: a kid who *doesn't* want to watch a ton of TV all the time.

And I can't decide whose side I'm on. Would it be better for Joey to *not* have a superpower when he grows up, so he won't be locked into a life like mine, beholden to the agency because of my special ability? But if the agency does cut him loose at some point—which I'm not even sure they would allow, given all that he's seen already and all that he knows about me and the secret Moon base and whatnot—what kind of a life would he be able to have then? Nothing special about him except being the first viable clone of another human being, but again, that would be a thing that he couldn't tell anybody else.

The kid's going to be messed up whichever way it goes. But, like most of the times when I revisit this situation in my mind, I fall on the side of wanting him to have his own pocket when he grows up. Not just so that he'll be guaranteed protection and access, but also because it would be nice to not be the only person in the world with a superpower.

It would be nice to feel a little less lonely all the time.

"Hey, I'll make you a deal, okay?" I kneel down so I'm more at Joey's eye level. I'm told this makes children more comfortable when speaking with adults. "I need to go away for a little while, but while I'm traveling, I'll have some time to watch TV. What do you say we both watch the same show, so we can talk about it when I get back?"

Joey shifts from one foot to the other and gives me a dubious look. "Does it have to be *this* show?" He waves one arm disdainfully back at the screen, where a man is having an argument with his talking car.

"No, it can be something else. A detective show, maybe? We've got a list somewhere." I glance up at Gryphon, who nods at me and makes a note on her wrist-mounted computer. "Gryphon's going to tell me what you pick, and we can message each other while I'm away, okay?"

"How much TV do I have to watch each day?" Joey asks.

I hesitate to answer, since I'm afraid any number will sound too big and will immediately diminish his enthusiasm. "Why don't you pick a show first and then we'll figure that out later. Okay?"

Joey makes a resigned flapping noise with his lips. "I guess."

"Great." I stand up, hopefully signaling to everyone that it's time to wrap this up and go our separate ways. Joey immediately lunges forward and hugs my legs again, even more tightly this time.

"When are you coming back?" he asks. "Can we go outside next time?"

Jesus, he's breaking my heart. "I'm sure Gryphon can arrange for you to spend some time on the observation deck." There are no windows in Joey's hab module, partly for environment control and also because we don't want him getting motion sickness from seeing the constant rotation. One of the wall screens is dedicated to a live view of Earth beamed from a geostationary satellite, but Joey knows that's not real.

"I wanna go outside!" he wails in a tone that could easily become very irritating after any more than a few seconds. "It's boring in here! I want to play!" He grabs my sleeve and yanks on it repeatedly.

I look at Gryphon again. "What happened to that simulation environment we talked about?" We've been trying to figure out ways to mitigate Joey's captivity, for lack of a better term. We don't lie to him about where he is, so he knows he lives on a space station in Earth orbit, and that unfortunately means he wants to "go outside" for a spacewalk, which his doctors have absolutely prohibited because of the radiation danger.

We're already rolling the dice, having him live up here, but we know he won't survive in heavier gravity until his body can adapt.

Nobody really knows whether the increased cosmic radiation exposure outside of Earth's atmosphere will have a huge influence on his growth and development. We just don't have much of a choice.

Gryphon shakes her head. "He's not into it. Doesn't like wearing the headset." Nobody has yet figured out a better way to do "virtual reality" than strapping tiny binocular screens to your face, possibly because there are still very few practical applications for the technology.

I make a monumental effort to avoid sighing or groaning with exasperation while being roughed up from below. "Hey. Joey. Joey? Let go now. Joey!"

Gryphon helps me pry his arms off my legs. I'm afraid he's going to start crying, so I talk fast, not really caring right now whether I'm making promises I can actually keep.

"Okay, this is the deal. You're going to pick a new show to watch, I'm going to watch it at the same time and we're going to message each other about it, and you're going to give the VR thing another try, okay?"

"I don't like it!"

"They're going to see if they can make it more comfortable for you. But I want you to promise me you'll just try it again, for a full session, and I'm going to bring you back a souvenir from my trip, okay?"

His face brightens a little at that. "What kind of souvenir?"

"What would you like?"

"Where are you going?"

"I can't tell you. Just, in general, what do you want?"

He scrunches up his face and says, "Can I have a cat?"

I'm caught off guard and hesitate before answering. "I don't think so. Pets aren't really a good idea in here."

"I want a cat!" This is the problem with asking children open-ended questions.

"Maybe," Gryphon says, "you could find something catlike instead, Kangaroo."

I frown at her. "What kind of catlike thing would I—"

"Let's discuss it outside," she says, giving me a hard look. "You need to go."

"Oh. Right." I pretend to check the time. "Okay, Joey, I'm going to bring you back the most catlike thing I can find on my trip. It's going to be a surprise."

"Okay!" Joey, apparently mollified, grabs his book and sits back down in his chair. Still facing away from the TV. "Bye!"

Gryphon swivels his chair around to face the TV before we leave. He's opened the book by now, and doesn't seem to notice much.

Once Gryphon and I are sealed in the airlock again, I say, "I can't wait to see your list of catlike things that I could possibly bring him."

"It's going to be fine," Gryphon says. "Even money says he'll have forgotten all about it by the time you get back."

"I wouldn't be so sure about that," I grumble. I remember how much I wanted a pet when I was young. Any kind of pet. And if Joey doesn't already know he's got leverage for demanding goodies from his adult caretakers, he'll figure it out soon. This kid's going to be a nightmare when he gets to be a teenager.

This is the part I've been both looking forward to, and dreading.

I don't actually see Ellie until we've boarded the spacecraft that's going to take us to Venus. I've just picked my seat when she floats into the ship, gives me a hard stare down the length of the passenger cabin, then turns and pulls herself into the cockpit.

I sigh and start the long journey forward to the cockpit, bumping against every goddamn seat along the way. At least that's what it feels like. Zero gravity sucks. Not literally. You know what I mean.

Ellie's strapped into the pilot's chair when I get there, running down her preflight checklist. I take a moment, floating in the doorway, to admire her. Even from the back, with her hair tied back in a ponytail that splays out into a messy weightless flare of brown strands, she's beautiful. I don't know what it is. Something about the way her shoulder curves, the way her arms and hands and fingers move. Maybe because I've seen all those parts without clothes on, and experienced how deft her touch is on my own body.

But I can't get distracted right now. I need to address the problem at hand—namely, that she seems annoyed with me. She didn't come back to the passenger cabin to talk, which means either she's avoiding the conversation or she wants me to initiate it. Probably the latter. But she's not going to tell me that, not verbally anyway, because then she'd be starting the conversation and that would defeat the purpose of her letting me have the opening line. She wants to hear what I have to say for myself before speaking her piece.

I've been a spy in one form or another for almost thirteen years now, but this is my first attempt at maintaining anything resembling a long-term personal relationship. And Jesus motherlovin' Christ, it's the toughest thing I've ever done.

Eleanor Gavilán was the chief engineer aboard *Dejah Thoris*, the Princess of Mars Cruises spaceliner that was hijacked two years ago and nearly crashed into Mars Capital City. I happened to be aboard at the time, and I helped stop that act of terror. But before all the shouting was done, I had also gotten emotionally involved with Ellie. And she had picked up some PTSD from being held hostage during the crisis.

We didn't talk too much immediately after the incident, except to make sure that we were both unharmed and still interested in seeing each other. We knew it was going to be tough, what with both of us working vastly different jobs and having to be apart for weeks or months at a time. But then Paul Tarkington stepped in and appeared to make our lives somewhat easier.

I still don't know how he convinced Ellie to join the agency. I know she was in the Outer Space Service, years ago, but she retired before the war with Mars began. It wasn't her military experience or connections that Paul was able to use as leverage. I'd be willing to bet that some sort of blackmail was involved—I have no illusions about how Paul operates—but I never asked Ellie, since I figured it would be something very private and personal and really not any of my business.

For a while, it was nice. It almost felt normal. I worked a number of operations on or close to Earth, and Ellie went through agency training in various sites around Earth, in orbit, and on the Moon. We saw each other almost every week, and we spent long enough apart each time that the first night together after every break was like getting together for the first time, rediscovering how to pleasure each other, catching up on our lives. It was remarkably freeing, being able to talk about my actual work and having more things in common due to Ellie's agency clearance. She already had a pilot's license and a spacecraft engineering degree, but she needed to learn tradecraft if she was going to work Operations.

And she learned pretty quickly. That turned out to be part of the problem.

As soon as Ellie finished her agency training, Paul started sending her out on missions. Usually into outer space, and usually not with me. I'm not sure if he did that on purpose—I'm never really sure how much Paul considers anybody's feelings when weighed against what he needs to accomplish, both operationally and politically. He's aware that the people who work for him are human beings, with independent thoughts and emotions, but he will also push people as far as he thinks he can without breaking them. It's always about the greater good. Or just his greater purpose.

So Ellie and I started seeing each other in person less frequently. We could send recorded messages back and forth, but with long and irregular delays that made actual conversation impossible, and we couldn't talk about anything too sensitive in those recordings. It's true what they say about long-distance relationships being hard to maintain. Human beings are built for physical contact and face-to-face communications. Not knowing how long you'll have to stay apart, not knowing when the next message will come—that's worse than almost any form of psychological torture I can imagine.

At one point, we almost called it off. We even talked about it, but we both felt like that would be giving in too easily. She didn't say that part out loud, but I could see it in her eyes and the set of her jaw. We had been through more than a few hellish situations at that point, life-or-death crises during shared operations, and if we could get through those, what was a few weeks of waiting here and there? It seemed like capitulation if we simply decided to stop trying.

But, like I said, torture. Never underestimate the cumulative effect of uncertainty and anxiety on a person's psyche. That's how captors wear down prisoners of war. That's how kidnappers turn their victims into Stockholm-syndrome'd accomplices. You can't live in limbo forever.

We're still trying. But it seems like every circumstance in the world is conspiring against making it easy for us to be together. Yes, okay, we could both choose less stressful jobs—or at least Ellie could; I'm not sure Paul would ever let me leave the agency—but that's not part of the deal. We're fighting to have our cake and eat it too.

I watch Ellie run down her preflight checklist for maybe half a minute, trying to figure out what the best opening line would be. Do I dive right in with a serious pronouncement about how to address our relationship situation? Do I break the ice with a joke? Or do I offer to help her with the work at hand?

Joking feels the most natural to me—hello, I'm Kangaroo, have we met?—but I don't want her to think I'm not taking this seriously. Offering to help with her work would show that I'm sensitive to her current needs, but again, maybe I don't want to imply that I'm avoiding the elephant in the room.

So that leaves the adult option: saying something about the relationship difficulty we're having. The trouble is, I'm not sure I want to open with such a grave tone. We're still okay, aren't we? Sure, we haven't seen each other in more than a month, but we were talking. The last message I sent to her was about my upcoming mission, to visit Korra Korra and retrieve a very special item. And to meet the defector who was bringing it to us. I did mention that I was meeting Rose Kim on the island—

Oh. Yeah. Ellie probably didn't like me taking a tropical vacation with another woman. That's probably why her last message was so short.

I call up the transcript in my eye—I don't have time to replay the whole thing—to see if I can read between the lines. She told me to be careful, said she couldn't wait to see me . . . what am I missing here?

And that's when I realize just how much of an idiot I am.

You might think that, with all this agency training to be vigilant and hyper-aware on mission, I would be more perceptive all the time. But that's not really the case. It's exhausting to be on guard every single second, and I don't want to use my tools on my colleagues or friends. Not that I have any actual friends outside of work. This might explain why it's been hard for me to adapt to treating Ellie like a romantic partner. Because I'm not sure what that's supposed to feel like.

Anyway, now that I'm actually studying the transcript for emotional cues, I can see what she's saying by not saying certain things and by her choice of words. I pull up the actual vid and scan to the middle to check on something I dimly remember and yup, there it is, a pause and a look away. Why am I such an idiot? I know what it means when someone breaks eye contact during a conversation, and I should have paid more attention.

Now I'm almost certain this is why she's upset. But how do I broach the subject without seeming like a heel? I want to be sensitive, but not too mushy. We established our boundaries, Ellie and I, and I didn't break them. Maybe I should lead with that.

Maybe I should have spent more time thinking about this before literally the last five minutes.

I sit down in the co-pilot's seat with my body turned toward Ellie. I don't want be looming over her while we talk, and I also don't want to seem like I'm distracted by the spacecraft controls while we're talking. I'm placing myself at her level, and we're having a conversation as equals, and I'm giving her my full attention.

Sometimes it does help to have all this secret-agent training for navigating social situations.

"Hello," I say, opting for something simple, and also to make sure she's in a talking mood.

"Hello." Ellie doesn't look up from her checklist.

Right. I'm doing the heavy lifting right now. Ball's in my court. "When did you get back to Earth?"

"Didn't. Got cleaned up here on the Eyrie. Lasher said we're tight on time."

I nod. "Yeah. Oliver said something about orbital insertion windows—" No. Stop. Don't stray off topic. "Is everything okay?"

"I'm fine."

"Are *we* okay? You and me?"

She finally stops and looks at me. "You tell me, Kangaroo."

"Well," I say slowly, "I thought we were. Until your last message. Which made me kind of uncertain." *Jesus Christ, Kangaroo, you can speak in complete sentences. Don't be an idiot. Or at least don't sound like one.*

"Sorry. I didn't have a lot of time to compose the message." She stops working her checklist and turns to look at me. It takes a monumental effort for me to not fall into her dark eyes. "You know you can ask me anything, right, Kangaroo?"

It still stings that she doesn't know my birth name, the one my parents gave me before they died. But I can't tell her. I may never be able to tell her.

At least she's calling me by a name and not an epithet.

"I know," I say. "But there remains the matter of whether you'll actually answer said question, and whether you'll be offended that I dared to ask it in the first place."

She lowers the checklist and stares out the window for a moment before turning back to me. The shuttle is docked with the Eyrie but pointed outward, away from the Earth, and the Moon isn't in our line of sight right now. The interior of the cockpit is bright enough that it washes out the faint stars visible from Earth orbit.

"You can talk to me like a human, Kangaroo," she says. I bite my tongue to prevent offering impromptu commentary on the ironic juxtaposition of the words in that statement. "Like a normal person. You don't have to watch what you say around me; I'm not an asset, this isn't some negotiation, it's just you and me. We're just two people trying to figure this out. Can we agree on that as a starting point?"

I want to agree with her. I want everything to be just fine, I want us to be happy and to do happy things together and not have to worry about scheduling our time together and keeping the right work secrets from each other and not knowing each other's true names. But this isn't the life I have, and it's not the life that she's opted into now.

We can't be normal people. I'll never be normal. And like it or not, the agency's personal-interaction handbook has been drilled into me by several years of training. I wouldn't say I'm particularly good at it —several incidents in the past two years have demonstrated that I really am not—but I still think about it. All the time. Because I don't know any other way to deal with people.

"You're thinking about it right now, aren't you?" she says. "Calculating the angles. Trying to come up with the best thing to say to keep yourself out of trouble."

"I'm sorry," I say, meaning it sincerely but unable to keep the exasperation out of my voice. "It's what I've been trained to do. I'm working on it."

"So work on it," Ellie says. "Just tell me the first thing that comes into your head, right now. Go."

"I'm not a normal person," I say, proud of how little thought I had to put into it. "I'll never be normal."

"So don't worry about it. Just be yourself."

"I wasn't myself when we met."

"Of course you were." She smiles and reaches out to take my hand. My skin tingles with delight at her touch. "There are some things you can't hide. Change your face, change your name, carefully choose every word you say—there will still be something unique about the way you talk. The way you move." She laces her fingers between mine, and I suddenly wish we had more privacy—and more time—before launch.

"I didn't sleep with her," I blurt out. "All I did was kiss her a little. And put my hands on, you know, her body. But it was part of the job. I promise, nothing happened."

Ellie frowns at me. "You kissed who? What are you talking about?"

I blink at her honest expression. Of course. She's only been on the Eyrie for six hours; she must have spent most of that time in debriefing from her last mission. Even if she had wanted to review the after-action report from my mission to Korra Korra—even if it was accessible at her security clearance level—she wouldn't have known about it.

So this is all new information to her.

Crap.

"You know what, it's kind of a long story," I say. "When we get back, I will cook you a very nice dinner and tell you all about it."

"Was it an operational necessity?"

That's the standard jargon the agency uses when it wants to describe distasteful things that it asks agents to do in the field. Usually we're talking about things like collateral damage to civilians, ignoring short-term gains to pursue long-term goals, things like that. Not turning down the opportunity for a night of passion with a very consenting partner.

"Absolutely. I just had to keep her occupied until our exfil arrived. And I did everything I could to keep us from, you know." I wave my hands around, not wanting to pantomime the obvious gesture.

"That's all you had to say, Kangaroo." Ellie shrugs. "I know what your job entails. And I know that if you do have to sleep with a beautiful foreign agent to seduce state secrets out of her, you'll feel terrible about it."

"So you're saying . . . it would have been *okay* if I had . . . slept with her?"

"Of course not," Ellie says, frowning again. "Don't be an idiot. I would dump your ass like a rotten grapefruit."

"But you just said—"

"I would *understand* why you might need to do something like that," she says, "but that is *not* something I'm looking for in a relationship."

"I'm very confused right now."

Ellie sighs. "I just want to be clear on where the lines are. Okay? I'm not going to hold a grudge if you have to do something unsavory in the line of duty. But there are some things that I don't want with respect to my romantic partner. I won't stop you from doing your job, but there are deal-breakers as far as our relationship goes. Is that clear?"

"So can you give me a list of these deal-breakers, or—"

She frowns at me. "Seriously? It's not a checklist, dude."

"I thought you liked checklists."

Oliver raps on the cockpit door and shouts through it, "I was under the impression we were on a schedule?"

Ellie releases my hand. "Let's finish this conversation later?"

"Okay." I hesitate before standing. "But we're okay. Right? We're okay."

She smiles at me. "We're okay. Talk later."

"That's not very encouraging."

"Well, you know me." She starts going down her checklist again. "Engineers are emotionless automatons."

I risk leaning over to kiss her cheek. "Good thing I love robots."

She kisses me back, then jerks a thumb over her shoulder. "Stop fooling around and get in the tank, agent."

CHAPTER
SIX

Here's a fun fact about military space travel:

I'm sorry, did I say "fun"? I misspoke. What I meant to say was "pretty much the worst thing ever."

So here's *pretty much the worst thing ever* about military space travel: *the tank.*

Humanity expanding throughout the solar system was a good news/bad news situation all around. It's a good thing that we no longer have to depend on planet Earth as our only option for a habitable world, since we seem to pretty regularly screw it up with some ecological or technological or political crisis that makes everybody miserable. Unfortunately, being able to live on other worlds—different planets, moons, asteroids, space stations—means that we get all the chances to screw those places up in exactly the same ways, or in new and exciting ways that we don't know how to fix.

Human beings: can't live with 'em, can't live without 'em.

And the thing that made all this expansion possible—the ionwell—was also a good news/bad news type deal. The good news was, we now had a compact, efficient fusion reactor that did not throw off deadly radiation during operation, which we could use to power all kinds of things, including spaceships that would go really fast without having to haul an unwieldy amount of fuel with them. The bad news was, ionwell engines could actually propel ships faster than it was safe for the humans aboard to survive the trip.

Most Earth civilian ships thrust at slightly less than one gravity, so it doesn't feel too strange to most of the passengers. And it does shorten the travel time between planets significantly—a trip that once took months to make, like going from Earth to Mars, can now be completed in as little as a week, depending on whether the planets are aligned in their orbits. Physics is still physics, but engineering can defeat a lot of problems these days.

Of course, the military isn't satisfied with taking a whole week to get somewhere when their engines could go even faster. So they focused on the weakest link in the chain: the human passengers.

OSS spent many years and many billions of dollars researching ways to protect the human body from prolonged extreme acceleration. They ran all kinds of experiments, from psychotropic drugs to exotic gene therapies to, I'm not even joking here, training banana slugs to pilot spacecraft.

Finally, though, it was a deep-sea-diving outfit that came through with the solution currently favored by most outer-space militaries. It involves filling an astronaut's lungs with highly oxygenated surfactant fluid and then immersing them in a tank of the same weird fluid and putting them into hypothermic shock for the duration of the voyage.

I did say it was pretty much the worst thing ever, didn't I?

Funny story, filling a person's lungs with fluid feels exactly like they're drowning, and the body generally resists drowning with as much violence as possible. So the person needs to be sedated while this initial drowning—excuse me, "pulmonary saturation"—happens, and you know what, at that point we might as well keep the person chemically paralyzed for the whole time, so they don't move around and risk damaging any part of their body while the ship is under high acceleration. And we'll just trust the ship's computer to wake everyone up at the right time later.

Civilians are understandably reluctant to submit to this procedure.

Most people would rather endure a couple of weeks aboard a luxury cruise spaceliner than get drowned and frozen just to reach their destination faster. But the military—and by extension, our intelligence agency—prefers the latter, since they frequently deal with time-sensitive matters. And soldiers and spies don't get to book their own travel.

No matter how many times I fly by tank, I still feel miserable coming out. The one thing that makes me feel better right now is that Oliver and Jessica don't look much better than I feel.

The three of us are huddled in the galley of our ship, bundled up in thermal blankets and hunched over hot beverages of our choice. What I can't figure out is how Ellie was able to recover so quickly. She's actually piloting the ship now, bringing us to our rendezvous with the OSS frigate *Tacoma* in orbit around Venus. Autopilot is good enough to manage a long-haul trajectory, but not for docking with another spacecraft up close and personal.

Ellie was the first one out of the tank, and she came in to check on us shortly after the med-bots had finished reviving us, and I swear she looked like she just stepped off the cover of *Sexy Astronaut Monthly*. Now I'm not a bit surprised that Paul put her into such a short turnaround from her last mission. Space travel clearly agrees with her. I wonder if that's something that got trained into her in OSS or her civilian engineering school, or if it's some innate ability that Paul discovered and was able to exploit. Like my pocket.

Well, that would give us one more thing in common to talk about, I guess.

I gulp down the rest of my coffee, scalding the roof of my mouth, then stand up and test the temperature with my blanket off. Nope, still too cold. I bundle myself up again.

"Where are you going?" Jessica asks shakily, both hands curled around a steaming bulb of tea.

"Going to talk to Marmosa," I say, nodding toward the cockpit. "We didn't get a chance to finish our conversation on the Eyrie."

"I imagine she's a little busy right now," Oliver says, dropping another handful of tiny marshmallows into his hot chocolate.

"She can multitask."

Oliver raises an eyebrow. "If you say so."

"We need to run a full diagnostic on your nanobots," Jessica says. "Five minutes."

"I'll set a timer," I say, intending to do nothing of the sort.

Ellie isn't doing much of anything when I join her in the cockpit. From what she tells me, most of spacecraft piloting is just about this interesting. The important thing is to get the initial calculations right, taking into account orbits and fuel consumption and trajectories, but then you just program the computer and let it run.

"So." I decide to cut right to the chase. "If you're not upset about my canoodling with the defector back on Earth, what were you so upset about when you sent that last message?"

She stares at me for a second. "'Canoodling'? What are you, two thousand years old? Who talks like that?"

"I'm oddly pleased that *that's* what you're focusing on out of that whole sentence."

"I'm buying myself time to figure out the best way to say this."

"I thought we were just talking," I say. "No tradecraft."

"It's not tradecraft," Ellie says. "I'm finding the clearest and best way to communicate my meaning to you. I don't want you to take this the wrong way."

"That's never a good preface."

"Shut up." She takes both my hands in her own, and I feel that tingle again. She needs to stop doing that if she wants me to focus on her words. But I also don't want her to stop touching me, so I let it slide.

"I want to be clear that I'm not expecting anything specific from you," Ellie says. "Okay? I don't know where this relationship is going. But the thing that was upsetting me at the time was, neither of us seemed to have a plan for this. And it was both of us, not just you. I apologize if it seemed like I was taking it out on you. I've had some time to think since then."

"So you were upset about not having a plan," I say, "but you also don't have a specific goal in mind? Isn't that the . . . definition of a plan?"

"Okay, maybe 'plan' isn't the best word." She shakes her head. "See what I mean? It's difficult to talk about this stuff. Our language doesn't really support this level of introspection."

"It's going to be hard for me to meet your expectations if I don't know what those expectations are," I say. What I don't say is: *This feels an awful lot like what I have to do on an operation, when people don't want to or can't tell me what they actually want, and I have to read other signals to try to figure that out and then give them what they want. So you can't blame me for falling back on tradecraft here.*

"I just want you to be yourself."

"But, see, there must be *something* specific you want." I stare at her, studying her facial expressions as much as I'm enjoying the view. "You don't think I'm being myself because of some particular thing. And you don't want to tell me what that particular thing is, because you want me to figure it out on my own, so I will then fit your idea of who I am. But maybe I'm not who you think I am."

"You're exactly who I think you are," she says. "You're a brown kid with a superpower who got sucked into a bigger and more terrible world than he ever expected, and you're still struggling to figure out where you fit in all this."

I smile in spite of myself. "Geez, who needs therapy when you've got a girlfriend?"

She smiles back. "You know, I think that's the first time you've actually called me your girlfriend."

"Well, maybe to your face."

"Well, I like it, *boyfriend*." She leans forward and kisses me, and I'm once again aware of how cold I am. Her lips feel almost uncomfortably hot against mine.

The radio chimes. "Incoming transport shuttle, this is *Tacoma*, ready for docking. Please confirm your trajectory and link for autopilot."

Ellie pulls back, and I lose my balance leaning forward to follow her. She chuckles and puts a hand on my chest to push me back into my chair. It feels like a hot iron through my thin medical recovery smock, but it hurts so good.

"We'll finish this later," she says.

"Yes, please," I say, squeezing her other hand before letting go and shuffling back into the galley to drown my sexual frustrations in a hot beverage.

———

"Welcome aboard the *Tacoma*," says the impossibly slender, tall, black-haired woman who meets us on the inside of the big ship's airlock. She's gripping a handhold with her right hand, and waves us into the adjoining corridor with her left palm. "I'm Commander Simone Naka-mura, first officer. Who's your engineer?"

"I am," Oliver and Ellie say simultaneously. They exchange a look, then Ellie shrugs.

Oliver turns to Nakamura. "What's the problem, Commander?"

"Not a problem as such. We've got your modified bluejay tied down on the hangar deck. But none of us has worked on this particular configuration before. Just wanted whoever's responsible on your team to check it out before we drop you off."

"I'm the pilot," Ellie says. "I can do the inspection."

"Brill." Nakamura waves another officer forward, a red-haired woman with a splash of freckles across the bridge of her nose. "Lieu-tenant Leng will show you the way. Does your other engineer also want to tag along?"

Oliver shakes his head. "No, I'd like to review the overall flight plan with you, Commander."

"The captain will brief you on that. I'll take you to the bridge. If you'll follow me?"

We divide into two separate groups headed in opposite directions. I trail behind Nakamura, Oliver, and Jessica, looking over my shoulder at Ellie following Lieutenant Leng the other way down the corridor. She turns and blows a kiss at me before we turn the next corner.

My girlfriend.

The captain of the *Tacoma* is a squat, barrel-shaped man named, ironically, Cooper. I don't make a joke about that. I also don't make any remarks about what an odd couple the captain and XO are, one looking like a burly lumberjack, the other like a malnourished stick insect. I suspect that Cooper grew up on Earth, still the highest-gravity, consistently habitable environment in the solar system, and Nakamura is one of the very first humans to be born off-planet and who has lived their entire lives in space. The combination of low-gravity habitats and high-protein diets makes for some unusual body adaptations.

"Which one of you is"—the captain squints at his tablet—"Enoch Wenceslas?"

"Wences*lao*," I say. If Paul's going to give me ridiculous legends, I'm going to make sure people pronounce the names properly. "Rhymes with 'chow.' Sort of. It's not important," I add when I notice Jessica giving me a dirty look across the table. "That's me. What's up?"

We're standing around a conference table, or as close to standing as we can approximate in zero-gravity. Technically it's microgravity, as Oliver would correct me if I said it out loud, since the *Tacoma* is orbiting Venus and that wouldn't be possible if there were no gravity involved. But the pull is small enough that it feels like we're weightless.

The table itself is hexagonal, which means each of us gets a side to ourselves with one left empty. Going clockwise from Captain Cooper, it's XO Nakamura, Jessica, empty space, me, Oliver. I'm sure it's not intentional that Jessica didn't want to stand right next to me. She probably just wanted to be closer to Nakamura. Study her unusual physiology for medical reasons or something.

"Welcome aboard, friends," the captain says, touching the tablet and then the tabletop. The surface lights up with an orbital diagram of Venus, with icons showing the *Tacoma* and other spacecraft in orbit and several floating habitats just above the troposphere. An animation draws a line from the *Tacoma* to one of the habs, then down into the clouds and back up to another hab, then into the clouds again before returning to *Tacoma*. The animation cycles as Captain Cooper continues talking.

"I just want to make sure we're all on the same page with respect to transpo on this mish," he says, using unnecessary military slang that I hate. "Since you three are the passengers, I wanted to go over the sched with you. And I understand that you, Mr. Wenceslao, are the primary?"

"That's me." I give him a thumbs-up. He gives me a puzzled frown. "So tell us about the ride."

"I don't know if you all have been to Venus before, but it's basically divided into two zones as far as where the habitat balloons float." He manipulates the tabletop display to zoom in on the first stop. "Most habs stay in perpetual daylight. The resorts so it's always sunny for their guests, the blue sites so that any escape attempt will be visible and obvious. I presume you're all familiar with the disposition of what we call 'blue sites.'"

"Wretched hives of scum and villainy?" I say.

Nakamura gives me a strange look. "Is that from a poem?"

"Sure." I direct my attention toward Cooper, because I don't want to start guffawing in the middle of a very serious mission briefing. "Azure was the first blue site built, right?"

"Correct." Cooper scrolls the display sideways. "The blue sites stay above the clouds, with camouflaged exteriors. The domes extend all the way down below the baseline ring, so unless you know where to look, anyone spotting them from orbit will just see more clouds."

He taps on one of the blue dots swirling around the equator, and it expands into a side view cutaway schematic of the habitat balloon. I bite my tongue before pointing out that Cerulean looks a little different because it needs extra shielding to stay in Venusian cloud cover all the time. Secrets within secrets, that's the agency's specialty dish.

"I'll need an up-to-date technical readout on blue-site security," Oliver says. "To develop countermeasures before we drop off Mr. Wenceslao."

"You got it." Cooper turns to Jessica. "And you're the physician?"

"Yes," she replies. "I'm going to want your latest on-site medical records for all blue sites. Patient profiles, treatment records, anything and everything."

"We can provide summaries," Nakamura says.

"I'd like the complete and unabridged files, if you don't mind," Jessica says.

"That's going to be a lot of data."

"Surge likes data," I say.

Nakamura frowns. "Surge?"

"It's short for 'Surgical.'"

"I prefer the raw data," Jessica says, ignoring my nickname shenanigans. "Let me worry about how to process it."

Nakamura shrugs. "Okay, doc, whatever you want. We're here to help."

"Thank you."

"You're welcome."

Jessica sure is being talkative. Is she actually flirting with this person? I'm severely tempted to blink my eye into sensor mode to see if they're both showing signs of arousal. But honestly, I shouldn't really want to know. Damn my own innate curiosity for making me speculate about information I don't actually want to have.

"Very well," Captain Cooper says. "We're currently adjusting the *Tacoma*'s orbit to take us above the civilian insertion point. Your bluejay will launch and drop into the spacelane where it'll look like just another inbound tourist flight." He highlights this maneuver on the tabletop display. "From there on in, it's up to your pilot to make the deliveries. First she'll drop off your Surgical and Equipment officers at the Sunstone resort, then dive into the clouds to hide her approach to Azure."

The display shows a glowing blue triangle traveling through an orange haze, then rising straight up and attaching itself to a dark blue half-circle.

"Docking facilities for all blue sites are on the bottom side of the hab," Cooper says, "to hide ingress and egress activities from eyes in the sky. Your pilot will drop you off, Mr. Wenceslao, and then make another dive into the clouds to circle back around and meet up with *Tacoma* near the north pole."

The tiny blue triangle slices through the orange haze again before rising to meet up with the green rectangle representing the *Tacoma* in orbit.

"We'll then move into our standard orbit until it's time for the bluejay to dive and retrieve you when it's time for exfil." Cooper looks at me, then at Oliver. "Seems like an awfully risky plan, if you ask me."

"Just the last part?" I ask. "Or do you mean the whole thing?"

Cooper gives me a sideways glance. "I was talking about the final exfil. We've dropped lots of bluejays into those clouds, but never just a rescue bubble. Are you sure the material will hold?"

"It's the same polytherm as used in the construction of the bluejay hulls," Oliver says. "We've done plenty of testing with Science Division. I don't anticipate any problems."

Yeah, but you're not the one who's going to be inside that rescue bubble falling through poisonous clouds of acid. "I have every confidence that Equipment is looking out for me," I say aloud. "You don't anticipate any problems with the final rendezvous, Captain? After the bluejay retrieves the rescue bubble and flies back up to meet the *Tacoma* in orbit?"

"Not at all," Cooper says. "We do a pretty good job of keeping these skies clear. Both to protect the tourists, and to make sure no bad guys try to bust out their friends. Lots of satellites watching to make sure nothing unauthorized gets through except space rocks. And those we track anyway just in case someone threw them at us as a distraction."

"I'm curious about your signaling protocol," Nakamura says. "Mr. Wenceslao, you're not going to have your comms implants on the inside. And you're not planning to secure the cooperation of the warden or any other prison authorities. How will we know when you're ready for exfil?"

"That's classified," Jessica says. "TS/SCI Silver Sunflower."

Nakamura looks at her, but not with surprise. I'm sure the XO on an OSS patrol frigate has encountered her share of Top-Secret-slash-Sensitive-Compartmented-Information before. "And we don't need to know?"

"Just be where you need to be," Jessica says. "We'll handle the rest."

"Let 'em have their secrets, XO," Cooper says. "State does right by us. We're happy to help, right?"

"Absolutely, Captain," Nakamura says, her eyes still locked on Jessica. "Shall I show our guests to their quarters?"

"Quarters?" I repeat. "I didn't think we were going to be here very long."

"Fifty-eight minutes," Oliver says, checking his tablet.

"XO's being nice to you all," Cooper says. "She thought you might want a private moment to yourselves. Freshen up, use the facilities, get your head in the game before your descent into madness."

"That's very thoughtful," Jessica says. "I would definitely appreciate some private time."

"All right then." Nakamura gestures at the door. "Let's float on over to the elevator and I'll get you situated."

She touches Jessica's shoulder, and I see the ghost of a smile flicker across Jessica's face. I suspect those two will be doing something very private for the next fifty minutes. Maybe I can go down to the hangar deck and help Ellie with something similar.

As it turns out, Ellie doesn't want any help. She and Lieutenant Leng are geeking out over how Science Division has modified our bluejay, and I feel completely out of place in the middle of their rapid-fire back-and-forth technobabble. So I go back up to the crew decks, taking the longest possible route so I avoid going past Jessica's assigned quarters —I don't want to accidentally hear anything through her door, or be tempted to use my eye to see through the walls.

That leaves just one person for me to hang out with, unless I want to make some new friends here on the *Tacoma*. And I'm not really in the mood for that when I'm about to go to prison.

I knock on Oliver's door three times, getting progressively louder, until he finally answers. He opens the door with a towel around his waist and his entire body still damp from a shower.

"Yes?" he says.

"Sorry," I say. "I didn't know you were actually going to make use of the facilities. I'll go away."

"Is there something wrong?"

"No. Just killing time. I'll leave you alone."

He pushes back and holds the door open. "Come in."

I float into the room and anchor myself on one of the stick-strips on the floor. Sometimes it's fun to turn yourself sideways or upside down in zero-gee, just because you can, but mostly it's just disorienting for everyone. Oliver closes the door and grabs another towel to dry his hair.

"So. Zero-gravity shower?" I say.

"Inconvenient but necessary," Oliver says, moving the towel to his shoulders and neck. "I still smell a bit like the tank, but at least it's mostly out of my hair now."

"I don't suppose you've looked at the blue-site schematics yet."

"I glanced at them. I'll review them in more detail once Surgical and I are settled in at Sunstone."

"So what did I put in my pocket for you?"

Oliver stops drying himself and frowns at me. "We've been over this. It's a private matter."

"Hey, I'm doing you a favor here."

"No," he says, "we agreed on a mutually beneficial bargain."

"Come on, just give me a hint."

He pulls himself over to the door and opens it. "Good-bye, Kangaroo."

"You know I'm just going to keep asking you," I say, moving slowly toward the door.

"If you must. I'll see you in half an hour."

He closes the door in my face before I can correct him: it's actually only twenty-nine minutes until we depart now.

CHAPTER
SEVEN

Venus—Sunstone Resort Habitat
Time to put on a show

"Welcome to Sunstone, Mr. and Mrs. Gorgon! . . . and friends!"

I wasn't expecting anyone to meet us at the spaceport section of Sunstone. I suppose it's completely feasible, seeing as how the whole habitat is contained and surveilled and whoever's in charge could keep track of goings-on anywhere they wanted to monitor, but given the amount of traffic arriving and departing, this personal treatment seems a little excessive. In fact, I see some of the economy-class passengers from other flights giving us dirty looks as the unreasonably attractive blond man approaches our party, followed by two similarly muscular but somewhat less strikingly visaged porters. They're wearing similar but clearly different uniforms, and it's actually quite impressive how well this resort has used common knowledge of regimental uniforms throughout history to design sartorial cues into their staff outfits. The man in front has just enough additional shiny bits on his shirt to indicate that he's more senior than the other two, and the porters are wearing flat hats and trousers with stripes down the side.

"Thank you," Oliver says.

"I'm Peter," says the blond man, placing both hands on his chest, "and this is Henry and Dorian." He waves one hand, then the other, at the two porters behind him. "And I'm so sorry! We didn't get the full details on your party, so we thought you would be coming with your family."

"Enoch and Kendra are like family to us," Jessica deadpans.

"Of course. How wonderful." Peter consults a small computer tablet attached to his left forearm. "Now we've got you in the presidential suite for ten days, is that correct?"

"Correct," Oliver says.

"I just want to be clear on the accommodations," Peter says. "The presidential suite is quite spacious, but it only has two private bedrooms. Is that going to be enough for the four of you? I can check to see if there's another available stateroom on the same floor—"

"That will be fine," Jessica says. "Enoch and Kendra won't be staying long. They're just here to help us get settled in."

"Noted." Peter taps on his tablet. "And do we have any more luggage for you that we need to deliver to the suite?"

"No, this is everything," Oliver says.

"It's our honeymoon," Jessica says.

"We don't need a lot of clothes," Oliver says.

I can't decide whether to laugh or cry at how terrible their performance is. Fortunately, Peter doesn't seem to care. I suppose they get a wide variety of people visiting Sunstone. And resort staff are, if nothing else, trained to be discreet.

"Well, we have a very well-stocked shopping center if you find you're missing anything at all," Peter says without missing a beat. "If there's anything we can do to make your stay more pleasant, please don't hesitate to let us know."

"Thank you," Oliver says.

"We really just want some privacy," Jessica says.

"Yes. Privacy." Oliver hooks his arm through Jessica's and yanks her toward him, ignoring her sudden stiffness. They didn't rehearse this. "We would like to be left alone for the entire duration of our stay."

"The whole time. Yes." Jessica tugs her arm loose and flashes Peter a ludicrously stiff smile.

"Of course," Peter says. "I should warn you that health and safety regulations do require our housekeeping staff to enter the suite at least once every three days. To ensure sanitary conditions. It's a legal requirement. I hope that won't inconvenience you too much."

"Not at all," Oliver says. "Just have them call before coming in."

"So we can put away our stuff," Jessica says.

"And put on some clothes."

"Maybe."

I want to smack both of them, they're so bad at this. I notice that Ellie is coughing into her sleeve. She finishes, looks at me, and turns away again to cough some more.

"I will make a note on your account," Peter says, tapping at his arm tablet some more. "Now, if you'll follow me?"

We walk behind him out of the spaceport, our robotic luggage rolling along behind us. The porters disappear to help some other guests—apparently they were expecting some more bags. Peter points out various amenities as we pass them: gardens, fountains, swimming pools, play areas for children, a whole laundry list of frivolity.

It's a little bit cruel, seeing as how I won't be able to enjoy any of this and will, in fact, be behind bars while Oliver and Jessica are romping around here.

I know they won't actually be vacationing. But it will take a day or so for my nanobots to repair the implants after I get into Cerulean, and they won't need to spend all that time prepping their command center in the hotel room, especially if they're keeping it simple so they can hide or disguise everything when the maids come in.

Paul insisted on stationing Oliver and Jessica here for support, so they'd be close enough to me that there would be no appreciable communications delay, and he didn't want them on the *Tacoma* just in case something happened in orbit that the warship needed to go and deal with. We never know what's going to transpire during an operation, so we need to prepare for any imaginable contingency. And Paul Tarkington can imagine an impressive number of worst-case scenarios.

Oliver's job will be to monitor my implants. Jessica's job will be to monitor my vital signs and the biotech interfaces. They'll need to work together if anything goes wonky with my nanobots. Hopefully not the comms part, because then I won't even be able to talk to them. Although it would also be hilarious if I ended up being able to transmit but not receive, so all they could do was watch while I improvised my way through a prison break.

Let's hope it doesn't come to that.

The presidential suite turns out to be grotesque in its luxuriousness. There's a fountain—a literal fountain, with gilded jade dragons squirting water out of their mouths into a shallow pool—in the middle of the foyer. A large bay window in an alcove above and behind that looks out over one of the perpetually sunny gardens, and the doors to the bedrooms are off to either side. Apparently each bedroom has its own bathroom as well. Our luggage-bots scoot off into the bedrooms while Peter demonstrates the rest of the amenities for us, including a fully stocked wet bar to one side of the entry doors and a giant bathroom featuring a large hot tub to the other side.

"That's a very large tub," Oliver observes.

"It's the largest on the property," Peter says. "You could probably fit all four of you inside." He winks at me for some reason.

"Ha ha. Why would we want to do that," Jessica intones, and I can't tell if she's actually trying to do a lousy impression of a robot, or if she really is just that awful at acting.

"Would you like me to show you the shower controls?" Peter asks.

"No, that's fine," Oliver says. "I'm sure we can figure them out."

"Yes, I think we're all set here," Jessica says, ushering Peter toward the entry doors.

"Enoch and Kendra need to get to work," Oliver says, "and my wife and I would very much like to start playing around."

"You mean fooling around," Jessica says. "Honey."

I bite my tongue.

"Absolutely," Peter says, backing out of the room. "Remember, you can call us for anything at all, any time, night or day—though, as you know, it's always sunny here!" That's apparently the official resort motto. "Any last questions before I go?"

Oliver and Jessica stare at each other, then at me. I sigh and pull some bills out of my wallet and hand them to Peter.

"Thank you very much," I say, palming him the money in a handshake. "I'm sure we're all going to have a great time here."

"Thank you, Enoch," he says, winking at me again. Why does he keep doing that? "We hope you all have a wonderful stay with us at Sunstone. Please don't hesitate to ask if you need anything."

The doors close, and Ellie starts laughing uncontrollably.

"Oh my God!" she says after a moment. "Did you two even get trained on maintaining cover? I mean, seriously, did you ever take an improv class in college?"

"They don't care how weird we are," Jessica says, snapping her fingers twice. Her luggage rolls out of the left bedroom and meets her at the bottom of the stairs leading up to the observation window. "It's a resort hotel. All they care about is how much we spend."

"Yeah, about that," Ellie says. "The presidential suite? Seriously?" She gives me a look. "If I'd known the agency had this kind of budget to throw around, I might have joined up earlier."

"This is a special circumstance," Oliver says, walking over to help Jessica unpack her bag—which, by the way, is full of computers, communications gear, basically anything except clothes and toiletries. "And your custom bluejay was not exactly inexpensive, either."

"Those were necessary modifications," Ellie says. "You all didn't just want a plastic spaceship that could survive in the Venusian atmosphere. You also wanted it to have a secondary, ablative outer hull that would make it look like a normal civilian transport until we had to dive."

"Wait, *you* designed the ship?" I ask.

"Of course," Ellie says.

"It was a team effort," Oliver says as he sets up a radio component. "Science Division had several people working on the modifications."

"But I signed off on all of them," Ellie says. "It's my bird. I want to know exactly what I'm flying." She looks at me. "And I want to keep my boyfriend safe."

Jessica makes a strange noise, somewhere between an exaggerated sigh and an almost geologic rumbling. "I wondered when this would happen."

"What?" Ellie says. "You don't like me talking about *my boyfriend*?"

She purses her lips and makes smooching noises in my general direction.

"Please don't encourage them," Oliver says to Jessica.

"Hey," I say, "it's not my fault Lasher wanted to assign *my girlfriend* to this operation."

"Yeah," Ellie says. "I just happened to be the best pilot available on short notice. Deal with it, EQ."

For some reason it's incredibly arousing to hear her use my nickname for Oliver. I'm tempted to suggest we retire to the other bedroom and close the door for a few minutes.

"How long before they can leave?" Jessica says, making a show of directing the question toward Oliver.

"Just another twenty minutes," Oliver says. "Or however long it takes us to verify the communications link."

"Work fast."

"Doing my best."

———

Much to my dismay, Oliver and Jessica finish setting up their gear very quickly. Ellie and I haven't even completed our nonverbal negotiations about how much fooling around we're willing to do in such close proximity to our colleagues. Are we going to take off some of our clothes? Yes? How much clothing? Wait, do shoes count as clothes? It's very difficult conveying all this information without using words. I'm still working on learning some kind of useful sign language, and Ellie still isn't keen on getting a comms implant for herself.

It only takes a few minutes to verify that my shoulder-phone can talk to the comms rig in the suite, and then it's time for Ellie and me to reluctantly get all our clothes back on and head off to Cerulean City.

We parked our bluejay in the short-term docking area used for incoming passengers. There are a lot of ships moving around Sunstone all the time, so it's easy for us to slip into the traffic stream of the robotic delivery vehicles underneath the floating hab, near the service docks, and then disappear into the clouds below.

Once we get into the thick of the toxic Venusian atmosphere, the ablative outer hull on our bluejay starts melting away, and it's really freaking disconcerting to see your spacecraft disintegrate all around you.

I'm not an expert, but here's what I remember from my mission briefing: the atmosphere of Venus is mostly carbon dioxide. Won't kill you immediately, but you can't breathe it. Some nitrogen, which again, won't kill you, but because the air is so thick, the pressure differential will give you the bends like crazy if you're not in a pressurized vehicle when you change altitude.

But never mind all that, because the real problem is the clouds.

They look fine, and they're everywhere looking pretty, which is good because the actual surface of the planet is a superheated hellscape. But the cloud formations move ridiculously fast, achieving speeds of up to three hundred kilometers per hour at the highest layers. Also, they're made of sulfur dioxide, and if there's any water around, the hydrogen catalyzes a reaction that produces sulfuric acid, which is incredibly corrosive to any kind of metal that you might use to build otherwise sturdy vehicles like spaceships.

No matter how much you scrub your spacecraft's exterior, even if you build it in hard vacuum in an orbiting drydock or at a deep-space construction facility, there's probably still going to be some kind of hydrogen compound on the outside, and even in trace amounts, that spells trouble with a capital *T* and that rhymes with *C* and that stands for *corrosion*. You really don't want three-hundred-kph winds blowing toxic gases into your spacecraft through an acid-worn hole in some important part of the outer hull.

This is why all the bluejays servicing Venusian habitats are built with sealed plastic or ceramic outer hulls, using materials that won't react with sulfur dioxide or sulfuric acid or really anything involving sulfur, because that's part of the volcanic hellscape thing. Except we needed our spaceship to look like a normal civilian transport when coming into the Sunstone resort, but then it had to change to look like a military bluejay when approaching Cerulean City. After that we didn't care, since everything from that point on was going to be super-secret plausible-deniability agency stuff anyway, but we needed to maintain cover while going into both places.

Ellie is a very good pilot. As good as she is at engineering, as far as I can tell, though to be fair I don't actually know that much about either discipline. She fixes things, she makes things go, and generally things are better after she's tuned them up to her satisfaction. Oliver respects her, which says a lot to me. Oliver can be very fastidious about other people's handiwork.

But even though she might seem to be keeping her cool while flying our bluejay through the maelstrom that is Venusian tropospheric cloud cover, I know her well enough to know that she's freaking out only slightly less than I am. It's only natural: the whole ship is shaking, and parts are falling off the outside, and even though we know on an intellectual level that this is what's supposed to be happening, our animal instincts are going wild and telling us THIS IS BAD, THIS IS REAL BAD, RUN THE FUCK AWAY ASAP.

"Everything good?" I ask, shouting over the noise as she slaps the console in front of her to turn off a new light that just started blinking.

"We're fine," Ellie replies. She adjusts a few other controls, then takes both hands off the wheel. My heart skips a beat as the bluejay lurches, but then our flight smooths out, and I see the autopilot indicator on the main screen. "There. Just had to retrain the autopilot for current conditions."

"You can do that?" I'm always impressed by her competence, but right now it's turning me on even more than usual. Maybe the knowledge that I'm going to prison for the next two weeks has something to do with it.

"It's been a while, but these systems are also newer than—the last time I flew a dropship in atmosphere." She doesn't like to talk about her time in the military, but I'm okay with that. Especially right now, since I have another topic we can discuss.

"So how long until we get to Cerulean?"

"These winds are a little unpredictable, but ETA is six minutes."

I don't try to stop myself from smiling. "Plenty of time for a little canoodling."

"Kangaroo," she says in the tone of voice that means *stop joking around*. "I'm serious. We should talk about what we're doing. With our relationship."

I don't know what it is about that word—"relationship"—but it's an instant buzzkill, every time I hear it. Maybe because I usually hear people say it in very specific contexts, like a therapy or evaluation session where an agency-appointed psychoanalyst is trying to get to the root of my psychological difficulties. It's certainly not something I look forward to discussing with my girlfriend. Even if I know that it's a healthy and necessary part of our . . . relationship. *Ugh.*

"Okay," I say. "Six minutes isn't long, so let's wrap up the convo in about three minutes. To leave enough time for the canoodling and all."

"Kangaroo."

"You are taking me to prison, after all, and they're not going to allow conjugal visits—"

"We do have fun," Ellie says, her tone now just shy of being sharp enough to snap. "But I don't just want to have fun with you. Okay? I want a little more. I think you do too, but it's not going to be easy. And if we want to figure this out, we have to do it together."

I lean forward and take both her hands in mine, in an effort to both focus my own attention and to remind her of the reward that's awaiting us at the end of this uncomfortable conversation. "I'm with you. You know I am. And it sucks that we didn't have more time together on turnaround, because there's so much that I want to talk to you about, but we're not going to solve all our problems in the next few minutes." I squeeze her hands. "I can, however, promise to accomplish one good thing in that time, if you know what I mean."

Ellie shakes her head, but I see her smiling. One thing I know for sure, she definitely likes having sex with me. "I can have an orgasm on my own, sweetie. I can even think about you while I'm doing it. But I can't talk to you when you're not here. And the most important thing to me, right now, is talking to you."

I'm disappointed, to say the least, but I can't argue with her reasoning. And I do want to make this work, if we can. I don't know if it's possible. That's what scares me. That's why I just want to do the easy thing, the straightforward thing, the immediately gratifying thing instead.

Why can't I just say all that to her, instead of making dumb jokes?

I open my mouth to start to say something—I think it might be an apology, just a placeholder until my brain catches up with something more meaningful—but I'm interrupted by a noisy alert and blinking lights on the flight console.

"Approaching landing zone," a computerized voice says. It sounds remarkably human for a computer-synthesized voice, and I idly wonder if Oliver had anything to do with that. Apparently I'd rather think about literally anything other than having this relationship talk with Ellie. "Pilot intervention required."

"Sorry, Kay." Ellie squeezes my hands, then pulls her hands away and turns to face the controls. "Gotta bring us in on manual."

"Sure. Yeah. Go ahead. I'll stay out of the way."

She gives me a brief sideways glance. "But I can multitask. You talk. I'll listen."

I should have known I wasn't getting out of it that easily. "Okay. Well, as you know, I really enjoy spending time with you. But we don't get to spend a lot of time together. So I guess I just, um, want to prioritize what we do when we are together."

"Uh-huh." Ellie continues working the flight controls, not looking at me. "And top of your list is sexytimes?"

"Well, that's *near* the top. I want as much skin-on-skin contact with you as I can get."

"What else is on the list?"

And that's the $64,000 question. I should have a good answer for this, any answer, but I just want to be together at the same time. Sometimes I really am an idiot.

"Talking," I say. "Talking is good. Like this. Talking in real time, face-to-face. This is good."

"I agree." She turns her head for a moment to smile at me. "So. Talking about anything in particular?"

"Our . . . relationship?"

"This isn't a quiz," Ellie says, taking one hand off her controls and reaching over to put her palm against the side of my neck. It's more distracting than I anticipated. "I'm not looking for one specific answer. I just want us to be able to talk. Openly, freely. About whatever's on your mind. You get that, don't you?"

"Sure," I say. "I'm happy to talk."

"You don't seem that happy."

"I'm very happy. I'm the happiest Kangaroo in Kangaroo-town."

"Are we going to be able to make this work?" Ellie takes her hand back, apparently giving up on trying to guide me through the conversational shoals and just cutting to the chase now. "Your job isn't going to change. My job—well, I never know where Lasher's going to send me next, but I'm sure he doesn't take our personal lives into consideration when he assigns missions."

"Definitely not," I say. What I don't say is: I've never had a personal life for Paul to worry about before. If I'm having this much trouble figuring things out with Ellie, what must Paul be going through, having to worry about each of us plus the two of us together on top of all the normal spy stuff?

"Do you want me to talk to him?" I blurt out before I can think about how weird it might sound.

Ellie gives me a strange look. "To Lasher? About us? God no."

"He might listen to me if I ask for—something," I say.

Ellie gives me a dubious look. "Really."

"Well, it would depend on the thing, obviously. But if he knows that two of his best agents—"

"I'm not sure that describes either one of us."

"Okay, two of his most unique agents, then. He can't replace me, and he won't let you go after putting so many resources into training you up so quickly."

"Still not convinced, but go on."

"He wants us focused on the job. Not distracted by personal issues. So it's in his best interest to make things easy on us, to give us as much time as possible to be with each other."

Ellie gives me a sad look. "Or it's in his best interest, and the agency's, to force us apart so there will be no possibility of distraction."

"What? No. Paul wouldn't do that to us." He wouldn't do that to *me*. Would he?

"Wouldn't he?" Ellie says, nudging her control stick forward and tilting the nose of the bluejay down. Gravity pulls us forward in our chairs, slightly off-balance. "I believe he'll do everything he can to protect *you*, Kangaroo. I'm not sure he cares that much about me. Even if I do make you happy."

"He cares," I say. But I have to admit, even though I have firsthand experience with the full force of how much Paul can care about something, I also know that he seldom cares about the same things that I do.

"It would be great if we could work together more," Ellie says, leveling out our flight. I see new shapes and colors on the forward-looking radar image. We must be getting close to Cerulean. "It would be great if Paul believes that's the best way to use us."

"I'll talk to him," I say, feeling some resolve now that I'm in the position of protecting my girl. I know it's a dumb, archaic, overly gendered stereotype, but it still grabs hold of me from time to time. I want to be the strong one in the relationship. I want to be the person who can do something that his partner can't. "He'll listen to me. I'm always going to need transportation, right? It'll be extra convenient if I have a dedicated pilot. And if that pilot also has a vested interest in me coming home in one piece."

Ellie nods, slowing the bluejay down. "Well, good luck with that, I guess. We'll have to pick this up later. We're here."

I look out the front window just as two rows of lights become visible through the dingy orange haze of the Venusian clouds. The bluejay floats closer, and the lights resolve into a rectangular shape, outlining an open hangar bay.

"Are there doors on that thing?" I ask as Ellie lines up our little bluejay with the mass of the floating hab, which we're now close enough to see the edges of. "It looks like the hangar's open to atmosphere."

"It is," Ellie confirms. "It's a wind shelter. Cycling the whole bay like an airlock would waste a lot of oxygen each time, but there's too much turbulence outside to dock safely. So we're going to land in there, then connect to a pressurized tunnel for egress."

"Speaking of pressurized tunnels–"

"Dude."

"Have I mentioned how much it turns me on to hear you talk technobabble?" I say. "You know, we still have a couple of minutes before we meet anyone—"

"Keep it in your pants, lover," Ellie says with a grin. "You're going to survive a couple of weeks without my touch."

"But I won't like it."

"I'm sure you can handle it."

The wind noise abates as the bluejay passes the threshold into the hangar. We touch down at the far end, close to the innermost wall, following a trail of animated running lights. Ellie rotates the bluejay to the left, positioning our airlock against the end of the docking tunnel.

As soon as we're on the ground, I unbuckle my safety harness, stand up, and lean over toward Ellie's seat.

She turns her face upward to look at me. "What are you—"

I move down and kiss her on the lips. She makes a muffled protest at first, then settles in and kisses me back. I reluctantly pull away after we have the moment.

"Just want to remind you of what you're going to be missing," I say.

She smiles. "Fair enough."

The control panel beeps, and she taps at it. The computer voice says: "Docking complete."

"Time to start the show, I guess." I lead the way out of the cockpit and back into the cabin. Ellie follows.

Before we left Earth, Paul transmitted my forged prisoner-transfer orders to Cerulean City. I suppose the orders themselves weren't actually forged—they had to be encrypted to agency standard, otherwise Cerulean wouldn't have authenticated them—but the reason behind them is definitely fake.

My cover is that during my latest op, instead of extracting Rose Kim and her superweapon, I succumbed to her feminine wiles and was fully about to defect with her to Pyeongyang when the exfil team showed up. Which I don't love as a story, but it's not like Paul asks me for notes on these things. Apparently he thinks it is totally plausible that I would have been seduced so easily, and in this amusing fiction it was only the heroic actions of SEAL Team Nine that prevented me from joining the dark side.

Of course, according to this legend, there was a big ruckus when the SEALs apprehended me, and I managed to kill two of those brave, selfless, courageous all-American boys before being taken down. So I'm also on the hook for double homicide in addition to the terrible treason. I very much do not approve of this wacko version of Kangaroo that Lasher's cooked up, but I suppose if I'm going into a prison environment, it might help if the other inmates' initial impression of me is that I'm a lethal badass with poor impulse control.

Anyway. All these fake details are super hush-hush, obviously. I've had access to a lot of sensitive information over the years, and the agency doesn't want me talking to anybody about anything until they can decide what to do with me.

Cerulean acknowledged the orders, so they're expecting us, but we still don't know anything about the situation on the inside here. We know they're still operating. They send regular reports on inmate status and they get regular shipments of food and supplies in from off-planet, but the information coming out is the bare minimum. We have no idea what conditions are like, whether it's a gulag or a country club. I'm really hoping for the latter.

Ellie, playing the part of prison guard, pulls both my arms behind me and fastens a pair of cuffs around my wrists.

"Don't say it," she says.

"What do you think I'm going to say?"

"I know it's going to be some kind of bondage joke."

"You are so wrong."

"What were you going to say, then?"

"I was going to say that we haven't really explored the realm of role-playing in the bedroom—"

"Okay, technically not bondage, fine." Ellie grabs my shoulder and pushes me toward the airlock. "Ready?"

"No, but let's get this over with." I hear her snickering behind me.

"Don't say it!" I blurt at the same moment that Ellie quips, "That's what she said!"

"Jinx," she says, then kisses the back of my neck.

I sigh. "I'll see you in a couple of weeks."

"Don't do anything I wouldn't do."

Ellie reaches forward with her other hand to cycle the airlock. A hissing noise comes from behind the door, and then the light above the round hatch turns from red to green.

The door irises open to reveal two guards waiting for us on the Cerulean side of the docking tunnel. They're both wearing featureless dark jumpsuits and standing on either side of a metal gurney. On top of the gurney is a black plastic—

"Is that a body bag?" I blurt out.

The guard on the left side of the gurney, a broad-shouldered woman with short green hair, looks past me at Ellie. "Prisoner-transfer orders?"

Ellie steps around me and hands over a small computer tablet. We have a split second to barely glance at each other and exchange a *holy shit what the fuck* look.

"Who's the body?" she asks the other guard, a platinum blond woman.

Blondie hands Ellie a different computer tablet. "Your transport authorization." Ellie frowns as she unlocks the tablet with her thumb.

"One side," Greenie says and shoves Ellie away before I can read the tablet over her shoulder.

Greenie grabs my left arm and yanks me toward the other end of the tunnel. "Welcome to Cerulean City, prisoner number eleven."

"Have the family been notified?" Ellie asks Blondie. I try to look over my shoulder to observe their conversation, but Greenie has some impressive upper body strength. She locks my wrist restraints to a handhold next to the inner airlock door.

"Number Eleven's family?" Blondie asks. "That's not our job."

"No. This guy. Martin Shimura. The guard who died, the body I'm taking out of here." Ellie says all that with emphasis and over-enunciation, for my benefit, I'm guessing. I make eyes at her and hope she can divine my meaning: *That's not good!*

"Also not our job," Blondie tells Ellie. "You just get him back to the agency morgue and file the paperwork. Home office will take care of admin."

Shimura was supposed to be my contact here. He was the one who was going to tell me all about getting around inside Cerulean City, so I could sneak my way to Jordan Elba. "How did it happen?" she asks Blondie.

Greenie makes a *bup-bup-bup* noise. "Not in front of the prisoner."

Ellie looks over at me, and I'm relieved to see that although she's hiding it, she's just as freaked out as I am. "He is an extremely high-value asset," she says to Greenie, and I'm surprised those words coming out Ellie's mouth are such a turn-on. "If you're having security problems inside, I'm not handing him over to your care." She takes a step toward me.

Blondie moves to body-block Ellie at the same time that Greenie shoves me behind her. I start calculating pocket angles, but I can't see a way to capture both guards with one portal—not enough unobstructed space in this tunnel—and as soon as I suck one of them into the pocket, the other one's going to strike back.

"Our security's fine," Greenie says to Ellie. "We'll file a full report later. Number Forty-Seven expired earlier today, and we've had other concerns in the meantime. Since you're here, we're offloading the body so the agency can start whatever processing they need to do."

"'Other concerns'?" Ellie repeats. "You're not helping your case here."

"This is not a debate. Our orders are clear. Yours and mine."

"Was it natural causes? Did one of the prisoners shank him? Give me something here, lady."

"It'll be in our report." Greenie nods at Blondie. "Load the cargo, Ninety-Nine."

"And what's your number?" Ellie asks Greenie. "For *my* report."

Greenie moves forward to get in Ellie's face while Blondie wheels the gurney into the bluejay. "I am Number Eighty-Six. You want me to write it down for you?"

Ellie glares at her silently for a long moment. "I got it."

Blondie returns with the empty gurney. "Cargo's loaded. You're good to go, pilot."

"Thanks. Appreciate the help." Ellie isn't even trying to sound sincere.

We lock eyes again. Her eyebrows move up just enough for me to notice. *Are we doing this?*

I shake my head once and shrug, making both motions as small as I can. *I've gotten out of worse situations.*

I had time to think this through during Ellie's staring contest with Greenie, and yeah, this is unexpected and unfortunate, but even if we can call it off, we won't have another chance at this for weeks or months.

And as much as I don't want to go to prison, I want to know what the hell is going on inside Cerulean. I want to avenge Badger's death.

Ellie returns to the bluejay and shoots me one final *good luck don't die* look before the airlock door closes on her and Shimura's body, and I'm left alone in the tunnel with Greenie and Blondie.

To my great surprise, both guards immediately begin stripping off their jumpsuits. I'm about to raise an objection when I see what they're wearing underneath, and then I'm just confused.

Both women are dressed in colorful striped outfits that coordinate with their respective hair colors. Greenie has a green and black horizontal striped shirt above a pair of gray slacks, looking like an old-timey Russian sailor, and Blondie sports a green-and-yellow-striped long sleeved shirt with purple trousers.

"Okay," I say, "what's happening now?"

"Just relax, Number Eleven," Blondie says, her toothy grin screaming *cult member*.

"Yes," Greenie says, patting my shoulder in a way that is absolutely not comforting at all. "Just take a deep breath and relax."

I hear a hissing noise above my head, and I look up to see an opaque white mist descending from hidden vents. "The fuck?" I can't move my hands, but I kick the airlock door to see if someone on the other side will open it. Not that I'm expecting anything, but I can't just stand around and do nothing.

I take another look at the two women and decide to risk using the pocket.

I can't pull anything out without using my hands, which are still cuffed together and locked to the wall, but I can open the portal without the barrier and suck any atmosphere in this universe into the other one. I think of a blue-and-white serving platter and open the pocket in front of my chest, close and small. The pitch black disk appears, ringed by a glowing white halo, and the white mist starts rushing into the opening.

Not sure how much time that's going to buy me. I frantically work my fingertip controls to send a message to Ellie in the bluejay: **THEY'RE GASSING ME. WHITE MIST. HELP!**

No response. I'm not even sure the signal made it out—this closed airlock might be shielded. I keep trying anyway.

Meanwhile, I've blinked my left eye into scanning mode and am trying to identify the gas. Mostly I want to know whether it's toxic, but having some idea of what it is might tell me whether this is an accidental leak or something more sinister. But my pocket is doing a pretty good job of holding the mist at bay, and with only spectroscopic information based on a visual scan, my eye can't tell me much other than it's heavier than air.

Still, I'm pretty sure I don't want to breathe in this shit. Greenie and Blondie now have their eyes closed and are inhaling deeply. Yeah, I definitely don't want to do that.

The hissing noise changes, seeming—deeper? More resonant? And the mist suddenly seems thicker, more opaque, blotting out my view of the two guards.

WTF WTF WTF, I text frantically.

The white cloud billows and rushes forward, starting to fill the tunnel despite the black hole that I've opened in its path. It seems impossible, but are those—solid gray tendrils forming at the edges, reaching forward around the portal, as if it knows to avoid the vacuum?

I stagger backward until I'm pressed flat against the side of the tunnel. **MIST MOVING**, I start composing. **LIKE ALIVE???**

A tendril of white whatever-the-fuck-it-is stabs upward into my right nostril.

I lose consciousness before I can send the message.

CHAPTER
EIGHT

Venus—aboard bluejay, circling Cerulean
Mission time 3'44

Ellie Gavilán has never had the unfortunate duty of transporting a corpse before. Well, not knowingly, anyway. There was that one time on *Dejah Thoris*, where she worked her previous job as chief engineer of that luxury civilian spaceliner, and someone smuggled aboard a dead body as part of an elaborate terror scheme. That was also when she first met Kangaroo.

She stares out the forward window of the bluejay into a roiling mass of sulfuric acid clouds. Wisps of yellowish vapor slide past the nose of her spacecraft, and she looks down at her instruments to confirm that the autopilot is holding a safe trajectory. She can't put this off forever.

Ellie unbuckles her safety harness, opens the cockpit door, and walks back into the passenger cabin where the black body bag from Cerulean is strapped to a sleeping mat against one wall.

Being in the middle of a Venusian cloud bank means that radio signals are blocked and she can't contact either Surgical or Equipment at Sunstone, or the *Tacoma* in orbit, until she surfaces again. That means

Ellie has to figure out on her own what the hell to do about this dead body.

She's not going to attempt an autopsy or anything, but Badger being dead is definitely a big problem for this whole operation. Will Kangaroo be able to accomplish anything on his own now? Should Ellie have called an audible while they were in the airlock? Could Ellie have actually changed the plan at the last minute?

But that's not her job. Kangaroo is the primary on this op, and it was up to him to call it off. He didn't look happy right before Ellie left, but he did look determined. Ellie has to trust that he can take care of himself.

Meanwhile, it's just her and this corpse for the next little while. Yay.

Ellie finds the bluejay's medical kit in one of the storage lockers at the back of the cabin, along with a protective face mask and exam gloves, all of which she puts on before even approaching the body bag. She sets up the med scanner next to the bag and takes a deep breath before unzipping the plastic enclosure. Yup, it's Martin Shimura all right, code name Badger, and definitely dead according to the med scanner.

She takes another few breaths to steel herself before unstrapping the body from the wall, lowering it to the floor, and unzipping the bag the rest of the way so she can access the whole body. Shimura's wearing the same type of jumpsuit as Eighty-Six and Ninety-Nine were, no signs of damage or external wounds. Ellie's not about to strip the corpse for a closer inspection, but she can use the med scanner's probe to do a quick blood panel and toxicology screening.

She just wants to know if she needs to keep this respirator on for the rest of her flight back to *Tacoma*. Ellie has sat through enough OSS and agency training sessions to know that sometimes bodies undergo weird changes after death, and sometimes decomposing bits leak or pop.

Ellie pulls the wireless probe out of the med scanner and makes sure it's synced to the main unit. Then she touches the business end of the cylinder to Shimura's forehead.

The corpse's eyes pop open.

Ellie yelps and jumps back. The corpse starts screaming.

"What the fucking fuck!" Ellie shouts as she looks around the cabin for a weapon. "Stop screaming!"

The not-actually-a-corpse stops and takes a breath. "Wh-who are you?"

Ellie grabs a pair of scissors from the medkit and brandishes them. "Who the fuck are you?"

"You first."

"I don't think you're in any position to negotiate, friend."

The man looks at the scissors, then up at Ellie's face. "The galette is in the oven."

That catches Ellie off guard, and it takes her a moment to recall the proper response. "But were the leeks fresh?"

"I did braise the celery, you know."

"Then I hope this side of dill is enough." Ellie lowers her arm but keeps her grip on the scissors. "I'm Marmosa, Outback Operations. And you are?"

"Badger," Martin Shimura says. "God, I can't believe that worked. And Paul—I mean, Lasher got my message!"

"He got *a* message," Ellie says. "We weren't sure exactly what you meant."

"Good enough," Shimura says. "Okay, before anything else, would you mind getting me some water? I'm really dried out from playing dead."

"Sure." Ellie puts down the scissors and moves slowly toward the galley station, not turning her back on Shimura. "How did you manage that, by the way? Playing dead? Even the med scanner thought you were a corpse."

"Juliet drug."

"What?"

"Sorry, I don't remember the actual name of the compound. It's a literary reference. You know, *Romeo and Juliet*? The Shakespeare play?"

"If you say so."

"Wow. Okay, short version, Romeo and Juliet are star-crossed lovers who can't be together because their respective families have been locked in a blood feud for generations. They meet at a masked ball—"

"I'm sorry, can we skip to the part where there's a drug that makes you look like you're dead?"

"Apologies. I've been inside for months. You can't imagine how refreshing it is to talk to someone who's not a villager."

"Villager?"

"This is a very long story. Can I get some water first, please?"

Ellie fills a drink bulb with water and brings it back to Shimura. They spend the next few minutes maneuvering him to a sitting position against the wall. His limbs haven't fully recovered from the fake-death drug, and he's heavier than he looks.

Shimura promises that he will regain full use of his limbs within the hour. Ellie nods but prepares herself for disappointment on that front. Given everything that's already gone wrong on this operation, it seems likely that they're in for more "unexpected variation."

While Shimura drinks his water, Ellie goes forward into the cockpit to check the flight instruments. As far as she can tell—and she has to trust the computer, since the only thing visible outside the windows is the same thick cloud bank—the bluejay's still circling below Cerulean, using as little fuel as possible to maintain position against the constantly changing and unpredictable winds.

When she returns to Shimura, he's finished his water, and Ellie gets him another. While he drinks, Ellie runs through a quick summary of what happened when she docked the bluejay and delivered Kangaroo as a new prisoner.

"So what do *they* think happened to you?" she asks. "How exactly did you fake your death?"

Shimura gulps down another mouthful of water before responding. "It was pretty easy, in the end. I knew they were going to use Rovor on me—"

"Rover?" Ellie asks.

"That's what they call it," Shimura said. "R-O-V-O-R. It . . ."

She waits for him to continue, but he just stares down into his half-empty bulb of water, slack-jawed.

"Badger?" Ellie leans down to look up at Shimura's face. His eyes are glassy. She waves one hand in front of his face. No response. "Hey, are you okay?"

Shimura jerks back, his pupils contracted, and he screams in Ellie's face while fumbling his bulb. Ellie stumbles backward and slams hard into the opposite wall.

"What the fuck!" she shouts.

Shimura pulls his legs up to his chest and shrinks back in almost a fetal position. "Who are you?" His eyes dart around the cabin. "Where am I? How did I get here?"

"Seriously?" Ellie unclenches her fists. "This isn't funny, Shimura."

He looks up at her, genuine and deep fear behind his eyes. "How do you know my name?"

Ellie takes a deep breath and counts to ten. "Okay. Let's start again."

It takes Ellie several minutes to reintroduce herself to Martin Shimura, and to assure herself that he's not putting on some elaborate charade simply to annoy her. The process is somewhat streamlined by the fact that she already knows what code phrase he's going to challenge her with, but then slowed by Shimura's confusion at Ellie already knowing certain details about his escape plan and the Juliet drug.

"Tell me about Rovor," Ellie asks, hoping to move the conversation forward. They're both sitting on the bench next to the galley station now.

"How did you—" Shimura shakes his head. "Right. I told you before, didn't I? And then forgot about it."

"So it would seem."

"I don't know what it is. I mean, I'm not sure what the mechanism is. It might be some kind of nanotech."

Ellie sits straight up. "That's illegal."

Shimura shrugs. "This entire facility is technically illegal. All I know is what Rovor looks like, and what it does."

"And?"

"They usually deploy it as a white mist, with anesthetic effects upon initial contact. With repeated exposure, subjects build up a tolerance to the anesthetic effects."

Ellie frowns. "So they have to stop using it after a while?"

"No. It starts doing . . . other shit to your brain."

"Could you be more specific?"

"I don't know how it works," Shimura says, more emphatically than Ellie was expecting or thought strictly necessary. "But it seems like some sort of brainwashing. Mind control. I know how that sounds, but this is what I've seen during the time I've been at Cerulean."

Ellie folds her arms across her chest. "But *you're* immune for some reason? How do I know you're not also brainwashed?"

"Why would I have contacted Lasher if I were compromised? And why would I even be telling you all this?"

"Maybe that's part of the ploy. Get access to Kangaroo, use him as leverage."

Shimura shakes his head. "Look, I'll take whatever medical tests you want. Do a brain scan and compare it against the baseline I recorded before leaving Earth. I promise you, I'm still myself."

"But how? If you've been breathing that shit for months—"

"They mainly use Rovor on prisoners who prove to be uncooperative. I was assigned here as a guard. I was only directly exposed a few times."

"That's nice. All I have is your word that any of this is true. And what about your little episode earlier?"

"You're right, I can't trust my memory entirely. They control the air in there, the water—who knows what else they've been dosing me with. We knew that was a danger going in. That's why Lasher gave me a way to record a secret journal." Shimura stands up and uses one hand to pat his left butt cheek.

Ellie purses her lips. "You hid something in your 'prison wallet' before faking your death?" She's heard of convicts concealing small objects inside their rectums, where they would be safe from all but the most invasive of body-cavity searches.

"Of course not. Foreign objects will show up on a basic body scan. I've been using a bio-scriber to store encrypted data in my lipid triglyceride cells."

This is beyond anything Ellie could have imagined. "You kept a diary . . . in your butt?"

"In the *fat cells* in my butt," Shimura corrects. "A little liposuction, a standard decryption algorithm, and you'll have all the information you need."

Ellie sighs. "Fine. It'll take us about half an hour to get back up to orbit—"

"What? No! We can't leave cloud cover," Shimura says.

"I'm not a doctor. You don't want me sticking a needle in your ass."

"It's a simple procedure. I can do it myself."

"Why exactly do you want us to stay down here?"

"Elba's planning to escape. I don't know when or how, but he's definitely been communicating with someone outside the facility."

"So we'll monitor from orbit."

"You don't understand. These are short-range comms, tightbeam. Whoever Elba's working with, they have ships in the clouds."

"That's highly unlikely," Ellie says. "We had to custom-refit this bluejay so it could survive prolonged exposure to Venusian atmosphere. Nobody maintains a standing fleet of cloud-divers."

"I'm telling you. But hey, don't take my word for it." Shimura points to his butt. "See for yourself."

Ellie considers her options. Shimura doesn't seem like he's joking around; he genuinely appears to believe that staying hidden is crucial to their mission. And though Ellie has never herself dealt with biological storage systems, she knows from her recent agency training that it is possible for field agents, especially those who undertake long-term, deep-undercover assignments, to store information using their bodies' natural biological mechanisms, and adipose tissue is one preferred method, both because fat cells are not regularly broken down as other cells might be, and because fats are already used by the body to store energy for later use.

In the end—so to speak—Ellie admits that she selfishly wants a reason to stay closer to Cerulean, so she can come to Kangaroo's rescue when something inevitably goes wrong. And, well, having to suck encoded information out of a stranger's backside is not the worst thing she's ever had to do in the line of duty.

She hopes Kangaroo's first day inside Cerulean is going better.

CHAPTER
NINE

My head feels like it's been stuffed full of cotton balls. Am I lying down?

I open my eyes and see a grid of softly glowing ceiling light panels. Yup, I'm in a bed. Pretty comfy, too. This pillow's real fluffy.

I stretch and breathe in and smell . . . What is that smell? It's not the slightly metallic scent that the bluejay's high-efficiency air scrubbers produce, and it's not the sterile odor of a hospital or medical bay. Why do they always smell like that, by the way? Is it the antiseptics? The medicine? The disposable materials used in surgical equipment?

Heh. Surgical and equipment, together again . . .

I sit bolt upright and look around. This is clearly a bedroom, but nowhere I've ever been before. It's way too fancy to be anywhere familiar. It almost looks like . . . a hotel room? No, it's not fancy enough. More like a house. A residence.

I throw off the covers—which are surprisingly light given how they felt against my skin, like super-high thread count—and make for the closed door of the bedroom. I blink my eyes to turn on the scanners in my left eye, but nothing happens.

I wiggle my fingertips to work the control implants there. No response.

I go for the emergency panic button on my shoulder-phone,

pressing hard into the flesh just above my left collarbone. I feel the mechanism inside, but I can't tell if it's actually registering the contact.

I pull off my shirt—wait, are these silk pajamas? Where did these come from? Where did my clothes go? Questions for another time. I do my best not to think about the fact that this means somebody saw me naked while I was unconscious. Multiple somebodies? Nope, don't think about that!

There's no scar on my chest, where Jessica said the Cerulean intake guards would zap my shoulder-phone. But it's definitely disabled. Along with all my other tech implants. I have no way to tell whether my nanobots are still functioning—the only way I'd normally know is by pulling up a diagnostic overlay in my left eye. And none of my usual equipment is working.

What the hell happened to me? And where am I?

I take another look around the bedroom. It's a pretty normal-looking room, except that it's very large compared to what I'm used to. And much larger than I was expecting on Cerulean. The blue sites aren't as space-constrained as interplanetary vessels, but they are still self-contained habitats with resource limitations.

This bedroom looks like it could be somewhere on Earth. Old Earth, even. The heights of everything are just a bit shy of what I'm used to, which as I understand from Jessica is because the human race has, on average, grown taller over time, mostly due to improvements in food nutrition and medical treatments for childhood conditions that would stunt growth. If someone from our time traveled back a couple thousand years, they couldn't really blend in with the population because they'd be much taller than the average person. Not to mention having better teeth.

There's a window on the far wall opposite the bedroom door, currently shuttered behind wooden panels. I go over to open them and get a look outside. I have to pull aside some frilly white curtains to get at the handles on the shutters. The fabric feels—strange? It looks like cloth, but feels a lot lighter and thinner between my fingers. I decide to investigate that more later, and pull open the shutters.

The light from outside momentarily blinds me, and I have to blink a few times before my eyes adjust. And before that, I hear sounds that I wouldn't expect inside Cerulean—if that's where I am: running water, like a fountain, and wind rustling tree branches. Those are sounds I know and recognize. But if that's what I'm hearing, I can't possibly be on Cerulean. Can I?

Which means—what? I've been kidnapped and taken somewhere else? This can't be on Venus; the heat and pressure at ground level would have crushed and melted me in seconds. But if it's another planet, that means I was unconscious for several days, at least. And that means somebody dosed me with very powerful drugs, in addition to doing whatever they did to disable my biotech implants.

I have even more questions when my eyes acclimate to the light and I see what's outside my room.

There's a hedge just below the window, a paved courtyard beyond that, and another cottage on the other side of the open space. There's a sign outside the front of my cottage, a small board hanging from a post with a single number painted on it, and a single word below: #11. PRIVATE.

A cobblestone path leads out of the courtyard and down a slope into what I can only describe as . . . the center of the village?

It looks like an old Hollywood studio backlot. Every structure looks authentic, but the way they've been placed—jammed together into a small space, frankly—suggests a very particular design, a specific purpose behind the layout of the place. There's a large pool with a fountain in an open area surrounded by storefronts that look like shops. Behind that, the spire of a clock tower rises over a large white building fronted by Greek columns.

There are no people anywhere.

The sky above is blue. Trees line the plaza around the fountain, and paved paths lead off in multiple directions. Beyond the immediate circle of buildings, I see what appear to be hills, forest, mountains.

I lean down to smell the hedge below my window, wondering if I can identify it by the white blossoms dotting it, and I get a whiff of salt. Seawater. This is near an ocean?

Where the fuck am I?

If my left eye were working, I could use its scanners to find out more about my surroundings. I could tell if these buildings are actually made of stone, and I could see if there were any heat signatures around indicating humans or animals or machinery. If my bionic ears were working, I could amplify the sounds I'm hearing and run software to detect patterns or even pick up distant speech. If my shoulder-phone computer were working, I could tell it to ask the nanobots in my blood whether that really is salt water I'm smelling.

But I can't do any of that. I'm on my own for now, at least until my nanobots repair whatever damage has been done to my implants. If they can repair it. Whatever's happened to me isn't anything that any of us was expecting.

I open the pocket to make sure I can still do that, at least. Yes, but . . . without access to my shoulder-phone, which contains Oliver's lovingly curated database of what I've got hidden in the pocket and which reference objects point to which actual objects, I have to depend on my faulty human memory to remember what's where.

The only scanner pointer I can remember is an old handheld training device. It's not quite state of the art, but at least I know how to use it. I pull the scanner and sweep it around the bedroom. Feels weird to be looking at a screen instead of just seeing the overlay in my eye, but I can deal.

Nothing suspicious hiding in the walls, no obvious surveillance devices. The weird thing is, there doesn't seem to be much of anything —I can't see any wires or cables that would normally deliver electricity to the ceiling fan and the lights. Maybe I've got the wrong scan setting or something. And wow, is this thing overheating already? Probably one of many reasons we don't use this model anymore.

I shut down the scanner and re-pocket it, turn back to the bedroom door, and then realize that underneath these powder-blue, two-piece silk pajamas—which are ridiculously comfortable, I have to admit— I'm totally naked. So however I got here, whoever left me also took my clothes. In addition to doing whatever they did to disable all my tech implants.

Man, I really hope this is Lasher playing a ridiculously elaborate prank on me.

I go to the bedroom door and take a breath before opening it, halfway expecting to see some kind of psychedelic landscape that would confirm that I'm dreaming. Except I don't usually experience all these sensory details when I dream. I certainly don't remember ever needing to pee this badly during a dream.

On the other side of the bedroom door is what appears to be the interior of a cottage. It looks like something out of an old-timey storybook, almost: decorated in soft pastels, everything just a little bit too short for me—I have to duck my head when passing through the doorway out of the bedroom—and all the furniture that I can see looking like it's from several centuries ago. Lots of wood. Lots of bare metal. No plastics or modern ceramics anywhere, nothing obviously electronic, no powered lights.

The cottage itself isn't very big. I check all the rooms quickly. There's a bathroom next to the bedroom, a living room in the center of the house, and an open-plan kitchen on the other side from the bed and bath. The only other door appears to be the front door, and that's where I head next.

I'm barefoot, but someone has thoughtfully left a pair of moccasin-type slippers by the door. In my size, too. I put them on and again note something unusual about the fabric that I can't quite pin down. It's soft and comfortable, but just doesn't feel quite right.

Not my most important concern right now. I yank open the front door and step outside.

Just as I step into the courtyard, a loud bell starts ringing. I turn and look up and see the culprit clanging back and forth in the clock tower I spotted from the bedroom. It sounds pretty much like I'd expect an old bell to sound.

The ringing stops a few seconds later, and then I hear other noises. Movement. Voices!

I move to the edge of the courtyard and look down the slope, toward the center of town, or whatever this place is. It was totally deserted before, but now there are people—humans—walking around, riding bicycles, sweeping in front of their storefronts. They're all wearing clothes that seem to have come out of a mid-twentieth-century children's television show: bright colors, stripes, hats.

If my left eye were working, I could zoom in and see more detail, possibly run some faces against the recognition database that Oliver downloaded to my shoulder-phone before we left Earth. But I'll have to do this the hard way.

I start walking down the path into the village.

The first person I encounter when I reach the town square is a middle-aged woman sweeping the stones in the plaza in front of a small CAFE, according to the signpost out front. She's using an old-fashioned manual broom, one that looks like it's made out of actual wood and straw, and I suppose that and her old-timey apron contribute to her matronly appearance.

"Excuse me," I say, walking up to her.

She stops sweeping and looks up at me with a blank smile. "Good morning," she says in a strange, lilting accent I can't quite place.

"Maybe for you," I say. "Where am I? What is this place?"

The woman looks me up and down, taking in my pajamas and moccasins, and her smile turns to amusement. "Had a rough night, did we? Perhaps you'd better pop round to the hospital. Do you remember how to get there, love?"

Her accent is definitely something from the United Kingdom. Irish? Scottish? Welsh? I'm not sure that's important right now, but it sticks in my head for some reason.

"Could you remind me, please?" I say, as if this is a normal conversation.

The woman points past the clock tower, at the far corner of the plaza. "Just back there, and follow the signs."

"Thanks." I start walking in that direction.

"Be seeing you," I hear the woman call behind me.

I do my best to take note of all the people now milling around the fountain in the middle of the plaza, once again bemoaning the fact that I don't have any of my tech implants to help me out with recon. Normally I'd be recording everything, or streaming data live back to Oliver for analysis, seeing things through a variety of filters that would give me information beyond what people tell me. I could have scanned that woman to see if she had any implants herself, and whether her autonomic body responses indicated surprise at seeing me walking around in my pajamas. But I don't want anyone to know I can access that kind of tech in here, not yet anyway. And without that analysis, all I know is I just had a weird conversation with a nice lady who might also possibly be a witch.

There are quite a few signposts all throughout the plaza, including a very tall one near the center, in front of the fountain, with several signs pointing in different directions. The labels mostly say generic things like HOSPITAL and SHOPS and RESIDENCES, but the one that catches my eye is GREEN DOME.

Honestly, there are a lot of weird things happening around here, but instead of dealing with any more oddball characters right now, I'd rather get the lay of the land first. At least figure out if I'm actually still on Venus, or if I've been spirited away to some other strange place. Get my bearings. Get some kind of solid information before I try to put myself back on track with my mission.

I follow the signs pointing toward the Green Dome, whatever that is. They lead me out of the plaza and up a winding street that wraps around a small hill. The path takes me past the clock tower, and on a whim I decide to see if I can climb up and get a bird's-eye view of this place.

There aren't any doors or velvet ropes preventing me from ascending the stairs in the clock tower, and once I'm up there, I take a moment to inspect the bell. I don't see any obvious automation mechanisms for ringing it, but there could be hidden motors or something. Why hide that, though?

I file the question away for later and look out over the town. Village. Whatever it is.

I don't have my eye to help me measure distances, but I estimate I'm a good twenty meters above the plaza here, based on my angle and how out of breath I am after climbing all those stairs. I can see over most of the buildings, except for the ones on the hill behind me—and now I can see the Green Dome, sitting on top of another white building with columns back there.

On the far side of the plaza, past the "residences" area where I woke up, is what looks like a sandy strip of beach. And an ocean. The water extends out to the horizon.

So I'm on an island? What the fuck?

I move around the tower in a slow circle, straining my unaided eyes to see as far into the distance as I can. The hill with the Green Dome building blocks my view in that direction, but the other two hundred and seventy-ish degrees around the circle show me the same thing: cute little storybook buildings, green trees, sandy beach, blue ocean. Sure as hell looks like a tiny little island in the middle of nowhere. Or at least that's what somebody wants me to think.

There are design tricks that a clever illusionist could employ to make a small, enclosed volume look like something else. Maybe this is part of what Cerulean's original designers were going for: the semblance of an environment different than the actual floating habitat, to mess with their prisoners' perception of space. Maybe the knockout gas, or whatever it was that got me back in the airlock tunnel, was part of that too—a forced discontinuity in perception, so you don't experience the actual transition from the real world into this fantasyland.

Again, I could tell more with my eye, but I suppose that's why they disable everyone's tech implants. You don't want the prisoners knowing more than you want them to know. You want to control everything around them, so you can—what? Manipulate them further? Makes sense as a form of psychological torture, but why go to all this trouble?

I figure I've seen all I can for now and walk back down the tower to continue following the path to the Green Dome.

When I exit the arched doorway from the tower and turn the corner to get back on the path, I'm surprised to see a vehicle there. It's a small cart with four actual wheels and a striped cloth canopy cover, otherwise open to the air, with two seats in front, one of them behind a comically large round steering wheel, and what looks like a flat cargo area in the back—basically, a bizarro golf cart.

There's a person sitting in the driver's seat, which I now see is on the right side of the vehicle. UK standard. Why is everything here so British-y?

"Good morning," the driver says to me. It's a dark-haired woman, also dressed in a striped shirt and wearing a beret. She makes a gesture with her hand, something like a wave, but with her thumb and forefinger touching to make a circle. "Care for a ride? Where are you headed?"

I hesitate before answering, wondering if this is a trap. Then again, I already seem to be caught in one huge freaking trap. Might as well save some energy in case I have to punch someone later.

"Sure." I climb into the cart beside the driver. "Green Dome, please."

The Green Dome is apparently only green on the outside. On the inside, the building looks remarkably like any number of old federal buildings that I've had the misfortune of getting lost in around Washington, D.C. Except that after I pass through the double doors from the outside, there's only one door anywhere along the single long corridor inside, and it's marked with a single number: 2.

This place is getting weirder all the time.

I briefly consider opening the pocket to pull out a hammer, so I can use that to knock on the door in the most annoying way possible, but I suspect that would raise some questions about where I got the hammer. And if there's any video surveillance in this building—which sccms extremely likely—some people who shouldn't know about the pocket at all might get an eyeful that they feel compelled to follow up on. So I settle for making a fist and using my knuckles to knock as loudly as possible, continuously, until the door swings open.

Through the open doorway, I see a long ramp leading down to a spherical chamber with what looks like a large white egg behind a semicircular desk.

"Do come in," says a male voice, echoing out from somewhere I can't see, speaking with a British accent.

I pad down the ramp toward the big egg. After I've fully entered the round inner chamber, a set of steel doors slams shut behind me. I turn reflexively to look at them, even though there's nothing I can do about it.

"So glad you could join us," says the voice.

I turn back toward the giant egg and see that it's rotated around to face me now—apparently it's some kind of chair, cut in half at an angle, with a padded and upholstered blue interior. More like a weird sculpture than furniture.

There's a man sitting in the egg-chair, his posture not looking very comfortable despite the wide grin on his face. He's got a plump face and a stocky build, and that creepy grin is nestled between a bulbous nose and thick gray beard. His weird village outfit is accessorized with a black scarf, showing lengthwise yellow and white stripes, wrapped around his neck. His stubby hands rest on the handle of a furled dark blue umbrella, which he's holding upright like a cane between his widespread legs.

I don't really like anything that's happening here, but I'm kind of stuck for now.

"You're Number Two?" I ask.

"At your service. Welcome to the Green Dome. Breakfast?"

This is all super weird, but if this guy's one of the guards . . . "The galette is in the oven."

Number Two laughs. "Not on the menu, I'm afraid."

That's no good. If he's a guard, he should have given a different response to that challenge phrase. If he's a prisoner . . . Have the inmates taken over this place? But then why are they all acting so strange? None of this makes any sense.

Before I can say anything else, Number Two snaps his fingers, and the double doors at the top of the ramp open again. A food serving cart rolls down toward us, pushed by a squat humanoid robot only slightly taller than the cart itself. On top of the cart is a silver tea service and three covered dishes.

"Is that a robot?" I point at the robot. It's unlike any of the industrial or maintenance models I've seen in use at other facilities around the solar system, either military or civilian. Most robots are purpose-built, designed to optimize a specific function, and unless it's a sex surrogate there's usually no need for them to look so much like humans. In fact, it tends to creep people out when they see fully human-shaped robots. This robot does have a distinctly humanoid upper body, but boxy and shiny so it looks cartoonish, and a round, three-wheeled platform for its base.

"Clive is a trusted associate," Number Two says. "Coffee or tea?"

I might as well go along with the weirdness for now. "Coffee."

"Oh, I'm afraid we only have tea, old chum."

I raise my arms in a half-shrug. "Then why did you even ask me?"

"Tea, then." He's clearly ignoring me on purpose. "Darjeeling. Sugar?"

"I'd appreciate you not giving me any nicknames until we know each other better."

"Oho!" Number Two taps his umbrella against the floor and chuckles. "Clive, would you make a note in Number Eleven's file: sense of humor, strong and unimpaired."

Clive, the robot, makes some whirring and clicking noises, and his square face lights up with multicolored blinking lights. I pinch the inside of my left wrist to make sure I'm not dreaming.

"Who's Number Eleven?" I ask, already knowing I'm going to regret hearing the answer.

"Why, you are, of course."

"And you're Number Two."

"Naturally."

"So who's Number One?"

Number Two's stupid grin becomes positively shit-eating. "That would be telling."

He nods at Clive, and the robot lifts the cover off one of the dishes, revealing two sunny-side-up eggs and two thick slices of back bacon. My stomach rumbles, and my mouth waters involuntarily. But it's probably not a good idea to eat or drink anything that this weirdo is offering me without testing it first.

"Do help yourself to toast," Two says.

What the hell is he talking about? "I don't see any toast."

Two snaps his fingers, and Clive reaches out both robotic arms to lift the covers off the remaining two trays. Resting on one silver tray is a small, antique, semiautomatic pistol. On the other is an even smaller, square, clear plastic package, with a flat purple ring inside—

"Is that—is that a *condom*?" I ask, reflexively leaning closer to get a better look. Yup, it's a condom. For some unknown reason. With my breakfast.

"Please choose," Two says.

I look up at him, expecting to see another smugly wry expression on his pale face. But instead, he's staring at me with an intensity that I've only ever seen on Paul Tarkington when he's about to explode with righteous fury.

"Why?" I ask.

Two's expression softens, and he leans back in his chair. "That is the question, isn't it?"

I shake my head. "What the hell do you want from me, dude?"

And the smile is back. "Information."

"Oh, good! I'm looking for some information too." Fuck it, maybe I should just try the direct approach. "Let's do a trade. Have you heard of a guy named Jordan Elba?"

"No names here," Two says, serious again. "Only numbers."

"Is *he* Number One?"

"Hardly!" The laugh takes me by surprise. I'm starting to wonder if Number Two has some kind of medical condition that's been exacerbated by his isolation here without proper care. "You are Number Eleven."

"I'm not a number. I'm Kangaroo."

"Interesting." Two lifts up his umbrella and taps the end of it against the semicircular table. Clive grabs the serving cart and pushes it back up the ramp.

"Are we done already?" I ask. "Can I get that breakfast to go?"

"It's six of one," he says, "or half a dozen of the other."

Forget it. I can find my own answers instead of wasting time with this dipstick.

I turn and start to follow Clive up the ramp out of the room, but the doors slam shut in my face. I turn back to look at Number Two.

"Why did you resign?" he asks.

"I didn't—" I start to recite my cover story but stop. If these yahoos have been compromised to the point that they aren't even reading the information coming to them from Earth, much less sending back reports, I don't see the need to recap the latest episode of *Let's Pretend Kangaroo is a Total Heel*. "That's none of your business."

"Oh, I'm afraid that simply won't do." Two stands up and walks around the table toward me. "They will keep you here for as long as it takes. And don't even think of trying to escape. It's impossible."

"'They'?" I ask. "Not 'we'?"

Two smiles. "It's very cosmopolitan."

"Seriously, what is your damage?" I don't know if I can stand two whole weeks of this ridiculousness. "I want to speak to your supervisor. Where's Number One?"

"Questions are a burden," Two says. "Answers are a prison for oneself."

For just a second, I contemplate opening the pocket to retrieve something I can use to smack this guy. Nothing that would cause serious injury, just a little love tap to manifest a physical expression of my exasperation with his insufferable behavior.

But I don't. The warders here do, in theory, have high enough security clearance that they could know all about me and my superpower, but they were sent here long before I became an active field agent, and there was no reason they'd get read into that new information without a specific need. Cerulean has been isolated for so long, nobody even knew they'd built this fake village inside their floating habitat.

I decide it's wiser to keep the pocket a secret. To keep it in my back pocket, so to speak. At least for now.

"Don't make me angry," I say out loud to Two. "You wouldn't like me when I'm angry."

"Why don't we go for a stroll?" Two says, walking to the bottom of the ramp. "I'll introduce you to your home from home."

"Don't you mean 'home *away* from home'?" It's like he *can't* say anything in a normal way.

He ignores me and waves his umbrella at the door. The door opens, and he walks out.

CHAPTER
TEN

Inside Cerulean's weird-ass village
One hour after I woke up, or did I?

I am really looking forward to the time when my nanobots, which I really hope are still working inside my bloodstream, manage to repair the other tech implants in my body. Because not being able to see through something as obviously fake as this "village" is frankly infuriating.

Number Two leads me out of the Green Dome building and back down the hill to what appears to be the main plaza, or town square, or whatever the hell you'd call a big pool with a fountain in the center of a shoddily re-created petroleum-age settlement. I've seen enough of these depicted in twentieth-century media to recognize that certain architectural styles or ornamentations are used to signify aesthetic intent without actually having a functional purpose—kind of like stone gargoyles on medieval cathedrals, which do nothing to help the building stay upright but definitely send a message to anyone looking at it from the outside.

"Ah, here we are, some of your neighbours," Number Two says as two women approach. They're both wearing very colorful pastel outfits and round puffy hats with tiny brims. They look ridiculous.

"Number Eighty-Six, Number Ninety-Nine, meet our newest resident, Number Eleven."

"Hello," the women say, nearly in unison, with identical plastic smiles. The one that Two pointed to when he said "Eighty-Six" has green hair and pale skin. "Ninety-Nine" has blond hair and a disturbingly even suntan.

They look vaguely familiar for some reason. Some reason . . .

"How are you settling in?" Eighty-Six asks me, with the same unplaceable accent as Two.

"No complaints," I say. "Number Two's been most hospitable so far." Wait, why the hell am I talking like this? I don't normally use words like "hospitable."

"Has he shown you the red square yet?" Ninety-Nine asks.

"No. What's that?" Something's wrong here. Something's very wrong. I wanted to crack a joke about Moscow's Red Square, where ancient Soviets used to parade on national holidays, but I can't. I literally *can't*.

Something's messing with the connection between my brain and my mouth.

"Oh, really, Number Two!" Ninety-Nine wags a finger at him. "Perhaps you ought to stick to governance and leave the hospitality to others more suited to such tasks."

"I agree," Eighty-Six says, sidling up next to me and hooking her arm through mine. "Let us introduce Number Eleven to the local color, and you can go back to whatever you do up on that hill."

Two shrugs, smiling. "Fair enough, friends. Number Eleven, you're in good hands. I'm sure our paths will cross again, sooner or later." He raises his left hand, his fingers curled down to meet his thumb so they make a circle. He holds that hand up to his left eye and peers at us through the opening. "Be seeing you." He splays his fingers apart and drops his hand, then turns and walks away.

"Thanks for the rescue," I say as the women lead me in the opposite direction down the path, away from the fountain. "I was afraid we were going to tour the sewers next." There! That's me again.

"Shush," Eighty-Six says.

"Not here," Ninety-Nine says.

"I beg your pardon?" Dammit. I don't talk like this!

"You're here to replace Number Forty-Seven, aren't you?" Eighty-Six asks.

That was Martin Shimura's assigned number. "Not exactly."

"We'll talk after we get to the red square," Ninety-Nine says.

I can't wait, I want to say in the most sarcastic tone possible. But it's like my mouth has a mind of its own now.

What the hell is going on around here?

The red square, as it turns out, is what might be called the exercise yard in a normal prison setting. But, as I've already learned and am getting hammered over the head with over and over again, this is not a normal prison. It's not a normal anything around here.

Eighty-Six and Ninety-Nine walk me away from the town square and take me down a narrow paved path that winds past a row of tall hedges with what look like marble busts on Greco-Roman columns displayed every few meters. I can't identify any of the people depicted —too bad I don't have my eye working, to do facial and image recognition—but they all look like the traditional classical dudes. Boring.

I hear crowd noises as we near the end of the path, when it curves around the last hedge, and I brace myself for yet another bizarre sight. I am not disappointed.

We stop right next to another one of the weird wooden signs, two painted planks hanging from what I now realize looks disturbingly like a gallows, the top one labeled RED and the bottom one labeled SQUARE. Why not just make one sign? Why go to the trouble of making two and having to hang them like this? For that matter, why make this weird kind of hanging sign at all? Why not just, I don't know, have an etched metal plate attached to a post, which would be simple and durable and doesn't waste a lot of materials or require special maintenance? Why would you do something overly complicated like this double hanging sign?

I look back at the sign as we walk past it. The other side of each plank is blank. It's not even good for usability or accessibility. I'm starting to get the distinct impression that the point of many of the things in this "village" is just to mess with us. Maybe most of the things. Maybe even all the things.

Something bounces off my head, and I turn to see a large, colorful beach ball spinning away to the ground.

"Careful there!" Eighty-Six calls out, much too cheerfully.

"I say, apologies, old chap!" says the man who comes running up after the ball and catches it with both hands. It's wider than his torso, and he has to crane his neck over the top of it to speak to us. "Terribly sorry about that. We've gotten a little carried away with our game, it seems."

I summon every bit of indignation I can muster in an attempt to say something scathing to this weirdo. Instead, what comes out of my mouth is: "Not to worry, my dear fellow, no harm done."

Goddammit, what the fuck!

Well, at least I can still *think* normally. But what if that changes? I need to get out of here, or at least figure out what's going on.

"Do you have room for more players?" Ninety-Nine asks the man. "I'm sure Number Eleven here would be interested in joining."

He looks me over with an unreadable expression. "New resident, are you?"

Jesus Christ, I sure as fuck hope not. "Just visiting."

The man's face goes pale. "Oh, dear."

What now? "I beg your pardon." Why do I even know that phrase?

On either side of me, I sense Eighty-Six and Ninety-Nine tensing up. Eighty-Six still has her arm hooked around mine, and she tightens her grip until it starts hurting.

"I'm afraid Number Eleven will have to take a rain check on joining your game," Ninety-Nine says. The man nods, whirls around, and runs back to his play area without another word.

"Is something the matter?" I ask, still unable to control my mouth.

"It is indeed," Eighty-Six hisses at me, as if she's embarrassed to be seen in public with me. "We'd better get you to the infirmary, tout de suite."

God help me, I actually understand what that phrase means. Even if I can't identify the language. German? Italian? Korean? If only I had my bionic ear working, my shoulder-phone could help with that. Eighty-Six and Ninety-Nine drag me away from the red square while I'm still trying to figure it out. Spanish? I hate not knowing things.

Without any of my implants functioning, I'm forced to rely on my own senses and memory—what Paul would call "good old-fashioned trade-craft." Well, I don't think that many old things are actually very good, with the possible exception of some cheeses, though I would never say that to Paul's face. But I suppose I should thank him for making me learn a few antique spy tricks before allowing me into the field.

I've started making a mental map of the layout of this place. My "residence," the place where I woke up, was on a small rise over-looking the town square with the fountain. The Green Dome was on a hill on the other side of that plaza area. And when Eighty-Six and Ninety-Nine walked me over to the red square, we descended to an even lower elevation. I try to recall the schematics of Cerulean City from my briefing, which now feels like it was very long away and far away. Was the habitat even big enough, vertically speaking, to account for all these hills and valleys?

But if I'm not in the hab, then where the hell could I be? I have to assume I'm still inside Cerulean. It'd be way too much trouble to transport me anywhere else.

Under normal circumstances, I might try to get away from Eighty-Six and Ninety-Nine—I hate this numbers thing, I'm going to have to start making up nicknames for everyone, I guess—but for some reason right now, I can't summon the gumption to struggle against their combined grip. They're on either side of me, each with one arm looped through one of mine at the elbow, guiding me in tandem toward the infirmary. I could definitely take them. At least run away. But whatever's been affecting my speech is apparently also inhibiting my impulse to escape.

As we proceed back up the hill from the red square and take a different turn, heading back toward the Green Dome, we pass an infor-mation kiosk showing a large map of the village. I can't make my feet move the right way to resist our forward motion, but I can and do turn my head to take in as much map info as I can while we're passing.

The map is displayed as a rectangle, wider than it is tall, but I know the hab is circular. That means there's stuff at the top and bottom of the map that they don't want us to know about. Or the map's not scaled properly. Whatever the case, whoever posted it is hiding information.

Eighty-Six and Ninety-Nine take me around to the back of the Green Dome building, and we enter through a door marked AUTHO-RISED PERSONNEL ONLY. But there isn't any kind of lock, not even a mechanical one, so I wonder how that's supposed to be enforced.

The door opens automatically as we approach, swinging back on its hinges to reveal a circular foyer with more doors leading off to other rooms. In the center of the entryway is Clive the robot. Or another robot that looks exactly the same as Clive. It's hard to tell. But I suppose having robot guards patrolling the whole place would work pretty well as far as security goes.

"Well, here we are," Ninety-Nine says, letting go of my arm. I still don't run away. What is wrong with me?

Eighty-Six guides me forward until I'm within possibly-Clive's reach, and then the robot stretches out one of its arms and clamps a metal claw around my wrist. I'm definitely not going anywhere now.

"Owen will show you to the doctor," Eighty-Six says, patting my shoulder. "He'll get you sorted, right as rain."

The two women turn on their heels and walk back outside. The door closes behind them. I can't see too much because Owen the robot is dragging me toward one of the unlabeled interior doors, which opens to let us through. Then it's down a long, straight, nondescript corridor with more unlabeled doors to either side. It's eerily quiet except for the whirring of Owen's wheels across the floor.

A single door stands at the far end of the corridor, and as we get closer I can read the letters printed on it: PRIMARY CARE. The door once again opens automatically, and Owen pulls me into a very plain room painted a pale green. There's what appears to be a dentist's chair in the center of the room, surrounded by cabinets and shelves of medical equipment. More than anything, I'm reminded of Jessica's Surgical office back on Earth, in our department's home base under Washington, D.C.

Except that the doctor here is not a dour-looking Asian woman—it's a bald, bearded Asian *man,* who turns to greet me with twinkling eyes and an enthusiastic smile.

"Owen! What have you brought me today?" He spreads his arms and walks toward us. He's a little shorter than I am, and a bit on the plump side. If his salt-and-pepper beard were white instead, he might look like a Korean Santa Claus. I don't know why I thought *Korean* instead of any other ethnicity. Something's definitely going wonky with my brain.

The alleged doctor raises his eyebrows as he looks me up and down. "Oh, yes, I see. Number Eleven, is it?"

"Apparently," I say, getting a tiny bit of my groove back. "And you are?"

"Number Twenty-Three." He points to a round button pinned to his lapel, with the number 23 printed in red against a white background, surrounded by a black line drawing of what appears to be a unicycle. "Now let's see, what seems to be the problem today?"

He turns to Owen the robot as he's asking the question, so it's clearly not directed at me. I can't tell how the robot communicates anything to the doctor, but he watches it and nods and says "mmm-hmm" a few times before turning back to me with a concerned expression.

"Well, it doesn't sound too serious, but I'm going to examine you just to make sure." He picks up an instrument that looks like a stubby silver flashlight, about ten centimeters long, and gestures toward the chair in the center of the room. "Please, take a seat."

I want to refuse. This whole time, I've been trying to move my legs and walk myself out of the room, but my body isn't responding. My head's feeling a little more clear now—I'm no longer confused about my own intentions, like I was before—but something here is still affecting me. It's more than a little unnerving.

I sit down in the chair and lean back. Doctor Twenty-Three waves his scanning rod over me for a moment, then turns to look at a display that lights up on the wall. It shows the same kind of incomprehensible visualizations that I've seen on Jessica's Surgical screens.

Twenty-Three makes additional thoughtful noises as he putters around at the counter to my right, pulling things out of the cabinet above and assembling some other medical instrument. When he turns back to me a moment later, I see that it's a clear canister attached to a face mask made to cover the nose and mouth. Like an emergency rebreather, except instead of oxygen, this one's set up to deliver some kind of cloudy, swirling white gas. I see it moving around inside the canister, and as Twenty-Three gets closer, I realize that it's actually composed of tiny discrete particles of a white substance moving around inside the air of the canister. And it's not moving because of the motion of the container around it. This stuff is forming clusters and changing shapes constantly, like some kind of agitated emulsion. Or an octopus. Yup, that definitely looks like a tentacle there—and then it's gone.

Whatever that shit is, I sure don't want to breathe it into my lungs.

But my body still isn't cooperating. And as much as I want to scream *I do not consent,* or at least hurl some verbal abuse at this quack, my mouth just hangs open as Twenty-Three seals the mask over my face.

"Now just relax," he says, turning a valve at the top of the canister. I hear a soft hissing noise and feel cool air puff against my face under the mask. "Breathe normally, if you would."

Against my better judgment and currently nonexistent will, I inhale the gas. It smells faintly of citrus and is cold and dry as it proceeds down my nose and esophagus. I shiver involuntarily as a chill spreads through my chest.

"Very good." Still holding the gas against my face, Twenty-Three picks up his scanning rod with his other hand and waves it around my head. The diagnostic screens show some different colors that still don't mean anything to me, but the change makes Twenty-Three smile. "There we go. We'll have you feeling better in no time."

I continue breathing, unable to stop myself. Then I feel a tingling behind my nose.

And my left eye goes blind.

I want to scream *what the fuck* and leap out of the chair, but I can't move. I want to throw this guy against the wall. I want to open the pocket and suck this hideous gas away where it can't hurt anyone ever again.

Instead, I keep breathing and think about all the ways I'm going to tear this place apart when I finally get back full control of my mind and body. I start making a list. So far, everyone I've met in here is fucking naughty, and I will summon a lot worse than coal to shove up their stockings.

After I finish sucking down all of Twenty-Three's goofy gas, the doctor calls two human attendants to strap me into a gurney and take me back to my residence. Oddly enough, being driven from the infirmary to my cottage and not being able to do anything about it is strangely soothing. Maybe this is what meditation is like, for people who can manage it.

The interval gives me a chance to think about what's happening and why. Not the villagers messing with me; I suspect that's part of their job description, and I'll sort out whatever weird cult this place has turned into later, when I get my implants back. And that's what I'm really considering right now: why I'm blind in my left eye.

What I've been told repeatedly by Jessica and Oliver and all the Science Division folks I've bugged about it is that my bionic eye is an enhancement to, not a replacement for, my original biological eye. Yes, there are extra sensors and relays wired into my optic nerve, but in terms of what I actually see, it's a transparent overlay film bonded to my retina. If the display is turned off, I see with my normal human vision. It's only when I turn on the implant that the overlay displays things in my field of vision, in an augmented-reality way.

So even if Twenty-Three's goof-gas did get into my implants, interfering with my bionic vision shouldn't have affected my ability to see normally. Which means that the gas, or particles, or whatever they are, they're doing something to my actual *body*. That's a little worrying. Especially if they're going to turn off more of my senses now that I've been dosed again.

I'm guessing, based on the appearance, that the white gas is the same thing that they pumped into the airlock with me after Ellie left. Assuming I'm still inside Cerulean.

Thinking about Ellie tightens a knot in my stomach. It's one thing to be unable to help myself; it's quite another to know that I can't do anything to help her. Or Jessica or Oliver, who might also be in trouble. If these people knew I was coming, knew to expect me, they probably also know about my support team.

On the other hand, maybe they just gas everyone who shows up as standard procedure.

I'm not sure which of those two options is worse to imagine.

The two attendants are completely silent for the entire trip. They bring me into my cottage, plop me onto the bed—on top of the covers, still wearing my pajamas and moccasins—and then leave without a single word. I do my best to give them dirty looks through all this. If they notice, they don't show it.

And then I'm by myself again, paralyzed and blind in one eye.

It could be worse, I tell myself. The evil doctor could have done something more drastic and invasive, like actually cutting me open or directly attacking one of my implants. But if the goof-gas is affecting my biological systems, could it be interacting with my nanobots? I know they're pure tech, not bio-based, but they do swim around in my bloodstream. Anything affecting my body is going to circulate the same way, and biologics and tech can affect each other. My nanobots in particular are designed to prevent and repair physiological damage.

What does it mean, if the nanobots weren't able to keep me from going blind in one eye?

This is one of the few times I really wish I could talk to Oliver or Jessica while I'm out on a mission. Normally I could do without their yelling at me and second-guessing my every decision, but right now I could really use some insight into all this technical and medical stuff that I'm not equipped to deal with on my own.

Or, maybe, since I can't do anything else right now, this would be a good time for quiet reflection. Upon my recent life choices and my place in this universe—

Okay, who am I kidding? I'm never going to do that. As soon as I can move, I'm punching something.

There's a noise from the other room. I reflexively try to wiggle my fingers and blink my eyes to activate my hearing implants, but I can only blink right now, and without the other control inputs those motions do nothing. I can't even turn my head to look toward the open doorway. The best I can manage is to roll my eyes to the side.

I can only see part of the other room from here, but there's definitely something moving in there. A cleaning robot, maybe?

Nope. The shape moves into the doorway, and I see that it's a distinctly human-shaped silhouette.

So why is someone creeping around my house? And why are they creeping around, when nobody else in this place has made the slightest attempt to be stealthy around me?

The human shape steps into my bedroom, and into the light, and I see that it's a completely average-looking adult male, clean-shaven, short brown hair, dark brown eyes, light brown skin. Older than me. Faint crow's feet around his eyes, a bit of sagging in the jowls.

The stranger is dressed in the same kind of clothes as everyone else in the village: solid color blocks and wide stripes. He walks quietly forward until he's standing next to my bed, looming over me. I still can't move.

"Well, hello there, old man," he says in a Midlands English accent. *Why do I know* that *now?* "What's your story, then?"

I blink and do my best to look menacing. It probably isn't very effective, given that I can't move any other muscles in my face.

"Hmm." The man uses one finger to poke my shoulder. I can't respond, otherwise I'd smack him and yell something profane. Oh, I'm going to use *so much* profanity when I can talk again. "Looks like Rovor got to you, eh? I would hang about until you've recovered, only my invisibility cloak won't last very long." He leans closer, until I can smell the garlic from his most recent meal. "Come find me later. Underneath the clock tower. Number Sixteen."

I do my best to blink angrily at him, but either I'm not very effective at it or he just chooses to ignore me. Even money. The stranger walks out, and I can just hear the soft click as he closes the front door behind him.

What the *fuck* is going on around here?

CHAPTER
ELEVEN

Venus — aboard bluejay, circling Cerulean
Mission time 4'49

Much to Ellie's relief, getting the data out of Shimura's adipose tissue isn't that bad. He only needs to expose part of one butt cheek for the initial extraction, and then she deposits the fat cells into the cabin computer for analysis. After the chemical separation and sequencing finish, it's just data on a computer screen, but Ellie can't stop thinking about where it came from.

And now she's thinking about Kangaroo, who would find this endlessly amusing and would keep cracking jokes about it long after it had ceased to be even mildly entertaining. He just doesn't know when to stop. It can be annoying, but more often it's endearing, a peek into his soul.

Ellie hopes Kangaroo is okay. She really hopes Shimura is right about Elba's escape plan. Because if he's not, they're wasting a lot of time and taking an awful risk staying down here in the clouds right now. The bluejay's ceramic hull is coated with a special composite to make it even more resistant to the corrosive properties of the Venusian troposphere, but it won't resist forever.

The good news is, Shimura had been able to access Cerulean's raw sensor data, before the automated systems filtered it for human review. So his butt data was unsanitized. The bad news is, he'd also gotten it before any of the scanning system's normal prefilters, so it contains a ton of noise that Ellie now needs to clean up to make any sense of the readings.

"What exactly do you think we're looking for here?" she asks Shimura as the cabin computer console fills with a seemingly endless listing of data files.

"Movement in the clouds," he replies, leaning over her shoulder.

"Can you be more specific?" The winds on Venus at this altitude never stop. As if to emphasize that point, the bluejay rocks from side to side, and the autopilot's computer voice calls out a warning. Oliver did have the foresight to build an environment-specific autopilot into this modified bluejay, with custom software to analyze the immediate vicinity for weather changes, but it's still unsettling to hear the vehicle's structure creak and whine when an unexpected gust hits it.

It makes the data analysis slower and more stressful, and Shimura breathing over Ellie's shoulder makes it even worse.

"Other vehicles besides our scheduled cargo drones."

"And that schedule is where?"

Shimura guides her through the byzantine file structure to a spreadsheet, and Ellie finds the clearly organized number tables a pleasant antidote to the chaotic sensor images they've been staring at. "So anything that doesn't match those timestamps—"

"Yeah, I got it. Are you sure you don't want anything to eat?" Ellie would really prefer to work alone for a little while. "We've got an assortment of shelf-stable protein rations, electrolyte drinks, candy bars—"

"What? Why candy bars?"

"Why not candy bars?" The actual reason is *because Kangaroo*, but she doesn't want to get into that right now. "You really should eat something."

"I'm not hungry." Shimura points to another block of data. "What about here? Aren't we approaching these coordinates right now? No, this other sector, that file—"

"Just getting there," Ellie says through clenched teeth. "Thanks."

"You're welcome." Jesus, this guy is oblivious.

Shimura starts babbling again as Ellie fine-tunes the analysis software, but she ignores him, focusing on the image data. There's definitely something unusual in that sector, an anomaly that she would have chosen to look at anyway, but it's still impossible to tell what it is. Could be some debris flying past, or a compression artifact, or—

The bluejay rocks from side to side again, and Ellie sits bolt upright. Red lights flash and alarm sounds blare from every corner of the cabin.

"That was a strong wind gust," Shimura says.

"No." Ellie locks the analysis console and runs back to the cockpit.

"Hey, wait! We're not done here."

"Shut up." Ellie switches off the autopilot and turns up all her instruments to active sensing. She doesn't care if anyone detects their signal now. "Something just ran into us."

Shimura pokes his head into the cockpit. "What?"

Ellie silences the hull damage alert just as the radar screeches out a new contact. "Gotcha."

"What is that?"

"Sit down and strap in." Ellie throttles up and shoves the stick into a hard dive, knocking Shimura back into the co-pilot's seat. "We're going to get a better look at whoever just gave us that love tap."

CHAPTER
TWELVE

Back in "my" cottage bedroom
Some time later, I don't know

It's dark outside by the time I can move my body again. My left eye is still kaput, but at least I can still see out of my non-enhanced right eye. I have no idea what time it actually is, since the habitat dome was designed to be opaque, with display projectors on the inside to simulate any kind of environment. This entire place was built to control the perceptions and behavior of everyone inside. Even if you know the trick, you can't escape what your senses are telling you. It's pervasive and insidious.

I get out of bed, crumple to the floor because my legs are still too wobbly, and lie on the floor for a few minutes, fuming and planning my outfit. I don't want to go wandering around in pajamas again, especially given that I have no idea what this Number Sixteen character wants with me. The least ridiculous outfit I can cobble together is a black-and-white striped shirt, light blue linen trousers, and black loafers.

There's a navy blazer hanging by the front door. I don't need a blazer though. Do I? I'll just try it on. Yeah, fits pretty well, almost like it's tailored for me. Looks fine. Sure, let's keep it on. But try as I might,

I can't remove the giant "#11" button attached to the left lapel of the blazer. Like it's welded in place or something? Whatever.

The clock in my house says it's half past six when I walk outside, still stretching and testing my legs. I have no idea what Twenty-Three's goof-gas might have done to my body or mind, and I'm very wary about trusting my limbs to do what I want them to. I've heard horror stories—mostly from eavesdropping at Science Division—about how some agents with malfunctioning motor-assist implants lost control of their muscles. There are fail-safes to prevent those kinds of accidents now, but the people who run this place nominally work for the agency and might have access to the same tech. Who's to say they haven't hacked their way into the prisoners here, so they can more fully control them?

I try not to think about it too much as I walk down the hill toward the village square, looking for the clock tower that Sixteen mentioned. If I didn't just dream all that in my delirium. But I don't really have any other leads right now to get more information about this place and the people in it, and a guy who can sneak around undetected seems like he might be a good ally to have. If he's not totally insane. Only one way to find out, anyway.

There's some kind of group activity happening around the fountain. Strings of lights hanging from poles surrounding the square illuminate the rectangular pool. The water has been turned off, and there are two clusters of people, one at either end of the long pool. I'm coming up on one long side as I approach, and to my left, the people are folding boats out of paper and floating them in the water, pushing them so they drift toward the other end. On my right, people are throwing coins at the paper boats as they get close, apparently trying to sink them with the weight of the coins before they reach the other end of the pool. Cheers and groans echo around the square each time a boat sinks or makes it all the way across.

I walk to the left edge of the pool and try to talk to some of the people folding boats, since they seem the least engrossed in what they're doing. Every single one of them ignores me. I only get a response when I nudge one of them in the shoulder, a stocky bald man.

He stares at me blankly as I ask him where the clock tower is, and finally grins and hands me a square sheet of paper.

"Good luck!" he says, and turns back to continue folding his boat.

Frustrated, I crumple my paper into a ball and throw it into the center of the pool. The babbling crowd of paper-folders suddenly goes quiet. I turn to look at them and see several dozen pairs of eyes glaring back at me.

I get the distinct feeling that I'm in the middle of a Shirley Jackson short story and I've just won the lottery. I stumble against the side of the pool while leaning over to retrieve my wad of soggy paper. The elbow of my right sleeve gets soaked in the process, but as soon as I've picked up my trash, the crowd goes back to their previous babbling and studious paper-folding.

I squeeze as much water as I can out of my crumpled paper wad and hold it in my left hand as I go to the other end of the pool to try my luck. Here, I watch for a moment, then decide that the woman fishing winning boats out of the water seems the least preoccupied, and approach her to ask my question.

The woman also ignores me until I drop my crumpled paper on top of her carefully arranged pile of winning ships, some with coins in them, in a small green wheelbarrow. She picks up the wad and shakes her head at me.

"Shipwrecked, eh?" she says, handing the wad back to me. "Terrible misfortune. You'll have to dispose of that elsewhere."

"Like the clock tower, maybe?" I say. "Can you point me the way?"

"Clock tower?" she repeats, forming the words in her mouth like she's never made those sounds in that order before. "Oh! You must mean on top of the old reclamation facility. But that clock hasn't worked in ages."

"Whatever. How do I get there?"

"It's on the map." She points at a signboard across the square. "Be seeing you!" She makes the same circle-exploding hand sign in front of her face as Number Two did, then turns back to monitoring the weird paper boat race.

I try to drop my wet-paper wad on the ground as I walk over to the signboard, but another helpful villager picks it up and gives it back to me before I reach the map. I grumble and briefly consider opening the pocket to dispose of the wad, but I don't want to risk revealing my ability in this crowd. Given how they responded to my minor disruption of their paper-boat race, I'm not eager to see how they react to someone lighting up the night with a genuine superpower.

The map on the signboard is the same one I've seen in other places around the village: a simple, black-and-white line drawing of this place, with a few buildings and areas labeled in all lowercase letters. But I'm sure, absolutely positive, that there has never been a "reclamation facility" labeled on this map before. I would have remembered two very long words overlaid on top of this simple image.

Unless there's something in that white gas making me forget things?

Nope. I'm not going down that paranoid road yet. It's much more plausible, and technologically possible, to construct a signboard display that looks like it's printed or painted but is actually an electronic display surface. Oliver's rigged up similar things for me, when I needed the same object to look different when showing it to different people. That's much more plausible than the wackos running this place coming up with some psychotropic gas that selectively alters memory. Right? Right.

I poke at the signboard with a finger, then get progressively more violent with it, checking over my shoulder periodically to make sure the crowd around the pool isn't offended by my mistreatment of village property. But I can't take apart the signboard with my bare hands, I can't tell what material it's actually made of, and this isn't getting me any closer to figuring out anything about this place and these people and their weird behavior.

I reluctantly step away from the signboard, which hasn't changed its appearance since I started messing with it, and walk down the path that supposedly leads me to the reclamation facility, soggy paper still in hand.

My briefing on Earth told me to expect surveillance devices—this place is a prison, after all—and the way this fake village is laid out, with curving streets and weird-shaped buildings and shrubberies every-where, it's perfect for hiding cameras and microphones and who knows how many other kinds of sensors all over the place.

If my left eye were working, like it was supposed to be by now, I could scan for at least some of those hidden devices. Anything that's powered will radiate something, even if it's only heat. Stealth compos-ites are super expensive and difficult to manufacture, and nobody's gotten them to work at sizes smaller than an interplanetary spacecraft yet. Something about how energy needs to be converted and the thick-ness of the material. I suppose that's good news for my job security: if every field agent could hide energy weapons on themselves, my pocket wouldn't be so special.

The problem right now is, special or not, it's always a bit of a light show when I open the portal. There's no way around that, and even if I only make it big enough to get one hand through, I need to leave the barrier in place so it doesn't start sucking in the air around me and making a lot of noise. So that's at minimum a ten-centimeter disk of bright white light, basically a huge torch. I could cover it up if I had a thick enough blanket or something, but these lightweight village-issue clothes are not made for that.

I really don't want to go into this meeting with Number Sixteen unprepared. Sure, he probably doesn't want to kill me—he could have done that quite easily while I was paralyzed in bed—but I don't know what he wants. And there are fates worse than death.

Given the choice, I'd rather be physically attacked than psychologi-cally manipulated. But that's just me.

At the end of the path leading to the reclamation facility, I see one of those little golf carts parked out front. That gives me an idea. I walk right up to the cart, kneel down next to the driver's seat, and take a quick look at the area under the steering wheel. No obvious cameras, or places to hide one. Good.

I think of a tin birdhouse, reach into the space under the dashboard, just above the brake pedal, and open the pocket for just long enough to reach in and pull out a hand stunner. Nothing fancy, just enough battery power for a dozen zaps. Small enough to hide inside most articles of clothing, big enough for someone else to see it and know what it is. Probably better suited for making threats rather than knocking down bad guys, but it'll do in a pinch.

With luck, anyone who might be watching will think that I was messing with something in the cart's drive system, and that flash of light was me short-circuiting something I shouldn't have. They'll be confused if they check and find nothing wrong with the vehicle, but that's to my advantage too. As long as they don't figure out what it is I'm actually doing.

Feeling better with the stunner tucked into the waistband of my trousers, I stand and size up the reclamation facility. It actually does look like what it's called, a run-down industrial site. Which is weird, because everything else I've seen in this "village" so far looks shiny and new, like a well-maintained theme park. Anything that looks weathered or less than pristine was obviously manufactured to look that way—it's not actually a centuries-old stone fountain back there, for example. There are obvious repeated patterns in the texture of the cracks and the placement of the moss, as if someone copied and pasted the same block over and over again to fill up the required space.

This area, on the other hand, looks legitimately used up. There was only one path from the plaza that led here—no turnoffs, no branches— so nobody's winding up here unless they're specifically coming *here*. The path ends in a small paved strip in front of the nondescript building, a big gray rectangular block. The golf cart is parked in front of a door set into the left side of the facade, which is otherwise blank except for the large nonfunctioning analog clock towering above the flat roof. I try to walk around the building, following agency protocol for scoping out the perimeter before entering an enclosed space, but a thick row of tall hedges hides the back of the building.

I pull open the door and see nothing but white light from inside. I step in, careful to keep one foot in the doorway so it doesn't close on me, and look around.

It's a completely featureless white room. Soft white light emanating from everywhere, softening all shadows, no obvious lines or corners demarcating the floor from the walls or ceiling. Super weird.

"Hello?" I call out. "Anybody home?"

I think I hear a sound and turn my head in that direction. I don't move at all, but apparently the distraction is enough for the force of the self-closing door to push my foot inside the room and click shut behind me.

"Hey! No!" I turn around, but there's no handle on this side. In fact, the lines that should show where the door is have become totally invisible to sight and touch. I run my hands all over the now-blank wall for a few seconds before I start cursing.

Then the lights go out.

I'm only in the dark for a few seconds, lamenting the fact that my left eye's night-vision mode is still offline, before a single spotlight appears overhead. Standing directly below it, face melodramatically half-shadowed, is Number Sixteen. His arms hang loose at his sides, nothing in his hands. I draw my stunner and point it at him.

"Why did you resign?" he asks.

Why does everyone keep saying that? "What the blazes are you on about?" Fuck, what am *I* on about?

"Why did you resign?" he repeats.

I consider the various ways this conversation could go. This guy obviously thinks I have some information that I definitely don't, but he also seems to believe that I'm just another inmate here. That was part of our original infil plan anyway, and I'm glad to see that part of my cover is still holding. So I should have an advantage, as long as I don't give away too much. I just have to find a way to keep him talking until he slips up and says too much.

"I beg your pardon. Who wants to know?" I ask.

He raises his left index finger and swipes it back and forth in a scolding motion. "No names in here, old bean. Only numbers. Why did you resign?"

So it's going to be like that. "Why did *you* resign?"

"Why do you think I resigned?"

Now we're getting somewhere. "So you volunteered to serve as a jailer here?"

He walks forward, and the spotlight follows him, until we're standing about a meter apart. "If I were a jailer, I wouldn't have needed to sneak into your residence last night."

"Unless you're trying to deceive me into thinking you're *not* one of the guards."

He folds his arms and chuckles. "Very good. You're ahead of the game already."

I point up at the glowing white spot in the ceiling. "Perhaps you'd like to explain how you're doing *that,* if you're not one of the swells who run this show? And how you were 'invisible' when you visited, nay, *trespassed into* my private residence?"

His eyes flick upward briefly. "Those are just parlor tricks. But let's get back to you, Number Eleven."

"You may call me—" My throat tightens up before I can say "Kangaroo." An involuntary reaction, like I'm literally choking on the word. What the hell did Doctor Twenty-Three do to me? How is this even possible?

"Cat got your tongue?" Sixteen's shadowed jowls look sinister in this light, but his tone of voice is light—almost sympathetic. "Or perhaps there's a frog in your throat. They have ways of *not* making you talk about certain topics. Shall we play a game?"

"I despise games," I lie.

"It's another word for stone, just four letters, rhymes with 'sock.'"

I decide I might as well play along, at least for now. "Rock?"

"Very good. Now take off that first letter, and replace it with the prefix for *five* of something."

That takes me a second. "Quinn. Quinnock." It's a given name. Unusual, but not unheard of.

I think I understand now. Sixteen can't say his own name, just like I can't say "Kangaroo" right now, because of whatever this Rovor stuff is doing to mess with our heads. But he can spell it out for me this way.

"Well done, you! Now the second part. What do you use to part your hair? Four letters, again."

"Comb?"

"Spot on. Now, in front of that, the acronym for Southern California's city of angels."

Los Angeles. "LA." I'm momentarily reminded of Joey, but push that thought aside. I definitely don't want to start talking about *him* in here.

"And finally, at the end, the short form of a hospital's urgent intake center."

I guess that's an emergency room. "ER?"

His eyes brighten for a moment. "You've collected all the pieces. Now just put them together, and you'll know what to call me, when you can speak freely again."

The syllables come together in my mind, and a geyser of rage fills my entire body.

Quinn-ock La-comb-er.

I know that name. Everyone at the agency knows who Quinnock Lacomber is. I didn't know what he looked like, or what his voice sounded like, because all that information was redacted from any files even remotely mentioning him.

After all, wouldn't you also want to run away and hide if you were responsible for causing the biggest ecological disaster in human history?

My mouth might not be working correctly, but the rest of my muscles are doing just fine. I squeeze the trigger on my stunner.

Nothing happens. I try two more times, then toss the stunner aside. Worry about that later.

I rush "Number Sixteen" and wrestle him down to the ground, out of the circle of light. The entire room illuminates again. This guy's definitely got something wired around here.

I've got a real good, close-up look at his face now. I don't know if he is who he says he is—though, honestly, why would anyone pretend to be a fucking mad scientist, just out of the blue like this?—but he's definitely got two or three decades on me. That would make him the right age to be Quinnock Lacomber.

Which then begs the question, why isn't he dead already?

If this motherfucker has been introducing himself by name to every new arrival here—even if he has to do it in a weird, roundabout way—I mean, why would he do that in the first place? Knowing the kind of strong negative emotion that just about anyone on planet Earth is going to associate with that particular name?

Something solid smacks into my jaw, and my vision goes blurry. The back of my head strikes the ground, and then Sixteen is standing over me, staring down balefully while I wait for the world to stop spinning and try to figure out what just happened.

Right. Maybe he trusts that he can fight off anyone who comes at him, and this is a fast and reliable way to find out who's an enemy and who might be a friend.

Specifically, in the latter case, someone who hasn't lived on Earth in a while and doesn't care about how many people died during the Fruitless Year or how long it took an international coalition of scientists to undo the blight. Someone who can't appreciate what we all lost. Officially, publicly, it was an accident—but sometimes the conspiracy theorists get it right, at least in part. Quinnock Lacomber wanted to see what would happen if he made tiny cyborgs that could evolve on their own. And, well, the answer was: nothing good.

"So you know who I am," Sixteen says. "Good. Then you know why I'm in here. What about you?"

I get to my feet and shake my head. "Nope. Not good enough. I need more answers."

The white light filling the room flickers—almost as if the walls are rippling and making themselves thicker and more opaque to whatever's lighting them from behind. But that can't be what's actually happening, right? Maybe I'm imagining things because I have a concussion. I mean, that would be a marginally better possibility.

I look up at Sixteen—Lacomber, maybe—and from the look on his face, I'm not imagining things.

"Sorry, old chap, we'll have to continue this later." He adjusts something on his wristwatch, turns on his heel, and walks away from me.

"Wait!"

In the few seconds it takes me to scramble to my feet, momentarily taking my eyes off Sixteen, he's disappeared. Completely vanished. I make a full 360-degree turn and can't see anything except the white walls, definitely moving now, and—getting closer?

"How the hell do I get out of here?" I shout.

The walls are definitely closing in around me. I run back toward where I think the door was—damn my poor sense of direction, and damn these stupid nanobots that haven't fixed themselves and my sensor implants yet—but just bounce off the wall, then fall back against another wall, less than a meter away now. Before I can turn around again, the walls are pressing up against me front and back, holding me upright in place, smashing into my face and starting to crush my skull ever so slightly.

Oddly enough, the thing foremost on my mind is how these walls don't feel like normal wall material. They're not hard; they're actually a little springy. And they smell a little like—vanilla?

Of course. *You're an idiot, Kangaroo.* If my comms were working, I have no doubt that's what Oliver would be yelling in my ear right now.

I've seen this before. Piezoelectric material—not programmable matter as such, since it can't rearrange itself on a molecular level, but a solid mass that can reshape itself without the need for any external mechanisms. You can have a solid wall that opens a portal on command, or you can have a blob that solidifies into a cocoon around a person you want to apprehend and restrain. You just need to supply power to—

Shit. Of course. It's an electronic device!

I know the nanobots haven't been able to repair my biotech implants yet. But they're still there, in my blood, able to do other things. I hope.

The walls have me pinned front and back, but they've left more space on either side of me, so I can still move my arms and legs a little.

The trick is going to be making myself bleed when there's nothing sharp nearby.

I fumble my hands up and down my clothes, but there's nothing there. I open my mouth to emit a frustrated noise, and my tongue grazes the wall in front of me. It doesn't taste like much—it's dusty, maybe some lint in there, I try not to think about why this stuff would be so salty—but the smooth, gelatinous sensation across my tongue is very unsettling.

This next part is not going to be pleasant, but again, limited options.

I catch my tongue between my teeth and, against every instinct, bite down hard until I draw blood, tasting salt in my mouth. Then I stick my tongue out again, smearing blood over the wall in a deranged parody of a French kiss.

Nothing happens.

I continue licking and bleeding on the wall.

A second later, I hear something faintly sizzling. Then I feel the wall in front of my face buckling and shifting. I push forward with my head. The material gives, bending back on itself, and now I see a ragged gray blotch where my nanobot-laden blood has disabled the piezoelectric workings of the wall, turning it back into a lump of dumb inanimate matter that can no longer resist my pushing back against it.

It takes a while longer for the nanobots to spread out enough so that I can free myself and move around inside my soft cage. But once I have enough room to open the pocket, I pull out the handheld scanner again so I can get some idea of what I'm dealing with here.

The scanner tells me pretty much what I had guessed: piezoelectric nano-weave, at least a meter thick on all sides. Some kind of programmable matter? The weird thing is, I don't seem to be inside the reclamation facility anymore. From what the scanner can see through the walls, there's empty space all around me now.

While I try to make sense of this, my nanobots finish disabling all the walls, and the light goes out, plunging me into total darkness. Good. It's unlikely that there are cameras or other surveillance devices in here anyway, given the nature of programmable matter, but I can play this tune.

I open the pocket—the portal flashes briefly just a couple times, and anybody who's watching can wonder what the hell I'm doing—and pull out a headlamp and a heavy-duty industrial laser cutter.

It takes me several minutes to slice through the walls with my laser. Not because I'm being careful—quite the opposite, in fact, I'm doing my best to completely wreck the progmat sheets as payback for trying to squeeze me to death just now. I know that's petty and unproductive, but there are precious few ways to entertain yourself when you're trapped on a prison habitat floating in Venus's upper atmosphere.

Oliver isn't on comms to answer any of my stupid questions about piezoelectric material, so I can only assume that the stuff has gone all squishy because my nanobots have killed its power source. So the good news is that I'm no longer being crushed between what felt like two big steel plates, but the bad news is that now there's what feels like an entire elephant's worth of stretchy putty pressing down on my upper body and attempting to suffocate me.

Under other circumstances, this might be fun. I can imagine a situation where this is a fun carnival game that people pay money for. Well, not that much money.

Finally hacking and slashing my way through to the outside is pretty satisfying, though. I let out a roar of triumph as I wriggle free of the giant mass of grayish goo and give it one final vengeful kick before taking stock of my surroundings.

I had half expected to find myself inside the wall of hedges behind the reclamation facility building, but I'm definitely not there. It looks—and I know this isn't possible, my brain is rebelling even as my eyes tell it to believe what they're seeing—but it looks like I'm standing on a beach.

Not a nice beach. Not like a tropical island resort. No, this is more like the sandy part behind the nice part where nobody wants to hang out because it's cold and wet and miserable. There isn't actually trash anywhere that I can see, but there's the distinct odor of rot that's specific to places with salt water. A big gray cliff face rising up on the side opposite the water. Nothing that I recognize from earlier.

None of this makes any sense. I must still be inside the Cerulean City habitat—transporting me anywhere else would be a matter of several days, at least, and if I'd been missing for that long, Oliver and Jessica would have come looking for me. If Paul Tarkington doesn't know where I am for a consecutive span of more than forty-eight hours, he will tear the world apart to find me. Q.E.D.

Wait. What does "Q.E.D." mean? Why am I thinking that? Shit. Whatever. Can't do anything about that, whatever's wrong with my brain is a problem for Surgical later.

For now, I have to proceed as if I'm still inside Cerulean, and the whole interior of the hab has been transformed into this wacky island village setting. Complete with this beach. And what looks like an ocean. If my bionic left eye were working, I'd be able to tell for sure whether that horizon in the distance is just an illusion generated by some kind of display surface. That's got to be it, right? There's no possible way anyone could have built all this inside the hab. There simply isn't enough volume inside, and you can't just add on another room to the outside of a structure that's only floating suspended inside a bank of toxic gases because the breathable atmosphere inside is lighter than the outside air.

If that's all true, then somebody went to an awful lot of effort to make this place look like a terrestrial island in the middle of nowhere. Weird, but okay. That still doesn't explain the strange behavior I've seen from all the people here, who act as if they're actually living in a rustic village somewhere in Earth's British Isles. Again, no idea why anyone would choose that particular setting. Bizarre all around.

I kneel down and stick my hand in the wet sand, digging my fingers down as far as I can. It definitely feels like wet sand. I use both hands to scoop out a hole, widening it to almost a meter across as I excavate farther down. If this is just an elaborate facade, I'm going to hit the actual floor soon, right? Like, they wouldn't have bothered filling this whole chamber, however big it actually is, with all this heavy sand and salt water just to fool the prisoners here into thinking they're actually on an island.

Several minutes later, I've doffed my blazer and sweated through the stripey shirt, and I'm standing inside a hole that's almost big enough to be a grave. That thought really creeps me out, so I spend the next couple minutes frantically scrambling back out of the hole that I've dug, getting dark wet sand all over my clothes and making myself feel even more uncomfortable all around.

When I'm standing back on the surface of what is apparently an actual beach, after I've made a half-hearted effort to brush the sand off my clothes, I notice something moving in the distance. The hell? Next to one of those big rocks. A rock that definitely doesn't look like a statue of some weird creature. Not from this angle, anyway.

The something-moving disappears behind the rock. I take a quick look around and behind me—I mean, sure I'm already caught in the trap that is Cerulean, but this could be a next-level trap like the reclamation facility apparently was—but when I don't notice any obvious immediate entrapment, I start jogging toward where the moving thing was.

It's a dog.

No. It's a horse?

What's wrong with my eyes?

The sun is setting. Why—how—what—

Where did everything just go?

CHAPTER
THIRTEEN

On Cerulean's weird-ass beach
Just after I went fully blind

So now I can't see at all. Great. Love it. Really makes my fucking day.

This should not be happening. Sure, we knew Cerulean intake was going to knock out my implants, but only my left eye is bionic. My right eye is the one I was born with, no cybernetic modifications, so whatever Rovor's doing inside my body shouldn't—

Unless. Except. Shit.

Rovor's fucking with my *brain*. That's why I've been talking funny, why I can only say numbers and not names. This means it's starting to affect even more of my brain, like the part that lets me see. What's next?

I hope like hell that my nanobots can fix this and it's just taking them longer than expected to adapt. They are programmed to repair basic cellular damage, so they can heal some minor injuries, but this—I have no idea what Rovor is doing to me. I just have to wait. And trust that Oliver's and Jessica's combined coding skills gave my nanobots the tools they need to pick up the pieces and put me together again.

Come on, nanobots, fight!

The good news, I guess, is that all my other senses are still working just fine. I hear the water lapping at the sand to my left side, I smell the salt, I feel the moisture on my skin. Probably not a good idea to move around too much right now. Maybe I'll just stand still until my sight comes back.

I mean, it's not terrible right here. Really does feel like I'm standing on a beach. I could almost pretend I'm actually relaxing by the seaside somewhere.

Maybe that's why whoever's running Cerulean decided to make all this fake scenery. Inmates are probably less inclined to think about escaping if their current situation is bearable, possibly even enjoyable, seeming more like exile than imprisonment. I know the agency really pushes the "first duty of every prisoner is to escape" thing, but come on. If the prison is better than your normal life, wouldn't you hesitate before trying to dig a tunnel with a spoon or something extremely hard like that? Why go to all the trouble when you can just relax and enjoy your prepared meals and private accommodations?

The obvious answer is because you know you're still trapped. A gilded cage is still a cage.

Shit. I think I just had an . . . epiphany? Is that what you call it? All these other people in here, acting so weird—the jailers must be doing something to them, brainwashing or something, so they don't *know* they're in a prison. Making them believe the facade, making them think they're actually in a seaside resort playing ridiculous games to pass the time. Diverting their attention so the thought of escape doesn't even occur to them.

The question is, *how* are they doing it? And why isn't it affecting me?

Except it is. The weird speech stuff, and the fact that they were able to zap my implants without sticking a cattle prod in my shoulder like Jessica did—it must have something to do with that knockout gas in the airlock. There's obviously a chemical component to the mind control, but there must be something else, too. Something that I can resist for some reason?

Yeah, get over yourself, Kangaroo. You're special, but you ain't *that* special.

I can still open the pocket. But I'm not sure what I might be able to retrieve to help me in this situation. All my most useful gadgets interface with my bionic implants, which are still offline.

Need to make a plan. One, find my way back to the village, obviously. Two, probably track down Number Sixteen so I can smack him around and get some actual answers—I don't know if he is who he claims to be, but I'm also not sure why someone would lie about that, it's just weird. I need to interrogate him for real.

Three, either find that quack doctor Twenty-Three and investigate what he's doing to all the people in here, or go looking for Jordan Elba. That's still the reason I'm in here, and I'll have to do it eventually. The question is priority. Will figuring out the brainwashing thing help me track down Elba? Or will it just be a huge distraction and cause more problems I'll have to deal with before I can go after Elba?

Man, I wish there was someone I could bounce these ideas off of. I hate talking to myself.

What's that sound? It sounds like . . . footsteps on the sand?

I call out, "Who's there?" I don't really expect an answer.

Much to my surprise, someone responds. "What do you smell?"

Okay, not what I was expecting. "Do you always answer a question with a question?"

"We don't have much time. What do you smell?"

It could be a trick, to get me to inhale some kind of poison gas. But hey, I've probably been breathing in toxins for the whole time I've been in here, starting with that white mist in the airlock tunnel. Whoever runs Cerulean can pump whatever they want into the air supply. I'm pretty much fucked here, whatever I do.

I take a deep breath and get something other than salt water. It takes me a couple of seconds to identify the scent. "It's . . . lavender? Something floral? Or herby? I'm really not good with—"

A small, cold object touches the back of my neck. I whirl around, waving my arms, trying to grab whoever is messing with me, but I don't connect.

Then I start feeling dizzy. Right. Of course they dosed me with something.

My last thought before my entire body goes limp and I fall face-first into wet sand is how much I hate this stupid place.

CHAPTER
FOURTEEN

Venus—aboard bluejay, tracking bogey
Mission time 5'55

Ellie realizes now that she should just have been ignoring Shimura all along.

The guy really loves to complain about everything, it seems, no matter how big or small the thing in question. And now, despite having no actual qualifications for piloting any kind of aircraft—Ellie distinctly remembers that from Shimura's personnel file—he is very emphatically offering advice on how best to maneuver their bluejay through the Venusian cloud banks in pursuit of their target.

"Watch out for that dark patch!" Shimura yells unnecessarily, also throwing an alert overlay from his navigation console onto the bluejay's forward heads-up display. Ellie silently dismisses the alert and then turns off the co-pilot station's access to her HUD.

"This bluejay has a custom-fabricated, nonreactive thermocoat layer bonded to its exterior hull," she says calmly while banking right to follow their target. "Unless you see something solid on that scope, please shut the fuck up."

That seems to get through to Shimura. He remains hunched over the radar display, eyes darting back and forth nervously and fingers tapping to enhance every stray sensor shadow. Ellie never thought she'd enjoy the random noise of acidified clouds and sudden wind shear slapping her ship around, but the wordless cacophony is easy enough for her to ignore. She can focus on flying. And she really needs to right now.

Come on, birdie, just hold together long enough for me to catch this son of a bitch, she thinks as hard as she can at the flight console while another sudden updraft nearly rolls the bluejay upside down.

Shimura says something else, but Ellie isn't paying attention. He's just part of the background noise now. They've caught up to the target vehicle, and though they're not in visual range yet, the bluejay's instruments paint a glowing outline of the other aircraft on the HUD, and Ellie does not like what she sees.

It's a flat, triangular vehicle, about twice as long and wide as the bluejay, with most of its footprint completely open and thrusters at each vertex of the triangle. A cargo skiff, normally a short-range utility craft used around suborbital shipyards and docking facilities. Resort habitats like Sunstone use them for loading and unloading supply containers from incoming supply drones, so the bulky cargo vehicles don't have to attempt docking with the habitat itself and risk bumping in the winds and disturbing the guests.

"We're too close!" Shimura shouts. Ellie only notices this time because he's also punching her on the shoulder. She grabs his fist before the next punch lands and shoves him back to the other side of the cockpit.

"We're not too close," she replies. "That's a drone anyway, the remote pilot will have limited instrumentation—"

"Not to the drone! To the hab!"

"What?"

"Cerulean!" Shimura bangs a fist on the cockpit canopy above his head.

Ellie looks up. She had been watching her forward sensors, tailing the cargo skiff through the clouds. She'd been careful to make sure their altitude didn't climb or fall too much and move them out of the clouds, making them detectable, but she hadn't kept an eye on the special sensors that watched for the hab. The blue site was designed for silent running, and even inside the clouds it emits limited radio and heat signatures.

Except now. One of the alarms that Ellie silenced would have been blaring, she now sees. *Heat bloom above current position.* She turns up the sensors just before the proximity alarm sounds.

A giant black cube is falling directly toward them.

CHAPTER
FIFTEEN

Still inside Cerulean's weird-ass village
Some time after I got dragged off the beach

I can't move, but at least my sight returns as soon as I get pulled up from the sand. Apparently that effect was temporary—just for the introductory phase of the abduction. Or my nanobots are fighting back better now. I can only hope.

I have a great view of the ground while being manhandled away from the beach and into a rocky cave. I get hoisted onto some kind of very cold stone slab, then rolled onto my back.

The room spins like a centrifuge. It's everything I can do to keep from puking my guts out. My fingertips wiggle out of reflex, just like they've been trained to do, but even if the nanobots in my bloodstream have detected and diagnosed a foreign substance, my implant network isn't releasing any antidotes from the reservoirs in my abdomen because none of those implants are working.

The only thing moving my fingers accomplishes is to tell me that whatever paralysis drug they hit me with is starting to wear off. Plus I'm feeling . . . sore everywhere, in what seems like all my muscles? What the hell?

I grunt as I roll off the stone slab I was lying on—it only looks and feels a little bit like a sacrificial altar; there's not even any dried blood as far as I can tell. My entire body is achy and stiff. What did I get injected with this time? Why does this keep happening to me?

Wait. I can see. Light! Find the light.

That's one thing that stuck with me from all the survival training required by the agency before they'd put me into the field as an operations agent. If you're ever captured by a hostile force and don't know where you are, start by looking for the light. Well, first, actually, feel if there's gravity: if not, you're in outer space, meaning you're trapped inside some kind of vessel or station, and that demands different strategies for escape. If there is gravity, see if there's any Coriolis effect —basically, throw something in the air and see if it falls straight down. If it does any weird spinning or curling while it's in the air, that means you're inside a structure that's being rotated to produce artificial gravity, and that tells you something about who your captors probably are.

I don't remember all the details for what I'm supposed to do in that case because I always figured, if I ever get captured in space and they're clueless enough to leave me alone, I'll just open the pocket and get out a spacesuit with a jetpack and a plasma cutter and suit up and start going to town.

Speaking of the pocket. It seems like my cover here's pretty much blown anyway, so I might as well take advantage of my biggest . . . advantage.

I think of a brown globe, open the portal, and pull out a marble. I throw the marble up in the air, and it comes right down. Seems like normal planetary gravity. If my bionic eye were working, it could tell me more precisely, but it doesn't look strange to me, and the feeling when the marble lands in my palm is pretty much what I'd expect.

I put the marble back in the pocket. So I'm still on Venus, still inside Cerulean, presumably, and someone decided to make this part of it look like a rocky cave for some reason. This can't actually be real rock, can it? That seems like it would be way too heavy for the hab. I mean, even if you could pump the dome full of enough breathable air to lift it, why would you spend the mass on that instead of, I don't know, food or water or something else more useful?

I crawl toward the nearest wall—I'm still a little dizzy and nauseous, but I can crawl just fine—until I can reach out a hand and touch it. Cold, rough, feels like rock. I make a fist and punch it.

Ow! Okay, maybe it *is* actual rock. But *why?*

I don't have time to contemplate this quandary because a doorway—previously invisible—opens in the side of the rock on the other side of the altar/bed. I pull myself back up onto the slab so I can get a better look, ignoring the cartwheels that my stomach is doing. I see three people dressed in blue jumpsuits walking through the opening. Behind them is a nondescript, off-white hallway—but it is a hallway, clearly built, not carved out of rock.

The "rock" flows back into place behind them, becoming a cave wall again. That explains it. Programmable matter, probably very similar to the stuff in the reclamation facility that trapped and then tried to suffocate me. Run an electrical current through it the right way and you can get it to mimic any number of other materials, including things as rigid as steel or solid rock, but using much less mass than the actual material. It's useful for things that are likely to need reshaping on a regular basis, but not recommended for structural support. Because, you know, if you lose power your whole building will collapse.

"That was fast," the lead jumpsuit says. They kneel down in front of me, and for some reason I can't get a good look at their face. I mean, I can see their face, it's less than half a meter away from me, but my eyes refuse to focus. I can't resolve any of their features. I can't even tell what color their skin or hair is.

But I can smell them, very distinctly. They smell like . . . cinnamon? And the two people flanking them on either side, standing a few steps back, they're similarly faceless to me but they each also have their own distinct smells. The one to my left smells like tree bark, and the one to my right smells like lavender. That must be the person who spoke to me on the beach. Even money which one of them got me with the paralyzing drug.

There are any number of legitimate questions I could ask at this point, but for some reason the one that falls out of my mouth is: "Who is Number One?"

I can't read Cinnamon's expression, but I can hear them laughing. "Well, that's another good sign. How are you feeling?"

"I am not a number, I am a free person!" I shout before I realize I'm raising my voice. "Shit. Sorry. Didn't mean to be so loud." What is wrong with my brain these days?

"No worries," Cinnamon says. "Comes with the territory. Your body's still trying to fight Rovor's influence."

"Who the what now?" Wait, didn't Sixteen say something about Rovor?

"Speaking of." Cinnamon gestures to Tree Bark, who hands them a small plastic container. "We're going to need a semen sample."

This one's easy. "Geez, at least buy me dinner first, sailor."

"Hilarious." Cinnamon pushes the vial into my hand. "We'll give you some privacy."

They stand up, and Lavender leads the way back to the far wall, doing something I can't see to the surface to cause the doorway to open again.

"Wait!" I roll to one side so I can at least watch them leave. "I'm going to need some, uh, reading or viewing material!"

Lavender holds the doorway open with one arm while Cinnamon turns back around, still faceless but I'm sure they've got a smirk on their face as they say, "I'm sure you can find something suitable in the pocket, Kangaroo."

Well, at least that answers my question about whether my cover's been blown.

CHAPTER
SIXTEEN

Venus—aboard bluejay, evading incoming
Mission time 6'08

Ellie now realizes that there is something worse than listening to Shimura complain all the time: listening to Shimura puke up his guts all over the inside of her cockpit.

Not only that, but she has to smell it, too. And she's still maneuvering the bluejay to get them away from both the falling cube and the cargo skiff that has now looped around and is heading back toward them on an apparent intercept course. Ellie doesn't want to crash into either of those things. Again.

Fortunately, the skiff ignores the bluejay as she dives away from Cerulean. Ellie keeps one eye on her rear-facing sensors as she skims the bottom of the clouds, wary of anyone who might be waiting for them down there. No human vehicles can survive the pressure below a certain altitude due to Venus' thick atmosphere, but someone could be piloting more drones inside the cloud cover, waiting to ambush anyone who emerges to take a break from swimming through cloud soup in favor of flying with visual range.

As she pulls the bluejay up at the bottom of the cloud bank, she sees the skiff collide with the cube from below.

No. Not a collision. The cube lands right in the middle of the skiff's flat cargo area.

That's a fucking *pickup*.

She makes sure the mission recorder is getting all this, then yanks the stick back to follow the skiff as it flies off carrying the cube. Shimura seems to be recovering, and he's found the drinking water dispenser tube mounted next to his co-pilot seat's headrest. Ellie lets him take a few more sips to wash the vomit out of his mouth before she starts asking questions.

"You know what that cube was?"

Shimura nods. "Garbage. Sorry. I tried to warn you."

"We're fine. Why the fuck is Cerulean dumping garbage?"

"It's standard procedure. Was this not part of your mission briefing?"

"I wasn't supposed to stick around for this long," Ellie says through gritted teeth. "Just tell me, please."

"Cerulean's a closed system, by necessity. But the people inside generate a significant amount of waste that can't be reclaimed or recycled. Doesn't make sense to carry all that dead weight around, so there's a periodic disposal drop."

"Why is it a giant cube?"

"It's not that giant, it's only a few meters across."

Ellie clenches both fists. "Why a cube?"

"Security measure. Loose garbage falling into the wind gets spread out." Shimura mimes falling debris with his fingers wiggling. "Makes it easier to see from a distance. Compact everything into a single, dense object, though"—he closes his hand into a fist—"and it falls real fast, disappears into the clouds, gets either burned up by the high temperatures or dissolved by sulfuric acid on the way down. If it survives all that, it lands somewhere on the surface, where nobody will ever be able to retrieve it, and still gets compressed beyond recognition anyway."

Ellie nods and relaxes her hands. "Sounds great. Unless someone intercepts the drop and steals your garbage."

"I can't imagine why they would want to do that. It's just garbage."

"Unless it's not."

"It does explain some of those sensor shadows I was seeing," Shimura says. "Wait. Are you saying that someone's hiding stuff *inside* the garbage? I told you it all gets compacted. What could you put in there that would survive the compression and then exposure to Venmo?"

Ellie frowns at him. "What the hell is Venmo?"

"Sorry. Venusian atmosphere, Venus-atmo, Ven-mo." Shimura shrugs.

Ellie shakes her head. She had her fill of gratuitous acronyms and abbreviations in the military. "Whatever. You're right, it's not really a viable escape route for a person, but there are materials you could fabricate that would survive compacting and exposure. What kind of production facilities does Cerulean have?"

"Not much. Most of the internal structures are made from progmat. Programmable matter," he adds quickly.

"Thanks, I knew that one."

"The advantage there is we don't need a lot of different specialized tools for handling different materials. Just something to composite together the progmat and flash it with control circuits, then we can use standard power and control modules to shape it into whatever we need."

Ellie thinks for a moment. "You said you think Elba's working with someone on the outside."

"I don't see any other way he could even attempt an escape."

"If someone inside Cerulean can print their own progmat, they could print a static sheet of polymer. They could write a message on that and hide it in the garbage for someone on the outside to pick up."

"Who would that be?"

"Whoever's driving that skiff." Ellie points to the drone carrying the black cube. "We'll find out soon enough. And then we can ask them how they're sneaking messages *into* Cerulean." Probably with the incoming supplies, but Ellie doesn't want to make assumptions. And she's really hoping this conspiracy doesn't extend that far out.

Shimura curses. "We have any weapons on board?"

"Nope."

He curses again and unbuckles his safety harness. "Don't approach or dock anything until I can find a sharp stick or something back here!"

"Sure. Take your time." She's not waiting for this asshat.

CHAPTER
SEVENTEEN

Inside Cerulean's weird-ass cave network
A little while after the smelly weirdos left

The fact that I didn't immediately object to providing a sperm sample probably says a lot about how generally messed-up my life is. My next therapy session is going to be real interesting. But right now, I've got more immediate issues. So to speak.

Like figuring out who my new captors are, and how they know who *I* am.

But since they already know about the pocket, I go ahead and start pulling equipment. In fact, I hope they're watching, so they understand exactly who the fuck they're messing with.

First I pull out the hand scanner again, and then I retrieve some thick work gloves, because now I remember that the deep-radar setting causes this thing to heat up even faster than the default sensing mode. Oliver modified this particular scanner to pump out a lot more power than is recommended, so it can see through a wider range of materials than just about any other hardware the agency has access to. But that also means I have to scan in short bursts, to avoid the damn thing bursting into flames.

What I'm seeing now is a whole network of chambers, separated by thin walls of programmable matter. The progmat's not doing anything to stop the scanning beam, so I can get a map out to a radius of several hundred meters, and it looks like I'm near the center of a huge honeycomb of these fake caves—although the other rooms could look completely different, depending on how they've set the progmat. They could look like featureless white rooms, like the inside of the reclamation facility, or like—

Or like a seaside village in the British Isles.

Holy shit. This whole place—at least, everything inside the outer shell of the hab, which needs to be made from acid-resistant material— must be built out of progmat. Well, not built, exactly. More like extruded, or fabricated. It would require an ungodly amount of power, but there's plenty of that here: Cerulean floats solar panels like kites behind it as it moves through the clouds, following the sun, using automated thrusters to keep the panels high enough to collect power but deep enough in the clouds to avoid detection from above. And there's also at least one ionwell reactor near the bottom of the hab, according to the blueprints I saw back on Earth, but the waste heat from that gets dumped down into the already-sweltering Venusian atmosphere, where it will barely show up on anyone's sensors.

And maybe that's part of the answer to *why*: if, instead of doing a normal prisoner intake, you can knock out your new arrivals and have them wake up in a weird fantasy village, and you can maintain that illusion indefinitely, you've got all the tools to thoroughly mindfuck them and make them question all sorts of things about their reality, their past, their allegiance to whoever they might have previously served. If you can convince someone that just one little thing that they believe to be true is demonstrably false, you start crumbling their entire conception of the world, and you can use that wedge to crack their mind wide open, if you work it right.

Why simply brainwash someone when you can break them down completely, and then reshape them into whatever you want?

They probably got to Martin Shimura and made him talk before killing him. Who knows how much these smelly villains know about the agency's current operations at this point, if they've been able to extract information from every single other prisoner in here? Plus all the guards?

This is bad. I need to get out of here and call for backup.

That means finding the edge of the hab—there's got to be an emergency airlock, or at least an exterior wall thin enough to transmit a distress signal through. I just need to get through these barriers down here.

Fortunately, as Oliver often reminds me, there's only so much anyone can do to reinforce progmat. I put the scanner back into the pocket and pull out the biggest, beefiest, most overpowered circular saw I've got—plus safety gear. Oliver claims that this thing can cut through anything short of solid titanium. I like it because it makes a cool noise.

I put on the work gloves and eye protection and power up the saw. The motor whirs like a whole hive of angry hornets.

"Sample this, assholes." I pick a direction at random and slice into the wall.

CHAPTER
EIGHTEEN

Venus—aboard bluejay, following target
Mission time 6'14

Ellie doesn't get much of a reprieve from Shimura, since he keeps yelling questions and unnecessary status updates at her from the back of the bluejay. She decides to try something different and see if she can get him yapping about something she actually cares to hear. The cargo drone doesn't seem to be aware of the bluejay tailing it—either it doesn't have great sensor range, or the pilot's not too worried about being intercepted—so flying isn't demanding all of Ellie's attention right now.

"Tell me how you know Lasher," she says after making Shimura put on a wireless headset so they don't have to shout at each other over the wind noise. "He said you two served together?"

"Is that what he called it?" Shimura chuckles.

"You weren't in the military together?"

"Depends on how you define military."

"I think there's a pretty specific definition for that word."

"Words mean what we want them to mean. You know how the dictionary people decide what words to include in the dictionary? Popular usage. It's not a prescriptive text. It's supposed to reflect what people are actually saying, without passing judgment on whether it's proper in a traditional constructionist sense."

"We're getting off track here," Ellie says. "How would *you* define military, in this case, with you and Lasher?"

"Well, you know he grew up in New Hampshire, right?"

"Yeah."

"And you know what the state motto is?"

"Something like 'live free or die'—wait. No. No way." Ellie's now sorry that she can't see Shimura's face. "Are you telling me that you and Paul Tarkington were in a fucking *militia group* together?"

"It's worse than that. We were teenagers, and our dads were super into it."

"Oh my god." Ellie can't fucking wait to share this bit of Lasher backstory with Kangaroo. "I really hope your therapy is going well."

"We've made some real progress the last couple years, thanks. Anyway, without getting into that whole thing, it went about as well as you might expect, and both of us got out of Dodge at the earliest opportunity. I mean, going off to college was a convenient excuse, but really we just wanted to get as far away as we could from the wackjobs with automatic weapons."

"Always a good policy. But I guess you and Lasher kept in touch?"

Shimura goes silent for a moment. "Indirectly. Through a mutual friend."

Ellie recognizes the tone in his voice, of someone reaching for a poor euphemism for something they don't want to talk about. "So were you Ashley or Rhett?"

"Excuse me?"

"In this adolescent love triangle. Were you the one she thought she should be with, or the one she actually should have been with all along?"

"It wasn't like that," Shimura says, sounding a little snippy now. Ellie must have touched a nerve. "She wanted . . . both of us. And that wasn't ever going to work out, for various reasons."

This is about as much as Ellie ever wanted to know about her current boss's past flirtations with polyamory. "And she was also in the same, uh, social group?"

"She didn't have the same options for getting out that we did. But she wanted to hear about what Paul and I were doing in the world, and whatever one of us told her, she felt free to share with the other one."

"Sounds like she didn't ask permission."

"We didn't find out until we ran into each other again. At her funeral."

"I'm . . . sorry to hear that."

"It wasn't a bad death."

While Ellie debates whether she wants to pull on *that* thread, her control panel starts lighting up with proximity alerts. She checks all her instruments, looks out the window, and sucks in a breath.

Straight ahead of them, the cargo skiff is approaching a large, spindly structure.

Several other skiffs are already docked to the structure in various places. It looks like the skeleton of a floating habitat like Cerulean or Sunstone, but not finished or furnished for humans. There are no signs of any modules or compartments that might contain breathable atmosphere or—now that Ellie notices—are even big enough for an adult human to fit inside. More than anything, it looks like an orbital drydock scaffold, but built only to service those triangular drone skiffs.

"Are you seeing this, Badger?" she asks, still staring at the bizarre sight as she throttles back and turns the bluejay. She wants to keep their distance from the scaffold while still keeping it close enough to see through the cloud haze.

Ellie circles the bluejay around the structure, counting at least a dozen skiffs now. One of them is docked near the bottom of the scaffold and carrying a standard cargo shipping container.

Bingo. Ellie nudges her stick down to aim the bluejay's nose-mounted telescopes for a better look.

"Fuck me," she says out loud as she sees what's written on the side of the cargo container.

CHAPTER
NINETEEN

Still inside Cerulean's weird-ass cave network
Even after several minutes of aggressive sawing

The good news is, my big-ass saw makes short work of the progmat walls. This stuff isn't designed to be super durable; it's mostly for looks. Almost entirely for looks. I'm pretty sure Oliver has yelled at me at some point about most progmat being only for interior use, don't leave it out in direct sunlight, blah blah blah.

The bad news is, it's not very satisfying to cut through. The walls of my cell turn out to be literally paper-thin—and I'm sure Oliver would object to that too. There are safety guidelines and physical limitations on how this stuff can be used structurally. And in terms of paper, it's actually more like corrugated cardboard. Except not corrugated; it's two thin sheets with perpendicular slats connecting them, and those slats are also arranged in a honeycomb pattern. I think that's to make it stronger and resist flexing. Oliver could explain it a lot better.

But each individual layer is still ridiculously thin, I'd guess barely a millimeter, and it falls apart as soon as the saw blade touches it. The sections that get separated from the rest of the surface dissolve into a grayish goop and collect around my feet like puddles of slime. At least it doesn't smell as bad as it looks.

Oddly enough, when I power down the saw and use my hand to try ripping the hole in the wall to make it bigger, the progmat feels as hard as, well, rock. Even kicking it just hurts my feet. There must be something about the saw blade—oh, right, it's metal, isn't it? Conductive. So it probably disrupts whatever electric current is flowing through the progmat to power it.

Back to sawing. I choose an empty chamber to cut into first, and I carve the hole big enough that I can step through it. This chamber looks nothing like the fake cave I came from. This one hasn't been programmed yet, apparently, so it's a smooth, featureless white room all around. Kind of like the inside of the reclamation facility was.

It now occurs to me to wonder if that facility was supposed to "reclaim" stray prisoners.

The corners of this chamber, and the lines where the walls meet each other and the floor and ceiling, are all rounded so it's hard to see them. And there's soft white light emanating from everywhere, it seems. I can't see any shadows as I walk around with the scanner, picking the next wall to cut through.

It looks like I'm close to the center of Cerulean's circular footprint. I can't tell how high or low in the hab I am, but if I had to guess, based on the height of the ceiling here, I'm probably "below the line" of the main dome. The blueprints we saw during our briefing showed that the prisoners were housed "above the line," in buildings inside the volume of the main dome, which was made of transductile display crystal. The TDC could be opaqued on the outside to camouflage it in the clouds, and lit up on the inside to simulate day and night views. The design always included some level of trickery to manipulate the inmates, but it seems like whoever's in charge now has upped the ante on that illusion.

Underneath the actual prison areas—"underground" relative to the village proper, I suppose—is where all the control and maintenance systems were supposed to be housed. That's where the guards lived, where all the computers and power generation stuff was located, where all the supplies were kept. Locked up and secured, so the prisoners couldn't get to it.

But this weird giant progmat hive that I'm in now doesn't resemble what the below-the-line areas are supposed to look like. Not even close. Where did they get all this extra space? Did they physically reconfigure the hardware that was installed here when the hab was first constructed? How the hell did they do that on their own, without any support from the agency or anyone else?

Unless they *did* have support from someone.

I stand there, holding the saw in one hand and the scanner in the other, while I contemplate this possibility, probably with my mouth hanging open. We didn't think it was possible for anyone to sneak past all the security measures in place around Venus—orbital satellites, telescopes on nearby navigation beacons, regular OSS patrols—or to get through the clouds and past the on-hab security without detection.

But what if the guards themselves were compromised?

What if whatever I've been breathing—whatever everyone in here has been breathing, the stuff that was messing with my ability to speak and who knows what else in my body and brain—what if they got that into the below-the-line air supply, and brainwashed the guards into doing their bidding?

Ellie. What's happening with Ellie? Did she get away?

Was that corpse they gave her also contaminated with Rovor?

Is everyone on the *Tacoma* infected at this point? Fuck!

I cut faster. I'm going in a straight line, I've got to hit the edge of the hab eventually.

My scanner also measures distances, and I've sawed halfway across the hab before I realize how much of an idiot I've been. I blame the Rovor fog inside my brain. If I want to get my bearings, I can try a different floor. The Cerulean hab is at least five levels tall, even if its current controllers have reconfigured its interior using progmat.

I've pulled a ladder out of the pocket and gotten on top of it, and am just about to power up the circular saw to cut through the ceiling, when the wall in front of me opens and three jumpsuited figures walk in. Their faces are still just blurs, which is still more than a little disturbing, but I take a few deep breaths as they approach. It smells like I'm dealing with Cinnamon, Lavender, and Tree Bark again.

I ignore the shouting as they approach, and shove the spinning saw blade into the ceiling. The saw digs in with a satisfying crunch and whine. I've barely pushed it upward a centimeter before Lavender and Tree Bark grab my arms. I wave the saw around in what I hope is a threatening manner, but apparently it's not that threatening, because Cinnamon walks right up and grabs it out of my hand. The scanner, hanging over my shoulder on a cross-body strap, bangs against my backside as I get wrestled down off the ladder.

"Leaving so soon?" Cinnamon asks while powering down the saw.

"The first duty of every prisoner is to escape," I reply, struggling against Lavender's and Tree Bark's grip, mostly for show. But also to determine how much leverage I have on them, physically. I cue up a couple of appropriate reference objects in my mind's eye.

Cinnamon smiles. "I'm glad you feel that way. I don't suppose you provided the sample we requested?"

"Oh, yeah, sure." I brace myself. "It's in my pocket."

Cinnamon's standing right in front of me. I open the portal right behind them, without the barrier.

Lavender and Tree Bark instinctively yank me away from the air being sucked into hard vacuum, but not before I can extend a leg and kick Cinnamon in the gut. They tumble backward and into the black. I close the pocket.

"What the hell!" Lavender yells.

"Don't let him go!" Tree Bark shouts from my other side.

That back-and-forth is enough time for me to adjust my aim and open the pocket again, smaller this time, with the barrier in place. It appears as a glowing white disk in front of my head and, as expected, Lavender flinches away, relaxing his grip just enough for me to slip my arm out at the same time that I close the pocket and open it again behind him—bigger, and without the barrier. I shove him inside and close up again.

Now it's one on one, and Tree Bark isn't that much bigger than I am. We grapple for a moment until I manage to shift my weight enough to wrestle their right foot over to the ladder, where it gets tangled up and throws them off-balance enough for me to topple them backward to the ground. The moment when they hit and get the wind knocked out of them is enough for me to open the pocket, pull out a new stunner, and shoot them in the face immediately.

After Tree Bark's knocked out, I take a moment to rest. Opening the pocket that many times in such a short period of time always takes a lot out of me. I pull one last portal to retrieve a water bottle. My nanobots still appear to be offline, so they can't help balance my body's internal workings. And I know from experience that using my power dehydrates me.

I finish up quickly, though. I don't actually want to kill Cinnamon or Lavender, so I need to get them out of the pocket, where the environment is essentially deep outer space. Too long in there without a spacesuit and they'll suffocate and freeze. After draining the water bottle, and taking a couple of analgesics for good measure, I check the stunner to make sure it's got plenty of energy left.

Then I open the pocket, rotated to drop Lavender out at my feet, and stun them as soon as they emerge. I do a quick medical scan to make sure they're stable. Finally, I retrieve Cinnamon, standing a safe distance away, and hold the stunner on them while they shiver and gasp for breath.

"That—what—" They struggle up to a sitting position.

"Nope. My turn to ask questions now." I wave the stunner in their face. "First question. Where's Jordan Elba? I know he's in here."

I still can't see the details of Cinnamon's face, so I can't read the expression on their face during the pause before they respond. *"I'm Jordan Elba."*

CHAPTER
TWENTY

Venus—aboard bluejay, circling mystery scaffold
Mission time 6'22

EMERALD KITTY OTHERWORLDLY SHIPPING. That's the logo emblazoned on the side of the cargo container now being ferried away from the drone scaffold by a robo-skiff—which is headed directly for the bluejay's position.

Ellie banks the bluejay and reverses thrust to maintain a safe distance as the skiff approaches, turns away from them, and disappears into the muddy orange clouds. Perfect cover for going wherever you want with nobody knowing.

"Badger, are you seeing this?" she calls over her shoulder. "Fuckin' A, we got these motherfuckers! That's how they're going to escape!"

EKOS is the shipping company that supplies Sunstone. Ellie remembers seeing their logo on an automated supply craft up in orbit, before Team Kangaroo left *Tacoma*. EKOS also maintains an uncrewed transfer station up there—Ellie saw it on the charts while mapping her infil trajectory—and that's a perfect spot for escapees to hide in while moving from aircraft to spaceships for the next, interplanetary stage of their prison break.

Oh, it's going to be real satisfying to intercept these assholes.

"All we need to do is contact *Tacoma* and—" Ellie suddenly realizes that she hasn't heard Shimura's voice in several minutes, and he's been talking practically nonstop since he woke up. "Hey, Badger? You okay back there?"

There's no answer. She calls his name over the radio a couple more times, then shouts over her shoulder through the open doorway. No response.

Ellie curses under her breath while piloting the bluejay to the far edge of its sensor range—hoping that the automated scaffold complex doesn't have superior instruments—and sets the autopilot to keep station at distance from target. Then she unbuckles herself and goes back into the cabin to see what the fuck is wrong with Shimura now.

She finds him unconscious, collapsed face-down on the deck with a pile of random supplies next to him. It looks like he was working on fashioning some kind of spear with an electric prod on the end. Not a bad idea, Ellie has to admit; it would be effective against both humans and machines, if the output voltage is set properly.

Shimura doesn't show any signs of having electrocuted himself, but Ellie does a quick medical scan anyway before rolling him onto his back and trying to wake him.

"Hey!" She shakes his shoulder, then pats her palm against his cheek—not hard enough to call a slap, but enough so that she's sure he'll feel it. "Badger! Wake up! What happened?"

Shimura's eyes pop open. He swats her hand away, then he sits up and gasps and shuffles backward until his back hits the wall. He starts screeching. "Who are you?" He looks around the cabin. "Where am I?"

Jesus Christ, not this again.

CHAPTER
TWENTY-ONE

Cerulean City—below the line
Right after I asked a stupid question and got a stupid answer

"Okay, nice try, Spartacus," I say, still holding the stunner on Cinnamon. "I don't know why I can't see your face, but obviously I'm not going to take your word for anything."

"You don't have to." Cinnamon points to the scanner I was using on the walls and ceiling. "That's agency issue, right? It's got an ident scan mode? Scan my right cheek."

This could be a gambit, a way to distract me so I won't be paying close attention when they make their move. But it's a weirdly specific thing to request me to do. And I'm curious about what the scan might reveal.

"Hands up," I say. "Don't move."

Cinnamon raises their arms and holds still while I stoop down to grab the scanner with my free hand and work the controls to get it into the right mode. Then I aim it at Cinnamon's face and wait for the instruments to lock on to whatever might be there.

I'm not sure what's interfering with my brain to make me unable to recognize faces right now, but the computer in the hand scanner is working just fine, and I'm able to read that display without any problem.

The agency likes to modify its agents in many ways, most of them invisible to the naked eye. One thing they stopped doing a few years ago is embedding a field of microscopic, nonconductive beads in an operative's face as a secure identification system. Each tiny bead has one hemisphere that will reflect infrared, and the beads can only be manipulated with very precise, localized magnetic fields. Basically, it embeds a small display grid in your face, and the pattern can only be changed with the proper equipment provided by Science Division.

But the ident beads can be read by any scanner tuned to the right frequency, like my left eye would be, or like the hand scanner is now. And the pattern it's showing me is a two-dimensional bar code that registers as a high-level security clearance. It doesn't uniquely identify this person, but there aren't many people other than someone at Jordan Elba's level who would have that clearance.

"No, that doesn't make sense either." I lower the scanner and raise the stunner. "They would have revoked your clearance before throwing you in here. What is this, a new trend in prison tattoos? Faking agency data?"

"Check your records," Cinnamon says. "They stopped using this security method at the same time I was framed. I'm sure Sakraida overhauled everything at Intel after I was ousted."

"So why didn't they remove the grid?"

Cinnamon shakes their head. "It's my scarlet letter."

"What is that, like a red key?"

"Wow. No appreciation for the classics."

I jab the stunner toward them as a threat. "You know what? I don't care. I'm taking you out of here so you can be someone else's problem."

"Why would I lie to you about any of this?"

"I don't know. I don't know why this whole 'village' is set up the way it, except to mess with people's heads. And I don't like my head being messed with."

I hear a noise behind me, and I turn to see Number Sixteen—Quinnock Lacomber.

I can think his name, even if I can't say it out loud. He steps through an opening in the wall into our chamber. I can see *his* face clearly for some reason. I move back so I can cover both Lacomber and Cinnamon with the stunner.

Lacomber stops in his tracks, holding a tablet computer of some kind. "Am I interrupting something, Number Nine?"

"You know this person?" I point at Elba with the scanner. "What is his name?"

Lacomber grimaces. "I'm sorry, I couldn't say."

"Fine, let's play another fucking word game, does it start with E? Like 'elephant'?"

Elba stands casually, as if I don't have a stunner pointed at his head. "Are they ready?"

Lacomber holds out his tablet. "Awaiting your signal."

"Nobody is going anywhere!" I shout. Fuck it. I level the stunner at Elba and squeeze the trigger.

Nothing happens.

I try again and again, and while I'm distracted, Lacomber passes the tablet over to Elba and then puts his hand over my stunner.

"My apologies, old chap," Lacomber says. "Rovor does get into everything here."

He yanks the stunner out of my grip and removes the battery pack, then hands the deactivated weapon back to me. I briefly consider pistol-whipping his stupid face, but settle for giving him a dirty look while shoving the stunner into the back waistband of my trousers. "You are not helping."

Now this fucking guy has the audacity to look upset by my perfectly fair criticism. "My life is my own."

Whatever. I see Elba walking away, looking over the computer tablet, and I'm preparing to tackle him when I notice something moving in the opening in the wall behind Lacomber.

Something big and round and white and blobby.

"Oh, come on, not this shit again!" I turn to run away and find that Lavender and Tree Bark have both regained consciousness. They grab my arms and swing me back around to face Elba.

"Don't even think about opening your pocket," Elba says. "My friends here won't hesitate to knock you out. We know you can't hold the portal open when you're unconscious."

The mass of white goop wriggles closer and closer to me. "Look, just tell me what you want. This doesn't have to be a whole thing."

"I want you to wait quietly here for a little while."

"I can do that."

"You can, but you won't." Elba nods, and I feel a cool, squishy mass wrapping around my legs and waist. "Rovor will just make sure you don't get up to any more tricks."

One of the two henchmen covers my nose and mouth with a breather mask before I can protest. Then the white mass envelops my entire body, blotting out my vision and plugging up my ears.

I get it. Elba knows all about my pocket power, apparently, so he knows that I can't open the portal inside solids or liquids or white gelatin-like substances. If I had an idea of how thick the stuff around me was, I could try opening the pocket outside that radius and dropping something against it, but I don't know that, either. A few experimental portals don't seem to have any effect. It's entirely possible that they reconfigured the progmat in the chamber to fill the whole space with thin strands, like a web, to interrupt any potential portal-forming spaces. And I can't see to figure out whether I have an angle anywhere.

But I keep trying anyway, until my head starts hurting. That's a sign that I'm starting to dehydrate myself from the exertion of even trying to open the pocket, and right now I don't have access to any fluids I can take in. At least this air doesn't smell too antiseptic.

Wait. Did Elba say that "Rovor" would make sure I didn't get up to any tricks? Is that what they call this white stuff? Weird. But, honestly, not the weirdest thing I've encountered this week.

Hmm. Number Sixteen—Lacomber—also mentioned "Rovor," when he visited me in my residence here. But the way he talked about it, made it sound like something different. And it was before I'd encountered this big ball of progmat, so could I have misheard him?

Unless . . . we're talking about programmable matter here, so it can be programmed to emulate a wide range of different materials. Including stretchy, gelatinous masses. And it's actually made up of many small, individual particles, not quite like my nanobots, but small enough to be—inhaled?

Jesus motherfucking Christ. Have I been breathing in this shit the whole time I've been here? I mean, it seems likely that this Rovor crap was the knockout gas that got me in the tunnel when I first arrived.

I really need to get out of here.

And I really need my stupid nanobots to finish repairing all my implants. My eye, my shoulder-phone, the remote-control-release capsules of medication in my abdomen . . . Without any of my equipment and not able to use my pocket, I'm pretty much useless right now.

To be fair, any other agent would also be useless while trapped inside a ball of white gelatin. That doesn't make me feel any better. Paul sent me in here because I was uniquely qualified to extract people in secret. But that was only supposed to be the last stage of the operation. Why didn't he prepare me better for all this weird stuff?

Because he didn't know about it, obviously. Nobody knew about it except the folks here on Cerulean, and they weren't exactly sending out a newsletter to keep the rest of us up to date on their shenanigans.

So what *are* they doing in here, anyway? Aside from the obvious messing with people's heads using illegal nanotechnology. Secret military prisons: perfect for all your unethical human medical-experiment needs!

Lacomber seems like the obvious culprit. And now he's mixed up with Elba, who is definitely up to no good. And who knows way too much about me. How in the hell did he get access to those records? And what's he going to do with that information? If he knew I was coming, why didn't he set a trap for me as soon as I arrived?

He's still hiding from the jailers—Number Two, that weird robot, all the other brainwashed villagers. So Elba doesn't have this whole place wired, if he needs to sneak around with his henchmen guarding him.

And he didn't try to convince me that he had information the agency needed, that I needed to extract him. That doesn't make sense.

If the reason Paul sent me in here was to make contact, to verify his utility as an asset—

Did Paul lie to me about why we're here? Did he lie to all of us? Why would he do that?

I know why, of course. Paul Tarkington will do whatever it takes to get what he wants.

The question is, what does he want out of this situation? Why would it be an advantage to send in me, Jessica, Oliver, and Ellie when he doesn't actually know what we're going to encounter? I thought it was because the potential intel was too valuable to pass up, but that's clearly not the case. Why would he risk handing all of us—and me in particular—over to someone as dangerous as Elba?

I mean, it's not a surprise that Elba has recruited henchmen in here. According to everything I've read and seen and heard from other agency folks, he's a natural leader, and very persuasive when it comes to getting people on his side. A smooth operator. So Paul must have suspected that Elba would have his own prison gang in here. Even if everyone else started out hating his seditious guts, he's had years to sweet-talk them into trusting him again.

There's way more going on in here than anyone on the outside suspected. The only people who might have a clue are the ones who've been here for the duration.

So I'm faced with doing something that I really don't want to do.

I'm going to have to talk to Number Two again.

CHAPTER
TWENTY-TWO

Venus—aboard bluejay, circling drone airbase
Mission time 6'43

Ellie's third introduction to Shimura is the shortest yet, but she's really getting tired of repeating the same challenge phrase and then having to recap all their previous interactions and conversations. She leaves out the part about how Shimura knew Paul Tarkington through a militia group and an old flame.

"Goddammit. It's Rovor, it's got to be." The fact that Shimura seems just as annoyed as Ellie at his random memory loss is a small comfort. "Did anything change when I got knocked out? Did we get closer to that skiff?"

"No, but a different one approached us as it was leaving the scaffold. Carrying an EKOS cargo container." Ellie plays back the vid recording for Shimura. "I'm guessing the agency didn't hire a civilian transpo corp to supply its secret prison."

"Absolutely not," Shimura agrees. "And those flying triangles aren't us, either."

"Drone skiffs," Ellie corrects, hoping against hope that he'll catch the hint. "Could they be broadcasting some kind of control signal? On an unusual frequency band, something that we don't normally scan for?"

"What are you getting at?"

"You blanked out when we left Cerulean, and then again just now when we approached this scaffold. It's got to be related to distance. Something that triggers the nano-stuff that's still in your system."

"But it's still opposite. Going *away* from Cerulean, but coming *toward* that cargo skiff . . ."

"We need to call this in." Ellie stops the vid playback. "All this science crap is outside my area of expertise. Yours too, right? We figured out what your sensor shadows are, we got decent images of their drone airbase, we know who they're working with on the outside. We haul our asses back up to the *Tacoma,* report in to the office, and Lasher tells us what to do next."

Shimura nods slowly. "Wait. Where are we?"

Ellie groans. "Jesus Christ, not this again."

"No, my memory's fine. I mean—" Shimura points at the screen, which is now displaying its default readout, a navigational schematic. "Weren't we flying away from Cerulean, following the skiff?"

"Yeah, but I turned back so we wouldn't get too close to that scaffold thing."

"Are we headed back toward Cerulean?"

"No. Why would we do that?"

Shimura taps a column of numbers on the left side of the screen. "Are these numbers right?"

Ellie leans over to take a closer look. She wasn't paying attention to their distance from Cerulean, since she figured the drone air base would be far away. But now that Shimura's directing her attention to the numbers, she also sees something strange.

"This doesn't make sense." Ellie returns to her pilot's chair so she can see her full panel of instrumentation. "We left Cerulean, circled below, then followed that garbage skiff away, found the scaffold, then I pulled back to avoid the cargo skiff that was leaving . . ."

She trails off as the numbers coalesce into a clear picture of their position in her mind. She double-checks, then triple-checks the navigation log, then verifies their current position once again.

"Fuck," Ellie says. "Fucking fucker!"

"You found something?" Shimura slides into the co-pilot's seat beside her. "What's wrong?"

"This is wrong." Ellie brings up her triple-checked navigational plots, two sets of shapes and lines in different colors. "Green is where we're supposed to be. Yellow is where we actually are."

"And all the red . . . ?"

"That's where this fucking drone base will be in less than two hours if nobody changes course." Ellie switches off the autopilot and banks them away from the scaffold. "We need to get back to Cerulean and extract Kangaroo."

CHAPTER
TWENTY-THREE

Cerulean City—below the line
Time has lost all meaning

Rovor's pressed so tightly against my face this time, I can't even attempt my previous bleed-on-it-and-break-it trick. Did they catch me doing that on camera? Fuck. At least I'm not being actively suffocated, thanks to the breather mask.

While I'm racking my brains for some other way out of this literal mess—the white goo cocooning me is pressing against my body everywhere and it's weird and uncomfortable—I hear an unusual noise vibrating through Rovor's gelatinous mass.

I can't identify it at first because it's being transmitted through the goo, which makes everything sound like it's underwater, muffling certain frequencies and amplifying others. It sounds like something elastic being stretched, like an old-timey rubber band or something.

And then the elastic . . . snaps?

The new, different vibrations move through Rovor and thump me in the chest, then ripple upward and buzz my ears. Something's definitely happening out there, but I can't see anything, and I can't open the pocket while there's all this stuff in the way. All I can do is wait, and be ready to punch someone.

More stretching and snapping, but stronger this time—I guess "louder" inasmuch as that means more intense vibrations. And it repeats, getting louder each time. After the first few I start getting the notion that the snapping is actually *breaking,* like someone pulling a rubber band hard enough to break it.

I don't know who might be coming to rescue me, but I hope they're not going to be weird about it. Then again, that might be too much to ask for in here, given everything I've seen since arriving at Cerulean.

A dark mass fades into view directly in front of me, on the other side of the white goo mass. The shadow moves and wiggles, and I feel more than just the vibrations of sound now—I'm feeling Rovor actually being stretched around and away from me. Some of the goo comes away from my head. I press myself backward, instinctively wanting to get farther away from whatever's ripping Rovor apart.

Then the white wall in front of me rips apart, and I squeeze my eyes shut as the ragged edges smack against my face, feeling like half-cooked cold pasta. After they smear away and off my skin, I open my eyes and see a robot holding the hole in Rovor open.

It's Clive. Number Two's trusted associate. Or one of the other robots I saw roaming the halls inside the Green Dome building.

I'm not one to look a gift horse in the mouth. Clive's arms telescope apart, opening the hole wider, and I struggle out from Rovor into the same white chamber as before. Only now, it seems to be filled with a haze of white mist or fog or something.

"Thanks, Clive," I say, brushing a few stray bits of Rovor off my clothes. "Now what?"

Clive releases the Rovor mass, which flows back together and jiggles before settling into a round sphere. While I'm watching that, Clive extends one arm toward me, clamps a hand around my throat, and squeezes.

Of course. Why would he be here to help? I'm a prisoner who's not where he's supposed to be. The robot's here to contain me.

Maybe even kill me? His grip seems to be getting tighter. Fuck!

I try opening the pocket. But it doesn't work. Shit! Elba and his cronies must have thickened the concentration of Rovor in the air here;

that's why everything looks hazy—are they forcing everyone to breathe in more of it, to enhance or reinforce their mind-control doping? Is this making everyone more susceptible to suggestion? I can't smell anything like before, when Doctor Twenty-Three was forcing me to inhale straight Rovor, but breathing in feels noticeably tougher than normal.

Or maybe that's because Clive is choking me.

The robot hoists me upward, his clamp-hand digging into the underside of my jaw. I'm getting real sick and tired of being pushed around.

I know my nanobots are still running the Weyland-Yutani program, even if they haven't been able to fully repair my other tech implants yet. And Clive is definitely a piece of electronic equipment.

I bite the inside of my cheek until I taste blood, then spit it onto Clive's boxy head. It takes a few expectorations to accumulate before I can see anything happening—first the blinking lights that serve as the robot's face go dark, then wisps of blue smoke escape from one corner of his box-head as my nanobot Davids melt through the silver Goliath's outer shell.

Finally, and mercifully before my vision tunnels to darkness from lack of oxygen, Clive's grip loosens around my neck, and I kick off his chest and fall onto my butt against the hard ground. The robot makes a few truncated blippy noises, then goes silent and immobile.

"Size isn't everything," I mutter while approaching the dead hulk. I poke Clive a few times to make sure he's not playing possum, then carefully pry open his head casing to get a look at what's inside.

I'm not sure what I was expecting to see, exactly, but it's just a mess of electronic guts that means nothing to me. Maybe I was hoping there'd be a tiny critter inside piloting the rig. Wouldn't have been the weirdest thing to happen in this wacky village, honestly.

And then I see it: a small access panel at the back of Clive's box-head, latched and locked from the outside, but there's some instructional signage printed on the inside of the panel. I slowly work open the side seam of the robot's head casing until I can yank the panel off its mounting and read it.

IN CASE OF MALFUNCTION: RETURN TO BASE, it says at the top. And below that is a map showing a circular area divided into concentric segments, with one section near the center highlighted.

Well. I guess that's where I'm headed now.

It takes me a few minutes to line up Clive's RTB map with the distances I measured with the hand scanner while cutting through walls below the line, but I get it done, and along the way discover that the emergency map also shows vertical-egress locations—cylindrical cutouts with ladders inside that run the full height of the hab for maintenance access, topped by hatches leading up into the main dome of the hab.

I suspect it'll be easier to move past the brainwashed villagers up top than to evade Elba and his minions down here, so I find the nearest ladder, double-check my bearing to the robot repair bay, and climb up and pop the hatch.

The egress port looks a lot like an old-timey manhole cover, or maybe the waterlock on a submarine. It opens right next to the fountain where I saw the weird paper-boat races earlier. I hear the babble of a crowd as I climb out of the hatch and close it behind me, but it's not until I stand up that I witness the total madness that I've stumbled into.

It's a full-on riot. People are attacking each other with makeshift weapons, some just using their hands as fists or claws, and at least two bodies are floating face-down in the fountain, presumably dead. I crouch down and slowly creep away from the mob.

One of those wacky golf carts is toppled on its side at the edge of the plaza. Nobody over there—and no bodies, either. I glance over my shoulder to make sure the mob hasn't noticed me. They seem to be concentrated on the lawn sloping up to the Green Dome building, their bodies forming a roiling assortment of colors that's getting redder all the time.

I reach the golf cart, scuttle around to the other side, and lift it back upright. The vehicle makes a loud creaking sound as its weight smacks all four wheels onto the loose gravel at the edge of the path here.

"Hullo, what's all this then?" says an oddly familiar female voice.

I turn around while taking a big step toward the back of the golf cart, putting most of its bulk between myself and whoever said that. It's a woman with green hair—Number Eighty-Six. She's lost her ridiculous hat, her hair is disheveled, and the rumpled front of her striped tunic is spattered with dark red blood. She's holding a length of pipe in both hands.

"Hey, I'm not looking for trouble here," I say, holding up both hands and still not able to open the pocket. "Just passing through."

"Well, that's a jolly crock, isn't it?" says a second voice. Number Ninety-Nine emerges from behind Eighty-Six looking just as disheveled, holding irregular chunks of what look like white marble in both hands. "Trying to sneak away from the party, are we?"

"An Irish exit, eh?" Eighty-Six makes a *tsk*ing sound with her lips. I hate it when people do that at me. "Definitely not cricket."

"Okay, I have no idea what you're talking about, and I don't care about whatever activity you're into now," I say, cutting my eyes down to check the golf cart's control panel. "Live and let live, that's my motto, so let's all just go our separate ways and—"

Ninety-Nine hurls one chunk of maybe-marble at my head, and I move out of the way, leaping into the driver's seat of the golf cart. Eighty-Six lunges forward and swings her pipe and I duck again, squeezing myself below the steering wheel as the pipe takes out one of the four struts holding the canopy above the cart body.

I find the power switch, then the accelerator pedal, and slam the cart forward. Eighty-Six dodges out of the way but Ninety-Nine goes under, and the cart wheels bump over her with surprising force. I ignore her wailing behind me as I struggle with the wheel, steadying the cart and heading away from the mad plaza.

A scene like that would be disturbing in any situation, but it's extra unsettling here given how . . . mild-mannered everyone was before. Clearly what I saw before was merely a facade of civility, but what changed? Is the nanotech mind control going haywire, or did someone flip the switch to "kill" on purpose? Both options are pretty horrifying.

I'm not going to get any answers up here. I haul ass toward the red square, the next landmark on my way to the repair bay. I try opening my pocket again, but still nothing but a headache. I can see a slight haze in the air up here, too. It seems likely Elba's taken over Cerulean and is escalating things . . . but to what end?

I just hope I can talk some sense into whoever was controlling Clive.

The red square, which was earlier bustling with recreational activity, is completely deserted now. Various balls and rackets and bat-like stick things are strewn all around the empty courtyard. The lower part of the RED SQUARE sign has been broken in half, and one half has fallen to the ground, so the letters ARE dangle below the word RED at a precarious angle.

I check my hand-scanner measurements again once I'm hidden behind the hedges from the mob that's still swirling around in the plaza. Following the map overlay leads me to a back corner, where a blindfolded marble bust sits on a pedestal above the gravel edge of the exercise area. I kick aside some gravel and see the telltale gray of an access hatch.

It takes me a minute or two to sweep enough gravel away that I can pull open the hatch, and the whole time I'm looking over my shoulder, hoping that all the noise I'm making won't attract the mob to come over and attack me. But nobody shows up as I climb down onto the ladder and clang the hatch shut behind me.

According to the emergency map, robot repair is on the first underground level. I ease myself off the ladder when I reach the first circular opening, and have to crouch a little to walk through the round tunnel into a larger, full-height corridor. I breathe a sigh of relief when I see that it seems to be made of regular metal and plastic and ceramic, not that crazy progmat stuff. I also try my pocket again, but still no dice. And I'm starting to get a headache from the exertion.

There are also helpful signs down here—this aesthetic is more what I expected from Cerulean's below-the-line areas, industrial and unadorned. I find the robot-repair bay and slap the wall panel to open the large double doors, which slide apart and disappear into the walls on either side. Again, like normal mechanical parts, not progmat.

I'm not quite prepared by what I see inside the repair bay. There are robots, yes, but the whole place looks like a large infirmary, with pale blue walls and at least a dozen beds with human people strapped down to them. An identical Clive-bot stands next to each human patient, waving medical scanners over their bodies. Number Two and Number Twenty-Three, the so-called physician, are conferring with each other to one side of the room, both studying a display screen showing a bunch of different colored graphs.

"What the fuck?" I say out loud before I can contain myself. It's been a long day.

Number Two and Number Twenty-Three look up at me in surprise. Twenty-Three smacks the wall next to the display screen, causing red lights to start flashing all around the room, and Two steps forward to confront me.

"You're not supposed to be here, old chap," Two says, pointing at me with his umbrella.

"Fuck you." I throw the access-panel map down at his feet, where the metal plate clatters against the ground. Two jerks backward. "Clive says hello. He won't be joining us at this time."

I notice that two of the robots here have left their beds and moved closer to me. I pull the stunner out of my waistband and brandish it. Twenty-Three taps his fingers against the wall again—a hidden control panel?—and the advancing robots stop. Good thing they don't know this stunner is missing its power pack.

"What did you do to Clive?" Two asks. "He wouldn't have hurt you; his program was merely to corral any stray villagers in restricted areas. Is he still functional?"

It's been a very long day. "Nope. It's my turn to ask the questions. What did you do to the people up top to cause them to start attacking each other?"

"*We* didn't do anything," Twenty-Three snaps. "Someone has co-opted our authority."

"Are you talking about—" I try to get the names out, but I'm still muzzled by whatever Rovor has done to my brain. "Number Nine and

Number Sixteen? You know they've been sneaking around down here, right?"

"We did have our suspicions," Two says. "Unfortunately, it seems that their influence has spread farther and deeper than we anticipated it could."

I briefly consider demanding the whole wacky backstory of this place, but there are more immediate problems to deal with. "Do you still have control of *anything* around here?"

Two tucks the furled umbrella under one arm with a huff. "That's none of your concern."

Twenty-Three steps away from the wall controls and moves up to stand beside Two. "We could use his help. Number Eleven seems able to resist Rovor's influence—"

"He's a *prisoner!*" Two shouts, recoiling from Twenty-Three.

"Oh, for crying out loud." I lower my stunner, just a little, and peek at the robots to make sure they're not rolling up on me. "Lasher sent me." I can say code names? Might as well try the challenge phrase again. "The galette is in the oven?"

Two and Twenty-Three exchange a confused look.

"Is that a challenge phrase?" Twenty-Three asks.

"Curious," Two says. "Parabolic mildew is the scourge of Great Slave Lake."

My heart skips a beat, and then jackhammers in my chest. This isn't happening. This can't be fucking happening!

That's also a challenge phrase. But not just any challenge phrase, not just something Paul made up so I could identify my contact in the field. There's about a dozen challenge phrases I have to memorize at least once a month, whenever the agency code sheet changes. Some phrases are general purpose, just so you know someone is working with the agency. There are different challenge phrases for different branches of service in the military, and sometimes for specific departments within the agency, or—very rarely—for specific individual people.

Number Two just gave me the current challenge phrase for direct reports to the Secretary of State.

"What the fuck!" That's not the correct response phrase, but I just need to get this out of my system first. "What the ever-fucking FUCK!"

Two stares at me and repeats, "Parabolic mildew is the scourge of Great Slave Lake."

I take a few deep breaths to calm myself and then reply, "Your slings and arrows are as anomalistic as a backspace."

"Vertical lineage is the burden of most."

"Two pillows, please; no more and no fewer."

Two exhales with apparent relief. "Well, I'm glad we got that out of the way—"

"You report directly to *State*?" I stomp forward and grab the white-striped lapel of his blue suit jacket with my free hand.

"Questions are a burden," Two says. "And answers, a prison for oneself."

I shake him for emphasis. "Tell me your name."

"You know the rules, Number Eleven, no names in here—"

"I'm Kangaroo!" Hey, I just said another name! Progress!

He frowns. "Is that supposed to mean something to me?"

I'm flabbergasted, and then I start laughing. I shove him away and turn to look at Twenty-Three. The other man is just standing there, watching blankly.

"Okay." I catch my breath. "Let's start at the beginning. How the hell are you controlling all the prisoners in here? I've seen brain-washing before, but never at this level of precision."

"It's not 'brainwashing,'" Twenty-Three huffs. "Rovor is a novel form of programmable matter, reconfigurable at nanoscale. I'm told that you've encountered Rovor in its macroscopic form recently?"

"Yeah," I say. "Didn't love it."

"That is the crudest manifestation of Rovor, though perhaps the one most familiar to outsiders, because of its similarity to standard programmable matter."

"Wait, you're saying this Rovor thing isn't progmat?"

"Much more than that," Twenty-Three huffs. "It's an infinitely malleable microscopic agent with atmospheric flight capability and a versatile biological interface that can permeate the blood-brain barrier."

It takes me a moment to untangle the thicket of technobabble. "Are you all *insane*?" I screech. Then the second realization hits me. "Holy shit. That's why Lacomber's in here!" And that makes it a hat trick. "I can say his name! Quinnock Lacomber! *Quinnock fucking Lacomber!*"

Two and Twenty-Three look at each other. "Who?"

"Seriously?"

"What is their number?"

I swear, after I help save these people I'm going to strangle them all. "Number Sixteen! I'm guessing Rovor was his bright idea?"

"Oh, heavens, no!" Twenty-Three laughs. "Sixteen wanted nothing to do with our project, at first. Took us some time to persuade him to our way of thinking."

"Indeed," Two says. "As you must know, Eleven, the agency has always wanted to do more research into the use of biological-interfacing nanotech agents. But such investigation was forbidden by law."

I feel my ears getting warm and hope my blushing isn't too obvious. "Yeah, well, that's never stopped them before."

Two shrugs. "The powers that be thought it prudent to situate their experiments here on Venus, far from prying eyes and also well isolated in case of any mishaps."

Right. That makes sense. Anything goes wrong with your illegal nanobots, you just turn off the hab's engines and let the whole thing fall to ground level, where it'll all get crushed and incinerated beyond recognition or recovery by Venus' intense heat and pressure. Complete plausible deniability.

"Rovor was already working at a rudimentary level when Sixteen joined us," Two continues. "At that time, we were focused on memory extraction and meeting little success. Sixteen suggested a different approach, using plant DNA as a guide, which has gotten us closer to the goal."

"Did you say *plants*?" I repeat. Then it clicks. "Like lavender, cinnamon, and tree bark?"

Two barely smiles. "The nose knows. That's the saying, isn't it? Rovor interacts with every person's microbiome differently. Causes each of us to sweat out unique compounds. It became an easy way to tell if someone had ingested an effective dose."

"Plants mutate slower than viruses," Twenty-Three says. "Using chloroplastic sequencing meant we wouldn't risk another incident like the Fruitless Year."

"Yeah, apparently you found totally new ways to completely fuck everything up," I say.

"The program showed great promise!" Twenty-Three seems way too excited about this disaster. "Can you imagine? No need for interrogation. Simply pump a healthy dose of Rovor into the holding cell, and then you can *download* whatever memories you need from the subject."

It sounds to me like the most horrifying thing ever, but I don't say that out loud. Maybe I'll do the strangling before the saving after all. "How close are you?" I ask, my mouth feeling a little dry.

"We're now able to suppress memory formation, and recall to a lesser extent," Twenty-Three says. "But along the way, we discovered that we could affect the subject's state of mind. We've refined that process to the point where we can, through Rovor, issue simple commands to a subject."

This is even more horrifying. It literally sounds like mind control. "But some people aren't affected. I'm not. Both of you. Sixteen."

"We *are* affected. Surely you've noticed our idiosyncratic, retrospective speech patterns," Two says.

"If you mean the weird fucking way everyone around here talks, yeah, it is super annoying."

"And how we can only address each other by number." He suddenly looks sad. "I've known Twenty-Three for years, but I can't remember what I called him outside Cerulean."

"Sixteen did devise a protective inoculation for us warders," Twenty-Three says. "Purely technological, hard-coded nanobots to counter Rovor's effects at a cellular level. Crude by comparison to our experiments here, but we maintained complete control over Anchor."

"Anchor?"

"Our designation for the antidote nanobots," Two says. "Anchor to keep us grounded. Rovor to expand our scientific horizons."

"Nice that you devoted so much thought to *something* about this insane setup," I say. "Can't you just turn Anchor up to eleven or something? Have the tech nanobots completely obliterate the Rovor bits?"

"That was, indeed, the first thing we attempted." He gestures to the patients around us. "This was the result."

"Rovor's become too advanced," Twenty-Three says. "Anchor is no longer an effective countermeasure."

"Except that Number Sixteen and Number Nine seem to remain immune," Two says. "Sixteen must have engineered some new twist without our knowledge."

Jesus fucking Christ. I don't have a response to that. Sure, I'm sympathetic to these two—apparently the only guards remaining on any sort of duty—unexpectedly getting brain-boozled along with their inmates, but they weren't exactly good guys to begin with. I tap the butt of the stunner against my right temple, trying to shake loose some planning thoughts.

"What is that noise?" Two asks, pointing at the stunner.

I stop, look at the weapon, and give it a shake. It makes a rattling noise. That's not right.

Then I remember that Lacomber pulled the power pack earlier. I pop open the bottom of the handgrip, where the battery used to be, and a small white figurine—shaped like the head of a horse—falls out into my palm. "The fuck?"

"May I?" Two steps forward, hand outstretched. I give him the little horse, and he turns it over and looks at the underside of the cylindrical base. "White knight." He rotates it so I can see what's inscribed on the bottom: XVI. "Number Sixteen always did enjoy chess."

"Your stunner wasn't even powered?" Twenty-Three squeals.

"Well played." Two walks back to the wall and sticks the chess piece to some kind of hidden magnetic docking plate underneath the display screen. "Now let's see what our former ally has to say." He works the controls. "No encryption? Interesting."

The screen lights up with a jumble of white letters on a black background: CUUJ MXUHU VEHJO IULUD TYUT

"Are you sure that's not encrypted?" I ask. "Is there any other data on that horse?"

Two shakes his head. "It's a knight, and no. Just this text string."

"A substitution cipher!" Twenty-Three says. "If we assume it's monoalphabetic—let's see—lots of U's there, if those are E's . . ." He picks up a tablet and taps on it with one finger. "It's ROT-16."

"Clever." Two taps the wall controls, and the on-screen letters change to: MEET WHERE FORTY SEVEN DIED

"You've had forty-seven prisoners die on you?" I ask. "That's fucked up."

"No," Two says, looking sad. "Just one. Number Forty-Seven. He passed shortly before you arrived."

"Okay, that's still bad, but we'll deal with that later." Something's tickling my memory, but I can't get a hold on it. "Where did he die?"

"I'll show you. We'll all go together. Strength in numbers."

That is a hilarious thing for this person to say to me. I'm just about to reply with a witty rejoinder when Oliver starts yelling at me.

"Kangaroo! This is Equipment! Please respond!"

CHAPTER
TWENTY-FOUR

Venus—aboard bluejay, returning to Cerulean
Mission time 7'37

"Look at this," Shimura says as he climbs into the cockpit beside Ellie, holding a display tablet.

"I'm a little busy right now." Ellie points at the HUD. They're almost within visual range of Cerulean City. "Can you just tell me?"

"Fine. Well, I was reviewing the sensor logs for that drone platform we saw back there, right? Like you asked me to."

"Can you tell what it was made out of?" There are only a few specific materials that wouldn't corrode after sitting in Venusian atmosphere for more than a few minutes, and all of them need to be imported from off-planet. Not a problem for an interplanetary shipper like EKOS, but they need to source those exotic materials from someone else. The agency's going to go after whoever the weakest link in this chain is.

"Not exactly. The material doesn't match anything in the standard construction database for Venus, but it matches something I remember from inside Cerulean."

"What the hell are you talking about?"

"It's Rovor."

Ellie grits her teeth. "I thought Rovor was a knockout gas."

"It's a type of programmable matter. Progmat for short," Shimura says. "Nonconductive, low albedo, very lightweight—"

"Hold on." Ellie knows about this from years of working on spacecraft. "Progmat needs to be conductive. You need electricity for power."

"Well, Rovor's technically nanotech, but you don't like that word—"

"I don't like it because—never mind." She's not repeating that whole conversation. "You're saying this Rovor stuff can form *solid shapes* on its own?"

"Not usually solid. The one shape I remember seeing is like a big bubble, hollow on the inside."

"But you're saying it's maintaining its own structure." Ellie realizes what Shimura's implying. "You think that whole fucking drone platform was made out of *progmat*?"

"Not all of it, but—look. Say you want to build something secret that can survive sitting inside Venmo for a long time, and you want it to be able to dock with a variety of different cargo drones. Why import materials and construct a bunch of static hardware when you can instead have a progmat platform that can reshape itself into whatever you need at a particular moment?"

Ellie's head is spinning. "Okay. Let's say you're right. How the hell are they controlling it remotely?"

"Yeah, that's the other thing." Shimura holds up his tablet. "Can I show you something on the HUD over here?"

"Please."

Shimura docks his tablet to the top of his co-pilot's console and taps a few controls to pull up a false-color-sensor schematic of the drone scaffold. "I detected a control beacon coming from the platform. And I picked up the same signal inside this vessel."

Ellie stares at him. "*What?*"

"It's just a radio signal!" Shimura waves his hands, as if that's any reassurance. "But I've still got some Rovor inside my body, right? That's what's been dicking with my memory. I think Rovor's programmed to wipe the memory of anyone who leaves Cerulean, and something about the control signal from the platform or one of those skiffs also triggered me. Like you described."

"Shit." Ellie studies the sensor schematic. "How strong is this signal? Can it get through a spacesuit?"

"Huh. They're radiation shielded, so . . . probably not?"

Ellie's been thinking about suiting up anyway, given how long they've been driving through Venmo and how much she doesn't want to breathe in acid at any point. "Better safe than sorry."

They both put on spacesuits, and then Ellie waits until Shimura buckles himself into the co-pilot's seat before nudging her controls forward. The clouds in front of the bluejay slowly thin until she sees the edge of the Cerulean City habitat dome. She continues forward until the ring at the widest part of the hab becomes clearly visible, then banks to the left and starts circling clockwise.

They're about a quarter of the way around the ring when Shimura makes a choking noise, then starts convulsing in his chair. Ellie curses and pulls the bluejay away from Cerulean.

"Can't—breathe—!" Shimura cries, opening his helmet visor and gasping for air.

"Hang on, don't do that!" Ellie hits the autopilot and starts to unstrap herself.

She's just reached out one gloved hand to Shimura when his head snaps back, his jaw yawns open, and a haze of white particles begins drifting up out of his mouth.

"What the fuck!" Ellie slams back into her chair. She closes and locks the visor on her own helmet and makes sure all her suit pressure seals are intact.

Then she watches in fascinated horror as a cloud of white smoke congeals in midair above Shimura's head.

CHAPTER
TWENTY-FIVE

Cerulean City—Green Dome
Time to kick some ass

"Stop shouting at me!" I don't think I've ever been so happy to hear Oliver's voice. Also because it means my nanobots are fixing my biotech implants. I try blinking my left eye into operation, but that's still offline. "Where are you? Is Marmosa with you?"

"She's not with you?"

"Obviously not, if I'm asking! Any more stupid questions?"

I hear Jessica's voice now. "Kangaroo, Surgical. There's no need for attitude, we're just syncing up on status."

"I'm sorry, I've been trapped inside a weird-ass prison! How's your day going?"

Jessica's voice gets quieter, like she's moving away from the microphone. "You talk to him. I can't deal with him when he gets like this."

"Kangaroo, Equipment," Oliver says. "We have reason to believe that the security forces inside Cerulean City are using modified nanobots on the prisoners. Have you seen any evidence of that?"

It takes me a moment to respond, because I have to laugh out loud first. "Oh, you have no idea. It's too bad my implants haven't been working, otherwise I would have some juicy footage to show you.

What the hell's going on there, anyway? Why was I offline for so long?"

Jessica again. Guess I'm not too annoying after all. "Project Weyland-Yutani is still in the prototype stage. We weren't sure how long it would take, and it looks like the Cerulean nanobots have been interfering with your bots. I'm working on an override program now. Wait one."

"Just so you know, it's not just nanobots. They're also able to assemble themselves into larger shapes, like progmat, and they have some kind of biological interface. And I can still bleed and break things, so that part of the project is working just fine."

"Good. And we are aware of the novel nanotech," Oliver says. "I'm working on countermeasures."

"You also know about the mind control, right?"

"The *what?*" Jessica gets back on mic.

"Oh boy." I look over at the bald doctor. "Hey, Twenty-Three, can you talk to my support team about Rovor? They could probably use your insight. Especially about that Anchor thing. EQ, how do I patch my comms through to someone else's tablet?"

"Not possible at the moment," Oliver says. "Your control implants aren't online yet, and I don't have remote access. We'll have to wait until your nanobots finish repairing those modules."

"Let's get back to the fucking mind control," Jessica says. "Tell me everything you know."

I quickly describe the experiments that the Cerulean City designers have been conducting, using tiny cyborgs to manipulate human brain functions. I hear a weird noise over our comms before Jessica speaks again.

"Kangaroo, Surgical." Her voice sounds like a rubber band about to snap. "Is there some reason you haven't already dropped those two into the pocket?"

"Yeah, funny story about that, the real bad guys—the ones trying to escape this place—have thickened the atmosphere in here so I can't open a pocket portal. EQ, any ideas on how to fix that?"

"I don't have sensor data from your implants," Oliver says. "They're still—"

"Offline, right, I get it." I blow a raspberry. "Well, we're on our way to meet someone who might have more answers."

"Stay on with Oliver," Jessica says. "I'll call *Tacoma* for backup."

"We'll have to sign off with you for Surgical to use her blue key," Oliver says.

"Right. Fine. Just get back to me soonest, okay?" I hear the comms channel close, and I look back at Two and Twenty-Three, who are standing in the open doorway. "Will all these people be okay if we leave them with the robots?"

"Of course," Twenty-Three says.

"Okay, then," I say, "let's go see a man about some spooky nanotech bullshit."

CHAPTER
TWENTY-SIX

Venus—aboard bluejay, circling Cerulean
Mission time 7'47

One of the last things Ellie expected to hear just now is Jessica Chu's voice coming through her spacesuit's helmet radio. But a lot of unexpected things are happening lately. Maybe Ellie should just fucking get used to it.

"*Tacoma*, this is Kangaroo Surgical. We need air support and exfil ASAP. Over."

Ellie's not sure what to say, especially given what's happening with Shimura and Rovor right now. She clears her throat and checks her radio before speaking.

"Surge, this is Marmosa, I'm a little busy right now, can I call you back? Over."

"Marmosa?" Jessica's voice crackles with static. Ellie's not sure if that's because of the white smoke-thing currently filling the bluejay cockpit, alternately trying to get into her spacesuit and poking at the controls. She also isn't sure which of those two situations she's more worried about.

"Yes, this is she," Ellie replies. "What happened to radio silence until exfil?"

"I was calling for exfil," Jessica says. "I thought I was calling the *Tacoma*. Which is where you're supposed to be. Are you still in the bluejay? Where are you?"

This is all highly irregular. Ellie needs to authenticate the identity of whoever she's talking to. "Some boneyards welcome jugs transposed for movement."

After a moment, Jessica says, "Other repositories maintain that starlight provides ideal paganism."

"When will we learn not to gamble with zucchini?"

"It is only wellness which salts our kettle."

"Nice to hear from you, Surge. Yes, I'm still in the bluejay." Ellie has her back to the cockpit door, which she closed as soon as the white smoke emerged from Shimura's mouth. She also switched the cockpit air to recirculate. She doesn't want this shit spreading throughout the rest of the ship if she can help it. So far, her spacesuit seems to be keeping it at bay. "I'm wearing my pressure suit. Is Equipment there with you?"

"I'm here." Oliver's voice sounds as drowsy as ever.

"Can I send you my helmet cam feed?"

Oliver rattles off some quick instructions for setting up a secure communication link. Ellie follows the directions, and a few seconds later a small red light starts blinking in the corner of her visor's HUD.

"*What* the *hell* is *that*?" Jessica asks with uncharacteristic agitation.

"Are you talking about Badger, the asset we were sent to extract, or the cloud of strange white particles flying around my cockpit?"

Jessica and Oliver both start talking at once. Ellie waits until the babble dies down and says, "On second thought, let's deal with the more immediate problem. Equipment, how the fuck do I get rid of this white shit?"

"Let me see the bluejay's internal sensor readings," Oliver says.

Ellie taps the controls on her spacesuit wristpad to send over the data, then waits in tense silence while Oliver and Jessica mutter at each other. The white cloud floating around the cockpit keeps changing shape, always coming back to a sphere but continually pulsing outward to extend tendrils toward different parts of the cockpit. Ellie wonders if it's touching everything because that's the only way it can sense things outside of a human body—and what it might decide to do once it maps out the whole space.

She sticks out her arm, putting one gloved hand right next to the hazy white sphere. When it expands out again, one side makes contact with her glove, then flows all around it, bringing the rest of the mass with it until it engulfs her entire gloved right hand up past the wrist joint.

"Shit." Ellie knows the seals around her gloves are airtight, but she also hopes they're . . . nano-tight. "Um, hey, Equipment, are you seeing this? Is this going to be a problem?"

After a second, Jessica says flatly, "What did you do?"

"This thing's been probing all around my cockpit, and I was trying to stop it from breaking anything." Ellie shakes her arm gently, but the white mass stays clumped around her hand. "It's not getting through my suit. It's not going to get through my suit, is it?"

"Probably not," Oliver says.

"You didn't breathe any of it in, did you?" Jessica asks. "You got your spacesuit on in time?"

"As far as I know." Ellie quickly summarizes Shimura's memory-loss symptoms. "But I haven't experienced anything like that."

"As far as you know," Jessica says.

The white mass has changed from a sphere to a cylinder, still wrapped around her right hand, and now seems to be slowly crawling up the arm of her spacesuit toward her shoulder. Ellie tries using her left glove to brush it off, but the cloud simply parts when she swipes through it and then re-forms itself in the same place. "Well, I'm guessing you would have mentioned if you'd noticed any strange behavior while talking to me just now. Can we for the moment assume that I'm okay and concentrate on how to get this white stuff out of here?"

"Equipment's working on that. Just hang tight for a few more seconds."

"Oh, I'm tight, sister," Ellie says. "Believe me, *everything* is clenched right now."

"Got it!" Oliver says. "Okay, Marmosa, I have a procedure for you. It should be showing up on your HUD right now."

The left side of Ellie's helmet visor lights up with a block of text. "Yeah, I see it, let me read . . ." She trails off as she studies the instructions, then reads them again to make sure she understands correctly. "The fuck! Is this a joke? Are you drunk? Or high?"

"I realize it may seem unorthodox—"

"The bluejay is designed to keep Venusian atmosphere *out*!"

"Yes, but this is a modified vehicle, and we added fail-safes—"

Something buzzes on the radio, and the blinking red light in the corner of her HUD goes out. "Hello? Equipment? Are you there? Surgical? Hello?" Ellie works her controls, but the connection's been broken, and because it was an incoming blue-key communique, she has no way of calling them back.

"Fuck," Ellie says to herself. The white mass is starting to encroach on the edge of her helmet visor. She doesn't have any better ideas than Oliver's procedure, and she needs to work fast before this thing blocks her view out of the spacesuit.

CHAPTER
TWENTY-SEVEN

Cerulean City—below the line
Five minutes after we got the band back together

Number Two leads Twenty-Three and me through the service corridors to another vertical egress tunnel, and we climb up the ladder and through the hatch and emerge next to the hedges at the back of the reclamation facility with the broken clock on top.

"Oh, fuck, no, what?" I shake my head at Two and Twenty-Three. "We don't want to go in there. That's bad news bears."

The two men exchange a look, then Number Two says, "You've been to the reclamation facility?"

Twenty-Three says, "Whatever for?"

"I guess it's where Sixteen likes to hold all his secret meetings." I stand up and try to open the pocket to get some water. Still no dice. I really wish Oliver would hurry up and figure out how to fix this. "Hey, EQ, any progress on finding a way to disperse this hazy air?" No response. "Hello? EQ? Surge? You there?"

Without my eye or my fingertip controls, I can't check my other implants to see if they're working. And I can't stand here all day with Two and Twenty-Three staring at me like I'm a weirdo for talking to the voices in my head.

"I'll deal with them later," I say, pointing to my ear. "So we're doing this?" I point at the entrance to the reclamation facility building.

Two nods. "Follow my leader."

Twenty-Three and I follow him up to the door. I hang back while Two reaches for the handle, but nothing explodes when he pulls the door open. I lean over to take a peek inside. Completely dark again.

"Hold on." I raise my hand scanner and turn on its front spotlight, which I used to think was a pointless feature, but now I'm grateful for the overengineering. "Let me go first."

Two moves out of the way. I make one final attempt as I step over the threshold to open the pocket and retrieve a weapon. No joy. Looks like Elba and his crew were pretty thorough in preparing their Kangaroo countermeasures. After Two and Twenty-Three enter, I take off my jacket, ball it up, and use it to prop the door open.

Then I turn around and sweep the light across the room, and there's Quinnock Lacomber, standing in the middle of the blackness. But he doesn't look quite as smug as last time.

"I was hoping you'd come alone," he says, holding up a hand. The entire ceiling lights up, the same soft white as before. Rovor. A shiver runs down my spine.

"How are you doing that?" Number Two asks.

Lacomber smiles. "That would be telling."

I step up and get in Lacomber's face. "If you're not going to be telling, we'll be leaving. I don't know if you've noticed, but people are killing each other out there for no apparent reason."

The smile goes away. "It's a smoke screen. Literally, to prevent you from using your ability, and also to cover Nine's escape attempt."

"What ability?" Twenty-Three asks.

Lacomber raises an eyebrow. "They don't know who you are?"

"They don't need to know," I say, giving him a shut-the-fuck-up-now glare. "Talk."

Lacomber glances at Two and Twenty-Three before looking back at me. "In for a penny, in for a pound, I suppose. Although the pendulum's swung the other way now."

"I should say so." Number Two steps forward. "It wasn't that long ago that you were our man."

"I've never been your man," Lacomber snaps. "It was merely convenient for me to have you believe that."

Twenty-Three walks up beside Two. "But you helped us develop Rovor's biological interface!"

"I helped myself continue my own research," Lacomber says. "I honestly couldn't believe it, the first time you came to talk to me. They throw me in prison for the rest of my life because I caused the Fruitless Year, so-called, and then I'm offered the chance to redeem that failure by creating 'proper' nano-borgs in a fully controlled experimental environment? It was almost like I was being rewarded." He turns to Number Two. "But it was never about me, was it? It was always about what your lot could use. Whether you could control the power that you had already seen unleashed on the world."

"No need to be so dramatic," Two scoffs. "It was a fortuitous inter-section of common goals. At least, until you began colluding with other prisoners and scheming against us."

"You're so obsessed with control." Lacomber waves his hand, and the whole room lights up like it did when I was here before—ceiling, walls, and floor—only much brighter everywhere. The rest of us blink at the sudden illumination, and while we're distracted, tendrils snake up from the floor and wrap themselves around Two and Twenty-Three. A noise behind me attracts my attention, and I turn to see the edge of the door deforming after it pushed my jacket out of the way and closed itself.

"Goddammit," I mutter.

But at least I'm not the one getting immobilized by Rovor this time. The white goo cocoons Two and Twenty-Three up to their necks, and Lacomber gives them a moment to get their very vocal objections out of their systems.

"It's never been about direct control," Lacomber says. "It's always been about influence. Persuasion. 'Soft power,' so-called. Finding the latent impulses that reside inside all of our heads, and finding the right way to push those buttons until a person thinks they're doing some-thing because *they* want to do it. Not because you've coerced them. That's the only true method of converting someone to your side. You have to make them want what you want."

I raise my hand. "I feel like that doesn't explain everything. How did you disable my stunner?"

Lacomber gives me a dirty look. "Everything inside Cerulean is of a piece. It's all connected. I'm sure the original designers intended it to allow surveillance and manipulation of the environment at all levels, down to the microscopic, but that interconnectedness goes both ways. If you can exploit one subsystem, you can find a way to exploit them all." He looks back at Two and Twenty-Three. "And Number Nine has had many years in here to find those ways and means."

"Why are you telling us all this?" Twenty-Three asks. "If you've cracked all our codes to this extent, where you can turn our own systems against us, why reveal that before your escape plan is complete?"

"Because it's not his plan," I say.

Lacomber gives me a thin smile. "Someone's been paying attention."

"You don't care what Elba wants, long-term," I say. "Like you said. You've always been in it for yourself. Nothing's changed. Always looking out for number one."

"You are Number Eleven," Two and Twenty-Three say in unison.

I blink at them. "What the hell was that?"

"Ignore them," Lacomber says. "Latent programming, can't be unrooted. *You*, though—you said a *name*." His gaze has become much more intense. "How are you combatting Rovor's influence?"

"Oh, I'm full of surprises," I say.

Sixteen nods. "They were right to be concerned about you, then. I overheard some things. But it seems that Nine doesn't fully trust me, either. Not at this juncture."

"And you passed me a note because, what, you need a new best friend?"

"I need an ally." Those eyes really are something else. "We can't let Elba reach a populated planet."

"Because he'll spread Rovor around." That definitely seems like a worst-case scenario.

"Rovor won't work independently without a control signal being broadcast nearby. Outside of this environment, the nano-borgs will deteriorate quickly, and the neurological effects will wear off within a few days. But that's still long enough for Nine and his cronies to cause a lot of damage."

I do my best to not think about how Jessica and I dispersed my nanobots on purpose inside *Dejah Thoris* a couple of years ago, and to not let the fact that I'm trying to not think about it show up on my face. Luckily, I've found that the best way to avoid introspection is to become outraged at someone else. "So you've grown a conscience inside the big house? I'm not your parole board. We can stop Rovor without you."

"Agreed!" Number Two says. "Escaping Cerulean doesn't do Elba any good if he can't get out of orbit. And that warship up there will not hesitate to shoot down a boatload of prisoners heading for open space."

"Unless they have civilian hostages on board," Lacomber says. "The military prefers to avoid collateral damage whenever possible."

"Where's Elba going to get civilian hostages?" I ask.

"What time is it?"

"Why does that matter?"

Lacomber calls across the room, "What time is it, please, Hope?"

A remarkably human-sounding female voice calls down from the ceiling: "Fifteen-oh-seven hours local time."

Lacomber gives me a hard stare. "They should be arriving at the resort any minute now."

CHAPTER
TWENTY-EIGHT

Venus—aboard bluejay, circling Cerulean
Mission time 7'57

Ellie is glad for one thing: the fact that she has very little time to execute Oliver's instructions means that she has no time to think about how ludicrous the whole scheme is, and having to devote all her concentration to doing things mostly one-handed keeps her from trying to come up with alternatives for getting out of this predicament.

First, she closes Shimura's helmet visor over his still-unconscious head and seals up his spacesuit. She can't tell if he still has any of the Rovor particles inside of him, but if he does, at least they'll be contained now. They seem to mostly obey the laws of physics, at least when it comes to airtight seals.

Next, she programs a parabolic trajectory into the bluejay's autopilot. She takes a few seconds to double-check Oliver's recommended flight plan, but she can't wait too long, otherwise the winds might change and she'll have to plot a new solution from scratch.

Finally, she opens the cockpit door, steps into the main cabin, and secures herself to the wall opposite the airlock with a safety tether. She makes sure the tether is secure, and then, as the white haze spreads to cover more than half of her helmet, slaps the control to cycle the airlock open.

Warning lights and alarms go off throughout the cabin. Ellie peeks into the cockpit to see if they might rouse Shimura, but he still seems to be out cold.

The airlock's outer door opens, and Ellie hears a *thump* as thick Venusian atmosphere floods into the lock. Through the inner door's small porthole, she sees thick lines of orange and yellow and brown whipping around. It barely even looks like gas. More like some deranged painter throwing colors all around with a thick brush.

Then the inner door opens, and her ears pop before her suit can adjust for the change in pressure. The rust-colored cloud rushes in and slaps her back against the wall. Her helmet HUD lights up and beeps angrily, warning her about temperature and pressure exceeding safety margins.

"Yeah, yeah." Ellie bends her right arm up until the sleeve of the spacesuit makes contact with her helmet visor. She sees the coating of white particles being burned off her suit by Venmo.

Well, at least the first part of the plan's working.

The bluejay lurches, and more warnings pop up in her HUD. Ellie can't see anything now except the roiling, dirty yellow cloud of toxic gas filling the cabin. She can barely see her own hands through the haze. She lifts her left arm until the wristpad controls are just barely visible, then brings her right hand over to slap the controls to engage the autopilot program.

The sudden acceleration yanks her sideways, and she hardly hears the whine of the bluejay's engines over the roar of the Venusian cloud-storm. All this shaking better be from the ship fighting to get out of the clouds, and not because Ellie's bird is being dissolved from the inside out by sulfuric acid and starting to fall apart.

Her helmet HUD is tied to the bluejay's navigation controls, and it's now showing a glowing-line plot of where the ship is supposed to be. The most unnerving thing is, she knows the navigation plot should be beeping loudly as it updates the ship's current position, but she can't hear a goddamn thing except the hot atmospheric gases as they whip around inside the cabin. And the other side of her HUD tells her that she's not imagining it getting hotter in here—the suit's external sensors register two hundred degrees Celsius and climbing.

"Come on, birdie, fly!" Ellie says through clenched teeth.

The bluejay shudders as it nears the top of its arc. Ellie can now see maybe a couple of meters through the cloud haze, which is dissipating as the atmosphere thins.

Oliver's plan—which actually seems to be working, miracle of miracles—was to open the bluejay cabin so the toxic clouds could burn away the white particles from Cerulean, then bring the ship far enough into the upper atmosphere to flush out those cloud gases, and finally close the airlock and let the interior repressurize and hope the ventilation filters are up to cleaning the air enough to make it breathable. Worst case, though, Ellie still has six hours of breathing air inside her spacesuit to figure out a plan B.

The danger, of course, is that flying the bluejay up out of the cloud cover means it'll be visible to anyone who happens to be looking at that part of Venus. They're counting on the fact that Cerulean City's flight plan is supposed to keep the hab far away from any other objects, so the exposure should be minimal.

Ellie feels her feet leave the floor as the bluejay hits the top of the parabola, and she's momentarily weightless. The tether tugs her back toward the wall, and she reaches out a hand to steady herself. It's quiet now that all the air's been sucked out of the cabin, and through the open airlock she sees the blackness of space.

"Hello, beautiful." No matter how many times she launches off a planet, that initial boundary crossing into the black is always breathtaking. This view never gets old.

The bluejay begins tipping forward, and the dirty-canary-yellow limn of Venus creeps into view through the open airlock. Ellie releases the wall and taps her wrist controls to close the doors. As soon as the inner door cycles shut, she unhooks the tether and pushes herself off the wall, enjoying a brief tumble in zero-gee.

"Back into the soup," she mutters as gravity reasserts itself, tugging her down to the deck. She lands on her side and checks the cabin air readings before opening her helmet. It smells like rotten eggs, but the sensors assure her that nothing in here now will kill her.

Ellie climbs forward into the cockpit, stows her helmet, checks on Shimura, then freezes when she looks out the window.

"What the fuck?"

There are two giant domes floating right in plain view.

She pulls herself into the pilot's chair, buckles the safety harness, and brings up a full tactical display on the forward HUD. The instruments confirm what she's seeing: two airborne habitats within seventy-five kilometers of each other, perilously close by any standard, one fully above the clouds and one just emerging, moving upward. Additional smaller shapes circle both habs, but the sensors can't identify those objects.

The tactical display identifies the habitat at a slightly higher altitude as Sunstone Resort, and the lower one as Cerulean City.

And they're on a collision course.

"What the ever-loving FUCK!" Ellie shouts. She switches the bluejay over to full manual control.

CHAPTER
TWENTY-NINE

Cerulean City—the Village—reclamation facility
Seconds before I beat down a lunatic

I don't bother to conceal my agitation this time, when I realize what Lacomber is talking about. There's a limited number of spacecraft that can safely enter Venmo, and only a few of those are scheduled to come and go regularly. And other than Cerulean, there's only one other habitat anywhere nearby.

"Sunstone," I say. "You're talking about Sunstone Resort."

He nods. "I don't know all the details. But I know they have confederates in a shipping company, EKOS. You've probably seen their green-and-white cargo transports."

That does ring a bell, visually. "Yeah. Okay. So that's how they're getting off-planet."

"And how they're infiltrating the resort to acquire hostages," Lacomber says.

"Quite nefarious," Two remarks. "Using human shields to cover their escape."

"Okay, now that we know their evil plan, how do we stop them?"

Total fucking silence. I look at Two, Twenty-Three, and Sixteen, but they all just give me blank stares.

"Seriously? No bad ideas here, fellas!" I say, waving my hands, palms-up in encouragement.

"I've done all I can," Lacomber says. "Hope, please release Number Two and Number Twenty-Three."

The Rovor material enveloping Two and Twenty-Three retracts into the ground. It's still super creepy to watch.

"You still have control!" Twenty-Three says, sounding both amazed and accusatory.

"Rudimentary, at the macroscopic level," Lacomber says.

"'Hope' is your own special countermeasure, then?" Two asks.

"A miniscule bulwark," Lacomber replies. "She keeps Rovor from restraining me. I'm afraid Nine and his cabal have frozen me out of everything else. Why else would I stay behind, waiting for certain death?"

I wave my hand in confusion. "Aren't you hiding in here so you *won't* die?"

He frowns at me. "Why would hiding in here protect me?"

I point back at the door. "You're hiding from the murderous mobs, aren't you?"

He coughs out a single laugh, then shakes his head. "They wouldn't hurt me. Hope and Anchor protect me. But we're all done for when the self-destruct goes off."

"*Self-destruct?*" I turn back to Number Two. "Fuck all this. How the hell do we get out of here?"

Two and Twenty-Three exchange a glance. "Whatever do you mean?" Two asks.

"I mean, obviously we're not staying here! Your security's compromised, Elba's escaping and taking who knows how many other prisoners with him, and I need to get out of this fog to use my pocket." I wave at the white haze that still permeates the air. I don't think I can bleed on the air. "Where are your escape pods? Are they back at the intake dock?" The two men exchange another look, and I don't like it. "What's the problem?"

"There are no escape pods," Two says.

I take a deep breath and exhale it. "Why," I say, "the fuck *not*?"

"This habitat is rigged to self-destruct. We crack the dome and let the breathable air escape, killing our buoyancy; then purge all the thrusters of fuel and make it impossible to maneuver. The wind tears us apart, and the pieces fall into the clouds and either get dissolved by acid on the way down or get crushed into oblivion once they hit the ground."

I gape at him, then look at Twenty-Three. "And everyone's okay with this?"

"We all knew the risks of this assignment," Twenty-Three says. "We were prepared to live out our natural lives here."

"Security includes secrecy," Two says. "If we do our jobs properly, no one outside of the agency will ever know that this facility existed, even long after we're all dead."

"Yeah, well, I didn't sign up for a suicide mission, and all those prisoners weren't sentenced to death! How do we stop the self-destruct?"

Two points back at the door. "You'll have to fight your way through that mob. Back to the Green Dome."

I can't even. "Not an option. You don't have a secret tunnel back into that building or anything?"

"There is one possible way," Twenty-Three says.

Two shakes his head. "That's infeasible."

"You don't even know what I'm going to say."

"You mean the airlock, don't you?"

I don't like where this conversation is headed. "What airlock?"

"There's an emergency service airlock just below the line," Twenty-Three says. "It leads outside the habitat. You'll need to be in a pressure suit, of course, and it will be quite treacherous to make your way around the outside of the facility."

I hate this idea, but at least I won't have to fight my way through a brainwashed horde. "Fuck it. Let's go."

———

"This spacesuit is rated for Venusian atmosphere exposure, right?" I ask.

"Pressure suit. Not spacesuit," Two says. "And yes, fully rated. You'll be fine out there."

We're in a below-the-line maintenance tunnel, standing at the outer perimeter of the hab next to a service airlock. The inner door is small and circular, with only a wheel on this side for opening and closing it. Manually, I might add. The only instrumentation on the wall next to it is three lights, red, yellow, and green. The green one is currently illuminated. The door looks barely big enough for me to fit through, but Two assures me that there will be a large chamber on the other side in which I can actually stand up.

While I'm looking around, my left eye comes back online, flickering and flashing before showing me the default heads-up overlay. "Hey, I can see again!" I work my control implants to tell my eye sensors to analyze the Rovor haze in the air.

Lacomber frowns at me. "Surely you haven't been blind this whole time?"

"Just in my left—you know what? Not important. Everything's fine now. Forget I said anything."

Lacomber came with us, grudgingly, and I suspect the main reason he agreed is so he won't die alone, as he seemed to believe he might. His face seems stuck in a permanent hangdog expression now. I can't decide if him being silently grumpy is better than him being annoyingly chatty.

My eye comes back with nothing. Apparently Rovor is too different from any known substances to register on these limited sensors. But I guess we'll have plenty of the stuff to scrape out of my head later for Science Division to dissect.

"Back to the task at hand," I say. "What is the exterior hull made out of?"

"Ceramic coated with a light-absorbing polymer," Two replies. "Why?"

"Mag-boots aren't going to work on that."

"Oh, your suit doesn't have magnetic boots or gloves," Two says, way too casually for my taste. "You'll have to use climbing tools."

I am not a fan of rock climbing. It is, believe it or not, actually one of the required skills for an agency field operative to learn—or at least pass a basic competency course—before the agency will allow them into the field for live operations.

It's not that I have any huge phobia or problem with heights. I just don't like the only thing between me and a fatal fall being my fingers, or some little claw-type things that I'm supposed to stick into the side of a boulder.

Even worse now, when I go crawling around the outside of Cerulean City, there's going to be some serious wind. Venusian atmosphere moves at nearly four hundred kilometers per hour all the time at this altitude. And it's going to push me around. Granted, I have a smaller profile than the massive bulk of the station, and the pressure suit won't have any big flat sections to really catch the wind, but I'm still going to feel it. And if I happen to drop any of my climbing tools, it's bye Felicia.

"I can help you," Lacomber says.

I turn to face him while Two checks my life-support backpack. "I'm sure you can. Why would you want to?"

"I told you. I don't want Elba to take Rovor off-planet. We barely have control of the nano-borgs in this controlled environment, and who knows what will happen once they're released into the wild, even briefly. I won't have another disaster on my conscience."

"Probably should have thought of that before you became a collaborator, huh?"

He scowls at me. "Do you want my help or not?"

Two pokes his head over my shoulder. "We only have the one pressure suit."

"I don't want to go with him," Lacomber says. "I'm not nearly physically fit enough. But there is a way you can break through Rovor's influence on a person, at least temporarily. Do you have medical supplies in the pocket?"

Twenty-Three raises a hand. "What is this 'pocket' he keeps talking about?"

"Don't worry about it," I say. Too many people already know about my big secret superpower around here. "Yeah, I've got some medical supplies."

"Do you have access to prithoxazine injector slugs?"

He's talking about small flexible packets of pharmaceuticals with measured doses inside. Tiny thin needles on the bottom of the slug puncture a person's skin, and a pressurized mechanism forces the slug-drug, whatever it is, into the body. Jessica always insists I keep some medications in the pocket, packed away inside temperature-regulated containers so they don't freeze in hard vacuum.

I ask him to spell the name and do a quick search. Oh, it's so great to have access to my local databases again. "Yeah, I've got a few of those. What are they?"

"A neural stimulant. It will interfere with Rovor's synaptic interface, and for a few minutes the subject will be highly susceptible to suggestion."

"It will hypnotize them?" Twenty-Three asks.

"Hypnosis is hogwash," Lacomber snaps. "I don't have time to explain the biochemical interactions. You'll be able to issue simple commands, and the subject will obey."

This is making my skin crawl. "How will I know it's working?"

"Use this trigger phrase." He holds up a computer tablet showing the text: WHY DID YOU RESIGN? I guess the mind control only works when it's transmitted verbally. "If the override is working, they'll respond with this." He swipes to the next screen: TOO MANY PIGLETS KNOW OVERMUCH. "You'll have about five minutes to issue your override commands to the subject, and thereafter the influence should last for maybe an hour, give or take. After that time the drug's efficacy will start to wane, and Rovor will be able to reestablish full control."

"And I'm just supposed to trust you on all this."

"You can trust that I'm the enemy of your enemy."

I swear, sometimes it's exhausting talking to secret-agent types. "Almost done back there, Number Two?"

He steps out from behind me and hands me the pressure-suit helmet. "Right as rain."

I put on the helmet while he opens the airlock door, then crawl inside and stand up. It's not bad. Only then do I think to ask, "Hey, has anyone ever actually done this before?"

"Probably," Two says. "During construction, I'd imagine. Can't do everything with robots. Godspeed."

The airlock's inner door closes. I grab the nearest handhold with both gloves and nod. Two cranks the wheel, then pulls open the outer door. I'm not expecting air to rush *into* the airlock—that's *not* how it works in space—and nearly lose my grip and my footing as the Venusian slipstream shoves me backward.

"All good out there?"

I steady myself, then raise one hand to give them a thumbs-up. "Didn't expect it to be quite that windy."

Two points to my right. "That way. Clockwise around the circle until you reach the antenna, then down. Good luck."

I turn to brace myself against the outer doorway. "Be seeing you."

The equipment belt on my pressure suit has been rigged with multiple tethers, climbing tools, other tools, and backups of everything. I can also pull quite a few other gadgets and gizmos out of my pocket—I give it a test, and am elated that I can open the portal and pull out a simple test object, a red rubber ball, which I immediately fumble and drop in the high winds.

Then I realize I can see blue sky.

"We're above the clouds!" I shout. "We're not supposed to be up here! What the fuck!"

I hear Lacomber muttering something in the background, and then Two's voice: "This may be part and parcel of the escape plot. It's out of our hands right now. Just get to the Green Dome."

"Fucking fuck. Moving!"

I'm supposed to pass ten range markers on the way to the antennas, and given how the habitat curves, I should be able to see some of the antenna protuberances by the time I get to the last three markers. I slowly drag myself along the outside of the hab, making sure I have a good grip with three of my limbs before moving the fourth. According to the clock overlay in my left eye, nearly six minutes have passed before I reach the first marker.

One down, nine to go.

The wind picks up in a sudden gust, and one of my boots slips as I reposition the crampon at the toe, jabbing it into a new section of the habitat's hull. I'm not too concerned about damaging anything. The surface is already pretty weathered and pockmarked.

As I move past the next few markers, I have plenty of time to reflect on how sideways this whole operation has gone and how some of that aggravation could have been avoided if some more people would have just talked to each other beforehand. People who nominally work within the same organization, by the way; and I don't mean the United States government generally, I mean the agency, and specifically Outback Operations. Paul is the director of operations, reporting directly to the secretary of state, and you might think that those two would talk about some of these issues in more detail than they seem to have.

Then again, State is the same person who secretly cloned me and hid that medical experiment on the Moon for years. So, maybe not the most trustworthy or dependable boss in the world.

Six markers down, four to go. The wind has calmed down somewhat, so I risk extending my arms to push myself away from the hab a little and crane my neck to see if I can spot the antennas from here. Nothing yet. Two did say "clockwise," didn't he? Because it would really suck if I had to double back. I think I'm getting a cramp in my left arm. Maybe it's just stress.

Get a move on, Kangaroo. You can worry while you're traveling.

Seven down, three to go. Where the hell are those antennas? Two did say "within three markers" I'd be able to see something, right? Crap. Nothing to do but keep going.

As I move around the curve of the hab, I see something else in the distance: the day-night terminator line, a planet-wide zone of shadow over the clouds. It's one thing to see that from orbit, but it's something else entirely to see it from just above the cloud line, while you're also feeling the wind that's pushing the clouds around under that shadow, billows and peaks and bulges getting swallowed up by the darkness.

Keep going, Kangaroo. You're on the clock here.

I turn back to continue my outdoor crawling adventure and see a glint of light in the distance. Which is weird, because nothing that naturally occurs in these clouds should reflect that much sunlight. So if

I'm really seeing something that shiny—there it is again—that means something artificial.

I blink my left eye into telescopic vision mode and move my head around slowly. It's always a bit of a challenge to aim this thing. Even if I think I'm looking directly at something when I switch to the telescope mode, I always seem to be a little bit off. Oliver explained it to me at one point—something about a few degrees of arc turning into a huge distance as you get farther away. But he didn't actually offer any helpful advice for dealing with it, operationally, so I kind of let it all go in one ear and out the other.

It takes a few seconds for me to find what's reflecting the light. It's something floating above the clouds. That's the good news, I guess; it's not moving fast, like an aircraft, so I don't have to track its motion and try to predict where it's going. But—wait, is that a dome? That sure looks like a glass dome, sitting on top of a ring, with service facilities below the line—

This can't be happening.

I'm looking at another habitat. I'm looking at another blue site, and it's dangerously close to Cerulean. It's also above the clouds, which means—

Holy hell. That's not a blue site, it's a resort. I blink my eye to maximum magnification and pan around slowly until I find the illuminated lettering above the spaceport entrance: IT'S ALWAYS SUNNY AT SUNSTONE RESORT HABITAT!

Mother of swirly shit balls, this is bad. This is completely and supremely fucked up.

I don't know how he managed it, but Elba's gained control of Cerulean's thrusters, and it looks like he's going to crash the hab into Sunstone and use the ensuing chaos to steal a shuttle and escape. A lot of innocent people are going to get dead or injured in the process, but he clearly doesn't care about any of that.

Nope. Not going to happen while I'm still breathing.

I make sure I have both legs and my right arm securely clamped onto the side of the hab ring exterior, then think of a pepperoni pizza and open the pocket, with barrier. I carefully reach in and pull out an emergency comms unit. I very carefully engage the stick-strip on the back of it and press it hard against the hab ring.

Once the comms unit is secured, I turn it on and make sure it's working. Then I imagine a red bird with bushy black eyebrows, open the pocket, and pull out the red key that Gryphon gave me last year.

I plug the red key into the comms unit, and after it verifies my identity—I have to yell for it to hear me through the helmet and over the wind, and it takes a few tries to get it to scan my retina through the pressure suit helmet visor—it starts up a secure communications program. I choose the option to connect me to the nearest secure government site, which is the *Tacoma* in orbit above us. The only other secure sites in range are the blue sites, and those aren't going to respond to a red key ping.

The display blinks and changes to a status screen saying CONNECTED. "*Tacoma*, this is Kangaroo, calling with an urgent request. *Tacoma*, do you copy?"

The line hisses with static for a moment—that's odd, there shouldn't be any interference up here—and then I hear a very familiar voice.

"Kangaroo?" It's Ellie. "What the fuck is going on?"

CHAPTER
THIRTY

It's only been a few hours since Ellie last heard Kangaroo's voice, but hearing him again now, it feels like spotlights are popping off inside her head. "I'm so glad you're safe, but—why are you calling the *Tacoma*?"

"Why are you answering *Tacoma*'s comms?" he asks.

"I'm not aboard the *Tacoma*."

"*What?* Why the hell not?"

"I'll explain later. Give me a sitrep, what's happening inside Cerulean?" She decides that she needs to ease him into the news about possibly colliding with another hab.

"Yeah, funny story, I'm actually outside the hab right now . . ."

"You're *outside*? What the fuck are you doing outside? Where are you on the ring?" She starts circling the hab.

"Well, I—wait. Why do you want to know that?" The bluejay's proximity alarms sound, and Ellie silences them. "Are *you* still *down here*? In the clouds?"

"Like I said, I'll explain later! Stay put, I'll come pick you up!" She banks the bluejay down so she can see clearly out the top of her forward window. She was keeping a safe distance from both habs, but this is worth the risk.

"No! I mean, it would be really nice to see you, but I can't right now."

Ellie matches altitude and speed with Cerulean, hanging about ten kilometers to the leeward side. "Kangaroo, for fuck's sake—"

"I need to get to the docking platform," Kangaroo says. "If you can get close enough to see me, I need you to help guide me there."

She hears it in his voice. He won't be talked out of this, and her choices are either to go away and let him do his thing, or stay with him and do what she can to help him not die.

Ellie nudges the stick and resumes flying around the circumference of Cerulean's habitat ring, going counterclockwise. "I'm coming around the ring now. Will advise when you're in visual range."

"Thanks. Glad you're alive and well, by the way."

"You too."

". . . I'm alive, anyway."

"Why were you calling the *Tacoma*?"

"Yeah, funny story, there's another hab over there, you might have noticed?"

"I did. Shit's fucked up. Blue sites are never supposed to be within a thousand kilometers of any other facility. If it's this close, it means someone compromised their navigation months ago and has been hiding it through all the regular inspections and automated security sweeps."

"Jordan Elba," Kangaroo says. "And his co-conspirators."

"How many co-conspirators are we talking about?"

"That's a great question for later. Right now, I need to get inside the docking area before these habs crash into each other."

"Can't happen. Proximity alarms would go off before the habs got within five hundred kilometers of each other. Even resorts have rudimentary propulsion, for safety reasons."

"But they need a diversion. While everyone's busy trying not to fall to their deaths, Elba and his crew can steal a shuttle and—"

"No. That's unworkable. They wouldn't be able to control the extent of the damage caused by a collision. There's no telling how badly the structures would be compromised, how quickly they'd lose air. No sense in killing yourself or running straight into emergency responders."

"Is there another reason they would want to get the habs this close to each other? I mean, it's not like they can put out a gangplank and walk across to Sunstone."

It takes Ellie a moment to recall what a "gangplank" is. And then she thinks of another wide, flat thing she saw recently.

"Fuck me!"

"Yes, dear, if we live long—"

"They've got drones in the clouds!" Ellie says. "Cargo skiffs. The habs use them to transfer cargo from incoming freighters—those are all automated with cheap-ass nav systems, so they don't want them trying to dock with the habs.

"If Elba and his crew have taken control of Cerulean, they probably also have remote control of the skiffs. They can walk onto one and ride it over to Sunstone, where they can steal a shuttle from the resort's low-security spaceport. Hell, they could probably hide themselves in an emptied cargo container on its way back up to orbit, and nobody would know until it was too late!"

After a moment's pause, Kangaroo says, "So have you always been this good at spycraft, or is this like a recent thing? 'Cause I'm getting really–"

"There you are!" Ellie slows the bluejay to a hover about fifty meters away from the pressure suit hanging off the side of the hab ring. She could get closer, but she doesn't want to risk being pushed into the side of the hab by a sudden shift in the three-hundred-kph winds. "Unless there's more than one idiot risking his neck climbing around out here."

Kangaroo waves at her, then looks upward and opens the pocket for a second. The glowing white disk almost looks like a halo above his head. Ellie can't help smiling.

Kangaroo says, "What do these skiffs look like?" There's an unusual tightness in his voice.

"Big flat gray triangles," Ellie says. Then, ". . . You see one, don't you. Fuck."

"I think you might want to—"

The bluejay's collision alarm drowns out the rest of his sentence. Ellie shoves the bluejay into a straight vertical lift—the maneuver will immediately tell her if the incoming is powered or purely ballistic; and if the former, how much thrust it's packing relative to her own vehicle.

The alarm silences almost immediately, but the radar shows the bogey following her upward. Ellie rolls the bluejay away from Cerulean and dives into the clouds. Beside her, Shimura groans but doesn't wake up. At least she hopes that sound was Shimura and not the bluejay's structure creaking because Venmo has been eating away at it.

The skiff is definitely not as maneuverable as the bluejay, both in physical design as well as its automated guidance systems. It follows Ellie down through the clouds for a few seconds, wobbling as the winds catch its large flat shape. A particularly strong gust flips it over, and it spins in the air for a moment, seeming confused, before it breaks off pursuit and heads up out of the clouds again.

"Broke its target lock," Ellie mutters. "Good to know."

"You still with me, hotshot?" Kangaroo says over the radio.

"Yeah. Just had to lose my tail. Coming back up now."

"Don't stop for me. Get into orbit and signal the *Tacoma*. They need to send reinforcements in hazmat pressure suits prepared to evacuate all the people still inside Cerulean. And, uh, prepare for them to resist a little, or act weird a lot. Numbers Two and Twenty-Three can explain."

"Sure, I can call—" Ellie can't establish a link on her comms panel. "No. Shit. They must be jamming us."

"Seemed likely," Kangaroo says. "I'll be fine. You go, and come back with the cavalry."

The bluejay rises up out of the clouds. Ellie spots Kangaroo again, hanging off the side of the hab ring. Now he really *is* hanging, turned face out away from Cerulean, one arm extended, holding what looks like a portable deep radar unit.

Ellie sometimes gets jealous of how Kangaroo can seemingly pull whatever he wants out of the pocket at any time. It's also been fun for her, sometimes. But she's not jealous of the life it forced him into, being the only person who can do certain secret things.

She watches him wave the radar around, then attach it to the chest piece of his pressure suit. His helmet lights up with some kind of tactical display, and he puts both hands on the wall behind him and plants his feet, knees bent. His entire body tenses up. He's getting ready to jump.

"Hey." Ellie's eyes feel wet. "I love you, man."

"I know, dude." The helmet turns toward her. "Be seeing you."

He turns back, looking down into the clouds, and launches himself off the hab. Ellie's about to wish him luck when she sees a black triangle surface out of the clouds. Then another. And another.

She stops counting after five and banks her bluejay in the other direction. Time to call in the cavalry.

CHAPTER
THIRTY-ONE

Venus—in the clouds
Moments after yet another poor decision

I did the math, thanks to a very morbid program that Oliver added to my shoulder-phone before we left for Venus, so I know exactly how long I can survive falling through the clouds.

I can't see a damn thing once I plunge into the cloud cover, and I can't hear anything except atmosphere rushing past me and hopefully not eating through this spacesuit too quickly. But the tactical display in my helmet HUD, being sent from the deep radar strapped to my chest, guides me toward one of the triangular skiff things well enough.

I picked the one that's lit up with a shit-ton of radio emissions. Seems likely that that's where Elba will be, controlling and communicating with all his minions. And with a little luck, I'll be able to fly myself there. Or at least do a semi-controlled freefall.

I hate rock climbing, but skydiving was one of my favorite training activities. It's still one of the most effective ways to sneak someone over a border, if they're not being smuggled in the pocket. But we still have to get the pocket-user, that's me, in and out of those inconvenient places, and Paul was right: I do get dropped out of airplanes a lot.

So I've had a good amount of practice guiding myself as a ballistic projectile, using my arms and legs as control surfaces. The Venusian winds, and the fact that this suit doesn't have the arm and leg webbing that would allow better control, don't make it easy, but I don't need to go too far anyway. I hope.

The real problem is, I can't control my speed. I line up the target well enough, and as the glowing triangle gets bigger and bigger in my HUD, I wonder exactly how big it is. I didn't get a good enough look earlier to compare it to the size of the bluejay, which would have told me when I can expect to crash into it now.

So I'm not prepared when I smack headfirst into the back of the skiff. I tumble forward on its flat cargo surface until I smash into something big and boxy and hard. It takes me a few seconds to catch my breath and steady my nerves.

There's a cargo container strapped to the skiff. Big and green. I don't recognize the logo. I start crawling to the side so I can check its registry information.

Then my arms are yanked upward.

I'm pulled to my feet by two spacesuited figures. One of them jabs a pistol in my face—not a stunner, but an actual projectile weapon that will for sure shatter my helmet and then allow the Venusian atmosphere to suffocate and/or acid-burn me to death. I hold up my hands. Both suits have mirrored helmets. I can't see the faces inside.

The other spacesuit yanks me backward, and I'm surprised when I fall into the cargo container through a gooey wall. Then the first spacesuit steps in behind me, and I see that they've cut away part of the side wall and covered the hole with progmat. Rovor, I presume. Making themselves a fully configurable airlock.

The outside seals, and then the inside opens. The spacesuits shove me forward into the center of the container, where Elba is sitting on a large white throne. Standing all around him are more prisoners, dressed in colorful, stripey village outfits, all staring blankly into space.

But I can see his face now. My brain's working again, and my implants, and my eye positively identifies him. I set it to start passive face reco on anyone it can get a good look at. I don't know how many people he left behind on Cerulean, but we need to account for everyone who was there to begin with.

"Ah, Kangaroo," he says, fingers steepled in front of him. "I thought it might be you."

Air. There's air in here. I open the pocket, no barrier, to suck it away—

Except I can't. Dammit. The Rovor haze is in here, too.

"Feeling a little lightheaded?" Elba waves one hand in the air, and I can see a faint swirl as the white haze clears for just a moment. "Breathing in Rovor at this density does take a little getting used to. Fortunately, our friends have all adjusted quite well." He gestures at the catatonic crowd.

"Just needed to get some air?" I ask. "These skiffs can't make orbit. You're not going anywhere."

Elba grins. "Just you wait."

The more time I spend with this Elba character, the more I hate his guts.

But waiting does give me time to reflect on how I'm going to get stuff out of the pocket. They haven't taken off my spacesuit, which means I still have normal atmosphere inside the suit. There's not a lot of empty space, but there's enough to open a small portal. Which limits what I can actually get out of the pocket. The other complication is that I can't use my arm to reach inside and pull something out.

I have some ideas for things I could retrieve—and I'm using my eye to review Oliver's database of what's stored in the pocket currently, and filtering the search results by size and use—but getting them out through the barrier without using my hands is going to be a real trick.

Similarly, I can open the pocket *outside* this cargo container—we're high enough up in the thin atmosphere, and Elba hasn't been able to spread Rovor across all of Venus. I confirmed that earlier, when I was crawling around the outside of Cerulean and pulling equipment out. But I don't usually put things into the pocket with any velocity. It's a special occasion when I throw something in so I can rotate the pocket when I open it again and have the thing come shooting out. I need to be prepared for that, because I'm always standing right in the path of the pocket, and the portal is always facing me.

Note to self: talk to Oliver about always throwing some stuff into the pocket before a mission, just in case. Including some heavy objects. Maybe an anvil.

"Listen," I say to Elba. "We can be friends, too. You and I. Things were weird back there, but obviously we both wanted to escape. And we're both on the agency's shit list. We have a common enemy."

Elba stands up and chuckles. "Tell me what you did, Kangaroo. Tell me why they sent you to Cerulean."

"I disobeyed a direct order."

"Not the first time you've done that."

"I failed to complete the mission," I say. "I was supposed to retrieve some weapons technology offered to us by a defector, but she double-crossed us. Seduced me."

Elba raises both eyebrows. "I see."

"It got ugly when my exfil arrived. I didn't mean to, but I—killed two of our guys. Accidentally." I look away, pretending to be ashamed of my actions. I'm pretty proud of my performance right here. "We can stop talking about this now."

"I'm impressed, Kangaroo," Elba says, smiling. "Normally it takes a lot more authority to fuck up that badly."

"Like enough authority to order an OSS ship of the line to the wrong coordinates during a battle?"

Elba's smile evaporates. "My intel was good. The Löwenthals fucked me over."

"You know, passing the buck is never a good look. At least I'm owning my fuckup." That name tickles something in my memory, but I can't get a hold on it. I can't wait to get all this Rovor shit cleaned out so my brain can work properly again.

"Who are you going to believe?" He steps closer to me, his face a stone mask of anger now. "The guy who's been stuck in prison for six years? Or the double-crossing snake who brought down the entire Intel Division and tried to start another war with Mars?"

We stare at each other for a few seconds. I've blinked my eye into biomedical scanning mode by now, and I can see the heat map of Elba's face glowing yellow and orange as he fumes. He's not faking this, and I've found a way to get under his skin, past his charm.

"I believe you can protect me on the outside," I say. "And I believe my abilities will be useful to you as you embark on your comeback tour."

Elba calms down a little. He nods, paces a small circle back to his throne, and sits down again. "You would be quite valuable, it's true. But this all seems a bit too good to be true. Too convenient."

"Convenient? I just jumped off the side of a goddamn blue site to get to you! I could have fucking died!"

"Oh, I believe that you're motivated, certainly. The question is what exactly you're motivated to do."

"I want to get off this stupid planet," I say. "Let me prove it. You want something out of the pocket? Some hardware that'll make this escape a lot easier to pull off? I can hook you up."

"An interesting offer." Elba steeples his fingers again. "But I'm feeling pretty good about the plan that I've spent every waking hour of the past six years working on. If we do need to improvise at some point, don't worry, I'll let you know."

The whole cargo container wobbles, and the spacesuited guard not holding a gun on me turns and goes back to the airlock corner. Our container shimmies for a moment, then shudders to a standstill, and the Rovor airlock peels open to reveal the side of another vehicle. The white progmat has extended from the cargo container to make a short tunnel leading to the other vehicle's airlock, which now hisses open.

Several black-suited commandos, all wearing helmets with mirrored visors, walk out holding stun rifles. I count a dozen of them, and after the last one files into the cargo container, I lean over so I can see through the airlock into the other vehicle.

It's full of unconscious people. Civilians. I use my eye to do a quick medical scan, which tells me that they're still alive, all thirty-two of them. They seem–drugged? They're lying on the floor of the vehicle, some of their bodies draped over others haphazardly. I see elderly couples here. I see *children* here, for fuck's sake.

"Who are all these people?" I say, staring at Elba and pointing back into the airlock.

"Our insurance." Elba addresses the lead commando. "Autopilot and distress signal are all set?"

"Affirmative," the commando replies. "Interior cameras will broadcast live vid."

That's when I get it. "These are your hostages!"

Elba makes a *tsk*ing sound with his lips. "Such an ugly word." He waves a hand, and the Rovor airlock seals shut again before I can figure out how to rescue anyone. "Now that our friends have rejoined us, those lost souls are just a diversion." Elba gives the lead commando's shoulder a fraternal squeeze.

What did he say? *Autopilot and distress signal.* Jesus. Of course. He just needs a diversion. Just long enough to get this cargo container out of range of *Tacoma*'s pursuit.

I can't do anything about the hostages, but I can fuck up the other part of his plan.

I really hope Lacomber was also telling the truth about using these slugs to override Rovor's mind control.

But first I need to convince Elba that I'm trustworthy. If I want to use the pocket, I'll have to get Elba to dissipate this Rovor crap in the air.

My left eye is still scanning the new commandos, and now it also picks up something else that it's programmed to always alert me to: an agency-issue signal necklace.

I locate the wearer at the back of the cabin. It's one of the black-suited commandos. I blink my eye into a scanning mode that can see through their mirrored face shield and get an ID hit.

Oh, this is perfect.

"Stowaway!" I push my way through the crowd—with the addition of the commando dozen, there's barely enough room to move around in here—and point an accusatory finger at my target. "You've got a stowaway here! An impostor! J'accuse!"

"What the hell are you talking about?" Elba says. At least he's willing to entertain the notion that I'm telling the truth.

I reach the commando in question and use both hands to lift up her helmet visor, revealing her face. "Et voilà!"

It's Jessica Chu, and she gives me an especially murderous look as my guard takes away her stun rifle.

Elba reaches us and studies Jessica. "I know this face. Isn't this your

Surgical officer?"

"Used to be."

"And what do you suppose she's doing here?"

"They probably sent her to keep tabs on me. Lasher knew I'd break out of Cerulean sooner or later." I do my best impression of a male chauvinist pig while feeling up her equipment vest and removing the handcuffs. "Looks like she's gotten all up in your business too." I put the cuffs around her wrists, using the opportunity to lean close to her and give her a look that hopefully tells her I'm still on mission, and she should just go along with this.

"Yes," Elba says thoughtfully. "But why not a more experienced field agent? Why Surgical?"

"Because you're fucking around with nanobots," Jessica snaps.

Elba takes a step forward. "Interesting. Lasher knew that? He told you that?"

"Of course not!" I'm pretty sure Jessica doesn't have to fake her indignation right now. "If he admitted knowing, he'd have to report it up the chain. But he knew I'd be able to deal with it. Let me tell you, it was a real fucking surprise when your errand girl tried to dose me. Not cool, by the way. It's hard enough to get a drink at the bar without worrying about ingesting illegal medical nanotech."

"You seem to have recovered just fine," Elba says.

"Better than your girl."

Elba sucks in a breath. Was that a flicker of emotion I just saw? "Where is she?"

"Sleeping with the baby Jesus." Jessica almost smiles, and I'm both intensely disturbed and impressed with her acting ability.

"I see Lasher remains as ruthless as ever. So be it. She knew the risks. And she would have been glad to sacrifice for these rewards." Elba nods at me.

"See? I'm a fucking reward," I say, thrusting my chin out.

"Congratulations, princess," Jessica spits. "So are you assholes going to kill me now, or what?"

Elba smiles and looks at me. "Kangaroo, would you care to do the honors?"

"Delighted." I shove Jessica backward into the only empty space at the back of the cabin, the short hallway next to the restroom. "If you wouldn't mind calling off Rovor in the privy."

"Ah. A demonstration for me. Excellent." Elba snaps his fingers, then puts his palms together and mutters something. It looks like a weird combination of casting a spell and praying, but I'm sure what he's actually doing is manipulating some control implants like the ones I have, and giving subvocal commands to his own shoulder-phone. Which then does something to wirelessly relay them to the Rovor particles nearby. It all makes sense, sort of, but it still looks super creepy and sinister.

The pressure and particulate matter sensing display in my left eye HUD starts changing, and in a few seconds the numbers turn green, indicating that it's clear enough for me to manifest a portal. I open the restroom door and think of a green boxing glove. I open the pocket, then reach inside to retrieve my decoy stun-stick. It looks just like a meter-long nonlethal crowd control weapon, but all it's good for is a light show. It won't actually deliver any electrical current into the victim's body.

I hope Jessica recognizes this piece of equipment. It might look more real if she puts up a fight, but we don't have a lot of time to spar right now.

"Thank you." I trigger the fake stunner a couple times to sell it, firing simulated arcs of electricity up toward the ceiling. "I hope this hurts, Surge."

"Don't call me Surge. I hope Elba eats your liver."

I think of a red-and-yellow hammock hung between two euca-lyptus trees—oh, man, I could really go for a nap right now—and open the pocket behind her, no barrier.

Jessica grabs the walls to brace herself against the vacuum sucking her backward. I shove the stun-stick into her belly, between the lower edge of her body armor and the top of her belt, and trigger the light show again. She puts on an adequate performance of being shocked, and when I pull the stick back, relaxes her body and falls backward into the pocket.

Be ready, I mouth at her, and close the pocket.

Elba laughs and claps his hands together above his head. "Wonderful!" I re-pocket the stun-stick before he can grab it and discover my deception. "Oh, that is a splendid trick. I think this is the beginning of a beautiful friendship, Kangaroo."

I give him the smarmiest smile I can muster. *You probably haven't even seen* Casablanca, *you prick, and I hate people who quote movies in the wrong context.*

"All right!" Elba's voice booms out as he moves forward, and why are all these people making way for him when I had to shove and fight my way through? Rude. "My friends, we will soon be free of this place and headed for new lives on other worlds. But we're not out of the figurative woods yet. Stay sharp, just in case we encounter any other unexpected guests."

While everyone's attention is focused on him, I quickly open a barely fist-sized portal to retrieve a compact emergency air tank, then open the pocket to Jessica's location and toss it inside for her. She'll have some burst blood vessels from exposure to vacuum before she closed her helmet, but at least she won't suffocate. I start a timer in my eye to make sure I get her out, or at least sneak her more equipment, before the air tank runs out. Then I slam the restroom door shut.

At least I'll be able to use the pocket, now that Elba trusts me not to stab him in the back. I'm going to have to tread very lightly until I see how these escapees are planning to get out of orbit.

My guard takes off their helmet, and I smell that it's Lavender—a middle-aged man with a receding hairline and scruffy gray beard. My eye identifies him as someone of minor importance—an analyst, no special file tag. I wonder what he did to end up at Cerulean.

"Nice to get out of that spacesuit, huh?" I say to him.

Lavender sneers at me. "I've still got my eye on you, boy."

It's never been my experience that any adult man who calls another adult man "boy" in that tone of voice will turn out to be a decent human being. I shrug off Lavender's tiresomely unoriginal insult. At least he smells nice.

I really, really hope Ellie got through to someone.

CHAPTER
THIRTY-TWO

Venus—still in the clouds
Not much time left to stop this maniac

I can see that we're disembarking onto some kind of loading deck, but the interior of this facility is unlike anything I've ever seen. It looks more flimsy than anything that should be floating inside a bank of corrosive acid clouds being blown around by gale-force winds. Spindly black struts are webbed together by translucent sheets of what must be more Rovor stuff. The only actual solid matter mechanisms are the twelve airlocks arranged in a ring formation, including the one that we're coming out of now.

It takes me way too long to realize that this freakish skeleton has been modeled after a commercial orbital transfer station, like the one in orbit above us that is how Sunstone and other resorts get their constant stream of incoming supplies to feed and water their guests. Some things can be recycled or manufactured on site from components or ingredients, but there's no substitute for actual fruits and vegetables, even if they're frozen. All those supplies get shipped in on robotic cargo carriers, guided by traffic satellites, monitored by ships like the *Tacoma* and their orbital security net.

And after they deliver their cargo, the drones drop off their crates and the freighters go back to Earth. They may be unmanned, but the company still wants their cargo carrier back, even if it's coming back empty. They're not going to scrap a whole interplanetary spacecraft after just one voyage.

So Elba's managed to replicate that transfer station down here in the clouds, where it's fully hidden from view, and automated it to work with those drone skiffs. I have no idea how Elba plans to evade detection after leaving Venus—cargo ships aren't known for having any stealth capabilities—but I'd better find that out and stop it before it happens.

I maneuver over to where a guard is dealing with a blank-faced prisoner and jab the guard in the neck with one of my hypno-slugs. The prisoner wanders off as the guard twitches, then settles.

"Why did you resign?" I whisper.

His eyes bug out for a moment. Then he says with eerie calmness: "Too many piglets know overmuch."

"Protect other people," I say. "Make sure nobody dies."

"Protect other people," the guard says in a drowsy monotone. "Nobody dies."

I repeat the procedure with the second guard as he grabs me and tugs me away, injecting him in his wrist and issuing the same instruction. His eyes go glassy, and he repeats back my command. It's really creepy to see up close like this. I make a mental note to ask Jessica to update my nanobots' poison- and toxin-detection algorithms. I wouldn't want to accidentally eat the wrong thing and wind up a zombie like these guys.

Speaking of nanobots, I blink my eye and twitch my fingertip controls to try my shoulder-phone. Still jammed. No talking to Oliver, wherever the hell he is, or Ellie in her bluejay. Jessica and I are on our own here. And I'm the only one who can move freely right now.

Another hand grabs my shoulder as I'm moving back through the crowd and roughly spins me around. I stare into the face of a man wearing a red-and-white-striped shirt.

"Come with me," he says. I recognize the smell on his breath. Tree Bark!

"Sure."

As Tree Bark turns, dragging me behind him in the air like a giant floating novelty balloon, I see that his red-and-white-striped shirt is slightly untucked. I stick him just above the left hip, then grab his shoulder and pull my face close to his head. He turns to look at me, and his disgruntled expression softens as the drug takes effect.

After verifying with the challenge phrase, I say, "I outrank Elba. If push comes to shove, you listen to me, not him."

"You . . ." Tree Bark stares off into space.

"I outrank Elba."

He shakes his head. "I obey Elba."

Shit. Maybe two slugs will work? This guy is in Elba's inner circle, he's probably snorted up way more Rovor than most of these other people. Hopefully more of Lacomber's anti-brainwash juice will overcome that.

I look around to make sure the coast is clear—fortunately for me, there's plenty of chaos to go around right now—and stick Tree Bark with another injector. "No, for reals, I outrank Elba. I am his superior. You follow *my* orders, not his. Got it?"

"Follow . . . your . . . orders," Tree Bark says, sweat beading on his forehead.

"Good enough," I grumble. "Let's keep going."

Tree Bark continues his footsteps, boots clanking against the metal walls. He's walking along the hexagonal perimeter of the loading area, avoiding the prisoners who are milling about mindlessly. We pass over two of the twelve docking ports, and I see that their airlock controls are lit up green. Other cargo containers are arriving. I don't have too much longer to throw a wrench into Elba's plans. But I need to know more about exactly what that plan is.

We approach Elba, who is surrounded by six guards and looking at a computer tablet. Tree Bark stops me outside the circle. "Here's the prisoner you requested."

Elba looks up from his tablet and gives me a wide, psychotic grin. "Kangaroo." Tree Bark pushes me down to the deck by my shoulders so I'm kneeling.

"So we're leaving the planet now," I say. "I'm guessing we're all going to take a ride in these nifty cargo containers?"

Elba chuckles, does something on the tablet, and hands it to another minion, who takes it away. Then he steps distressingly close to me and leans in toward the side of my face.

"I want to talk about your pocket," he says.

Well, I figured we were going to have this conversation sooner or later. "Sure. What do you want to know?"

"There is no air inside," Elba says, leaning back. "Is that correct?"

"Right." I blink a display into my eye, a preset grid that Oliver helped me create. It's titled "How to Lie About the Pocket" and includes a variety of different things I can choose to reveal or hide about the pocket. My advantage here is that Elba can't corroborate what I say with anyone else. "Basically deep space. No air, no light, no heat, no gravity."

"Hmm." Elba rubs his chin. I wish he would stop staring at me like that. Like I'm an object and he's trying to decide what to do with me— whether I'm useful, or whether I'm junk. "So in order to survive inside, a person would need to be wearing a spacesuit."

"Yup. Surgical's probably fully freeze-dried by now. Want me to bring her out?"

Elba waves a hand. "Perhaps later." Good. I didn't actually want him to call my bluff on that. My go-to then would have been to fake a pocket "performance issue," which does happen in real life if I'm not careful about how much I exert myself with pulling portals. "What about putting vehicles inside?"

I tick off a box in my fibbing grid. "I can put anything inside, as long as it's not too big. It has to fit through the portal. And I can only make that about one meter in diameter." This is a lie.

Elba studies me closely. "You've never tried to create a larger portal?"

"Oh, sure, I've tried," I say, calling on every resource I can to make this lie as convincing as possible. If Elba even suspects me of not being straight with him, he might decide to just throw me out of an airlock. Twelve of which are handily located very close by. "But I can only do so much with my ability. There are limits."

"Science Division hasn't come up with any ideas for enhancement? Chemicals, implants, hypnotherapy?"

Crap. Maybe Elba didn't have clearance to know about me before he got thrown in here during the war, but he knows enough to speculate pretty well about what the agency would have done once they found a kid with a superpower.

"They keep fucking trying," I say, allowing resentment to bubble up from the natural well that's been building inside me for years. "You want to hear about the time they broke both my legs? That was a goddamn laugh and a half."

"Please focus, Kangaroo," Elba says. "I'm simply working out how you can be most helpful during our current operation."

Damn, this guy's good. If I weren't all keyed up and on guard, he might actually be able to get that smooth voice under my skin a little. If he gets away, he won't need Rovor to recruit more criminals to join his crew.

"Yeah, cool," I say. "And I do want to help out. But I'm just telling you what's what. There's things I *can* do, and there's things I just *can't.*"

Elba nods. "And you are the only one who can access the pocket?"

"Yup. One and only Kangaroo, right here." I indicate myself with both thumbs and flash a stupid smile. I want him to underestimate me.

"So if you could put one of these cargo drones inside the pocket," Elba says, "you are the only one who could retrieve it later."

"Right on, daddy-o."

He ignores my archaic slang. "Or you could choose to leave that vehicle inside the pocket forever."

I shrug. "In theory. But what good would that do?" I snap my fingers, feigning a revelation. "Oh, I get it! You want me to hide all of *you* inside, so nobody will find you, and then pull you out later. Yeah, sweet plan, but I can't fit an entire one of those ships through the portal. Are there spacesuits here, though? You could—"

"I appreciate the offer," Elba says, holding up a hand to cut me off, "but it seems foolhardy to trust my well-being to a single point of failure."

I frown and draw back. "Did you just insult me?" I turn to Tree Bark. "I think he just insulted me."

"Not at all," Elba says. "I'm sure I will find your services very valuable in the near future. But I have spent many years crafting the operation we are currently running, and adding another variable at this late stage seems ill-advised."

"Fine, whatever," I say. "But you want to hide something, you know where to find me."

"Indeed."

Another guard approaches, carrying a different tablet. I can see the display bordered by flashing red lines. Elba takes the tablet, looks at it, and nods. "Very good."

I lean forward, trying to get a better look at the display. "What signal is that?"

Elba hands the tablet back to the guard, who leaves. "Cerulean City. It's automatic." Elba smiles, sending another chill down my spine. So fucking creepy. "Unlike resort habs, when a blue site's proximity alarm is triggered, the self-destruct activates and the site begins broadcasting a warning beacon just in case it's near anyone who isn't already aware of its location. Safety first, you know."

I hope my spiking heart rate hasn't affected my facial expression too much. I blink the medical alert out of my eye. Elba has to expect that I'm going to respond to this news.

"Isn't that a bit, I don't know, extreme?" I ask. "I mean, you already got everybody you wanted out of there, right? Why blow it up too?"

Elba chuckles. "Well, they do call us extremists. We must live up to our name."

I stare at him for a moment, waiting for him to say something else, but he just grins.

"Shit. It's part of the diversion," I say.

"Of course," Elba says. "Even in a secret cargo container, we could hardly be guaranteed escape with a US-OSS warship in orbit." The creepy smile intensifies. "But a terror attack on a resort habitat, combined with a blue site about to self-destruct directly above a shuttle full of innocent civilians . . ." He spreads his hands. "Safety first. Security second."

Oliver's still out there. Ellie, too. And inside Cerulean, Number Two and Twenty-Three and who knows how many of the prisoners Elba didn't deem useful enough to bring along.

I stare back at Elba. "Good thing you aren't constrained by things like ethics or morality."

He laughs in my face. "I learned from the best! Honestly, secret prisons? Where experiments are conducted on unwitting human subjects? Inside facilities programmed to self-destruct rather than risk letting any prisoners or secrets out?"

The smile disappears, and it suddenly seems like his face is all skull.

"I'm not the bad guy. I'm just playing the game."

Maybe he has a point. But he is going to hurt a lot of innocent people unless I stop him.

Elba waves me away, and after he turns his back, I inject the guard with the tablet and tell him to follow my orders when the time comes. He acknowledges me and releases me into the throng of prisoners milling about.

I try my shoulder-phone again. Still jammed.

You better think of something fast, Kangaroo.

It's too packed in here for me to open the pocket and sneak Jessica any more equipment, or to pull anything for myself without risking notice, though I keep looking for opportunities. My eye is also cataloging everyone here. Elba's crew has more than a hundred of the prisoners from Cerulean City, and twelve of the guards. I've jabbed three of them so far.

There's a lot of commotion when the twelfth and final cargo drone docks with the transfer station. Two guards flank the airlock as the lights go from yellow to red to green.

"Get back!" one guard says as I drift over.

"Whoa, easy there, fella," I say, stopping before I get within reach of his stun-stick. "What's with all the hubbub, bub?"

"None of your concern," the guard snaps. "Stay back."

I haven't had a chance to dose this guy. I look at the other guard beside him. It's Tree Bark again. I push myself over to him and say, "Tell me what's going on."

Tree Bark turns his head slowly. "The final cargo drone is coming in heavy."

The other guard snaps his head around. "What the fuck?"

"We're friends," I say, adding a wink. "You know, special friends?"

He rolls his eyes. "Just stay back."

"'Heavy' means it's carrying cargo, right?" I ask Tree Bark.

"That's right," he replies.

"Why is that a problem?"

"Supposed to be empty," Tree Bark says.

"Maybe it just didn't get unloaded properly before you guys, you know, hijacked it? Seemed like Elba's in a hurry to keep his schedule."

Tree Bark looks at me blankly. "I don't know."

The airlock hisses open, and the first guard starts shouting again. "Hands where I can see them! Don't move!"

Two more guards move up and into the open airlock, standing on opposite walls of the square cargo container, and pull out a single person with a mop of dark hair.

It's Oliver.

CHAPTER
THIRTY-THREE

Venus—aboard bluejay, running away
Mission time 8'31

"About time you rejoined us," Ellie says as Shimura wakes up, strapped into the co-pilot's seat next to her and sealed inside his spacesuit. "The galette is in the oven?"

Shimura blinks at her through his helmet and frowns. "I remember who you are, Marmosa."

She still makes him talk through the whole challenge-response sequence. It's the least he can endure after putting her through the whole amnesia song and dance multiple times. Then Ellie brings Shimura up to speed on what's been happening.

"I'm guessing the Rovor incident is why I'm still in this spacesuit?" Shimura says. "And why the helmet latches seem to be welded shut?"

Ellie did that to avoid any possible repeat of the earlier "incident," so-called. "Yeah. You've got well over five hours of air in there, and if we're not all back on *Tacoma* by then, Rovor will be the least of our problems."

"And right now we're headed where, exactly?" Shimura points out the forward window. Their current view is assorted swirls of churning clouds in various shades of dingy orange-brown, as the bluejay drives through an especially thick section of Venmo. Ellie doesn't love doing this, especially given all the new moaning noises that her bird makes every time they hit a strong patch of wind, but it's the fastest and safest way to get to their target.

"Somewhere we can make contact with *Tacoma*," she tells Shimura. "Cerulean was jamming us back there. We had to get out of range."

"How do you know what their jamming range is?"

Ellie side-eyes him. "Was kind of hoping you might have a clue."

Shimura shakes his head. "If I ever did, Rovor's erased it."

That's about what Ellie expected. She checks the navigation display and tips the bluejay back into a climb. "Never mind. We're going to see what we can see up here."

"I hate to ask, but where is 'here'?"

Ellie lets the view do the talking. The bluejay emerges from the clouds headed directly toward a giant shiny floating donut. "An oversized civilian radio that we can borrow."

Their helmets automatically darken against the light, so Shimura now looks like a marble-headed doll as he leans forward. "Is that another hab?"

"That is the Rainforest Preserve Habitat," Ellie says, maneuvering the bluejay into a station-keeping course directly underneath the hole in the donut of down-facing solar panels. Venusian clouds reflect a lot of sunlight, so it's worth building power generators on the tops and bottoms of these floating habs. The cutout in the middle is there for visual spotting and maintenance access. "A resort destination that also contains a carefully tended collection of unique flora and fauna collected from Earth's tropical ecosystems, managed by an international coalition. And the agency has a backdoor into their comms relay."

"How do we know *their* comms aren't also being jammed?"

"I'm hoping we're far enough away, and they've got enough extra transmitting power, that we can punch through. Let's find out."

She calls up the procedure from secure storage in the bluejay computer, and Shimura helps her make the connection. Ellie holds her breath for a few seconds, until they get a green light on their radio, and then crosses her fingers while dialing up the *Tacoma*.

"*Tacoma,* this is Marmosa, please respond, over." And holding her breath again.

Shimura leans over. "If this doesn't work—"

"Just give it a minute, will you?" Ellie nudges him back to the other side of the cockpit.

"I'm just saying, we could ascend into orbit, we'd have a better chance up there—"

"I'm not leaving him behind," Ellie snaps before she can help herself. "Kangaroo. We need to stay close. We are his exfil transpo."

"We can come back. Or someone can. *Tacoma* can send a fresh bird, fully fueled, one that hasn't been exposed to Venmo."

Ellie understands the reasoning behind Shimura's argument. In another situation, she might agree with him. But she's not going to leave Kangaroo. And she's the goddamn pilot here.

The radio buzzes. "Marmosa, this is *Tacoma,* where the hell have you been?" It's Commander Nakamura, her tone as snippy as ever.

"That is a very long story," Ellie replies. "But I'm fine, I just need air support to halt two floating habs that are on a collision course."

There's a long pause before Nakamura says, "Coordinates?"

Ellie rattles off the numbers so *Tacoma* can point their sensors to the right place and verify what she's saying. She's glad Nakamura didn't feel the need to ask a lot of follow-up questions.

"Confirmed, Marmosa. We're working the problem. RTB before your bird falls apart, we're seeing a lot of red on your telemetry."

Ellie has to unclench her jaw before speaking. "*Tacoma,* I'm sending you a secure data packet for relay back to Earth"—she waves at Shimura, who pushes buttons to make that happen—"and then I'm heading back to save some fucking lives. Please confirm air support, over."

"Negative, Marmosa. You're unarmed, let us take care of this."

Ellie isn't going to return to base, and she's pretty tired of being second-guessed all day. "I'm going to be very clear about this, *Tacoma.* I don't take orders from you. I am telling you what I'm going to do now, and you can do what you want, I don't care."

Another long pause. "Wait one, Marmosa, I'm conferring with the captain."

"Data's uploaded," Shimura says.

"Terrific." Ellie pulls the bluejay away from Rainforest, heading back down into the clouds. "*Tacoma*, Marmosa, I am headed back down now. Expect loss of signal in—"

"Negative, Marmosa," Nakamura says. "We are tracking you in and sending air support to your position. Switch to secure tightbeam, stay above the clouds and stay on comms."

Ellie exhales and almost smiles while Shimura adjusts their comms. It's going to take a few minutes to get back to Cerulean anyway, and talking to *Tacoma* will at least keep Shimura out of her hair while she figures some way to engage enemy drones in a crippled transport with no weapons.

CHAPTER
THIRTY-FOUR

Venus—in the clouds—aboard secret drone airbase
I hate ticking clocks

"You!" I shout, almost flinging myself into one of the robot arms in my haste to get to Oliver before the guards can do anything terrible to him. "I know this guy! What the fuck!"

It's only when I get closer to him that I notice that he's wearing some kind of jumpsuit—but not a flight suit or anything fancy like that, more like worker's coveralls, like the non-commando conspirators. The guards who pulled him out of the cargo drone yank his arms behind his back, and I see the Sunstone logo over his left breast pocket.

Crap. Probably shouldn't have called the play so quickly, but I wanted to lay claim to the fresh meat before the other predators could move in. Reflex. I think I can still salvage this situation. I need to know what the hell Oliver thinks he's doing here, but it seems unlikely that I'm going to be able to get him alone.

"I'm sorry, friend," Oliver says, staring daggers at me, "I think you must have me confused with someone else."

"What's all this, then?" Elba says. He's looking over my right shoulder.

I only have a split second to decide how I'm going to play this. If I walk back my recognizing Oliver, it might look suspicious at best, and at worst will make Elba think I'm incompetent or impulsive and make him more inclined to exclude me from his inner circle, despite my unique superpower. I need to demonstrate to him that I'm more than just a tool—I'm a multifaceted resource who can think for himself.

Sorry about this, Oliver. I would text that to him, but he's not carrying his customary computer tablet to receive the message. And ironically, my Equipment officer has never jumped on the biotech implants bandwagon. Something about how he likes to tinker with his personal gadgets all the time, and that becomes much more difficult if they're buried under his skin or grafted onto his central nervous system. Computer hacking is a little more dangerous than usual when the computer's wired into your brain.

"Nice try with the costume," I say, giving Oliver's shoulder a shove, hoping he can feel the extra pressure I put into every other finger. We've established a lot of emergency code motions for use in the field, and that one is a nonverbal gesture to indicate that I'm running a legend and he should just play along. I hope he remembers the signal. I hope he understands what it means.

"But I'd recognize those beady eyes anywhere," I continue, pointing at Oliver's face. "This guy's agency."

"How very interesting," Elba says. "And how do you know him?"

"He's the spook who escorted me to Venus aboard the *Tacoma*," I say. "I thought he would have stayed in orbit after sending me down in a bluejay. But I guess he wanted to take a little vacation while he was here."

"Perhaps not a vacation," Elba says. "Kangaroo, I don't suppose you have any truth serum stashed away in that pocket of yours?"

Oliver's eyes widen slightly when Elba says my name, but I'm impressed by how Oliver isn't exploding in a fit of rage right now. I glare back at him with an expression that I hope he understands to mean *keep a fucking lid on it, I've got this under control.*

"Sadly, no," I say, putting as much scorn into those three syllables as I can. "The agency controls my inventory pretty tightly."

"We'll have to remedy that situation later," Elba says. "For now, I suppose we'll have to conduct a more conventional interrogation. We can't have any other loose ends interfering with our plans."

"Let me do it," I say, turning to face Elba. "I've got history with this cocksucker. He wasn't very nice to me during the trip out here."

Elba studies my face for a second, then nods. "Very well, Kangaroo. Just make sure he can still talk when you're finished."

I grab Oliver by the collar and move toward the open airlock. "I'm going to take him in there. Too much noise out here."

"Leave the door open," Elba says. "We're going to start loading the other drones now. Be quick."

It's difficult maneuvering both Oliver and myself forward, since he's doing a real good job of pretending to struggle against my grip, but I manage to catch a foothold just inside the inner airlock door of the drone and use that leverage to slam Oliver down to the floor. He emits a loud grunt when his back hits the hard surface.

Keeping my toe in the foothold, I plant my other foot on the floor and then grab the collar of his jumpsuit with both hands. He raises a hand and clamps it against the back of my right hand. For a moment, it feels like he's trying to claw his fingers under my palm to break my grip, but then I realize he's actually passing me a tiny capsule. I release his collar and take the capsule and close my fist around it.

"Swallow that," he says under his breath.

"Shut the fuck up," I say, hoping my left eye overlay is correct about the sight lines from behind me into the drone's boxy interior. I raise my right arm, draw back my fist like I'm preparing to punch, and open it just enough to release the capsule as my hand passes my face, hopefully blocked by my head from the view of any guards who might be watching.

I catch the capsule in my mouth and gulp it down at the same time I deliver a right hook to Oliver's jaw.

His head snaps to the side, and a glob of what looks like blood flies out of his mouth.

I hope that was a prepared feint and that I didn't just actually hit him hard enough to draw blood. I've never actually punched Oliver in the face before. Wanted to, sure, especially when he wouldn't stop talking about some unimportant technical detail of a device I really needed to deploy in the field on a very tight timeline and I didn't have time for yet another lecture from Professor Pedantic. But he was almost always light-seconds away, just a voice in my ear that I couldn't stop from talking. Kind of like my conscience, but infinitely more annoying.

I'll apologize to him later.

"Talk!" I shout. Then, much more quietly: "How did you get here?"

"Long story," he whispers. "Commandos on Sunstone. Surgical went undercover."

I punch Oliver again. "What did I just swallow?"

"More nanobots. Should fix your comms, circumvent jamming. Also, sorry."

"You're sorry about fixing my comms?"

"No, sorry about this."

He slams his forehead directly into my nose, and a blinding pain explodes inside my skull. As I mentioned just now, I've never actually engaged Oliver in hand-to-hand combat, and I was kind of expecting him to be not very good at it.

Sometimes I wish my life were less full of surprises.

I wasn't braced against Oliver's sudden attack, and I lose my foothold as he tucks his legs under him and pushes up. This time it's my turn to get my back slammed into a hard surface. The interior lining of the cargo drone is incredibly hard and dense. I know these things need to be airtight and shielded against cosmic radiation, and extra thick to protect from micrometeoroid impacts while they travel long distances through deep space at high speeds, but I still wasn't expecting to feel like I was falling from a nontrivial height onto a solid concrete block.

"Ow," I say at the same time Oliver uses his free hand—the one that's not holding my left hand against his collar, which is good, because I probably would have let go by now and possibly blown our cover—to swipe my nose. He actually pushes my whole head to the side, and it probably looks like he's slapping me, but he actually gets a good amount of blood off my bloody nose. Then he smears it on the wall next to my head.

"Move us away, half a meter or more," he mutters.

I think I know what he's doing. I let out what I hope is a bloodcurdling cry, not something that sounds like a whiny baby who just got his nose broken, and use both fists to batter Oliver's abdomen, sending him stumbling back into the center of the empty cargo hold.

I blink my eye into spectroscope mode and follow Oliver, crash into his side as he's trying to turn around, and we tumble as he kicks at me. Jesus, is he *actually* fighting me now? Good thing he's not very good at it.

While he claws at me ineffectively, I turn my head to look back at the wall where he smeared my blood. The stain is lit up in all sorts of interesting false colors, indicating that the nanobots have started dissolving the wall material.

Project Weyland-Yutani is still online. Acid for blood, basically. I guess Oliver wasn't sure if my nanobots were fully functional yet, but now he knows.

"Good to go," I say, a little louder since that could be interpreted in a torture-relevant way by any eavesdropping guards. I don't see anyone standing too close to the open airlock, but there were at least two of them guarding this particular space.

"Did you get Surgical?" he hisses.

"She's in the pocket."

"Can we stop now, then?" Oliver is actually trying to break my hold on his torso now.

"Sorry," I say as I release both hands and then slam both palms against either side of his skull simultaneously, right in front of his ears. Not hard enough to break anything, just enough to rattle his brain inside his skull. Brains don't like that. A hard enough rattle is called a concussion, and it can cause permanent brain damage. This hit should just give him something to think about, stun and daze him momentarily. And I even pulled my punch, because I just want him to play along.

Oliver doesn't seem like he's acting as his head wobbles and his arms go limp. I grab both his wrists and pull them behind his back, then spin us around. He's still wobbling when I stabilize us and push him forward against the wall.

"Tell me!" I yell into his ear, hoping that it will focus him more than it hurts him.

"Forty-two!" he replies in kind.

"Forty-two what?" I don't actually know what he's talking about now.

"Forty-two point three six!"

I press my head close to his. "We can stop now, yeah?"

"Please."

I raise my head and turn toward the open airlock. I'm glad to see that no guards are watching us—they're too busy keeping an eye on the crowds they're herding into the eleven other cargo drones. "Hey! Guard! Give me some cuffs here!"

One of the guards—a woman I don't recognize, she's not someone I dosed earlier—stomps into the drone in mag-boots, holding out a blob of Rovor. "Here."

I make a face and pull back. "Maybe you should do that."

She wants to roll her eyes, I can tell, but instead she wraps the blob around Oliver. That distracts her long enough for me to open the pocket, pull another hypno-slug, and slap it onto her neck.

"Ow! What the fuck!" She turns to me. I pull the slug back and watch her pupils dilate. "What . . . what?"

"Why did you resign?" I ask.

"Is that really relevant just now?" Oliver hisses.

"Too many piglets know overmuch," the woman says.

"Stay with this man," I say, turning her back to face Oliver. "Keep him safe."

"Stay with him. Keep him safe," the guard repeats.

"Is that really going to work?" Oliver asks me.

"Seems to be working so far," I say. "You. Guard. What's your name?"

"Willis," she says.

"Okay, Willis. Tell me what you're going to do with this guy." I point at Oliver.

Willis looks at me blankly, then turns to Oliver. "I'm going to stay with this man and keep him safe."

"You're in good hands," I say to Oliver.

I move back into the central loading area. A sudden cacophony of sound in my ear makes me cringe. I look around, but no one else seems to be hearing this. And then I make out overlapping voices.

"Blue Seven, you've got another one on your tail!"

"Thrusters at maximum, Captain."

"We're still losing dome pressure!"

My comms implants are back online. Fuck yeah.

I drop my arms and wiggle my fingers to filter out most of the transmissions. My mission recorder's going, and I send a series of commands to push that buffer through a speech-to-text module and display the results in my eye. It can be incredibly distracting to have extra data floating in my field of vision, but right now I need to know what's happening with those other folks if I'm going to run the right play in here.

A guard walks over to me. "You okay, sir?" It's Tree Bark again.

"Yeah, I'm fine." I jerk a thumb over my shoulder. "Little twerp's tougher than he looks."

Tree Bark nods. "I know you wanted to take care of him yourself, sir, but would you like me to have a go?" He pulls his stun-stick out of his holster.

I pretend to think about it, rubbing one palm against my bloody nose and then holding out my hand. "Let me see that for a second."

He hands over the stun-stick. I turn it over in my hands, making sure to get my blood all over the area right above the handgrip, where I believe the main power connections are. Then I shake my head and hand it back to him before he can notice anything dissolving.

"Later," I say. "Let's go see if the big boss needs help."

Tree Bark holsters his stun-stick and nods. "Yes, sir."

I give Oliver one final look over my shoulder, then follow Tree Bark out into the loading area and study the transcripts scrolling up in my eye.

Looks like everyone out there has their hands full. I can't expect any more help to show up here. Oliver and I—and the few guards I've managed to brainwash to our side—are going to have to foil Elba's escape on our own.

"Give me your radio," I say to Tree Bark. He hands over the portable unit clipped to his belt. I turn it on and tune it to the channel that Oliver specified, hoping he was actually prepared to give up that bit of information.

The voices coming from that channel sound like the *Tacoma*, but it's a decoy feed. I can see the discrepancies between the ship's actual transmissions, shown in my eye, and the misinformation being broadcast here.

I have to say, sometimes I absolutely love working with smart people who think of even worse-case scenarios than I do.

Tree Bark and I approach Elba, who's standing in the middle of the loading area surrounded by guards. Almost all the prisoners, commandos, and other helpers have been loaded already.

Elba turns to face Tree Bark and me. I hand over the radio, still broadcasting the fake feed from the *Tacoma*.

"The jailers have their hands full," I say. "Are we blowing this Popsicle stand soon? Because I don't particularly like the decor." I jerk a thumb over my shoulder, toward Oliver. "Or the company."

Elba smiles and hands the radio to another guard. I've noticed that he's been keeping the same six guards as his personal escort.

"You have a very strange way of speaking, Kangaroo," Elba says. "But it's growing on me."

I shrug. "I talk like I talk. So what's the deal?"

"We're almost ready," he says. "But I'm afraid you will have to spend a little more time with your nemesis. We are leaving in that drone." He points to where Willis is holding Oliver, and I realize that all the other airlocks are closed and locked.

"Fine," I say. "But there might be some screaming."

"We can live with that." Elba makes an expansive gesture, and the whole cluster—Elba, all the remaining guards, and myself—move into the last airlock. "Have you ever tortured someone inside an airlock before, Kangaroo?"

I shake my head. "Can't say I've had the pleasure."

"It's a very convenient way to suppress noise." Elba steps over the threshold into the cargo drone. "Granted, neither of you has more than a few minutes before the victim loses consciousness from lack of fresh oxygen, but it does add a nice frisson of tension to whatever physical pain you're inflicting."

All the guards are inside now. The station-side airlock door closes behind us. Elba makes another gesture, and they close into a circle around him, leaving Oliver and me still inside the airlock.

I've got a bad feeling about this.

"We got seat belts in this jalopy or what?" I ask. "Seems like it might be a rough ride, especially if we run into those defense satellites."

Elba smiles. "You won't need to worry about that, Kangaroo."

He gestures again, and four guards clomp forward and shove Oliver and me back against the outer door of the airlock. The inner door closes before we can recover our footing. Now we can only see Elba and company through a small porthole on the inner airlock door.

"I have a bad feeling about this," Oliver says, holding on to the floor with his feet.

I quickly smear some blood on his blob-restraint before going over and slathering more blood on the airlock manual release. I can see the nanobots working in my eye, but not nearly fast enough.

Elba's face appears in the airlock porthole. The lighting illuminates his face from below, making him appear even more sinister.

"What the hell, Elba!" I shout at him. "You do remember who I am, right? Kangaroo? Pocket superpower? We're going to work together!"

"It was a nice idea, wasn't it?" Elba says. "Unfortunately, you would make me too much of a target. The only secret agent with a superpower in the entire universe, as far as we know? And I have to worry about protecting you as well as myself while we're on the run?" He clucks his tongue. "I'm safer on my own."

"You don't know what I can do for you!" I say, smearing more blood everywhere I can while Elba can't see what I'm doing. Then I remember: *Move us away, half a meter or more.* The nanobots aren't going to do anything until I'm farther back. "I haven't shown you everything I can do with the pocket!"

"Oh, it is rather tragic," Elba says. "But I have been putting together this plan for quite some time. And I can't risk such an extreme variation at this point. Besides, you'll make rather a nice diversion for our would-be pursuers. I'm quite sure they'll prioritize saving you over catching me. Finding one target, instead of trying to determine which one of twelve identical cargo drones is hiding me? Much better odds."

"Eight point three bar percent," Oliver says.

"Not helping," I say, turning my head to the side momentarily. Then I face Elba again. "Look. Forget the pocket. We have information, both of us, current and actionable against the agency. Ditch us later, on whatever planet or rock you're heading for. We can go our separate ways. No muss, no fuss."

"Oh, I've got my own . . . *inroads* to the agency," Elba says, still disturbingly calm and unemotional. "Besides, why waste any of my decoys? Once they found you, they would be that much closer to me."

"But you'd still have a head start," I say. "You can work with that, right? Listen, I was very close to Lasher, he's D.Ops now in case you hadn't heard, I can tell you all about—"

"Good-bye, Kangaroo." This motherfucker actually winks at me. "I'll tell the aunties you said hello."

"Why did you resign! Protect other people! *Keep everyone alive!*" I shout, not at Elba, but at the guards I managed to override. I hope it's enough.

Yellow lights flash inside the airlock, and I'm still screaming when the cargo drone decouples from the airbase and Oliver and I are left standing on an exposed ledge, clinging to handholds as the wind slams acid vapor up against us.

CHAPTER
THIRTY-FIVE

Venus—aboard bluejay, approaching Cerulean again
Mission time 9'48

Ellie's tongue is sore from being bitten after many long minutes of hearing Shimura recap their adventures in Venmo so far, but she's determined to let Nakamura soak up all that damage. She still hasn't figured out how she's going to do anything useful with her possibly disintegrating bluejay when they get back to Cerulean.

She's pretty sure her bird, with Oliver's modifications, is still sturdier than those flimsy drone skiffs she saw circling the secret scaffold air base. But if Shimura's intel about Rovor is right, and those skiffs have progmat parts that can reshape themselves—this might be a long drive to a quick end.

That doesn't mean she's not going to try something, though.

The nav console beeps, telling her they're approaching the target. Ellie brings her attention back to the cockpit and Shimura's conversation with *Tacoma*.

"Yeah, both habs are above the clouds now," Shimura is saying. "You should be able to see them real clearly."

"Can confirm, Badger," Nakamura says. "Keep your distance, but we're closing on your position to deliver air support."

"What? No!" Now Ellie needs to say something. "Stay up there, *Tacoma,* you need to keep scanning on orbit. Elba's escaping, trying to get off-planet. The habs are just a diversion."

"We're on top of it, Marmosa," Nakamura replies. "We've deployed additional monitoring satellites. But our priority has to be the thousands of civilians in danger right now."

"The prisoners escaping from the blue site are the danger!"

"Do you know what the emergency evacuation plan for a blue site is?"

Ellie blinks in surprise. "No. I don't."

"That's because there isn't one," Nakamura snaps. "If a blue site loses control of its inmates or suffers a major security breach, the hab is programmed to vent internal air until it's heavier than the Venusian atmosphere."

A chill flashes down Ellie's spine. "You're going to let all those people die."

"The blue site's navigation system has obviously been compromised," Nakamura continues. "Our standing orders are very clear. The only way to make sure *more* people *don't* die is to protect Sunstone."

"I'm telling you, the self-destruct is a diversion! Prisoners are escaping. They've got drones in the clouds, remote-control cargo skiffs, they're using those to move people out of the blue site. One of them almost crashed into us a while ago!"

"Shit." Nakamura says something Ellie can't quite make out, probably talking to someone else in her control room. "Okay, captain's scrambling our birds now. Blue Squadron's coming in hot. Stay out of their way."

"I'll do my best. I still need to extract our operative."

"Yeah, I'm aware," Nakamura pauses. "Lieutenant Leng says she'll watch your six."

It takes Ellie a moment to remember the *Tacoma* officer who helped her complete the preflight inspection for this bluejay. "Lieutenant Kahara Leng?"

"Affirmative. She's Blue Leader. Don't piss her off and you'll be fine."

Ellie feels a tingle of both excitement and fear. "Copy that."

Shimura turns to look at Ellie. "Hey, are you okay? You look a little—"

"Hey, Badger, how about you do me a favor and keep an eye on the radar there?" Ellie says, hoping her voice doesn't betray the trembling she feels through her entire body. "And strap in to your seat. I'm going to do some flying now."

"Haven't you been flying all this time?"

"Oh, honey." Ellie starts switching all her instruments over to manual control. "That was just driving around. Now we're going to have some fun."

———

Ellie is a good pilot. She knows that. She didn't need to log as many flight hours as she did when she signed up with US-OSS as a corp of engineers candidate, but she figured it might be her only chance to get that kind of advanced spaceflight training. And it was a blast.

Now, though, following *Tacoma*'s Blue Squadron into the crowded clouds around Cerulean and Sunstone, Ellie understands that she is a talented amateur at best.

She managed to stay out of the Independence War with Mars. She's glad that she never flew in combat, never served in a war zone. It means she never had to witness all that death and destruction up close. It also means that this is the first time she's seeing real-life dogfighting up close, and as terrifying as it is to be in the thick of aerial combat, it's also undeniably thrilling.

As Ellie twists her bluejay into another spiraling dive away from one of the robo-skiffs, making space for Blue Four to strafe its coilguns across the width of the triangular craft, she feels her stomach lurch and finds it oddly reassuring.

"Who's left, Badger?" she asks Shimura, who's working the radar panel on his side of the cockpit.

"Coming up at ten o'clock low," Shimura says. He's actually not bad when he's got a job to do.

"Blue Leader, what do you think? Missile?" Ellie has her own radar overlay on the HUD, and she's still seeing a big traffic jam on the far side of Sunstone. They need to keep that evacuation path clear while *Tacoma* does what she can to push Cerulean away.

"Aye," Lieutenant Leng replies in her lilting yet raspy voice. "Blue Two, take care of that tango, I'll escort Marmosa back around Sunstone."

"Copy that," Blue Two replies.

Ellie isn't prepared for the explosion that follows a split second later, as she's banking her bluejay to the right, back toward the resort hab. It's close enough to rattle the bluejay cockpit. "Fuck me!" She grips her control stick tight.

"Splash tango foxtrot," Blue Two says, sounding almost nonchalant.

"Incoming!" Shimura shouts.

Ellie sees it too. She rolls the bluejay over to avoid colliding with the skiff that shot up out of the clouds below them. Shimura gurgles as they turn upside down, and Ellie catches a glimpse of Blue Leader chasing down the skiff as she rights the bluejay and resumes course for Sunstone.

"Splash tango mike," Blue Leader calls out. "You good, Marmosa?"

"Five by five," Ellie replies without thinking.

"How many of these buggers do they have hiding down there?"

"Too many. Just keep swatting them, please and thank you."

Blue Leader chuckles. "Happy to be here."

Ellie looks over at Shimura. "You good, Badger?"

Shimura gives her an annoyed look. "Be nice to get out of this spacesuit someday."

The radio lights up on a frequency Ellie doesn't recognize. "New contact?"

"It's an agency handshake," Shimura says.

Then Ellie hears a familiar voice.

"Marmosa! Do you read?"

CHAPTER
THIRTY-SIX

Venus—stuck in the unfriendly skies
Time is never on my side

I have no idea who Elba was referring to when he said "the aunties," but we'll have to deal with that later. Assuming we don't die right now.

My eyes are squeezed shut, but I can feel the Venusian atmosphere burning my ears and nostrils. We don't have much time. I grab Oliver first, make sure we're together, and link my arm through his. The nanobots have had time to eat through his cuffs. That's the good news.

I think of an orange firefighter's hat and pull an emergency survival kit out of the pocket. There's no time for finesse, since Elba's cargo drone could fire up its main engines to escape velocity at any second.

Supplies go flying everywhere as I rip open the kit and grab only what I need. Two breather masks, one for Oliver, one for me. At least we won't suffocate now. And hey, Jessica can treat our acid burns when I pull her out of the pocket. Go team.

The breather masks also have built-in radios, tuned to the same emergency band. "You okay?" I ask Oliver.

"I'll live," he says. "Jetpack. Red balloon."

Good old Oliver. I would have needed to look up my inventory list in my eye to get the right reference object, wasting precious seconds, but of course he remembers every damn detail. If I had to choose someone to get blown around in corrosive, howling winds with, it would definitely be Oliver. Though I hope I never have to actually make that choice. This sucks right now.

I open the pocket and pull out the jetpack that Oliver makes me carry for every mission. He helps me strap on the backpack, then we both turn around so my front is pressed against his back, like we're doing a tandem skydive. Which we sort of are, I guess. I close the safety harness around both of us as Oliver works the jetpack controls— he's a better pilot than I am anyway, and I need to concentrate on this next part.

I blink my eye over to range-finding mode, doing my best to ignore all the radio messages that are still being transcribed and displayed in my eye. I should really just turn them off, but I can't abide the thought of being disconnected from all that activity. Even if there's nothing I can do about it. I still need to know.

"Ready!" Oliver calls out.

I step off the ledge, and we fall into the clouds, spinning for a few seconds until Oliver gets attitude control from the jetpack. I clutch him tight against me as he propels us forward, in a wavy path toward the drone.

"You sure that's the right one?" I ask him. There are, after all, twelve identical ships all around us, their matte gray hulls fading into the orange-brown clouds. Their transponders have been disabled. Bad for navigational safety, but good if you want to escape undetected from a floating prison.

"You can verify," Oliver says. "Scan for the nanobots."

I probably would have thought of that myself, sooner or later, but it is really nice to have Oliver here to help out. I blink my eye back to spectroscope mode and see the now-familiar green glow of the nanobots eating their way through anything technological, barely visible through the tiny porthole on the back of Elba's drone. "Verified! Fifty meters out. Need to get closer."

"Moving," Oliver says, and I feel the jetpack push against my back, transitively pushing my groin against Oliver's buttocks. Neither of us is going to mention how awkward this is. Bigger fish to fry and all that.

"Forty meters," I say. "What's the farthest we've done in the lab?"

"Thirty-one," Oliver says without missing a beat. "But that was a much smaller portal. This one needs to be at least five meters across. Are their engines spun up yet?"

I add a heat map to my eye. "They're close. Thirty-five meters. I need to try it. Level out?"

"Doing my best."

We're still bobbing and weaving a lot. This little jetpack wasn't designed for two people, and the vectors must be all off from what Oliver's used to piloting. Not to mention all the buffeting wind. At least we're still going in the same direction as the drone.

"Thirty," I say. "I'm going to try it now. Give me a pointer?"

Oliver barely hesitates before saying, "Black swan."

I picture a long-necked black bird with an orange beak and open the pocket directly in front of the cargo drone.

The drone doesn't have forward windows—it's designed for cargo, not passengers. So there's no way Elba and his cronies can see the giant black hole ringed with glowing white light that appears directly in front of their getaway vehicle. Oliver's flying us slightly above the drone, so we won't get caught in the engine blast, so the portal is at a slight angle below the drone's nose. That's going to make getting it back out again interesting, but I'm sure Oliver will be able to calculate all the right angles from my mission recording later.

One thing at a time, Kangaroo.

"Are we good?" I ask.

"Looking good," Oliver replies.

We've been rushing to this point, but now it feels like forever before the drone starts its engines. I catch motion out of the corner of my eye, but I can't turn my head—the portal will move with it.

"The other drones are leaving," Oliver says. "Hold the portal."

"Holding," I say. I'm starting to feel those very specific sensations inside my skull that tell me I'm starting to overexert myself by holding the pocket open too long.

Finally, after interminable seconds, Elba's drone fires its ascent engines. I feel a wash of heat as the thrusters light up blue-white. My left eye automatically polarizes to block the blinding light, and I squeeze my right eye shut, my neck muscles starting to cramp from holding my head as perfectly still as I can. I'm really glad Oliver is here to work the jetpack thrusters to keep us in position.

The drone shoots forward into the portal. I close the pocket and let out a breath I didn't realize I'd been holding.

"Fuck yeah!" I shout. "Got you, asshole!" I envision a multicolored beach ball and pull out the reinforced rescue bubble, my original exfil plan. Oliver has already stopped the jetpack, so I deploy the bubble around us and gasp loudly once it's inflated and filled with cool, refreshing, nontoxic, breathable air.

It's almost relaxing in here as the rescue bubble slowly rises through the clouds, rocking back and forth as its auto-stabilizers work against the winds. I raise one arm, ignoring the pain as I flatten out my acid-burned fingers. "Okay, I know you don't normally like high fives, EQ, but you gotta give me this one. Teamwork, am I right?"

Oliver doesn't respond.

"Oliver!" I lower my palm and smack the side of his face gently. "Hey, come on, buddy—"

He's unconscious. I switch my eye to medical scan mode and see that his vitals are dropping.

"Shit!" Time to get Jessica out of the pocket.

But of course now I can't pull a portal. Maybe it's stress? Or breathing in too much poisonous Venusian atmosphere, or stupid fucking Rovor again—the one person who could tell me for sure is still trapped inside the pocket. Just great. Plan B, then.

I blink open a radio channel to the *Tacoma*. "*Tacoma*, this is Kangaroo, do you read?" No response. "Come in, *Tacoma*, this is Kangaroo, I have an emergency!"

Nothing. I'm still seeing their actual transmissions, so I know they haven't fallen into the clouds or blown up or anything. Maybe my transmitter isn't working and I'm only receiving? Why didn't I try that earlier, when Oliver might have been able to help me fix it?

Because you were busy conning a psychopath, Kangaroo. Get over it.

I blink over to a different channel. "Marmosa! Do you read?" She should recognize my voice, but . . . "This is Kangaroo!" I'm not sure what else to add. "Help!"

I hear the fast beeping of an encryption handshake, pulsing almost as fast as my heartbeat.

Then I hear my favorite voice in the whole wide world.

"Kangaroo, Marmosa, I'm here!"

There are so many things I want to say to Ellie in this moment, but I start with the most important one: "EQ is unconscious! We're floating in the rescue bubble. Help?"

"Where are you? I need coordinates!"

"Uh—" The bubble has floated to the top of the clouds now and is bobbing, like it's in a sea of fluffy orange cotton balls. But there are no landmarks anywhere. How do I tell Ellie where we are?

"Blue Leader, I've located my friendlies," I hear Ellie saying to someone else. The radio in her cockpit is separate from the agency earpiece she's also wearing to talk to Team Kangaroo.

"I can't contact the *Tacoma*," I say. "Are you still in the vicinity?"

"Their comms might be jammed," Ellie says. "They're still dealing with the drone skiffs attacking Sunstone."

"They couldn't stop the self-destruct?" Oops. I was supposed to do that.

"Not our problem right now," Ellie says. "I need you to activate your distress beacon."

"Oh. Right." I blink and wiggle my fingers until a red triangle appears in my left eye HUD. "It's on."

"Shit. You're on the other side of the planet. How did that happen? Never mind." I hear Ellie hitting controls, and then the whine of her engines spinning up. "Buckle up, Badger!"

"Wait. You've got *Badger* with you? He's not dead?"

"Long story. Tell you later," Ellie grumbles.

I hear groaning next to me. "Oliver! Are you still with us?" I tap my hand gently against his cheek, careful to avoid the most obviously burned spots, and he finally stirs. "Jesus Christ, you scared me."

Oliver makes a low whining noise. "I think I soiled myself."

"Thanks for sharing. Can you move your hands and feet?"

He blinks and wiggles his extremities. "Yes."

"Okay. We're both alive. For now." I bring him up to speed on my brief conversation with Ellie. "Marmosa's coming to us. I'm going to get back on the horn with her."

Oliver nods. "Okay."

I unmute my radio. "Marmosa, Kangaroo. EQ and I are both good now. What's your ETA?"

"I've got your beacon," she says in a tone of voice that is, shall we say, not encouraging. Also she didn't actually answer my question, and that's never a good sign. "Track looks good. Expect loss of signal in eighteen seconds."

"Um, why is that, exactly?" I ask.

"The most direct route to you takes us through some bad weather. Ionization in the cloud bank will probably knock out our comms."

"Uh, so maybe you should go around? Or get out of the clouds?"

"I'm not taking one second longer than I need to get to you. And we can't risk detection by surfacing," Ellie says. "Just sit tight."

"Marmosa, Equipment," Oliver says. "Perhaps consider that your bluejay is not—"

"Yeah, I know we're not rigged for weather! Not a lot of options here. I'll see you on the other side."

"Not the best way you could have phrased that," I point out.

She doesn't respond. I guess that was eighteen seconds.

"I have another request, Kangaroo. While we have some privacy here," Oliver croaks. "Please retrieve my personal item."

"Your what?"

"The stuffed animal. The pony-monkey monster. My brother. Robbie."

Sure. It's a stressful situation, Oliver needs some comfort, I get it. Still a bit weird. "So you named the stuffed animal after your brother?"

"My brother's ashes are inside."

I stare at Oliver. "WHAT?"

CHAPTER
THIRTY-SEVEN

Venus—still in the toxic atmosphere
Sure, we've got a few minutes to talk about death and dying

"Please, Kangaroo," Oliver says. "I don't know what reference object you used to tag this pocket location. I'd like to spread Robbie's ashes here and now."

There's really nothing I can say to that. I think of a plastic lab rat, open the pocket, and pull out a freezing cold half-pony, half-monkey stuffed animal.

I close the portal and slide the stuffie over to Oliver. "Thank you." He takes the stuffie in both hands and tears it in half along one seam, revealing a small ceramic cylinder. I watch him struggle to unscrew the top of the cylinder and briefly consider offering to help, but this seems like something I should let him do for himself.

He gets it open and stares down into the neck of the container for a moment, his eyes wet and dark.

"Robbie killed himself," Oliver says. "Not quite a year before I met you."

He reaches into the cylinder and pulls out a clear plastic bag of gray dust.

"I'm sorry for your loss," I say.

"It wasn't my fault." Oliver turns the bag over in both hands, deforming the mass of ashes into various bulgey shapes. "I know that now. But even after I got over the guilt, I still felt . . . bad. About not having done more for him."

"You couldn't have stopped it." I've had more encounters with suicidal people than I ever cared to, starting when I was a young orphan in a group home. "It's never about you. And you're not responsible for whatever Robbie had to go through."

"He always wanted to go to space." Tears stream down Oliver's cheeks, and even though the salt must be making his burns hurt like a motherfucker, he doesn't react. "I thought putting him in the pocket would be close enough."

I could have told him that it wouldn't be. But I think I understand what's happening now.

"Now he's on Venus," I say. "Your brother got to visit a whole different planet. And he gets to stay here."

Oliver nods. "We'll need to open the feeder port."

He directs me to a small round tube built into the lower portion of the rescue bubble, kind of like a tiny airlock. Because these bubbles can also be used as short-term quarantine, there needs to be a way to pass food and water in, and also get blood or tissue samples out.

All the port controls are manual, so I have to hold the inner door open while Oliver pours Robbie's ashes into the tube. I'm a little surprised that they all fit at once. Then I close the doors and move back. Oliver sits in front of the port for nearly half a minute, mumbling to himself. I can't quite make out what he's saying, and I don't try.

Then Oliver puts both hands on the port controls and opens the outer door. Robbie's ashes burst forth, get caught in the howling winds whirling all around us, and return to the universe that they came from.

I don't know what I can say to Oliver in this moment, so I just reach out a hand and grab his arm. He clutches me in return and starts weeping loudly. I can feel his body shaking, even on top of the continued cloud turbulence.

And I have time to think about another kind of dust that we've been dealing with: Rovor, the insane nano-borgs developed by the wackadoodle Cerulean designers and supercharged by Quinnock Lacomber's mad science.

I was supposed to get back to the Green Dome to shut off the hab's self-destruct, but I got sidetracked by not wanting Elba to escape or to kill thousands of innocent civilians. We took care of Elba, but we've still got two habs to rescue.

We can save everyone. More than that, we need to know who escaped, and hold the people who've been running amok on Cerulean accountable for their actions. This can't be the end of it.

Oliver's done crying now, and seems to be reset to his normal deadpan personality. I hope he can find some peace now. Or at least start to.

My radio buzzes. I don't recognize the incoming frequency, but there aren't many people who could be calling me right now. "Kangaroo here, your one-stop shop for pocket needs large and small, over."

Oliver frowns at me during the ensuing silence. Ellie would have gotten that joke. Maybe I need to work on my timing.

"Kangaroo, this is *Tacoma*, please confirm signal, over."

"*Tacoma*, Kangaroo, reading you four by four. What's the scoop, troops? Over."

"I'm concerned you may have suffered some brain damage," Oliver says to me. I shush him with a grimace.

"Kangaroo, *Tacoma*, we have comms from blue site and are patching you through. Wait one, over."

"Who the what now?" Oliver smacks the side of my head. "Ow! What the fuck!"

"Go secure," he hisses at me. "*Tacoma*'s not read in for whoever's contacting you from that blue site."

I grumble as I blink and wiggle my fingers to switch my comms to an isolated channel that *Tacoma* won't hear once they hand off the signal. The radio buzzes with static for a moment. Then I hear a voice that I never expected to hear again.

"Hello, Number Eleven."

"Number Sixteen?" I should probably call him by his actual name, but that just feels weird at this point. "We're still working on the self-destruct issue. Just—"

"Never mind that," Lacomber says. "I've had some time to think, since it seemed as if you had abandoned us. But I am glad you're still here, so I can say good-bye."

"I got sidetracked, but we're coming back—"

"You needn't bother. I used my Hope and Anchor to execute one final override on what remains of Rovor here. All of Cerulean City's docking ports and airlocks are sealed shut. We'll meet our fate as it comes."

"What? No! Where are Two and Twenty-Three? You don't get to fucking decide—"

"I've locked them out of this control room. I'm not your man. And I'm not their man. As I told you and the others earlier. I was never in this for anyone but myself. That's always been the problem, I suppose."

Did this idiot call me just so he could perform a dramatic monologue? "Look, old bean or whatever, I get that you're seeking redemption for your sins, but this is a meaningless gesture. You can still do good things with your research. The agency has other blue sites, other safely isolated lab facilities in the asteroid belt—"

"I'm sending you all my research from the Rovor project," Sixteen says. In my left eye HUD, I see a whole slew of encrypted data packets arriving over the carrier frequency and getting autosaved to my shoulder-phone's internal memory. "Numbers Two and Twenty-Three added their data, and I believe my personal notes will be able to shed additional light on how the nano-borg technology can be safely deployed in the future."

"Hmm," Oliver says. "That's a new one. 'Nano-borgs.' I'm not sure I like it."

I shush him with a glare. "Sixteen. You're not thinking rationally about this. You've been breathing in that Rovor shit for years, who knows what it's done to your brain. Come back with us, we can figure out a way—"

"You're absolutely right, Eleven. I'm compromised, and probably in myriad ways of which I'm not even aware. That's the problem, isn't it, fundamentally? The agency didn't confine us here in the village to punish us. They locked us away because they simply didn't know where we belonged anymore, after the singularly devastating things that each of us had experienced or witnessed or caused. They couldn't leave us in the world, so they built us a new world. And they tried to mold it—and us—to their purposes."

"Okay, this is all very interesting, and we can discuss it at length back on—"

"But they failed, Eleven. They failed because a world can only be as good as the people who are in it. And all of us in the village were at worst villains, at best scoundrels, and every one of us lacking in empathy. I was always willing to sacrifice others before even considering giving up any modicum of my own comfort."

This is ridiculous. There are still other people on that hab, and even if they're hardened criminals, they don't deserve to die this way. "I forgive you. Is that what you want to hear? You're not a lost cause."

"That's quite kind of you to say, Eleven. But I've had more than my share of second chances. I'm glad you're the one carrying the burden now."

Oh no you don't, asshole. You don't get to pawn this off on the rest of us. Not this time. Not again. And you don't get to decide for everyone else over there.

I mute Lacomber and look over at Oliver. "I don't suppose there's any way you could run a remote override on the self-destruct?"

He squints while thinking about it. "You said you left an emergency comms unit attached to the outside of the hab ring?"

"Yeah. With a red key still plugged in."

"Perfect. I need a control tablet. Reference object, Atari joystick."

I am constantly amazed at the random information Oliver can memorize. I open the pocket and retrieve a ruggedized computer tablet for him. He fastens the safety strap around his torso and starts working.

While he does that, I keep sight of Cerulean through my eye and think about how we're going to extract everyone. There's no point in saying anything until Ellie picks us up, but Lacomber doesn't get to kill anyone. Not today, Satan.

CHAPTER
THIRTY-EIGHT

Venus—above the clouds
Mere minutes after I learned to appreciate life anew

"Tallyho!" I hear Ellie say over the radio. "Look to your nine o'clock. Or your three o'clock. I can't tell which of you is which."

I turn to my left, dial my eye's magnification up to maximum, and see the speck on the horizon expand into the beautiful sight of a battle-scarred bluejay headed straight for us. I spend the next few seconds, as Ellie circles our position to line up the bluejay airlock with the rescue bubble's auto-docking collar, deciding whether I should kiss her immediately or exercise some measure of restraint.

It turns out to be a moot point, because she throws herself at me as soon as I'm out of the airlock inside the bluejay with my helmet off.

"Missed you," she says after our thirsty lip-lock.

"Missed you more," I say, taking her face in both hands.

"Hey," says another voice behind her, "are you . . . Kangaroo?"

Ellie steps aside, and I see a dark-haired man sitting on the bench in the cabin, holding a medkit and gaping at me. It's weird to be a minor celebrity in certain specific circles.

"Badger?" I step forward and hold out my hand. "Glad to see you're not dead."

He shakes my hand with a smile that fades quickly. "Oh, wow. You're suffering from severe exposure. We need to get you and your friend into treatment right away." He snaps open the medkit while Ellie helps Oliver sit down on the bench behind us.

"I've got one more incoming," I say, and open the pocket to let Jessica out. Fortunately, it's been long enough since my last portal that it works this time.

She falls out of the black hole and lands on her back on the bluejay deck. She pulls off her commando helmet and stares daggers at me. "Never do that shit to me ever again."

"You're welcome for saving your life, and I can't promise anything." I try to distract her by quickly describing how we're going to rescue Quinnock Lacomber and the others from Cerulean City. It works.

"What," Jessica croaks beneath a fiery glare after I'm done talking, "the fuck. Are you serious right now?"

Oliver maneuvers the straw of a beverage bulb into her mouth and encourages her to drink some more water. "I did manage to override the self-destruct. But something has damaged the habitat dome—possibly drone skiffs crashing into it while harassing *Tacoma*'s raptors —and it is leaking air. We have less than eight minutes before Cerulean is no longer buoyant."

"So we go with my plan," I say. "It's the fastest way to get everyone out of there."

"Have you ever done this before?" Ellie asks me.

"Sure."

"Successfully?"

"Yeah."

"*Not* in an experiment at Science Division?"

I can't lie to her. "I can do this. We need to do this."

"Why, exactly?" Shimura asks. "You said he sent you all his data. And we still have samples of Rovor to study, obviously." He taps the side of his head.

"That's not the point," I reply, still looking at Ellie. She's the one I need to convince here. "We were sent here to bring people back alive."

"We've got both of those people. You and Badger."

"We didn't know what was going on inside Cerulean," I say. "We didn't know Quinnock fucking Lacomber was inside. You think Lasher wouldn't want us to extract him?" I turn to Jessica, whose expression has turned contemplative. "Don't you have a lot of fucking questions you'd like to ask him, Surge?"

Jessica avoids my gaze and clenches her jaw before speaking. "It's too risky."

"I agree with Surgical," Oliver says. "The risk-benefit calculation—"

"This isn't a democracy," Ellie snaps. "We're not voting here. I know what the upside is. But the downside is we might all die. You're asking me to risk everyone aboard this bluejay to go save a bunch of criminals."

"Oh, I'm sorry," I say. "I thought you were a good pilot."

Her face twitches, and I know I've got her. "I'm the *only* pilot here. We don't have a backup plan if we run out of time or I suddenly lose my memory or anything."

"Oh, that won't happen," Shimura chimes in. "We're right on top of the Rovor control signal."

Oliver blinks and leans forward. "What's this, now?"

"*Later*," Ellie says emphatically. She squints at me. "Is your mission recorder back online?"

"You're on candid camera," I say.

She rolls her eyes. "I'll assume that's a yes. So this entire conversation has been on the record, and I'm just going to clarify, for the record, that Kangaroo assumes full responsibility for this imminent operational variation."

Jessica mutters something that I'm pretty sure is a curse in Mandarin. Oliver and Shimura both sit down and buckle their safety restraints.

Ellie points at Jessica. "Get Surgical secured back here. Then join me up in the cockpit."

"Aye, aye, captain," I say.

"That's not—never mind."

While Ellie goes forward, I move Jessica into the seat next to Oliver and strap her in. When I turn back around, Shimura is staring at me with dinner-plate eyes.

"Is this really going to work?" he asks me.

I shrug. "It will or it won't. EQ, you're doing the math?"

Oliver's already hunched over his tablet. I head into the cockpit and close the door so Ellie and I won't be distracted by Shimura's chattering.

My left eye overlay starts lighting up with range-finding markers before I've finished strapping myself into the co-pilot seat beside Ellie. Oliver works fast, as always.

"You thought I was a good pilot," Ellie grumbles, giving me a sideways glance. "Fucker."

I bare my teeth in a flat grimace. "It worked, didn't it?"

"Listen." Ellie turns the bluejay, heading for Cerulean. "I sincerely hope we don't die in the next few minutes, but just in case we do—"

"Jeez, Wally, don't jinx it or nothin'."

"Just shut up for a second, okay?" She turns her head to raise her eyebrows at me, then turns back to face forward after I give her an apologetic nod. "I know we've got issues. But we—you and I—it just . . ."

She trails off. I give her some space to formulate her thoughts. After a few seconds, I open my mouth to attempt to say something non-jokey, but am interrupted by a large object crashing into the side of the bluejay.

"What the fuck was that?" I shout, grabbing at my console and leaning forward just in time for my eye to paint distance targets on a receding black triangle.

"Shit. Those skiffs are still harassing both habs. And us, since we're so close." Ellie checks her controls. "Stupid robots. We're okay. No breaches."

"Are you sure? 'Cause if there's even a crack—"

"Blue Leader, this is Marmosa, are you still engaged?" Ellie says to her radio.

A husky female voice buzzes from the overhead speaker. "Marmosa, Blue Leader, we've been mopping up so there's a clear ascent path out of the resort hab to evacuate civilians. Looks like you're headed back into the soup for some reason?"

"Yeah, funny story, we left something important inside that blue site and we can't leave Venus without it," Ellie says with an incongruously casual tone. "Should just take a few minutes. Can you spare any raptors to run interference for us?"

"Anything for a fellow Wrexham supporter," Blue Leader says. "I'm sending Blue Four and Blue Seven to escort you."

"Much obliged. I won't keep them long."

"See you at the pub. You're buying."

"Fair enough."

"Blue Leader out."

I cock my head at Ellie. "She seems nice. Should I be jealous?"

"Okay, this is what I was trying to say." Ellie reaches an arm across the center console, and I take her hand. I'm surprised at the tears that well up as soon as I feel her touch. "I'm glad I met you. I'm glad we're together. But it all happened so fast, and we just don't have normal lives. I'm happy for the time we've been able to share, and if we make it out of this—I want us to work on our relationship. I mean really work on it."

"Just so I'm clear on this," I say, "you're enticing me to stay alive with the promise of prolonged couples counseling in our future?"

She smiles at me. "You're a fucking idiot and I love you."

I squeeze her hand. "Challenge accepted."

The radio buzzes again. "Marmosa, this is Blue Four, forming up on your ten o'clock, and Blue Seven is coming up at your two o'clock. Here to plow the road."

Ellie releases my hand to tap the radio controls. "Very happy to see you, Blue Four, Blue Seven. Tying you in to my navigation now."

While she works her console, I look out the window and wave to our two escorts, who salute back from the cockpit bubbles of their sleek-looking fighters. The raptors aren't rated for cloud-diving, but they can shoot things down, and that's very helpful right now.

I blink my eye into heat-sensing mode and focus on Cerulean, which is big enough now to fill our entire forward view.

The hab is listing now, and its left side is just touching the top of the clouds. At least five different cracks are leaking white smoke. I work my implanted fingertip controls to filter out ambient heat sources— basically anything that isn't human-sized and radiating at human body temperature. It's easy enough to locate Lacomber that way, but of course there's bad news.

"He's below the line," I tell Ellie, mirroring my eye-sensor output to the bluejay's windscreen HUD. "You're sure that impact didn't do any damage?"

"I didn't say that." Ellie banks us downward as our escorts blast two more skiffs out of the sky, turning the large dark triangles into bursts of black particles that get immediately swept away by the high winds. "I said there were no breaches. We'll be fine. This will only take a minute, right?"

"Right." I see Lacomber's heat signature changing. "Wait. He's— moving? What?"

"Looks like he's going up into the dome," Ellie says. "Taking one last look around?"

"Shit."

"How close do you need to be?"

"Farthest I've ever done was fifty meters." I don't know why everything has to be sports-related, but someone at Science Division decided it would be useful to measure my pocket performance in terms of a regulation football pitch. I was able to stand at midfield and open the pocket inside one of the goals. "The hab dome's deeper than that, isn't it?"

"By quite a bit." Ellie bites her lip. "We could ask our Blue friends to crack the dome wide open, but with the winds out there—"

"Four hundred and ten kph right now," I read off the weather display.

"I'd rather not chase a rag doll into the clouds. Or risk us getting caught in a sudden gust, not to mention exposing him to Venmo."

"Venmo?"

"Venus atmosphere. Sorry, Badger was rubbing off on me."

"Should I be jealous?"

Ellie frowns. "Focus, Kay. How do we get you close enough to make this work?"

I find the cabin intercom controls and push the talk button. "Hey! Badger, can you hear me?"

"Yes?" Shimura's voice comes back through the cockpit speakers. "Should I come up there with you?"

"No, I just need to know about Cerulean's layout. When Lacomber was talking to us earlier, where would he have been transmitting from?"

"There's a radio room below the line," Shimura says, and describes where it is.

"Is that within fifty meters of the exterior wall?"

"I think so?"

I get him to tell me exactly how someone would get there from the village up in the main hab area. Then I get Oliver to tie my shoulder-phone in to every available receiver inside Cerulean City.

"This is Number Eleven calling Number Sixteen!" I say, hoping Lacomber hasn't already committed suicide or anything. His heat signature appears to be up in the bell tower now—a great vantage point for watching the hab fall apart—so he should be right next to a loudspeaker. "We need you to retransmit your Rovor data! Your previous transmission was corrupted! Please return to the radio room for further instructions!"

Oliver sets a recording of that on an endless loop while Ellie maneuvers the bluejay down to hover outside the radio room. This puts us deep into the sickly orange clouds, and our escorts circle out to patrol for any incoming skiffs. I swear I can hear creaking above the whine of the wind outside.

"He's moving," I report when Lacomber's heat signature starts descending from the bell tower.

"Shall I stop broadcasting?" Oliver asks over the intercom.

"No! We don't want him to know that we know where he is."

"Approaching position," Ellie calls out as the side of the hab fills our window. "These winds are picking up. I don't want to get too close and risk a sudden wind shear smacking us into the hab."

"Almost there."

Something creaks, then audibly cracks right above my head. I look around wildly, then turn to Ellie. "Are we sure that's not a problem?"

"Just some debris from the hab," she says, staying focused on her controls. "Relax and talk to your friend."

"Wouldn't call him my friend."

"Well, don't tell *him* that."

The radio beeps, and I answer it. "Number Sixteen?"

"At your service, Number Eleven," Lacomber replies, sounding very tired. I hear my own recorded voice echoing in the background and wow, is that really what I sound like? Distracting. "Shall we try this again?"

"Need you to make a few adjustments first," I say, wiggling my fingers to send a text message to Oliver. "To make sure nothing goes wrong this time. Can you see the instructions on the screen in front of you?"

"Yes." This is all busywork. Now that we know he's in the radio room, Oliver's excessively complicated directions should distract Lacomber long enough for me to do what we came here for. "Just a moment while I make these adjustments."

"Great." I double-check the range-finding overlays in my eye to make sure we're lined up. "Hey, can I ask you one last question? Since you're about to die and I'll never have the chance again."

"Yes. What would you like to know?"

"What was up with all the British accents?" I ask. I ignore Ellie giving me the eye and mouthing some words at me, words that might be *Seriously just do the thing*. "I even started talking funny at some point, and I don't do accents."

Lacomber actually chuckles. "A side effect. An unintended consequence. I honestly don't know why, except maybe it carried some cultural valence."

"Um, you're going to have to explain what that means."

"An ancient television programme. Are you familiar with twentieth-century entertainment media?"

Is this guy serious? "Nothing like this was ever on American television. I would know."

"Who said anything about America? It was a British concoction. A mid-century response to popular espionage fictions. A meditation on power, and control, and individuality, among other things."

"Sure, great, fascinating—"

"But we were never fully in control," Lacomber continues. "Of anyone or anything. Yes, we were able to affect people with Rovor, make them more susceptible to suggestion, even control certain mental and bodily functions, but there were always—peculiarities. Things we couldn't account for. Things we didn't understand."

I start to say something, but the targeting overlay in my eye goes green.

"Rovor was supposed to loosen people's tongues, but instead it was more likely to keep them from speaking certain things. We still don't know why." He exhales heavily. "I suppose I should have learnt my lesson, after the Fruitless Year."

"Yeah." I open the pocket behind Lacomber, filling the height of the room, with no barrier, and watch his heat signature tumble backward into the freezing vacuum. "You really should have. Be seeing you."

I close the pocket and turn to Ellie. "That guy talks too much. Let's go retrieve the rest of our villagers."

CHAPTER
THIRTY-NINE

Venus—Rainforest Preserve Habitat
No time like the present

"You've got some real balls, Kangaroo." Jessica looms over me, hands on her hips.

I look down at my crotch. "Are my swim trunks too revealing?"

"And what the hell is that thing?" She points at the jaguar maquette sitting on the low table next to me, a souvenir that I just purchased. It's not the greatest, but I didn't have a lot of good options.

"It's for Joey. He likes cats."

Jessica grumbles. On my left, Oliver groans—we're obviously disturbing his nap. On my right, Ellie makes an amused humming noise. Possibly remembering what we got up to last night in our hotel room.

We're all in the main pool area of the Rainforest Preserve Habitat, where we decamped after delivering Quinnock Lacomber into Commander Nakamura's loving care. I did have to pull him out of the pocket in the bluejay, since it was going to take a little while for us to rendezvous with the *Tacoma*, and I daresay Jessica was more than happy to render him unconscious with a sedative slug. She also wasn't too gentle while sealing him into a spacesuit, using it as a temporary quarantine. Lacomber's almost certainly got Rovor embedded in every nook and cranny of his body, and we don't want to witness any more "unintended consequences" if we can help it.

Jessica did extract some of my nanobots, after confirming that they had eliminated any trace of Rovor from my body, and reprogrammed them for injecting into the rest of our party. Nobody seemed to think it suspicious that she knew exactly how to do that. If there's a silver lining to all this nanotech fuckery, it's that the government might be motivated to move faster on clinical trials for the technology to be used for good, more widely and publicly.

Meanwhile, the OSS hospital ship *Karikó Katalin* arrived in orbit to take everyone from Elba's cargo drone into quarantine, where they could then deploy Jessica's anti-Rovor to decontaminate all those fuckers. I would have loved to see Elba's face as he realized he was losing control over his goopy white monster and being reduced to just another prisoner. They're also caring for the civilian hostages from Sunstone, who need to be processed by Intel Division before they can go home.

Other OSS ships are going after the many freighters with cargo containers from Venus, searching that haystack for the remaining eleven drones, to retrieve those prisoners and collaborators. Cleaning up all that will take some time—after getting disinfected, the prisoners will get delivered back to other blue sites on Venus—but at least my team doesn't have to do it. We've had a pretty rough time. We've earned a rest.

Martin Shimura stayed aboard the *Tacoma,* presumably to keep an eye on Number Two and Doctor Twenty-Three and the other jailers. Maybe he also missed living within the structure of a military vessel, after being stuck for months inside a bizarre mind-control prison-experiment village. There's a clear chain of command, he knows what's supposed to happen and what the consequences are for stepping out of line. Plus, no weird gooey monsters hiding behind corners waiting to encase you and ooze into your brain.

I'm certainly not going to miss Rovor either. That is going to be a big, big problem for all of us, but not until we get back to Earth and Science Division can go hammer and tongs on Lacomber's files. I wonder if some high-ranking officer with a grudge is going to demand the unique privilege of interrogating him directly.

I was definitely enjoying this more-or-less-actual vacation until Jessica decided she'd had enough of moping in her room and wanted to take in some of this singular Venusian sunshine with the rest of us.

I have to say, I only have eyes for Ellie, but I can appreciate how many heads are turning as Jessica looms over me in her own swimsuit.

"You *are* wearing sunscreen, right?" Jessica asks. "How long have you been lying out here?"

I shrug. This lounge chair is mighty comfortable, and the poolside drink service is very attentive. Especially given that I have a high-limit black credit card saved in the pocket for occasions just like these.

"Don't the *you-know-whats* take care of fixing all that skin cancer before it starts?" I ask.

"Shut up," Jessica snaps. "Lasher is going to have your hide for this."

"Well, there's more than one way to skin a Kangaroo."

Ellie sits up in her lounge chair. "As much fun as this banter is, I think it's time for lunch. Anyone else?"

"Doctor Chu?" a new voice says from near the pool. "Doctor Jessica Chu?" It's a Rainforest staff member holding an envelope.

"Right here." Jessica waves at the staffer.

"We're not using legends anymore?" I mutter at her.

"We're on vacation."

"Could have fooled me, with all the shop talk."

The staffer ambles over and hands the envelope to Jessica. She uses her wristband—Rainforest's combination room key and account-management device—to scan the staffer's name tag and give them a gratuity.

"Thank you very much, Doctor," the staffer says, clearly delighted by Jessica's overtipping. "Please enjoy the rest of your day." They walk off with a goofy smile on their face.

"Well, we're going to lunch," I say, taking Ellie's hand. "Neither of you are invited."

"Don't be a jerk," Ellie laughs.

"I'm just communicating clearly." I slip an arm around her waist. "Room service?"

"Stop."

It takes me a second to realize that it wasn't Ellie teasing me back; it was Jessica saying that word. I stop walking and turn back toward her. She's opened the envelope and is looking at the note inside. The card appears to have a string of random letters and numbers printed on it, but I'm sure it's some kind of encryption. The really unsettling thing is how Jessica can decipher it in her head, without even using scratch paper.

Oliver has also stood up at this point and is frowning at the paper. "What's wrong?"

Jessica looks directly at me. "We need to leave. Now. Go get packed, I'll charter us the next available flight back to Earth."

She's freaking me out a little. "Why?"

Her eyes are deep and dark. "Something's wrong with Joey."

A B C D E F G H I J K L M N O P Q R S T U V W X Y Z

⇕ ⇕

Q R S T U V W X Y Z A B C D E F G H I J K L M N O P

ACKNOWLEDGMENTS

This novel has been seven years in the making, and it was only possible because of the many people who encouraged me to continue this series and helped me figure out how to do that:

First and foremost, my amazing wife, DeeAnn Sole, who has stuck with me through more than two decades of all kinds of random bullshit and never stopped loving me, helping me, and pushing me to do better all the time, even when I wasn't sure I wanted to.

I owe no debt to Erin Wilcox, Lauren Hougen, or Skyla Dawn Cameron, because I have paid them all fairly for professional services rendered. If you're an indie author looking for a developmental editor, copy editor/proofreader, or cover art designer, respectively, I highly recommend all three of them.

Thanks to Lilith Saintcrow and Kate Ristau for their continued support of all my writing, publishing, and community building activities. It's not an easy life that we've chosen, friends, but I'm glad we're in it together.

My gratitude to editor Bryan Thomas Schmidt, who originally solicited the following Kangaroo prequel short story "Fire in the Pocket" for the space opera anthology *Infinite Stars: Dark Frontiers* (2019), and who also invited me to contribute a short story for *Aliens vs. Predators: Ultimate Prey* (2022). By the way, that latter story, "Better Luck to Borrow," is why Kangaroo uses a saw blade when he's below the line inside Cerulean. #IYKYK

Finally, thank YOU, reader, for sticking with me. We're not nearly done yet, so buckle up.

"FIRE IN THE POCKET"

A KANGAROO TALE

The apartment was cold and dark and empty. Oliver almost called out when he closed the door, and had to remind himself that there was nobody waiting for him at home anymore. He wondered how long it would be before the habit faded.

"Welcome home, Doctor Graves," said a gravelly voice.

Oliver yanked open the drawer of the table by the door and reached inside. The pistol was missing. He grabbed the letter opener instead and slapped at the light switch on the wall.

The living room lights came on, revealing a dark-haired man, graying at the temples, wearing a tweed three-piece suit. He sat in Oliver's armchair. His hands were raised next to his shoulders. One hand held Oliver's pistol, slide locked back to show it was not loaded. The other hand held the empty magazine.

"Who the bloody hell are you?" Oliver said. He couldn't decide whether he should advance toward the stranger, or duck into the kitchen and look for a better weapon, or reach for his phone to make an emergency call.

"Just a fellow firearms enthusiast," the stranger said, nodding at the pistol in his right hand. "Tell me, why is a materials engineer with a doctorate in physics so interested in keeping and modifying his own small arms?"

"I like working with my hands," Oliver said.

"You could build ships in bottles."

"I also enjoy loud noises."

"More to the point," the stranger said, squinting at Oliver, "why would you keep the gun that your brother used to kill himself?"

Oliver gripped the letter opener tighter.

"What kind of a person does that?" the stranger asked.

"I want to know who you are and what you're doing in my flat."

"I work for the United States government." The stranger slowly lowered his arms and put the empty pistol and magazine on the coffee table. "And I'm in need of some technical expertise."

"You're a spy," Oliver said.

The stranger's mouth twitched. "Not exactly."

"And I'm not exactly looking for a job."

"You resigned from Bradford Macro-Composites this morning," the stranger said. "It was either that or face a civil lawsuit. You won't receive any severance pay, and more importantly, if you spend too much time alone in this apartment, you will go mad with grief."

Oliver felt the emptiness in the pit of his stomach yawning open. The wall behind the stranger displayed the default screensaver, a vacant beach at sunset overlaid with a clock and calendar. Had it really been only two months since Robbie's death? It felt so much longer. Oliver couldn't summon a memory of the last day he'd felt in the least bit happy.

The stranger was right. An arrogant, presumptuous scofflaw, maybe, but still right.

"What do I call you?" Oliver asked.

"I'm Paul Tarkington," the stranger said.

"And what are you actually offering, Mr. Tarkington?"

Paul smiled.

Half a year later, Oliver sat in a state-of-the-art secure conference room, sipping his morning coffee and waiting for the daily debate to subside.

He could always count on his three lab assistants to have big ideas and bigger egos.

"I've got a new battery design," Karen said, her dark eyes twinkling.

"Here we go again." Raquel shrugged her broad shoulders.

"Shut up." Karen punched Raquel on the arm, then touched her left thumb to one of the data ports in the conference table. The optical storage mesh bonded to the keratin in her thumbnail glowed as the tabletop downloaded her files, and then the wall display lit up with a series of schematics.

"Wait, you're putting the heaters *in the magazine* now?" Philip said incredulously. His mouth hung open beneath his pencil-thin mustache.

"It's the only place we need them," Karen said. "We've gotten rid of lubricants with the new composites, so the mechanisms won't suffer from frost lock. The only thing that still cares about temperature is the chemical propellant inside the cartridges."

"Yeah, and if it gets too hot in there, *kaboom*," Raquel said. "I still say we should revisit my coilgun designs."

"Again with the coilguns!" Karen threw up her hands. "Did you even read the spec?"

"If we're making a weapon for use in outer space, a coilgun is much more practical than this Frankenstein refit."

"You're assuming it's outer space," Karen said. "What if it's Antarctica? Or the inside of a supercooled particle accelerator?"

"Yeah, 'cause you're really going to want firearms in there," Raquel said.

"All right," Oliver said. His coffee was getting cold. "We're not having this argument again. We've already spent five months developing cold-resistant composites for our 'Franken-gun,' and more to the point, our requirements specify that the weapon must use standard NATO ammunition." He nodded at Karen. "Tell us about your new battery."

"Electrostatic nanocapacitors." She touched the table surface, and the display zoomed in on a series of alternating vertical lines. "We store electrical charge directly on the surfaces of two conductors. No chemicals or moving parts. High power, fast recharge."

"And low energy density," Philip said. "I've played with these before. How are you going to generate enough heat for the whole magazine?"

"We don't have to," Karen said. "We just need to keep the chamber and the first round warmed up. The heat from firing that round feeds a thermocouple that recharges the battery and pushes the heat envelope down."

"This gets better and better," Raquel said. "How do you intend to regulate temperature if the operator gets trigger-happy and overloads the capacitors?"

"Way ahead of you." The display changed to a schematic of the pistol itself. "We add flanges just below the breach to vent excess gas—"

"Great! More moving parts!"

"Relax. They're electrically deflected."

"More energy requirements!"

"So what's your bright idea, smarty-pants? And don't say coilgun."

"But your battery would be perfect for—"

Karen slapped a hand over Raquel's mouth. "Since nobody seems to have any better proposals, Oliver, can I get some time on the salad shooter to build this thing?"

Raquel mumbled something unintelligible into Karen's palm.

"What do you think, Philip?" Oliver asked.

"Couldn't hurt," Philip said. "We're not going to know what the output curves look like until we have a prototype. And we need *something* to deal with the temperature issue."

"Very well. I'll get you the fab time, Karen," Oliver said. "Go work up your control files. And take Raquel with you."

"What? Why?"

"She'll be highly motivated to help you construct an efficient battery," Oliver said, "since she'll be able to include it in her coilgun proposal for the Outer Space Service."

Karen sneered at Raquel. "Traitor."

Raquel shrugged. "I seem to have a lot of free time these days."

After they had left, Philip said, "Oliver, I need to talk to you about something."

"You're leaving the project," Oliver said.

Philip looked startled. "How did you know?"

"It only makes sense. We've finished practically all the materials development, and the SALD fab is working perfectly." Philip's design for a single-atomic-layer-deposition 3D printer would revolutionize manufacturing—if the US government ever declassified it. "I appreciate your loyalty in joining me here, Philip, but I always knew you'd leave. God knows this agency can't compete with corporate salaries."

Philip smiled. "Actually, I'm taking a teaching position at University of Maryland."

"Ah. Fame instead of fortune." Oliver nodded. "Thank goodness. I was afraid you might be going back to Bradford."

"I'm pretty sure we both burned all our bridges when we left."

Oliver offered his hand, and Philip shook it. "Good luck. Not that you'll need it."

"Thanks for everything." Philip took a step toward the door, then stopped and turned around. "Sorry, just one more thing. I wasn't sure I should tell you, but I'd feel terrible if you thought I'd been hiding anything from you—"

"Karen and Raquel," Oliver said. "I know. They're leaving too."

Philip frowned. "How did you—? I mean, sure, they've been getting more affectionate in public, but—"

"Karen's been wearing the engagement ring," Oliver said. "Not here at work, but everywhere else. The tan line on her finger is starting to show. And once they're hitched, OSS is going to recall Raquel to duty and deploy both of them to, I would imagine, some manner of deep space research vessel." He shook his head. "God, I hope they decide to elope. I'm not sure I could handle going to their wedding."

Philip chuckled. "You really need to get out more."

He walked out, leaving Oliver alone in the room. All alone. Everyone was leaving him again. Like his parents had left. Like Robbie had.

It took a few minutes for the tightness in Oliver's chest and stomach to go away.

"I need more people," Oliver said.

Paul looked up from the report on his desk. He removed his reading glasses and stared at Oliver with eyes the color of pale blue ice. "No, you don't."

"I'm losing all of my research assistants next week," Oliver said. "Do you expect me to complete this project on my own?"

"Yes," Paul said without hesitation.

Oliver resisted the urge to grab the report off Paul's desk and fling it at the wall. "We've only test-fired the prototype under controlled lab conditions."

"And I'm told it worked very well."

"Something will go wrong in the field," Oliver said. "And when it does, I'll need a team to help me redesign and rebuild the prototype."

Paul shook his head. "I'm afraid we haven't the budget for that."

"The military isn't willing to overspend for a useless weapon? I don't believe it."

"We are not the military," Paul said. "And you've worked for seven months without a result."

"My lab has invented materials that will fundamentally alter spacecraft design principles, and electronic components that can function near absolute zero. Whatever shell corporation the agency has set up is going to make a bloody fortune licensing our technologies throughout the Solar System."

"Yes, and you'll receive a lovely Christmas bonus," Paul said, "but that is not the result I require."

"Are you ever going to tell me what I'm *actually* doing here?" Oliver asked. "All this can't possibly be just to design a handgun that can stored and operated in hard vacuum. What are these components actually going to be used for?"

"I haven't been lying to you, Oliver," Paul said. "The project requirements specified exactly what we need. Now, are you ready to release the prototype for field testing? Or would you like to wait until you alone are held responsible for its performance?"

Oliver gritted his teeth. "I'll have the prototype ready for transport tomorrow morning."

"Good," Paul said, going back to his report. "I'll send the operator to pick it up. His code name is Kangaroo."

"Doctor Oliver Graves?"

The young man standing in Oliver's doorway couldn't have been more than twenty years old. Wide eyes, darker than Karen's, stared out from a boyish face.

He didn't look a thing like Robbie—his brown skin was hereditary, not a suntan, for one—but he had the same youthful, innocent gaze. Oliver couldn't speak for a moment. Then he had to look away before too many memories came flooding back.

"Yes," Oliver said. "May I help you?"

The young man held out a requisition form. His slender fingers were too smooth to be a soldier's. "I'm Kangaroo. I'm here to collect the prototype?"

Oliver took the form. "You're the operator?"

"The one and only," Kangaroo flashed a smile.

"Did Paul assign you that code name?"

The young man looked uncomfortable. "I think he prefers to go by 'Lasher' when we're in the office. But yeah, he picks all our code names. What's yours?"

"I don't have one."

"Oh. You're not Operations? Are you with Science Division?"

"No."

"Are you—"

"I thought you were just here for a pickup."

Kangaroo frowned. "Rude."

Oliver signed the form, handed it back, and unlocked the wall safe behind him to retrieve the prototype. He laid the ceramic carry-case on his desk and opened it for Kangaroo to verify delivery of all the necessary components.

"Why is it green?" Kangaroo asked, holding up the pistol.

Oliver considered making up some story about the new synthetic composites. He also considered telling the truth: that Philip had been amused by the "Franken-gun" nickname and added some green dye to the final fabrication run.

But Oliver didn't really want to get into a long conversation with this boy. He already reminded Oliver too much of his dead brother.

"Does it matter?" Oliver replied.

"I guess not." Kangaroo slapped the empty magazine into the pistol, cocked it, released the slide, sighted down the barrel at the wall, and pulled the trigger. "Good action."

A wave of nausea washed over Oliver. It was almost too much, watching this young man who seemed so much like Robbie: full of impatient energy, wide-eyed and gangling.

But it wasn't Robbie. Kangaroo wasn't playing with the gun like a toy; he had clearly been through some rigorous weapons training. He handled the prototype correctly and carefully, never pointing it toward Oliver, checking the mechanisms one by one in a way that suggested he actually knew what each part did.

Not playing with a toy. Using a tool.

Kangaroo ejected the magazine, put it and the pistol back in the case, and closed the case. "Thanks, Doc. I'll let you know how it goes."

Oliver croaked, "The ammunition. You'll want. Rounds."

"I can get my own," Kangaroo said. "This thing's supposed to work with any standard parabellum ammo, right? Might as well test that first."

Oliver couldn't argue with that. "Watch out for the recoil. We've had some issues with the ceramic spring, and if your cartridge load is too hot, you might find yourself spinning backwards."

Kangaroo frowned. "I don't understand."

"In zero-gravity, I mean. You are planning to do a full field test, aren't you?"

Kangaroo grinned. "I'm not going to be shooting this thing in space, Doc. I'm just storing it there."

Oliver narrowed his eyes. "That doesn't make any sense."

"Sorry." Kangaroo shrugged. "If you're not Outback, that's all I can tell you." He turned, holding the gun and leaving the case on the desk.

"You might not want to walk around this building with a firearm," Oliver said.

"Don't worry," Kangaroo said. "I'll put it in my pocket."

Kangaroo came back a week later and unceremoniously dropped the prototype on Oliver's desk. "It doesn't work."

"Please tell me you haven't been throwing it around like that all week." Oliver avoided looking at Kangaroo's face and inspected the weapon. It seemed to be fine.

"No, I haven't, but it should be shock-safe anyway," Kangaroo said defensively. "The problem is it won't fire. At all."

"What type of ammunition did you try?"

"All of them! I loaded it with every type of parabellum round I could get from the armory, put it into cold storage for an hour each time, and nothing."

"You checked for duds?"

"I'm not going to get twenty duds in a row, am I?" Kangaroo said. "And yeah, I tested all the rounds after warming everything back up to room temperature. Then it worked just fine. I think you've got a heating problem in this prototype."

"All right," Oliver said. "I'll run some tests."

"How long is it going to take to fix?"

Oliver suddenly heard Robbie's voice in his head—*how long do we have to wait here? How far is it to home?*—and he hesitated before answering. "I need to determine what the problem is first."

Kangaroo actually pouted. "Come on, Doc, you gotta help me. Lasher won't let me go into the field without this."

"I don't suppose you'd be willing to tell me exactly what your field conditions are?"

Kangaroo pursed his lips. "I can't. I'm not allowed."

"I'll do what I can," Oliver said, "but it might take some time, since Lasher won't let me hire any more lab assistants."

Kangaroo's face brightened. "If you have assistants, you'll be able to work faster?"

"Yes, but—"

"I'll talk to Lasher. Thanks!" Kangaroo ran off down the corridor.

Oliver heard shoes slapping against the floor in overexcited rhythm. He thought of Robbie again, and it took him almost ten minutes to stop crying.

The prototype worked without any problems in Oliver's lab. He put it in the freezer, along with the ten different types of 9x19mm ammunition he had on hand, then dialed the temperature down as far as it would go and waited for two hours. Every round fired on the first try, and when he measured the temperature in the chamber, the readings were exactly what he expected.

After stripping off his cold suit, Oliver called Paul and said, "I need to accompany Kangaroo on his next field test."

"That won't be possible," Paul said, his face stern-looking even on the tiny vidphone screen.

"You can spare me for a week," Oliver said. "This is my most important research project, isn't it? And Kangaroo can't have gone farther than the Moon or L2 last time. He was back in less than a week."

"Time is not the issue," Paul said. "You don't have clearance to see the facility he's testing in."

"I don't have clearance to see the Moon?"

"This is not open to discussion. You can't go with Kangaroo. Tell him how to collect the data you need."

Oliver spent the rest of the night packaging up portable sensor modules and writing a detailed procedure document. Kangaroo groaned when Oliver handed him the reader tablet the next morning.

"Fifty pages?" Kangaroo said. "Do I *really* need to do *all* of this?"

"Lasher won't let me come with you to wherever you're conducting your field tests, so you need to collect enough data for me to diagnose the problem."

"But this'll take *forever*," Kangaroo whined. "Can't you, I don't know, build some kind of a robot to handle it?"

"I don't have time to test the automation that would require,"

Oliver said. "They're all very simple procedures. If you have any questions or problems, just call me."

"Pressure sensors?" Kangaroo was flipping through the procedures on the reader tab. "Radiation meters? We don't need all this!"

"It's not actually that much—"

"Can't I just take some temperature readings? That's got to be the problem, right?"

"Just do as I say, Robbie!" Oliver shouted.

Kangaroo cowered for a moment before asking, "Who's Robbie?"

"I'm sorry," Oliver said, turning away. "I had—I didn't sleep well last night."

He heard Kangaroo packing up all the sensor equipment. "I'll do my best with this stuff."

"Start with the temperature readings," Oliver said. "Don't worry if you don't have enough time to do everything."

"Okay."

Oliver heard Kangaroo shuffling toward the door and opening it. Then Kangaroo said, "I hope you sleep better tonight."

"Thank you."

"I won't tell Lasher."

For some reason, Oliver heard *I won't tell Dad.*

Seven days later, a mailroom courier delivered the suitcase containing Kangaroo's sensors back to Oliver's lab. Oliver couldn't decide if he was happy about not seeing Kangaroo again, but he was glad that he could work the problem without any further emotional distractions.

The first sensor Oliver downloaded to a lab computer was the tracking device he'd hidden inside the reader tab. He had installed planetary GPS receivers for Earth, the Moon, and Mars, and added an interplanetary nav-beacon receiver for good measure.

People might lie to him, but data never did.

He was surprised to see hardly any movement recorded on the tracker. He checked the device for faults and double-checked the logs, in case there had been some kind of triangulation error, but the unit had recorded no loss of signal. There were no signs of tampering on the tab casing or in the firmware.

Wherever Kangaroo had gone to test the prototype, it hadn't been more than a few kilometers outside of Washington, DC.

And the radiation meters showed something even stranger.

Oliver stormed into Paul's office and slammed the reader tab down on his desk. The rear access panel was open, clearly showing the tracker. Oliver knew Paul would recognize it.

"I want to know what the hell's going on here," Oliver said.

"I'll call you back," Paul said, and hung up his desktop phone. He glanced at the reader tab. "What is that?"

"This is the tablet of diagnostic testing procedures I gave to Kangaroo last week," Oliver said. "Because neither of you would tell me where he was going to perform his 'field testing,' I hid a tracking device inside so I could find out for myself."

Paul leaned back in his chair. "You shouldn't have done that, Oliver."

"Kangaroo didn't go into outer space," Oliver said. "He didn't even leave DC. So where did he go? Underground? Underwater? But why would he need a firearm that was operable in hard vacuum? What in the world could you lot be keeping down there?"

"It's not what you think," Paul said.

"Oh, but you haven't heard my guess yet!" Oliver said. He flipped the tab over to show its display. "You see, these are the readouts from the environmental sensors I asked Kangaroo to attach to the prototype while it was in 'cold storage.' According to the timestamps in each unit, he decided to attach all of them at once, presumably to save time."

"Oliver," Paul said quietly.

"You know what those readings show? I'll summarize. They show that the prototype was stored in hard vacuum, in total darkness, and in zero gravity, all at the same time. Deep space, right?" Oliver wagged a finger. "Not so fast, Mr. Holmes! Take a look at these temperature and radiation readings. What's this? Two *hundred* degrees Kelvin? In deep space? That can't be right; the cosmic microwave background radiation is only *three* degrees Kelvin. And look at the average proton collision energy level! That can't possibly be outer space.

"It can't be *our* universe, at any rate. Because our universe hasn't been that hot for at least *thirteen and a half billion years.*"

Paul stared at him in silence for a moment. "If I read you in, this will be the last job you ever have."

"And what's the alternative? 'You could tell me, but then you'd have to kill me'?" Oliver heard himself laughing.

"Nobody's going to kill you, Oliver."

"Well, why the hell not?" Oliver screamed. His vision had gone blurry, as if he were looking through a waterfall. "Why should I have to live with this? Why can't I be as brave as Robbie and just end it all?"

Oliver wasn't sure how he ended up on the floor, but he felt Paul gripping his shoulders and leaning him up against the wall. The old man's eyes looked different now—not icy, but like a clear blue sky far off in the distance.

"Your brother was not brave," Paul said. "He was very ill, and you did everything you could to help him."

"No," Oliver sobbed. "No, I didn't."

"What more would you have done? Quit your job so you could watch him every waking moment for the rest of his life? Become a medical doctor so you could suddenly invent a cure for congenital neurodegenerative disorders? You know what's possible and what's not." Paul let go of Oliver and stood up. "You can't fix everything, Oliver."

It took Oliver a few minutes to pull himself together. Mostly he just didn't want to cry so much at work—or yell at people, or throw things, or break things or people. That had been a real problem during his final months at Bradford.

Paul held out a hand and helped Oliver to his feet.

"I'm right, aren't I?" Oliver said, focusing on the science to distract himself. "You've got some sort of machine that opens a portal into a parallel universe. An alternate dimension. Whatever you want to call it."

"That's entirely possible," Paul said. "We don't actually know where it goes."

"Are you sure about this, Lasher?" Kangaroo asked.

He stood in a triangle with Paul and Oliver, at the center of a large, empty concrete bunker. Oliver had expected Paul to take him into some kind of secret research facility, but this appeared to be an old, abandoned, mid-twentieth-century bomb shelter. And there was no equipment anywhere in sight.

"Oliver has signed all the paperwork," Paul said to Kangaroo. "He's going to be joining you in Outback Operations."

Kangaroo beamed at Oliver and shook his hand vigorously. "Wow, that's great! Welcome aboard. Lasher's been looking for a good EQ for I don't know how long."

"EQ?" Oliver asked.

"Equipment officer," Paul said. "You'll be working very closely with Kangaroo. And a Surgical officer to be named later."

"So what's your code name going to be?" Kangaroo asked Oliver.

"His code name is Equipment," Paul said.

Kangaroo made a face. "That's not very interesting. And what if we have more than one person working on 'equipment'?"

"Then we'll use numbers," Paul snapped. "Or Greek letters. Just show him already."

Kangaroo shrugged and turned back to Oliver. "Okay. You ready to see it?"

"I gather that's why I'm here," Oliver said, still confused.

"Okay, come and stand next to me," Kangaroo said. Oliver stepped over to just behind his right shoulder. Paul took two steps back.

Kangaroo extended his right arm, and a whirling disk of translucent white light appeared in midair in front of him. Oliver saw blackness behind the light, which shimmered like a mirage.

"How are you doing that?" Oliver asked.

"Nobody knows," Kangaroo said.

"What do you mean, nobody knows? Where's the machine?"

"There is no machine. It's just me."

"My God." Oliver looked at Paul. "*That's* where you've been storing the prototype?"

"We call it 'the pocket,'" Paul said, his expression impassive. "It looks like deep space in there. No stars, galaxies, or other discernible light sources. Up until now, we've always believed it opened on a distant part of our universe, possibly inside an exotic dark matter structure or some other radiation-absorbing phenomenon."

"One Science Division labcoat thought it might be the inside of a black hole," Kangaroo scoffed. "That was pretty ludicrous. I mean, if it were a black hole, I'd have destroyed the whole planet the first time I opened the pocket."

"And when was that, exactly?" Oliver asked.

"I'll brief you later," Paul said. "But if you're correct about that being a parallel universe in there, Oliver . . . well, that makes things quite a bit more interesting."

"Did you figure out why your green gun wasn't working?" Kangaroo asked Oliver. "Was it a heating problem? Can you fix it?"

Oliver didn't even notice how much Kangaroo once again sounded like Robbie. "It's the cosmic background radiation. We tailored the ceramics in the magazine insulators to only generate heat if they were actually in deep cold. It's a failsafe, so the cartridges won't overheat and explode. The higher temperature and increased high-energy particle bombardments fooled the material into thinking it was never out of sunlight."

Kangaroo nodded. "Okay, and now in English?"

Oliver pointed at the pocket. "That universe is much younger than ours. Its Big Bang happened much more recently—probably less than two hundred million years ago—so it hasn't been expanding for as long, and that makes it hotter. The cosmic background radiation averages two hundred degrees Kelvin inside the pocket, which is two orders of magnitude higher than in our universe, and there's a significantly higher cosmic ray density."

"I meant American English."

"Your pocket universe caused the heater in the Franken-gun to malfunction."

"And do you know how to fix it now?"

Oliver nodded. "I'll need to take some more detailed sensor readings, but yes, I believe—"

"Great!" Kangaroo dropped his arm, and the portal vanished. "Hey, did you bring the gun? The prototype, I mean?"

"No," Oliver said.

"Oh. Well, do you have something small and—your watch! Let me borrow your watch for a second?"

Oliver handed over the antique wristwatch. The actual timekeeping mechanism had been replaced long ago with modern electronics, but the elaborate metal case was a centuries-old family heirloom. "I'm going to get that back, right?"

"Yeah, sure," Kangaroo said. "Trust me, this is a great trick. Just watch." He chuckled and held up Oliver's wristwatch. "Hey! Watch! That's funny."

"If you say so."

Kangaroo frowned and opened the pocket again, but this time the portal appeared as a solid black disk surrounded by a glowing white rim. Oliver heard a whooshing sound and felt a breeze blowing past him. Kangaroo let go of the watch, and it flew into the pocket, which then disappeared again.

"Hard vacuum," Kangaroo said.

"How exactly do you intend to retrieve that?" Oliver asked.

"Relax," Kangaroo said. The pocket opened again, this time with the light barrier—Oliver imagined it had to be some kind of airtight force field—and the watch flew out. Kangaroo caught it before it fell. The portal vanished.

"There you go." Kangaroo gave the watch back. It was freezing cold in Oliver's hands. "Cool, huh?"

Oliver looked up at Kangaroo, then over at Paul, but couldn't think of anything to say. Or maybe he simply couldn't move his mouth because of the ridiculous, childish grin covering his entire face.

"Welcome to the family," Paul said, smiling back. "I'm glad you passed the test."

Oliver snickered. "What, you mean not losing my kit at the sight of Kangaroo's 'pocket'? Who do you think I am?"

"That wasn't the test," Paul said. "The test was whether you would actually give a working, loaded firearm to a young man who reminded you of your dead brother."

Oliver felt lightheaded. Next to him, Kangaroo said, "The who the what now?"

"I won't lie to you," Paul said. "I am not a nice person. I will exploit all your talents to the best of my ability in the service of this agency and this country. But you're a bona fide genius, Oliver, and I want you around for as long as I can have you. I'm going to find the best Surgical officer in the Solar System, and that person is going to keep both you and Kangaroo healthy for a very long time."

"So we can spy for you," Oliver said with a dry mouth.

Paul's expression didn't change. "Your assignments will be varied."

"I'm sorry," Kangaroo said, "can we go back to the 'dead brother' thing?"

Oliver ignored him and took a step toward Paul. "You want me to make more weapons."

Paul shrugged. "We'll see. This project was necessary to satisfy my superiors that Kangaroo would not go into the field unarmed."

"He's—" Oliver did a double take. Kangaroo waved. He seemed so young.

"I'm an only child, thanks for asking," Kangaroo said.

"Are there others like him?" Oliver asked Paul. "Other people who can also access the pocket?"

"No. None that we know of."

"He's the only one? And you want to send him into situations where a *gun* will be necessary?" Oliver said. "Where people are going to be *shooting* at him?"

Paul remained motionless. "Kangaroo was using the pocket on his own, for many years, before the agency recruited him."

"I'm sure there's another very interesting story there."

"You're not cleared for that information," Paul deadpanned. "We didn't give him the power. We just gave him a purpose. A focus for his talents. As I hope to do for you, Oliver.

"Your life didn't end when Robbie died. It wasn't your fault. Most things in this world are out of our control, but we have an extraordinary opportunity here to take actions that no one else can accomplish." Paul pointed at Kangaroo. "He is the key. But he can't do it alone."

"This is a very long speech," Kangaroo said, coming up to stand beside Oliver again but addressing Paul. "I feel like he doesn't actually need this much convincing."

Paul ignored him. "None of us can do this alone. And you don't have to, Oliver."

Oliver sighed. "I suppose you'll want me to go into therapy."

"Oh, it's worse than that," Kangaroo said before Paul could respond. "Every single one of your 'debriefings' is going to be recorded for Lasher's later viewing pleasure."

"I would hardly call it a pleasure," Paul grumbled. "But it's necessary. Our job is keeping secrets from our enemies. We don't keep secrets from each other. Is that clear?"

Oliver nodded. "I think . . . I'd like to talk about Robbie. To tell someone else what he was like. So I won't be the only one who remembers."

"That's a good start," Paul said.

Oliver turned to Kangaroo. "You remind me a lot of him, actually."

Kangaroo blinked. "Is that a good thing or a bad thing?"

"It's good," Oliver said. "It's very good."

KANGAROO WILL RETURN

.

ABOUT THE AUTHOR

Once a Silicon Valley software engineer, **Curtis C. Chen** (陳致宇) now writes stories and runs puzzle games near Portland, Oregon. He's the author of the KANGAROO series of funny science fiction spy thrillers and has written for the Realm original podcasts *Echo Park*, *Ninth Step Murders*, and *Machina*. Curtis' shorter works have appeared in *Playboy* Magazine; *The Year's Best Fantasy, Volume 2*; *Aliens vs. Predators: Ultimate Prey*; the ENNIE Award-winning *Kobold Guide to Roleplaying*; and many other publications. His homebrew cat feeding robot was displayed in the "Worlds Beyond Here" exhibit at Seattle's Wing Luke Museum. Visit him online: https://CurtisCChen.com

xoxo.zone/@curtiscchen
instagram.com/curtiscchen
facebook.com/curtis.c.chen

Milton Keynes UK
Ingram Content Group UK Ltd.
UKHW020750071024
449371UK00014B/1126